D0034443

Wish Bound

J. C. NELSON

ACE BOOKS, NEW YORK

An imprint of Penguin Random House LLC
375 Hudson Street, New York, New York 10014

WISH BOUND

An Ace Book / published by arrangement with the author

ISBN: 978-0-425-27291-6

PUBLISHING HISTORY
Ace mass-market edition / September 2015

PRINTED IN THE UNITED STATES OF AMERICA

10 9 8 7 6 5 4 3 2 1

Cover art by Tony Mauro. Back cover image: Bridge at Carrer del Bisbe in Barri Gotic,
Barcelona © Nejron Photo / Shutterstock Images.
Cover design by Danielle Abbiate.
Interior text design by Kelly Lipovich.

Penguin
Random
House

For Allison, who makes the decision every day

Acknowledgments

This book is the product of several years' worth of work, many long nights and quiet weekends, but it's also the product of several other people's hard work. First off, my agent, Pam Howell, whose patient advice helped keep me on target. Secondly, Leis Pederson, my editor at Ace. Without Leis's help, this book wouldn't be nearly as much fun.

Thanks once more to Andy, Leslie, Laurel, Chris, and John at critiquecircle.com. You stuck with me through seven books, a novella, and a Christmas short story. That's world-class dedication, and as always, I'm grateful.

Finally, my intense gratitude to my wife and family, who put up with me as I obsessed with a set of stories that kept me up at night and woke me early in the morning. It's been an adventure. Now, on to the next one.

One

❧

WHEN I WAS a little girl, my mother used to say, "A little birthday party can't hurt anyone." She stopped saying that after my seventh birthday, when the ponies they rented stampeded. Then it was "How bad could a birthday party be?" which lasted until my tenth birthday, when the microwave oven exploded, coating everyone in melted frosting. Then it was "Let's get this over with," followed the year after by "You know, this year let's let Marissa celebrate her own way." Which meant I spent my birthdays reading alone while my parents went out for drinks.

And that's how I planned to spend my twenty-eighth birthday, which fell on a Monday, which, statistically, it does once every seven years. Mondays, in my experience, are lousy, and birthdays are even worse.

I ran to work that day, keeping my girlish figure looking slightly more girlish than trash-can-ish, and Liam ran with me. Liam. Almost six feet, built like a barrel, with arms like tree trunks. My fiancé. My other half. The man who'd stood by me through the end of the world. Also, a man in lousy shape.

"Marissa, could we take a break?" Liam limped along a few dozen feet back.

I learned to run earlier in my life. Run to get away from things that wanted to kill me, run to get away from things I couldn't get away from. Technically, these days I could eat the buffet and the table it came on, and still not gain a pound, thanks to the gift of a harbinger of the apocalypse, Famine. Being the apocalypse bringer had its benefits, but I wasn't taking chances, so we still ran.

In case you're imagining a romantic run through the city, two lovers getting an endorphin kick to keep us ready for work, stop. We had company. A few feet behind Liam came a bombshell blonde, curvy and pale, with brilliant blue eyes and a figure that stopped hearts.

"You can run on. I will stay with my liege." Svetlana, the aforementioned beautiful disaster, waved to me. I wasn't about to leave her any more than she ever left us. Which was never. It wasn't just devotion to my fiancé; it was a form of contract. Thanks to the machinations of an evil queen and her team of assassins, Liam wound up holding a stake in, well, everything Svetlana's people owned. Given that they were all vegetarian vampires, they objected to stakes of any flavor.

I jogged in place, waiting for Liam to gain his breath.

"This is a lot easier when I have four feet," called a six-foot-eight man with curly brown hair. The head of our shipping department and full-time Big Bad Wolf, Mikey, never passed up a chance to chase people, even if he wasn't allowed to devour them. The crowd parted for him in a way that would have made Old Testament Moses envious. Crowds in the city don't move for anyone, but even city folks had a healthy self-preservation instinct. "I'll see you at the office," Mikey shouted. He loped off, nearly sprinting.

We took another forty minutes to arrive, mostly due to my fiancé, partially due to a flower vendor who insisted I wanted a dahlia. What I really wanted was to shove the dahlia somewhere he'd find painful.

When we arrived at the Agency, I left Liam and Svetlana to take the elevator. I, on the other hand, sprinted up the stairs for a final calorie-burn burst, and exploded through the front door, ready for a Monday.

Our receptionist, Rosa, hunched over a man, shocking him repeatedly with a stun gun.

I nodded to her. "Morning, Rosa."

She made the sign of the cross with her middle finger, blessing herself and telling me off in one pass, and muttered under her breath.

Since Rosa obviously had the morning crowd under control, I checked the schedule. In my office, a six-by-four mirror pulsed, glowing orange in the darkness. I used masking tape to divide the mirror into slots for each day and hour, keeping a schedule that Grimm couldn't claim to not see. Monday morning. Liam had an appointment in the sewers, where a group of mud men awaited the "Final Flush." I hoped Svetlana brought her muck boots.

Mikey needed to be down at the docks, where something on a container ship kept eating the night watchmen. If you are what you eat, something had a cholesterol count that might kill it.

I looked at my name, and saw the whole day blocked out without explanation.

The column next to mine looked identical.

"Morning, Marissa. Does this outfit make my eyes look more or less yellow?"

I recognized Ari's voice, and couldn't help but smile. In the doorway to my office, Arianna Thromson stood, dressed in a yellow tracksuit. The yellow made her red hair look two shades lighter, and it made the diseased yellow of her eyes look even more diseased and yellow.

Arianna Thromson, my best friend. Also, princess, and witch. Don't hold those last two against her—the first you could blame on her parents, the second on an evil queen who forced Ari to use too much magic at once.

"Looks better." I looked at her dead-on, to remind her that regardless of how other people treated her, she was still just Ari to me. Witches didn't get many smiles, and most folks would stare at the ceiling rather than meet her gaze. "You and I have some sort of all-day engagement."

"I'm meeting Wyatt for lunch. I wish it were an engagement." Ari narrowed her eyes at me, then looked past me to the board. Despite the fact that her eyes had neither pupils nor irises, she could see perfectly well. In fact, if what you were looking for was a spirit, spell, or curse, she saw better than me.

Ari read the schedule, then put one hand to the bracelet on her wrist. A simple gold bracelet, the key to our communication with the Fairy Godfather. "Bastard Grimm, you come here this instant." Using Grimm's first name was something even I avoided, and I outranked Ari.

The calendar faded from the mirror, and Grimm swirled into view. He adjusted his coat, looking every bit the English butler I always imagined him as. "Ladies, how may I assist you?"

"I was going to have lunch with my prince." Ari crossed her arms and tapped her foot.

Grimm took off the heavy black glasses he wore, revealing eyebrows like a yeti. "Young lady, I'm sorry. We require your assistance. I'll make it up to you. Reservations to anywhere in the city."

"What exactly are we supposed to be doing?" I went around to my desk and opened my ammo drawer.

"Marissa, you always say I never let you travel for business. I think today I'll correct that. You are going to visit another realm." Grimm's calm smile left me worried.

I'd traveled to other realms. Inferno, a few times. It was better than the department of licensing. I'd been to a fairy's realm as well, and would rather not go back. "Which one? Avalon? Say Avalon. Or Atlantis."

Grimm looked down. "Nowhere near as extravagant. We've suffered an influx of goblins for the last few weeks, and I believe it prudent to check the health of the realm seal."

Of course. The realm seal, if it looked like the others, was a giant ball of lightning that acted as a barrier between realms. Part magic construct, part physical creatures, the realm seals required constant attention to keep them healthy. Grimm couldn't go himself, but that didn't mean he couldn't send others. "I don't want to go to the Forest. I want to go to Avalon."

"You don't have enough frequent-flier miles built up, but

we'll talk about it afterward. Meet me at the portal in fifteen minutes." Grimm faded out.

"Look at it this way: You'll get to shoot at least one goblin, and I'll be that much happier to see Wyatt tonight." That was Ari, always trying to salvage a bad situation.

"There's no point in shooting goblins. They're dumber than the bullets in my gun. As a matter of fact, in a trivia contest, I'd bet on the bullets—"

Grimm reappeared in a burst of light, in every reflective surface in my office. He spoke from all of them at once. "Code Mauve, Marissa. I need you in my office immediately. Alone." Grimm kept his tone calm, his eyes fixed on me. Not good.

I ran down the hall, threw open the door, ready for murder, mayhem, or destruction. The air conditioner's hum competed with the murmur of the crowds in the waiting room for loudest noise. "Yes?"

Grimm appeared in his mirror, his regular gray silk suit changed out for black, his look stern. He ignored me, keeping his eyes on the high-back chair, where I noticed two feet in penny loafers.

"Ah, so good of you to come at once." I knew the voice. Knew the man, if you could call him that.

I shut the door behind me. "Nick." Nickolas Scratch. The Adversary. King of demons, ruler of Inferno, and first-order paper pusher.

He rose from his chair, barely as tall as me, with heavy wrinkles around his eyes and a bald spot that could blind a girl. "I hate to bother you here, Marissa. I really do, but I have a problem, and you only lose your driver's license every couple of weeks, so I couldn't just wait for you to come in and replace it." The Adversary's second job, at the department of licensing, allowed him to be truly evil.

Since offending the commander of demon armies could have immediate impact on my life span, I chose my words with care. "Anything that's bothering you is way out of my league. I'm trying to pick on things my own size." Refusing the Adversary directly could be bad, but not, in my book, as bad as agreeing to help him.

Nick walked over and put one hand on my shoulder. "I know. I wouldn't ask, but I don't have anywhere else to turn. There's been a theft."

Grimm disappeared in a flash, leaving me alone. And for once, I didn't feel abandoned. Grimm had mastered the art of foretelling the future in a dozen ways, all of them bloody enough to make me lose my lunch. I was convinced he secretly made no effort to evict the rabbits that haunted his home, because they came in handy when a quick fortune needed to be told. Right now, I needed the knowledge he'd gain from slaughtering a few bunnies as much as he did.

"Where?"

"The Vault of Souls." Nick's eyes glowed like fireside embers as he spoke. "Think of it like a bank vault, only instead of your mortgage papers, or some certificates of deposit, I keep valuable things. Mass murderers. Tyrants. Genocidal maniacs."

"Who broke out?" I slipped around the desk and sat down in Grimm's chair.

Nick's hands clenched, turning white, and he trembled with barely contained rage. "There's never been a breakout. Someone broke into Inferno and took three souls from the vault." With each word, the lights in the office flickered, as if each shadow siphoned away the light. I'd stood face-to-face with demons and dealt with the harbingers of the apocalypse, including Death himself, but the Adversary was so far out of my league, my best hope was to let him rant and hope Grimm had a plan for how to contain the damage when his temper exploded.

"The angels did it?" The angels were the only creatures I could imagine being dumb enough to mount an attack on hell itself. Now would be a great time for Grimm to make an appearance. The Adversary could squash me like a bug if I said the wrong thing.

He rumbled like a thunderstorm. Anger or laughter, I couldn't tell. "Are you kidding? They want most of the souls in the vault locked up just as much as I do. You know, most of those souls are mine by agreement. And those three were mine by right. Given to me freely." Blood dripped from Nick's hands as his nails cut into his palms. It burst into flames that licked the edges of his fingers.

For just a moment, my curiosity got the better of me. "Don't you have armies? You know, the sort that you'd need to bring about the end of the world?"

The Lord of Destruction looked at me over his bifocals, his eyes round. "I can't admit there's been a lapse in security. My own children would rise up against me. So, you are going to retrieve those souls. If they've been lashed into another body, you have my permission to take them apart in any way you find convenient. Death will take care of bringing them back to me at that point."

The friendly grin on Nick's face made my spine tingle. "I'm sorry. I'm your girl if you need a pair of slippers returned, or a library book, but souls? Maybe Fairy Godfather can find them and—" The words strangled out in my throat as Nick began to belch black smoke and sulfur.

"You *will* do it. If I don't get them back, I'm going to start killing random people on the off chance that one of them has the soul I'm looking for. And you won't have to find the other two. They're going to come for you, Marissa. I'd bet on it."

I think his final words scared me more than his threats. "Who?"

For just a moment, Nickolas Scratch looked almost concerned. "An ex-queen and her son. Both of whom have issues with you."

Where two seconds earlier I could have baked bread just by setting it on my desk, now beads of sweat formed on my head and I shivered. I knew who he meant, and had barely survived the last time she tried to kill me. Maybe they hadn't meant to get her. Maybe—

"Marissa, don't kid yourself." The Adversary crossed his arms and shook his head. "That was no accident. There were murderers in that vault a thousand times more deadly; hell, Rip Van Winkle's soul was in a Mason jar two shelves down."

I nearly died at the hands of Rip Van Winkle, Kingdom's own boogeyman. "Who was it that broke in? And who else did they take?" I couldn't have moved from Grimm's seat if I had to, wrapped in a spell of fear as I waited for an answer I dreaded.

"You should probably have that discussion with your Fairy Godfather." He rubbed his hands together, extinguishing the flames. "I'll see myself out, assuming that receptionist of yours doesn't shoot me again. If she ever wants a night job, send her over. She'll fit right in below." Nick put his clipboard under his arm and marched out, leaving scorch marks on the carpet with each step.

I can't tell you how many minutes passed until my skin tingled from Grimm's presence in the mirror at my back. I didn't speak. Didn't move. Prince Mihail and his crazy mother were some of the few people who truly deserved their spot in Inferno. The thought of them out and about, watching, waiting—that I couldn't stand.

"Marissa, I listened in on your conversation. You have a special rapport with the Adversary, and I felt it wiser to allow you to deal with him."

"Is he telling the truth?"

"Yes, my dear. I'm afraid he is. I know in the past you've been reluctant to use deadly force, but in this case, I want you to shoot first, reload, and shoot again. Leave the question asking to me." The concern in Grimm's voice only amplified my fear. The Fairy Godfather feared nothing.

"We have to take care of Ari. Prince Mihail might come for her." Mihail had meant to marry Ari. Then murder her.

"His mother won't waste time on Ari or anyone else. I would comfort you, but fear will keep you alert. Alive. I confess I'm considering having Jess released from the hospital to accompany Arianna. Anywhere you go in this realm, Liam must remain with you at all times."

The thought of half-djinn Jess roaming the streets of my city worried me almost as much as the Adversary's threats. Once one of Grimm's agents, Jess was violent death given flesh when her bipolar medication wasn't working, or when she wouldn't take it, which was most of the time. "We can't do that. Too many innocent people might get hurt. What if, for once, you actually did some form of magic? Can't you influence fate to keep her safe?" Grimm had a way of influencing events that worked best when the person being influenced didn't know what was happening. He could bring two people together in a crowd of thousands—or, hopefully, keep them apart.

Grimm ignored my dig at his stinginess, his eyes unfocused. "I could, Marissa, but I can't do so for two people at once. That means, my dear, that I can't provide the same protection for you if I'm doing so for Arianna."

"Then there's no decision. You keep both Mihails away from Ari. If the Mihails want revenge, they can take it up with me."

"Marissa—" Grimm stopped for a moment, his forehead wrinkled and lips pursed. "You shouldn't endanger yourself so lightly."

"Better me than anyone else."

Grimm just shook his head and faded from the mirror, leaving me alone. Which meant I could spare a moment to worry for myself.

AN URGENT KNOCK on Grimm's door roused me from my worry. Grimm himself disappeared half an hour before, saying he needed to spend quality time divining the future. There'd be a food bank receiving donations of hasenpfeffer for days.

"Little pig, little pig, let me come in." I recognized Mikey's voice through the oak door.

"Oh, all right." I rose and unlocked the door, looking up to meet his eyes. "What?"

Mikey grabbed my arm, a move which would have earned him a silver bullet two years earlier, and dragged me along. "Emergency in the kitchen. You're in charge." He let go and sprinted off, rounding the corner like he'd just spotted a whitetail deer, or a cheerleader.

I followed him to the kitchen, throwing open the door and marching in, ready to lay down the law.

Darkness engulfed me, absolute darkness, as the door

swung shut behind me, and the sounds of shallow breathing made my heart race.

"Surprise!" a hail of voices shouted, and the lights flickered on. A shiver ran from my feet to my ears. In the center of the table sat a cake with "Happy Barmitzvah, Joshua" written in pink gel frosting.

"I got it on clearance at the bakery." Mikey reached out and lit a candle on the cake, oblivious to the terror in my eyes.

The kitchen door opened, and Liam shouted, "What idiot brought a cake? Grimm, we need you." He banged on the wall so hard, it shook the door.

The patter of light feet meant everyone was leaving. I clenched my teeth and tried to look away. "It's going to be okay, M." Ari stepped forward. "Everyone out of the building. Move, people." She barked orders while I struggled to contain a wave of nausea that made the world spin.

Grimm flashed into the microwave door, glanced around the room, and glowered at Mikey. "What exactly do you think you are doing?"

"Stairs." Ari cupped her hands and shouted. "Only use the stairs. Remember what happened to the elevators last time?"

"Marissa, take a deep breath. Close your eyes." Grimm's voice calmed me, though the panic still swirled in my stomach like a gallon of cheap rum.

Liam snuffed out the candle and threw his jacket over the cake. "It's fine, M. Nothing to see here. We're all going to just go for a walk down the stairs, out onto the street, and take the day off."

That's when the sprinklers went off.

Then every light in the building went out at once.

Then a bubbling noise like some monster from the depths gurgled up from the sewers, and a stench like rotten sheep entrails stung my nose. From the floors above and below, cries of terror and disgust echoed from vents.

"Deep breaths. Eyes closed." Liam put a rough hand on my face and pulled me toward him. "Mikey didn't know."

Mikey didn't know. Didn't know that I avoided every

birthday, anniversary, wedding, or funeral for exactly the same reason. They all ended in disaster. If we were unlucky, it required the hazmat squad. If we were lucky, there'd only be a couple feet of raw sewage spilling into the building.

"Grimm, you've got to help me with this." I pushed away from Liam as the emergency lighting came on, flooding the Agency with a dull red glow.

"Marissa, everyone has situations in which things do not go well. Little things, where the universe reminds them they have better ways to spend their fleeting days." Grimm spoke like a schoolteacher.

"Do you remember what happened when Ari baked me cupcakes for my birthday?"

Ari tromped back into the room, wearing yellow muck boots and carrying a matching parasol. "Asps. There were no asp eggs in the batter, Grimm. None. Would you like to guess how many cupcakes had asps in them when Marissa cut into them? What does that tell you?"

"It tells me cupcakes are bad for your figure. Now, if you don't mind—" Grimm cut off, his eyes losing focus, then snapping wide open. "Ladies, I need you to check on that realm seal immediately. There isn't a moment to waste."

I followed Ari to the back of the Agency, where Grimm kept portal runes ground into the concrete, having long ago given up any pretense of getting his security deposit returned. This birthday was turning out as bad as the rest.

"Proceed directly along the path to the Seal, contact me when you arrive. Do not waste time shooting goblins." Grimm stood in the full-length mirror, waiting. He looked to Liam. "Sir, I need your assistance as soon as the ladies have departed. We have a minor invasion to deal with."

"You got it." Liam rubbed his hands through his hair, wringing it out.

The portal lit up like a rainbow and solidified, revealing a land that looked like a barren fall landscape.

Grimm waved his hand like a host. "This is your stop. Please keep your hands and feet inside the portal, or a team of surgeons will be required to reattach them. I will reopen the gate once we have inspected the realm seal and understand what is wrong."

Ari stepped through, appearing on the trail visible through the portal. The portal rippled and shook, like it was made of cold, clear water.

"That normal?" I studied Grimm's face.

"Not exactly. Hurry, Marissa. There's a tremor in the fabric of magic itself coming, which might strand Ari." Grimm concentrated, his eyebrows arched.

I dashed forward, ducking down, and stepped across. As I did, the building shook again, and it felt like my insides twisted like a pretzel. Then a grip like iron seized my hand. Ari screamed. Liam cursed, and I disappeared into darkness.

Two

~❧~

I OPENED MY eyes to absolute pitch black. Nothingness, no sound or smell. Only the iron grip on my arm kept me from fleeing into the void.

"Happy birthday, Marissa. You're one day closer to dying." The voice came straight into my head, a voice like dried leaves and cracked bones rattling in the October wind.

"Death. That's you, right?" A few years earlier, Death, a harbinger of the apocalypse, spent quite a bit of time hanging around my apartment. "I didn't see it coming."

"You aren't dead yet. I came to give you a present. You know, I never did get you a proper present for almost ending the world."

I looked around, but couldn't see. Movement, eyes open or closed, nothing mattered.

In the inky black, a match struck and flared with the stench of sulfur. Before me, a single candle glowed to life, planted on a cupcake. I stared across it into a skull, its empty eye sockets leering back at me.

His grip held me fast, stifling my involuntary attempt to flee. "I'm sorry, I didn't have time to change skins. I'm very busy, and I have the feeling I'm headed into a holiday season of sorts." Death placed the cupcake in my hands. Then with a bony claw, he reached toward my left eye.

Scream? Hell yes, I did.

His claw tips met a gnat's width above my eye, and a sound, a feeling of tearing, ripped through me. With a puff of air like the gust of a coffin lid closing, he blew out the candle, and darkness wrapped itself about me once more.

"I'm sorry, Marissa. You need to be able to see to understand." His voice began to fade out.

The darkness seeped into me, freezing me to my core. "What did you do?"

"I've made a hole in the veil for you. So you won't be fooled."

A pinprick of light in the darkness caught my eye, the only light in the world. Rushing toward me, growing larger by the second, moving like a train. At the last moment, I saw forest, leaves, and then I went flying into the light.

"M?" Ari's voice, soft and sweet, distant. I tried to open my eyes, but after the darkness of the void, even the gray light of the Forest seemed to stab me.

"Ari." My own voice came from a distance.

Something clicked, and Ari spoke, "She just arrived. The portal opened on its own and threw her out face-first."

With my hands over my eyes, I sat up. "I'm fine."

"My dear, you were gone for nearly half an hour. I feared we lost you." Grimm's voice trembled.

"Death spoke to me." I opened my eyes, squinting. "Said I needed to see through the veil."

"What?" Grimm practically roared. "That's completely illegal according to the celestial laws, and not good for your health. Cosmic radiation, and so on."

Ari jerked her hand back, almost dropping the compact.

"He said it would help me understand. Why? And what?" I stood and dusted rotten leaves out of my shirt. The remains of a smashed cupcake said I'd landed on my birthday present.

"Arianna, please find the realm seal and return quickly. I need to examine Marissa." Grimm faded out.

Ari took my hand and stared at me. At one time, her dead eyes made my skin crawl, but these days, I just saw my best friend. She was using her spirit sight, for sure, looking down through my skin to see if there was damage inside.

"Well?" I arched one eyebrow.

"You look like you always do. Come on, let's get this over with." She started down the path, and I followed her.

The Forest Realm certainly wouldn't win any tourism destination awards if I were handing them out. It's not just the fact that every goblin, ever, made their homes there. The thing that really killed it for me was the endless array of brown, gray, and black. Not a green leaf or yellow flower for as far as the eye could see.

Combine that with the perpetual October-evening twilight, and I needed a beach vacation just to recover. Still, any realm visit was one worth remembering, if only so I could remember I didn't want to come here again. As Ari followed the path through blistered trees, I stopped her. "I never get to travel to other realms. Take a picture?" I handed her my phone.

Ari shook her head. "You have to come with me to Fae next time I tend my Seal."

A seal, in this case, was neither a small, furry aquatic mammal nor an imposing navy warrior. Seals, magical entities that served as barriers between realms, resembled living thunderstorms. Attempting to club one might get you electrocuted.

"Grimm says no. Actually, he doesn't say no. He just always has some emergency for me to handle. 'Marissa, I need you to find this missing child,' or 'Marissa, you have to prevent them from poisoning the city's water supply.' It's always something." I made a mental note that next time, I was going, no matter what. "This dump's the first place he's let me go on my own." I gave her a fake smile for the camera.

"Say cheddar." Ari waited. And waited.

I glared at her. "That's not funny." She knew darn well why. In the office fridge lurked a wheel of cheddar, which arrived of its own accord the day Grimm threw me a "welcome to the Agency" party. The number of interns who attempted to remove it matched exactly the number of interns who died horrible, bloody deaths within hours of touching it.

"Fine. Say 'Grimm's a bastard.'" Ari snapped the picture before I could open my mouth and handed me the phone. "You know what I'm noticing about this place?" She twirled around, taking in the breathtakingly dull landscape.

"Nothing. There's absolutely nothing of interest."

"No goblins. Shouldn't we have met at least one?" Ari peered into the forest.

She had a point. Goblins served as the cheapest, dumbest enforcers anyone with a little Glitter and an axe or ten to grind could afford. Now that I'd seen where they came from, I understood why they left. Goblins also tended to be as territorial as trailer park residents, so the fact that we'd made it twenty steps without having to give one lead poisoning didn't bode well. "Come on. Let's go for a jog, get this over with, and go someplace with sun, or at least fluorescent lights." I took off at a trot, with Ari close behind.

The path opened up to a vast meadow. Not the sort of meadow where forest animals frolicked in the sun. The sort of meadow where sick and dying animals would stagger, wounded and rabid, while making noises reminiscent of a band of drunken bagpipe players before dying. Like the rest of the Forest, it seemed frozen in a late autumn, dead grass, dead trees. The mounds of dead goblins, that was new.

Ari caught up with me, both of us reaching for our handguns at the same time. Goblins lay piled like cordwood, their black blood coagulating in pools like an oil slick.

Ari poked one with the barrel of her Desert Eagle. "What do you think happened?"

"No idea." With each step, I watched, waited for something to attack. I think I preferred the endless dead trees to the maze of goblin bodies. The closer we got toward the center, the worse the carnage. Bodies gave way to shredded mounds of barely recognizable flesh.

A glint of black caught my eye, and I approached, digging into the mound. "Take a look at—" A flash of pain shot up my arm, and I yanked back my hand. From my palm, a gush of blood welled up.

Ari grabbed my hand and chanted, turning the air cold as magic swept into her. I expected the wound to close. Instead, a filthy Ace bandage materialized, cobwebs and dust covering the outside.

"Seriously? Can't you do healing yet?" I poked at a spider, turning it into a splat.

Ari wound the bandage around my hand. "You have no idea how much power that takes when I have to do it on my own." Then she turned, and without a word, fire burst from her palm, incinerating the corpse on which I'd cut myself.

Roast goblin smelled a lot like roast goat. In spite of the pain in my hand, my mouth watered, imagining black beans, corn tortillas, and some fresh salsa.

"Oh no." Ari stopped the flamethrower act, looking back to me, rubbing her fingers together. "We need to get you out of here."

Where a mass of goblin flesh once stood, ashes drifted. Entwined in the bones of the goblin, a tangled mass of thorns twisted, still burning. My stomach twisted itself into a Gordian knot while my brain packed its bags and began considering the contortions necessary to escape via my left ear.

I'd read about deaths like that. Deaths that hadn't happened for more than four hundred years. Such bodies were the standard, the hallmark of the Black Queen. I reflexively covered my wrist, where the handmaiden's mark peeked out from beneath the bandage.

Grimm thought she'd take several hundred years to return.

The bodies said otherwise.

I looked around and didn't see Ari. While I'd stood, lost in my thoughts, she'd kept going. Quelling the fear that danced up and down my spine, I ran through the maze until I reached the center.

Ari stood there, on a black stone block I recognized as a

realm gate. In her arms, she cradled something. It crackled and popped like an electrical transformer.

As I approached, Ari sang softly, a Kingdom lullaby.

Ari looked up, her mouth open, lips turned down. "I don't know if we got here in time."

She opened her arms a bit, and I finally saw what she cradled. In her arms lay a wisp of blue energy. It shifted as I looked at it, sometimes almost resembling a baby, sometimes an octopus with hands. I'd seen one before, once, barely. That one was covered in lightning and wrapped in mist.

I opened my pocket compact. "Grimm, we've found the realm seal. It's not good."

Seconds passed without an answer, and then Grimm's eyes appeared, and only his eyes. "I am somewhat occupied, Marissa." His gaze went to the realm seal, and his eyes shut. "Thank goodness Arianna is present. Princess, I need you to take care of the Seal. It is starved, as the previous royal family has not had a seal bearer for two decades."

Ari continued to cradle it, sometimes petting it like a dog, sometimes just cuddling it like a child. Ari, in case you were wondering, was a seal bearer, as if being a princess and a witch wasn't bad enough. Each royal family had one seal bearer per generation. The seal bearers cared for the realm seal. In return, they received access to pure magic, sorcery at a discounted price. I'd never asked exactly what caring for a seal entailed. "What happened? It doesn't look like the Fae Seal."

Ari answered before Grimm could. "This one's sick. Realm seals need love and attention, or they weaken. I visit the one in Fae every week."

I'd seen the Fae Seal, touched it, nearly been electrocuted by it. I dropped my purse on the ground so my phone didn't get fried, then approached the Seal, holding out my hand. A tentacle of blue reached out, pushing my hand away. While the power in it buzzed like a drill, it didn't shock me. "Can I hold it?"

Ari frowned. "I don't think that's a good idea. Frankly, I'm surprised it let you get this close. The Fae one would knock you flat for getting within five yards, now that it's back home and at full strength."

"I believe this one would almost tolerate Marissa," said Grimm. "It belonged to Queen Mihail and her family, which explains the poor condition."

"So it belongs to me now." I reached out for it, and it shrank from me. That was just plain rude. I'd won her title (didn't want it), her throne (currently in storage in Queens), and apparently, one extremely sick Seal a few years ago.

"Marissa, we've had this discussion." Grimm sounded exhausted. "You cannot simply become a princess, and aside from the original seal bearers, they've all been born, not made. We must find someone to take over the role soon." His gaze flickered to Ari. "In the meantime, princess, I'd like you to care for Marissa's seal."

Ari frowned. "That's like asking me to scoop her litter box." The Seal let out a low whine, and nuzzled, wrapped all eight of its arms around her in a hug. "Oh, all right." She stroked it like a puppy. "I'll do it."

I'd owned a cat once, and the ending was definitely not happily ever after. Far as I was concerned, Ari could keep the Seal. "Grimm, I know why the goblins are coming. They're not invading. They're fleeing." I pointed the mirror toward a goblin body, where black thorns grew out of the eyes. "The Black Queen was here."

"I know."

Ari gasped at the same time I did, and if the Seal hadn't been latched on to her like a frightened toddler, she'd have dropped it.

"You what?" we said together.

"I recognize her work, but she is not in the Forest any longer." Grimm spoke slowly, calmly. "She is on Earth, in Kingdom."

Three

～⚬～

GRIMM'S WORDS HUNG in the dead air, striking more fear into me than a pack of gremlins armed with grenades or an army of lawyers.

"You said it would be hundreds of years before Isolde had enough power to return." My ears rang, and when Ari put her hand on my shoulder, I couldn't help flinching.

"I was wrong, or perhaps right, and the timer simply started at her death. I told you my daughter's actions were a blind spot for me. She arrived in Kingdom during the time you were . . . delayed. I suspect that her inability to locate you may have been a blessing. For now, you are safe. I will reopen the portal for you when I can." Grimm disappeared, not even waiting for me to respond.

I put my hand on my bracelet, which was far more than a simple piece of jewelry. Made of pure magic, it allowed me to summon the Fairy Godfather in any reflective surface, but for what I had in mind, I didn't need a mirror. By agreement with Grimm, I could contact a select few other people, though I wouldn't be able to see them. "Liam." I waited for the gentle touch of my fiancé's mind. And waited, and waited some more.

"M, we're a little occupied. Had a few thousand goblins arrive all at once." Liam's voice had an echo behind it, meaning he'd let the curse take control in return for the strength that came with it.

"The Black Queen was here, in the Forest." I waited, counting seconds, listening for his reply. At last, his presence swept around me, the same feeling when we were sitting in my living room together, that simple pressure that said he was here.

His panic spiked through our connection, matching my own. "Marissa, hang on, I'll be there—"

"Calm, Mr. Stone." Grimm cut in on our conversation, something he almost never did. What exactly Liam said in response, I couldn't hear with Grimm interfering, but Grimm's side of the conversation came through loud and clear. "I assure you, Marissa is in the safest place possible. She's in an entirely different realm. Your presence there would not assist her, while it may make the difference here. Please, Marissa, tell him."

I wanted him there with me. I wanted to hold him and be held. To know that with his love, a few bullets, and a touch of magic, we'd find a way through this. The business side of me cut that desire to shreds. "I'm okay. Take care of the goblins, then take care of me."

"I want to be with her." Liam's passion came through loud and clear, making me almost as happy as holding his hand. "I'm not playing around anymore. Any goblin that looks at me funny gets barbecued."

Our link cut off, leaving me in the silence of the Forest. Not quite silence. Ari stood on a black stone obelisk, her hands clasped before her, chanting.

"What exactly are you doing?" I walked toward her.

With a wave her hand, a wall of wind pushed me back to the clearing edge. "Stay out of this, Marissa."

At her feet, the runes carved in the stone lit up, one by one. With a gasp, I recognized the spell. Ari was attempting to open the portal.

"Stop! You can't even program your DVR, let alone tune a portal." I pushed my way through her barrier, though it buffeted me like a hurricane gale.

"I've spent a lot of time in Fae, M. I listened to everything the Fae Mother said." Behind Ari, the portal blossomed like a rainbow rose opening. "I don't have to tune it. Just open it to wherever it went last."

"Grimm! Stop her!" I shrieked, holding my bracelet and broadcasting to the world. "Ari, stop! You might open a portal straight to the Black Queen."

Ari opened her eyes for a moment, looking at me with a cold stare that left me frozen. "I know."

The gale knocked me to my knees as Ari's portal stabilized. "I don't understand."

Ari drew in the last of her magic, and the rush of wind ceased, leaving only the patter of leaves to the earth. "I'm going to fulfill my destiny."

"Be what you are." I'd repeated those words so many times, even Ari gave up complaining.

Ari shook her head. "I asked the Fae Mother how to stop the Black Queen, and I understand. I'm the last to challenge her before she is defeated. I'm going to save you." With those words, Ari turned and walked through her makeshift portal.

The moment Ari left, her spell weakened, becoming nothing more than a strongly worded suggestion that I stay in place. I'd never been one to take suggestions, or commands for that matter. I paced back and forth, and waited for Ari to return. Waited for Grimm to answer me.

The stone slab where she'd summoned her portal stood empty. The light from the portal runes faded as the minutes passed, and the only sound was the occasional crackle of the Forest Seal, which rested in an altar-manger combination you'd never find on a baby registry on Earth.

Every crackle of magic from it reminded me of goblin feet crushing dead leaves. The last thing I needed was a close encounter of the green kind on their home turf, alone. As I glanced about wildly, searching, a flash of light hit me, like a glint from a mirror. When I turned to look at it, I saw nothing, but it hit me again as I scanned the slab. Wincing, I closed my eyes, then peeked out. Like a spot in the corner of my eye, if I looked just right, a beam of light shot out from the portal slab.

When I realized what I was looking at, it took my breath away. Death told me I needed to see, and I did. Through the veil that hid most of the spirit world, I saw where Ari had opened her portal.

And it wasn't gone.

The last faint echoes of it hung, still outlined in the air. Invisible to human eyes, but maybe—

I sprinted toward the fragmenting vortex of light, curling into a ball as I leaped. My stomach swirled as the portal tore me from the Forest, casting me into the beyond.

I landed shoulder first, rolling onto my back and knocking the breath out of me, but the good news seemed to be that both of my feet, my hands, and all of my fingers made the trip with me. Even better, they weren't rearranged into some sort of Picasso painting, where I'd pick my nose every time I moved my lips. The lights above looked familiar. Fluorescent.

The carpet underneath felt much too comfortable for the Agency. Grimm never paid for anything but the cheapest remnants available, on account of how often our carpet caught fire, got doused in blood, or transmuted into moss. Light streamed in from stained glass windows, and wooden chairs lay scattered like leaves before me, in a—

"Rise, handmaiden." A voice like a silver flute, lilting with a French accent, laced with power. "I have awaited you."

I rolled to my feet and froze.

Twenty feet away stood a face I recognized from a dozen history books. From half a dozen documentaries that showed on the Kingdom Channel late at night. From an oil painting that showed up on my front doorstep, sent by the doorman at the Court of Queens. Her beauty entranced me, regal, unreal. From the gentle sweep of her arms to brown eyes that mesmerized me, everything about her said she was as powerful, as beautiful, and probably even more dangerous than the documentaries claimed.

Her hair hung in long brown tresses to her waist, without

the annoying curls that would have turned mine to springs at that length. Her figure, I'd call it killer, as in "that's got to kill her back." Like anyone else famous, she wasn't nearly as tall as pictures made her look.

"Isolde Faron." I practically spit her name, reaching for my bracelet. "Grimm, she's here. Time to do your thing."

The edges of her rose-pink lips curled up. "Yes, Father. Come and rescue your pet. Come and negate my power."

The bracelet on my arm began to glow, almost white-hot, but Grimm didn't even appear in the glass windows.

"Is something wrong?" The Black Queen glanced around. "Father, it's going to be hard to have our family reunion without you present."

Though my bracelet continued to glow like fire, Grimm showed no signs of coming to my rescue. I looked the Black Queen in the eyes and kept my tone firm. "Where is Ari?"

Isolde stepped to the side, and behind her, Ari hung in midair, spinning lazily like a top. "She challenged me to a contest. She, a peasant's princess, not even trained."

"Put her down." I reached for my purse and the gun inside, realizing too late I'd left it behind in the Forest.

"Or?"

"I won't let you hurt Ari." I stepped to one side, watching her turn to face me.

"Take your place at my side, handmaiden, and I will forgive her challenge."

I looked around, searching for something to throw, something to hit her with. "Not going to happen."

I know exactly what a tennis ball feels like, when someone lines up and smacks it so hard it breaks the sound barrier. I can't say what she hit me with, just that I went flying so hard and fast I hit the ground before I had time to flinch.

"You bear my mark." Isolde appeared at the edge of my vision, gliding toward me like a phantom, staring down at me like Death himself. "You wear my ring. A ring you chose to put on. You declared yourself my handmaiden before the Court of Queens."

Now, I can explain the mark. That was so not my fault,

using the Black Queen's bones to kill a fairy. The ring, I could almost explain. I really, really needed to get into the Court of Queens. As in, "The world will end if I don't get in there." That said, when I did those things, I still believed the Black Queen was dead. Standing before her never appeared anywhere on my "Things Marissa needs to do" list.

I kicked myself to my feet, unwilling to let her stare me down. "You want the ring back, take it." I'm not entirely crazy. The debate in the Court of Queens over whether or not it was possible for me to be a handmaiden ended with the decision to seal the ring on me, until such time as Isolde took it from me.

I held out my hand, beckoning. "You want it?"

"No, handmaiden." Isolde shook her head once. "You will be my emissary to the Court of Queens."

Some people just don't listen. So I picked up a chair and swung it at her, getting a nice smooth arc that would make a professional wrestler proud.

The chair *exploded* across her, shattering into a thousand pieces.

She didn't move. If I'd hit her with a foam bat, I'd have done more. Splinters of wood rained like confetti all around her, and she had the absolute gall to ignore me.

"I don't force my handmaidens. They come to me willingly." She raised her hand toward Ari, and Ari convulsed. "I also don't challenge lesser opponents, but I don't deny them that right."

I flung myself at the Black Queen, reaching for hair, clawing at eyes. I'd learned more martial arts than you'd think possible, but all of that was self-defense. In a brawl, a good hair pulling works perfectly well.

From what I could tell, I didn't fall, the carpet zoomed up to smack me, then bounced me into the air and hit me like a fist again. And the building began to shake.

See, there was this one time when I impersonated a genocidal fairy-tale character and shot up a village full of wolves (in retrospect, it doesn't sound so great). In the process, I rescued a Fae child, and his mother rewarded me with the worst pets in existence.

The windows split, spiderwebs running through them, and blew inward.

My pets were fifty percent cat, fifty percent ghost, one hundred percent psychotic. Creatures of pure magic, living spells called harakathin, they started out cute and cuddly, like a pirhana. You know how people pick a puppy at the shelter, and a few years later it weighs three hundred pounds and eats ponies?

My harakathin did something like that. The only good thing was the older they got, the less inclined to leave the house they were. Long as we sacrificed a daily can of cat food to them, they were happy. And when people made the mistake of threatening me, my harakathin objected in ways that required replacing the carpet, the windows, and every bone in the person's body.

A pressure wave burst past me, heading for Isolde.

Where she'd regarded me as nothing more than a nuisance, Isolde glanced at the air above me and switched to a battle stance. Of course she had spirit sight—I'd never seen it mentioned, but from the way her eyes tracked movement, I had no doubts. She held one arm in front of her, and with the other, held a whip of raw magic, which bubbled out of her hand. She lashed out with it, twisting her whip through the air to strike.

I closed an eye and peered through the veil. There, I could see my harakathin. Each stood at least twelve feet tall, with long arms that trailed on the ground. One glowed pure white, the one called blessing. The other, technically a curse, shone with violet light. In my experience, the term *blessing* or *curse* was completely arbitrary.

Isolde swung her whip, slicing a cut open across blessing's chest. A shower of golden sparks trailed to the ground as my pet bled magic, and I winced, losing my tenuous view through the veil. Before me, Isolde twisted and sidestepped, lashing out again and again. A storm gathered on her face with every act, and every time she swung, a hint of fear crept into her eyes. A gash tore open in her dress, and her whip faltered, fading away.

And for one split second, fear found footing in Isolde's

eyes. The carpet rippled toward her, and all sound ceased. My ears rang in the silence.

Then the world breathed out.

At least, that's the closest I can get to it. Like Isolde had sucked reality itself inside her and blew it out. From the corners of the room, a wail like all the voices of the dead and every wounded cat to ever grace a highway split my ears.

"Oblivion." Isolde spoke the word, and the air snapped, like static electricity.

I felt them die. My blessings. My pets. Torn away in an instant, blown to shreds by a force of magic so strong, I'd never encountered anything remotely like it. Sharp pain flared inside me as two lives guttered out like candles in a hurricane.

It's a good thing I was already on my face; I wouldn't have been able to stand.

Ari's gasps roused me, choking cries, like a hamster caught in a blender. I pushed up, looking for her, and the spotlight-in-the-eyes hit me again as my vision momentarily aligned with my peephole in the veil. This time, I understood how to use it, tilting my head just so.

If I'd eaten breakfast, I'd have vomited.

In flesh, Isolde resembled the paintings. Breathtaking beauty that seemed to only grow richer each time I looked at her, sleek white skin, and grace I could only dream of.

Through the veil, I saw the truth, a truth that would haunt my nightmares from that moment onward.

Isolde spent a few years trapped in a thorn tree, according to Grimm. Through the veil, I saw that perhaps she'd never truly left it. The best I can do is to say she looked like a thorn tree grew legs, borrowed a set of teeth from a shark, and grafted octopus tentacles into its branches. Actually, any self-respecting octopus would tear those limbs off and take up life as a jellyfish before waving appendages like that.

Ari shone like a spotlight, the source of the beam that caught my attention, golden light like a thousand suns welling up, churning inside her. And then the tentacles wrapped around her, pulling her in, breaking off chunks of light and swallowing them.

I once heard a witch claim the Black Queen could drink souls. Now I no longer considered it a euphemism.

Ari didn't scream. Her body convulsed in bursts, the guttural moan from her lips telling me she had seconds, maybe less.

"Stop." I don't remember making the decision. Just knowing what I had to do. "I'll do it."

Ari went stiff, a convulsion gripping her.

Isolde, her lovely lady form cloaking the monster that lay inside, turned back toward me. She spoke with leisure, each word measured. "Yes, handmaiden?"

"Let her go. I'll serve you. Just let her go." The words left me winded, nearly broken. My left arm dropped to my side, like I'd been shackled to an anchor.

"Yes, you will, darling. We have an agreement." Isolde jerked her hand at me, and the weight of a black hole forced me to kneel. She walked over, each step filled with menace, and raised my chin to stare into her radiance. "You have until the new moon to set your affairs in order. Arm yourself appropriately. The hand cannons you favor are no weapons fit for my servants."

Ari collapsed to the floor, her head flopping to the side.

Isolde looked at her with distilled, frozen contempt. "There is no part of your friend's training I have not observed. She had great promise, and so I will let her live with another promise: If she challenges me again, I will rend her soul from her body."

Rays of light burst from the carpet around Isolde, forming a portal, turning her body into vaporous light. "When you see my father, tell him that he knows my only request, my only demand." She dissolved into a river of light, leaving me to crawl over and cradle Ari.

I can't tell you how long I held her before the voices and the shouting pulled me from the whirlwind of fear that surrounded me.

"Arianna? Where are you, Arianna?" Only one man called Ari that to her face without fear. Wyatt. Son of the first royal family, MBA major, complete wimp. He rushed over, straining to lift her from my lap.

"Marissa!" Liam roared, and I do mean roared, as the curse that shared his body fed off of emotions. He nearly tackled me, checking me for cuts (none) and bruises (a few new ones for the collection). "Fairy Godfather told us where we'd find you, but I needed Wyatt here to get me into the Court of Kings."

"Tell him it's worse than he feared. Get the Fairy Godfather *now*. I mean, if you don't mind." Wyatt's tone bordered on panic.

Liam headed for a set of double doors with a sign that said "Men's Room." "I'll handle it." The sound that followed was either glass breaking or him tearing a wall apart. A moment later, he returned, carrying a shard of mirror the size of a guillotine blade.

From the mirror, Grimm watched, his eyes brimming with concern. "Stand clear. I need room to work."

Now, here's the thing: In nine years, I'd never actually seen Grimm work big magic. The odd potion or portal? Sure. Some of that came from the fact that he spent a few hundred years with his power constrained. The rest of it came from his stingy nature, unwilling to spend a fleck of Glitter where normal means sufficed.

A block of onyx erupted, oozing like lava through the carpet. Seconds later, a miniature blizzard formed overhead. Snow hissed against glowing hot stone, and a cloud of steam obscured the portal. When it cleared, a block of polished, black rock remained. Then runes slithered from fissures, crawling their way like snakes to coil across the stone. As each reached its point, it froze, dying, and locked the rune into place.

When the portal exploded into existence, a wave of heat like a blast furnace singed the edges of my hair. Liam stepped between me and the portal, letting the heat soak into him.

"Do not panic." Grimm's voice barely registered above the roar of the portal. "I've summoned help. Wyatt, please accompany Princess Arianna. I will inform your mother of your unauthorized field trip."

About then, the first figure stepped out of the portal, and my heart sank. Seven feet tall, willowy, with gray tattoos covering his face, I recognized him as fae. While the fae weren't exactly enemies, they weren't remotely friendly either. Another emerged, and another, fae warriors with weapons held at the ready.

Then another figure came through the portal, and my not-good-o-meter went from bad, straight past "ten-year audit," and stuck so far to the right, I'd never come up with a term. The Fae Mother. Not quite queen, not quite prophet, one hundred percent alien.

"Rise." Her voice echoed in my head, reminding me of the peal of church bells, or an approaching storm. She held her hand over Ari, and Ari's limp body floated into the air, then back through the portal. Wyatt threaded his way past fae warriors, who regarded him like I did convenience store clerks, and disappeared into the portal. With Ari gone, the warriors stepped one by one, backwards.

"What did you do? What sort of stupid prophecy did you tell her?" I pushed Liam aside, confronting the Fae Mother face-to-face. Well, as close as I could come, given that she stood a foot and a half taller. Afraid? I would've been afraid, but I'd encountered her before. She had a habit of spouting lines that made me almost think I understood them.

She gave me a sympathetic look like I was a toddler in need of a nap. "That she would be the last to challenge the Black Queen to a duel."

"I saw her. Through the veil, I saw her, tearing parts of Ari's soul off." My mind flicked from Ari to my harakathin, destroyed with only a word by the Black Queen's power.

"I wish I'd been here. I'd like to see the Black Queen survive without lungs." Liam shook with rage, a sure sign his curse just about had control.

"You must not come into contact with our half sister. If you come before her, there is no hope. To stand before her is to choose your own death." The Fae Mother spoke softly to Liam, so my ears only rang a little. "You must protect the princess, until she can become what she is."

I looked at Grimm, tears welling in my eyes. "You didn't come. I thought you would come."

Seconds, minutes passed before he finally spoke. "I could not. My daughter has consumed the power of another fairy, and I can no longer approach her." His voice sounded hollow, defeated.

"You said I had nothing to fear from her."

Grimm wouldn't look at me.

Then Liam caught my arm, his grip stiffening until it almost hurt. "M, what is this?"

On my wrist, below the handmaiden's mark, hung a gold band like a wide bracelet. Seamless, it fit so snugly it wouldn't even rotate. "She was killing Ari."

Liam looked past me, to Grimm. "What is this?"

The pain on Grimm's face made him look even older than normal, his voice nearly a whisper. "Marissa has promised her services as the Black Queen's handmaiden."

Four

~⚬~

I MIGHT HAVE mentioned that Liam carries a curse older than fruitcake, with enough power to level several square blocks of fruitcake. I might have failed to mention that he only carried it because I gave it to him. When we first got together, I figured his relaxed, calm attitude was just a side effect of being an artist. Over time, I grew to understand that in reality, it was his only hope of keeping the curse in check. Something he completely failed to do now.

His clothes caught fire, his arms grew even thicker, and red scales with a tint of green beaded his skin. I won't lie—I loved the man either way, and found him attractive even as a reptile. He rampaged about the room, then pushed me with his nose farther from the Fae Mother and Grimm's portal, setting the carpet in front of me on fire.

Not that I minded.

My engagement ring from Liam came with several nice side effects—first off, it made other women jealous, since my diamond looked like a baby tooth. The other key effect was even better, an enchantment that made me immune to fire. That's an absolute necessity when your lover's flaming passion isn't just a metaphor.

Then Grimm spoke from the mirror, in a language I'd never heard. Like the sound a vacuum cleaner makes when it sucks up a penny, only it went on, and on.

And Liam answered. At least, the dragon did. Liam always said he couldn't speak, but here they were, carrying on a back-and-forth conversation that I could only replicate with shop tools. After a soliloquy long enough to inflate a tire or vacuum out my car, Liam curled up in a ball around me, wrapping his stubby tail around to touch his nose.

"I didn't know you spoke dragon," I said to Grimm.

"I speak many languages, my dear. French, Spanish, Latin, pig Latin, all the useful tongues. It seems that both the curse and Mr. Stone would prefer to lock you in a tower and guard you." Grimm looked around. "But as you can see, that will not work."

And I think that's the first time I actually noticed where I was.

The Court of Kings, incidentally, was a dump that more resembled the mess left by a group of teens in their mother's basement than the seat of power for Kingdom's government. The collection of beer bottles, the dozens of poker tables, a podium that sported a stripper pole instead of a microphone. While the Court of Queens resembled a mall and spa, the boys' version left almost everything to be desired.

Hands down, the strangest part were the statues, gray metal statues of kings and princes playing poker or drinking beer. Then my skin started to crawl while my brain refused to accept what my gut said. I stepped over Liam, feeling him shudder and growl. "It's all right. I'm just going to look at something."

"What did she do?" The statues weren't stone. I'd seen people turned to stone. The perfect details always gave it away, stone eyelashes, stone lint on their clothing. These looked like caricatures, or roughs that a sculptor would finish.

The Fae Mother answered. "She has quelled them. An ancient spell, beyond the capabilities of even the most powerful mortals. They are neither dead nor alive. The world has stopped for them."

"The amount of power needed to quell someone is staggering." Grimm spoke now, his composure recovered. "I once did it for an entire castle until the crop blight could pass. I couldn't perform another spell for nearly one hundred years."

"You mean, like *Sleeping Beauty*–style?" Grimm was, after all, the Fairy Godfather. No surprise he'd been involved, or at least acquainted.

"Like you, the young lady's beauty manifested more on the inside. A charming personality, a sense of wit. Yes, I held their entire kingdom quelled until the wasted soil had years to recover."

"And then a prince broke through a forest of thorns and ended the spell?"

Grimm's eyes narrowed. "I told that idiot there was a perfectly serviceable road, just a mile down, but he refused to listen. Just like a man to ignore directions. He wandered around in a blackberry patch for fifteen minutes and came out looking like he'd fought a war with a polecat. And lost."

I tried chipping at the spell covering a prince, but I'd have had more luck chipping off a rubber glove.

"He goes riding into the castle just as everyone wakes up and decides that because the alarm went off while he was near, he must have been the reason it happened. The point is, quelling these people must have taken vast amounts of her power. She is weakened."

Again Liam hissed, the sound of teakettle filled with ball bearings.

Grimm shook his head. "Even weakened, she had the power to repel me. I appreciate the offer, but the result would be worse than suicide. The question, as always, is 'why.' My daughter has never been one to act without reason."

"She says you know her only demand." I rubbed at my wrist, rotating the golden band.

When the Fae Mother spoke, she sounded like a dozen voices at once, whispering to Grimm. When Grimm answered, it sounded like a sea of soccer fans, whispering in unison, all of them saying something different. She nodded toward me. "I go to tend the princess. Without her, there is no hope." Then she rose into the air, drifting back into the portal, and it folded up behind her into a wisp of light that disappeared.

"I know her demand. She knows I cannot supply it." Grimm spoke with an air of finality I didn't expect.

Liam spoke once more, like a mountain of pots and pans being turned over.

Grimm looked at me instead of him and shook his head. "You are asking me to perform the impossible. When the harbinger Death spoke to you, did he ever explain why he takes the souls?"

Talking to the manifestation of death had almost always left me feeling sick to my stomach, so I avoided question-and-answer sessions. "He said he offers them the choice to go. And that only hate or love could pin them to the world."

Grimm nodded. "Truth, but not all of it. A soul could remain, absent enough love or hate to keep it intact, but only for a month. On the thirty-first day, it would dissolve. So the choice is to go onward with Death, or face true oblivion."

I had a feeling I knew her demand now, which implied that something else Death told me was also true. "Can you raise the dead?"

Grimm always told me that he wouldn't raise souls, never couldn't. For the longest time, I thought it was to make him appear more powerful. "Yes, if the soul is still available. Creating flesh is easy, those bodies humans wear are little more than primitive, chemical machines. Without a spirit to guide it, the flesh is empty."

"And she wants you to raise someone from the dead. Someone dead more than thirty days." The pieces fell into place now.

Grimm nodded, his eyes downcast. "Someone dead more than four hundred years, Marissa. And since you will ask, she wants me to resurrect Rouge Faron. Her mother. My wife."

According to the history books, Grimm once allowed a princess to work for him as his agent. He considered it similar to keeping a pet lizard, except that this lizard talked and wore pink dresses and so on. After seven years of service, he granted her a wish.

"I wish you loved me" was never on the list of things he expected, but Grimm followed through, seeing it as an opportunity to learn more about these ridiculous humans. Together, they had a daughter, Isolde. Princess of Roses, according to the doorman. Later, Queen of Thorns.

On my right arm, the golden bracelet I wore fused into a seamless band, as tight as the manacle on my other arm. I shook it and pulled uselessly. "What are you doing?" When I first worked for Grimm, the bracelet had been our link. Fear of once more being Grimm's slave swept me, making me shake.

"You are bound to my daughter as her handmaiden. Now you are bound to me as well. It will prevent her from making more—drastic—changes to you. It will also give you respite, as for at least some of each day, you *must* be available to my commands, and I would command you to rest."

"Take it off." I yanked at the bracelet, pulling until it cut my skin.

"I will not. As her handmaiden, you would be subject to her spells, her changes, her desires. She would mold you in her own image. As long as I maintain a grasp on you, neither of us has complete control. You are, to the best of my knowledge, the only being ever bound to two fairies at once."

"All I ever wanted to do was be free." I stumbled backwards, holding on to Liam while I pulled at the golden manacle.

Grimm spoke softly. "That bond between us is your life preserver in a sea of magic, not an anchor meant to drown you. In this matter, I must insist that you trust me. Will you agree to it?"

The logical part of my brain knew the alternative was worse. My heart, on the other hand, didn't care about alternatives. It cared about *now*. I swallowed the fear inside me and forced myself to open my eyes as I nodded. "Only until—"

"Absolutely, Marissa." Grimm's power surged out, connecting to me in a way that I could only feel.

I shrugged it off like a mosquito bite, turning fear to anger, and anger into determination. "I'm not going to serve her. Don't you have anything you could kill her with? Bullets? Bones? Some blessed sword?"

Liam swept his tail around me, pinning me against him.

Grimm flashed to a bottle on the table so he could look me in the eye. "You are her handmaiden. A handmaiden's fate is tied to her queen. What the queen experiences, her handmaiden bears as well. Without a doubt, this is why she chose you to begin with."

For nearly ten years, I'd lived with realities so strange they made weird seem normal. Always facing the truth, always taking things as they were. Now I wanted, more than anything else, to hide away and pretend this wasn't happening.

Between being used as a repo man by the Adversary and as a human shield by the Evil Queen of Evil Queens, I'd nearly reached a breaking point. But the key to not breaking was to bend. I'd done the whole "bound to a fairy" routine once before, and hiding, running, those things never worked. This time around, I'd try something different. I'd fight her every step of the way. I pushed away Liam's tail. "So tell me, Fairy Godfather. What's the plan?"

Five

GRIMM DISAPPEARED AND remained gone so long I figured he wasn't coming back. In the ensuing quiet, Liam slowly transformed back into his normal self. The scales melted from his skin, which faded from red to tan. His limbs slimmed down, losing claws. As usual after one of his romps, he snored, and I let him.

When a crew of Kingdom police burst into the court, I honestly thought we were going to get another round of dragon rampage, but Grimm had apparently notified the rest of Kingdom's government about the Black Queen's intrusion. They offered Liam a towel, then ushered us out of the court, sealing the doors behind us.

Liam looked back, wistfully. "I wanted to check that place out. Looked like a nice hangout." He walked down the street, arm wrapped around mine, a towel wrapped around his waist.

"We have got to work on your sense of style." I'd never change him. Didn't want to. Didn't want him to change at all. My thoughts turned to Ari, and I put my hand to Grimm's bracelet. "Grimm, how's Ari?"

Grimm appeared in an oil stain, distorted like a rainbow. "The ritual to re-anchor her soul is complete, my dear. She is spending time with her Seal to complete her healing, and will return to work tomorrow." Without waiting, Grimm faded away.

"What do I do now?" I watched an ogre pass by, its trainer sitting on the ogre's shoulder, guiding it through the streets.

"I don't know. I'll be with you, though. What did she say to you?" Liam waved to a couple who'd apparently never seen a half-naked man walking down the street. Which meant they must have been tourists; I saw at least one buck-naked man on the way to work, every day.

"She said I had to get my affairs in order and arm myself. Let's head to the gates. My purse got left in the Forest."

"My wallet was in my clothes. Sounds like a great day for a walk."

So we strolled together, through the crowds, out of Kingdom. Just outside the Gates of Kingdom, a delivery van pulled up. From the driver's seat, out stepped Mikey, in his brown Agency uniform. "I was out making deliveries, and Fairy Godfather sent me to pick you up. He said you need to come now."

WE ARRIVED BACK at the Agency, where I kept seven spare sets of clothes, a spare set of keys, everything except an extra driver's license. I went straight to Grimm's office while Liam sang in the Agency showers, belting out show tunes from the fifties.

With a sigh, I flopped down in one of his chairs. "Grimm, any chance of retrieving my purse from the Forest?"

"We could retrieve the scraps and ashes, no doubt. The goblins are purging everything associated with the Black Queen with fire."

The buzzer rang, and Rosa spoke in fluid Spanish, more words than she'd said to me in three months. Grimm answered in English. "Bring her right in."

"Ari?" I shot to my feet, grabbed the door, and opened it to find Mrs. Pendlebrook. Wyatt's mother, ex–High Queen of

Kingdom. Taller than me, with pale blue eyes and silver gray hair, she radiated majesty in a way that didn't at all affect me. "You aren't Ari."

She brushed past me. "Your friend and my son are both still in Fae. Frankly, I think that's for the best given the situation here." She sat in one of Grimm's chairs, placing her purse in her lap. "Fairy Godfather, how may I assist you?"

Grimm bowed his head to her, earning a dour frown from both of us. "Mrs. Pendlebrook, you are aware of the Black Queen's attack on the Court of Kings?" He disappeared, leaving an image of the court in his mirror, the kings and princes frozen in place.

"Of course I am. I would offer Arianna and Marissa shelter, but while I consider myself protected from most dangers, if the Black Queen decides to come for me, my wards will not deter her." Mrs. Pendlebrook still lived in a three-story cracker-box house surrounded by enough celestial crystal and wards to strangle even a witch's magic.

I shook my head. "Those wards wouldn't even hold back a moving truck."

Grimm reappeared in his mirror, taking a moment to wipe it from the inside with a handkerchief. "For the time being, I have arranged a temporary apartment for you one floor above our offices here. My daughter will not dare approach me." Grimm crossed his hands and looked down.

Mrs. Pendlebrook took a cuticle trimmer from her purse and fastidiously worked her fingers. "While I'd welcome your protection, Fairy Godfather, I must ask—what could I possibly offer you in return?"

"Patience, please. Arianna was not meant to challenge my daughter when she did, if at all. Her actions have disrupted centuries of my predictions. Even worse, other fairies report similar effects. Well understood, near-term possibilities have unexpected outcomes. This leaves me unable to foretell what may occur."

I sat rock still, wondering what happened to Grimm. The Fairy Godfather always knew, and if he didn't, he sure as hell didn't let on to the clients. "I can find out" was the closest he ever got to admitting lack of knowledge to clients. "Grimm, Ari told me she would be the last one to challenge the Black Queen."

Grimm nodded in agreement. "I wish Arianna had discussed this matter with me, but I will entreat the Fae Mother to understand what her prophecy was. Always remember, even the simplest statements from the Fae are expressions of a dozen possible outcomes. A direct challenge to my daughter was only one of many ways that could be interpreted."

I knew that only too well. Once, I'd been the subject of such a prophecy, that the Black Queen would strike through my hand. The Root of Lies, the only remains of the Black Queen, had in fact ripped through the flesh of my hand to kill Fairy Godmother.

Grimm faded out again, showing a scene worthy of any slaughterhouse: chunks of flesh scattered amid a pile of gore. Grimm spoke over the image. "This is what remains of High Queen Wang Mi."

I don't know whose jaw fell open farther, mine or Mrs. Pendlebrook's. She closed her mouth and put away the nail file with a shake of her head. "I refuse to assert my claim to the title."

Grimm glared at her, and the building trembled. "I would appreciate your hearing me out. Though Arianna's actions have disrupted my predictions, I have already begun to rebuild my knowledge. I am well aware that you do not ever intend to take the throne again. I ask for your advice in exchange for protection. Who do you believe will win the title of High Queen, as Wang Mi's successor?"

"Irina Mihail would be my primary guess, were she still alive. Failing her, it will either be Muwende Takala or Gwendolyn Thromson." She looked to me as she spoke.

A surge of murderous rage blasted through me. "I'll put a bullet through Gwendolyn before I let her take the throne." The moment the words left my mouth, the rage passed, leaving me shocked at my own response. See, I'd killed people before, but only when they'd set out to kill me. One of them came within an inch of doing it too. This felt different, both wrong and on a level that made me queasy, terribly right.

"Forgive Marissa. She's had a rough day and isn't feeling herself at the moment." Grimm gave me the same look he used back when I was his servant, a look that said I wasn't to speak at all.

"Girl, murder is hardly new to the Court of Queens. Nor would this be the first time someone killed a potential heir to the throne. I didn't have you down as a killer, though." Mrs. Pendlebrook spoke with the tone of a school principal, leaving me wanting to burst into tears.

"I'm sorry. It just slipped out." I put my hand over my mouth and focused on my feet.

"Mrs. Pendlebrook, to be honest, I do not believe my daughter intends to involve herself with the Court of Queens. Her disdain for them was always quite clear. My expectation is that she will have one of her servants claim the throne as her proxy." Grimm kept his eyes away from me as he spoke, not betraying my situation.

That couldn't be it. Grimm had always been quite clear. Some people could be made princes or princesses, and some could not. I never minded being in the not group, but now I worried. What if Isolde planned to use me as High Queen?

Mrs. Pendlebrook nodded. "It would be a step down for her. Within the court, only Seal Magic and Wild Magic are permitted. According to history books, she had power approaching that of a fairy. She will send one of her handmaidens to ensure her pawn wins. Has she chosen them?"

I caught my breath, my lungs aching.

"Yes. A handmaiden volunteered, in order to save Arianna." Grimm didn't look at me.

Mrs. Pendlebrook pursed her lips. After a moment, she nodded. "I'm sorry to hear that, Marissa." I know I couldn't have held in the shock, because she gave me a pitiful smile. "After Arianna met my son, I began listening again to rumors from Kingdom. The tale of your challenge to Queen Mihail, declaring yourself the handmaiden, made me proud. You have the mark. And her ring. Who else would offer their services for Arianna's life?"

"Wyatt, though he'd probably want a few days to meditate on it first."

At that moment, Grimm's office door swung open, and Liam walked in. "Fairy Godfather, tell me you have good news." He waited in silence, and the normal smile fled his face. "You have a plan, right? You at least have a way to kill the Black Queen."

"Liam. How are you holding up, young man?" Mrs. Pendlebrook took a comb from her purse and offered it to him.

"Doing fine, Mrs. P." He shrugged off the comb, running his fingers through his hair a couple of times.

Now she turned the principal tone on Liam, pointing the comb at him like a weapon. "I know about Marissa's predicament. It isn't polite to lie to your elders. She will need your love and support even more."

Liam walked up behind my chair and put his hands on my shoulders, such heavy hands, with callused skin from swinging a hammer. "I'd do anything for her."

My face turned hot, and I didn't bother trying to hide the tears that came to my eyes, but Grimm cut my moment short. "Excellent news, Mr. Stone. The first thing I'd like you to do is forge a weapon for me. A weapon with which to kill the Black Queen."

Six

∿

OVER THE OFFICE intercom, a voice announced, "All licensed bear handlers report to loading dock A with porridge." Grimm waited until the hubbub died down to continue. "Mr. Stone, in the storage room, under the table, in a box labeled '6-21-A,' you'll find the materials required." Grimm spoke as though he were revealing the location of a bag of garbage Mikey missed.

Liam squeezed my shoulders and ran his hand up my neck as he walked out of Grimm's office, whistling as he went.

"Mrs. Pendlebrook," said Grimm, "if you don't mind, I would like you to tour your temporary living facilities. I will make reasonable adjustments."

"Of course." With that, Mrs. Pendlebrook marched out the door. Though she'd abandoned her position decades before, she still carried herself like the High Queen.

Now that we were alone, I waited for Grimm to reassure me. To tell me things would be fine. And waited. And waited. I'd been in trouble before, made mistakes that nearly destroyed the world before, and always Grimm functioned as a calming influence, explaining how we'd fix everything. "I need to do something. I can't sit around waiting, ticking off the hours and days. I can't take Liam home and spend the next week in bed with him. I need to work." As I spoke, I picked at the scars forming the handmaiden's mark, wishing I could pick them away.

Grimm nodded with understanding. "While Mr. Stone works on your weaponry, I will consult with Mrs. Pendlebrook to understand who Gwendolyn Thromson's supporters will be. In the meantime, I have a task, if you don't mind. One you are uniquely suited for, that perhaps I could not entrust to any other."

If I'd been a wolf, my ears would have perked up. "Dangerous?"

"Potentially deadly." Grimm smiled as he spoke, which in no way meant I might not get killed.

"Count me in." I was supposed to be settling my affairs, but the only affairs I had going were the love affair with Liam and my addiction to dark chocolate, neither of which I had any intention of ending.

Grimm nodded. "Excellent. I need a package retrieved from the Kingdom Post Office. I leave it up to you as to how you want to accomplish it." Grimm immediately disappeared, leaving me to curse at an empty mirror.

I swore my way out of his office, down the hall, out into the lobby, where I returned Rosa's sour look with a phrase she'd always claimed meant "Merry Christmas," at least until I learned Spanish. It was time to catch a bus.

I ENTERED KINGDOM the normal way. That is to say, the most normal way one can enter a second plane of existence layered on top of the normal city. All it took was turning a corner in the right place—and magic.

I froze at the gates, uncertain of what would happen. I had no magic powers. No special lineage, or powerful curse. My harakathin had been my ticket into Kingdom, as a person both blessed and cursed. Before that, Grimm always paid to get me in. Like paying a parking fine, or feeding a meter, his magic made the difference, allowing me to access a part of the city I had no right to.

And now I was afraid to pass the gates.

See, the golden manacle on my arm belonged to just about the most evil person ever, and the gates, they could take you to High Kingdom, sure, or let you past to walk down the normal Avenue, but they could also take you someplace else.

The gates could also take me to Low Kingdom, a place where darkness held sway, where every creature to get the short shrift in a fairy tale wound up. I didn't dine on human flesh, I never worked for the IRS, and serial killing as a hobby just didn't appeal to me. So Low Kingdom wouldn't normally have been an option.

But I wasn't clear whose power would transport me. Grimm would see to it I wound up in High Kingdom. Isolde would see to it that I wound up in hell. Not literal hell. I went to Inferno every now and then; that wasn't so bad. The demons gave me a fair amount of grudging respect as one of the few living apocalypse bringers. They also gave me a fair amount of pure hatred as one of the few living apocalypse enders.

I closed my eyes and took a step forward, and another. The air charged with static electricity. One more step, and when I peeked, the crowds around me drifted like mists, around me, past me, through me.

Holding my breath, I took one final step. For a moment, the sky darkened, and black cracks etched into the road, with the foul stench of open sewage drifting in the air. Shadows drifted toward me, taking form, reaching out. Then Grimm's power surged through my bracelet and up my arm, enveloping me.

The world flickered like a bad video feed.

This time, the river of colors ran golden and red, the colors of High Kingdom, turning the streets to gold, and instead of sewage, a blast of rose-scented air washed over me. I took a few more steps, nearly sprinting just to be sure, then sat down on the sidewalk, up against a Smiling-Large Golden Dentures shop.

Putting my hand on Grimm's bracelet, I called him. "How much did forcing me into High Kingdom cost you?"

Grimm appeared in a discarded champagne glass, a miniature version of his usual self. "Consider it simply a bump in the road, certain to be ironed out. And I am in no way concerned with the cost. Be careful at the post office, my dear."

I don't know what scared me more, Grimm's warning to be careful or the implication that the stingiest fairy on earth no longer cared how much magic I cost him. And it had cost him. He tried to hide the pained look on his face, but I'd spent too many years with him to miss it. I'd been in Kingdom earlier, when I followed Ari's portal, but I couldn't expect Grimm to spend the magic on a portal anytime I decided to make the trip.

With the gates behind me, I could relax. Get some additional cardio in. Run to the post office, get Grimm's package, run back. No stopping to smell the singing flowers, no talking animals, and no parades. I checked my laces, grabbed my purse by the short handles, and took off.

When the first squirrel began to scamper along behind me, I didn't panic. When he began to sing, trilling away a happy tune about the joys of Kingdom on a sunny day, I refused to toss him into a wood chipper, even though that was probably the only option to prevent what came next.

One squirrel became two, two became three plus a family of rabbits, and I'd only gone about two blocks when I looked back and found I'd gathered an entire procession. From the flock of forest creatures who had no business being in the city, to the singing minstrels who had no business being in the city, to the couples twirling and dancing with absolutely no regard for the normal rules of traffic, as usual, everyone wanted in on a parade.

I hated parades almost as much as I detested parties.

The longer this parade gathered steam, the worse the eventual disaster would be at the end of it. I skidded to a stop and spun on my heel, nearly crushing an unobservant cottontail. "What exactly do you think you are doing?"

A group of skipping children with baskets of rose petals stopped short, throwing uncertain fistfuls of petals into the air.

"Who's going to clean those up? You?" I surveyed the

buffet of woodland creatures. "You? That's littering." I caught one of the minstrels by his lacy sleeve. "You have a license for street performance? No? Well, stop. This isn't a parade. I'm going to pick up a package."

One of the dancing couples continued to spin and twirl, their eyes locked on each other, until I separated them. "Let me guess. You just met and can't wait to live happily ever after?"

The girl nodded, leaning her head up against the young man. "We're in love."

That touched a spot in my heart that I didn't often admit existed. Even after a decade in the business, I still believed in love at first sight and happily ever after, at least when no one was looking. I took a business card from my pocket, wrote a few instructions on the back, and handed it to her. "When I got engaged, the Fairy Godfather himself gave me a gift. It's a terrifying experience. A dark ritual that will force you to face truths you want to keep hidden. It's the best chance you've got."

She turned the card over and read aloud. "Rosa—arrange premarital counseling, at least eight weeks."

"Real relationships take time." I spun around, examining the remains of my accidental parade. "Does anyone else still think it's a good idea to follow me through the streets?"

The thick stench of crushed party hung in the air, and one of the flower girls began to weep.

The Agency business was built on tears. Not literally—the concrete in our building was normal enough, but I dealt with enough weeping on an average day to dehydrate a dolphin. "Listen—back by the gates, I saw a young girl who looked like she fell and scratched her knee. If you hurry, you could get there in time to serenade her." The group stampeded down the street, singing at the top of their lungs.

If there wasn't a girl who'd scratched her knee near the gates, by the time that crowd pushed their way through, there would be. And I'd be safely in the post office. I just couldn't wait to get in line.

Which, incidentally, should have been my first tip-off that something was wrong. I rounded the corner to the post office and saw only an empty marble entrance. On a normal day, the Kingdom Postal Service had a line that snaked out of the door like an anaconda made of pure frustration. I walked right up to the door, threw it open, and nearly choked.

The air indoors had enough humidity that every minute I spent inside would go down as scuba diving practice. The interior of the building held only darkness, and the odor of mud mixed with a smell like someone scooped up a quarter mile of rain forest and dumped it in Kingdom.

"Hello?" I pushed through a stand of bamboo just beyond the marble arch, wondering if a spell had gone wrong, or maybe a bomb and a spell.

With a *whoosh*, a row of torches flickered to life, leading off into the darkness. A distant drum thumped like the beat of my heart echoed, constant and worried.

"Is anyone here? I just want a package. That's all I need, and you—" On the edges of my vision, forms swarmed in the darkness, flickers of shadow, glints of torchlight in sharp steel.

"Come." A gnome's voice echoed from about the height of my knee. I swiped a torch from its holder and swung it in a circle. In the guttering light, gnome eyes gleamed back at me from every angle.

They'd completely destroyed the interior of the post office. The last time I was there, it had been decorated in "Old-Style Government," which meant marble floors and ceilings mixed with plastic chairs and cheap plastic "Now Serving" signs. Once, giant chandeliers lit vaulted ceilings. Now vines hung like ropes, and gnomes hung like rope-hang-y things from them, every last one sporting a spear that looked like a guitar pick tied to a chopstick.

Grimm could get his own package, as far as I was concerned.

"You know, I think I'll just come back later." With a swing of the torch, I cleared a path through the gnomes, took a few steps back, and pushed on the door.

Only smooth granite met my fingertips, cold and impersonal as a "We tried to drop off your package, but you were unconscious" note.

"Someone open the door." I pounded for a moment on the stone, then spun and put my back to it. It might not let me out, but the wall wouldn't stab me either.

"Come. Make your sacrifice. See if you live." I couldn't tell you which one of the gnomes said it, but the rest took up hooting like a pack of two-foot-tall monkeys. I don't have a problem with the occasional sacrifice, though I'd had to remind people on more than one occasion that virginity was a state of mind. The whole "See if you live" bit didn't exactly give me warm cuddles, but at least it wasn't "And then you die." That's almost always bad. So I followed.

Puddles do not belong on the inside of a government facility. The crocodiles were a complete violation of the Exotic Animal law, but I wasn't going to ask for their facility permit. Turns out, there's an easy way to tell if it's safe to cross a given stream: toss a gnome in first.

After what felt like an hour of listening to tribal chanting, punctuated by the occasional "I'm being eaten by a crocodile" gnome scream, I finally reached what I believed was once the main service counter.

Torches on either side lit the window, and a beaten brass gong replaced the service bell. I kicked it like a soccer ball, sending a reverberating crash through the post-forest. "I just want my package. I'll sign. Eight copies, if you want."

The gnomes began to chant and stomp their feet in a way that passed way beyond normal into flat-out weird. Then a new one approached from behind the counter, a pair of guitar-pick spears across his back, a miniature hockey stick in his fist. "Make your sacrifice." He pointed behind me with the stick.

There, a ring of torches illuminated a carven image of the dark jungle god. Goddess. In fact, the longer I looked at it, the more familiar it looked. "Oh, you have got to be kidding me. Seriously?" I swore at myself again. In the middle of the wreckage that remained, surrounded by a tribe of feral gnomes, I stood before a fourteen-foot statue of myself.

"Where did you get the picture to carve this from? I don't look like that most of the time. And while I'm flattered, if I had a bust like that, I wouldn't be able to stand up, let alone walk. And my hips do *not* look like that. Do they?" I almost missed the ring of pointy spears.

"Make a sacrifice." The young gnome at the counter screamed, leaping up and down like a gorilla in a rampage.

"Not going to happen. Let me out of here, give me my package, and for the love of god, carve a new face on the statue." I could send them a picture of Ari's stepmother, if they wanted to kneel before a monster.

Something hissed in the darkness, and a stinging fire lit up my arm. I pulled away a dart the size of my fingernail. For one moment, I thought about calling for Grimm. About screaming for help. Without a mirror to catch his reflection, Grimm couldn't watch, let alone help. A chorus of hissing, a flurry of pinpricks, and my body lit up all over with pain.

Then one of them lassoed me with a vine as I felt my hip and pulled out another dart. Like a five-foot, eight-inch tree, I collapsed, crushing a gnome or two as I fell, and the world became very fuzzy.

WAKING UP LEFT me in a worse mood than ever. My first urge was to strangle the nearest gnome, but with my hands tied behind my back, I didn't have a huge number of options.

"Put her in the pot," said one gnome, dressed in a purple loincloth to match his purple hat. "Our goddess demands we make a broth of you, with mint, dill, and just a hint of cumin."

The gnome before him held up his hands in a convulsion. "She don't fit. I don't know what she's been eating, but our largest pot won't hold her rear."

"Get the saws," they said in unison.

Now, their insults to my posterior I could deal with. Their glee at the thought of chopping me up, that I could get past. The thought of being boiled down as an offering to a grotesque misrepresentation of myself bugged me. "I demand a trial."

The blank look adorning their faces told me trials weren't common.

"I demand the right to defend myself in hand-to-hand

combat." If they wanted to go *Lord of the Flies* on me, I could spear a piggy or three.

The two looked at each other, a look of dread passing between them. "She challenges the chief." The way they said it, I wondered if the bone saws might have been a more kind option.

"Yes, she does." I assumed my normal boss tone. "Get him, let me face him in combat."

They scampered away, disappearing into the flickering shadows. The drums grew faster, louder, like the pounding heart of a gnome caught in a crocodile stream. Then the chanting began, low and long. A figure emerged, a torch in one hand, a guitar-pick spear in the other.

"You will sacrifice to our god, or be sacrificed to our god." The chief kneeled, pointing with his spear to the statue. His skin, covered in tattoos, shone blue in the torchlight.

"I have a strict policy against offering sacrifices to myself." I wrenched a hand loose, picking half a dozen darts from my skin. "Also against being sacrificed to myself."

With a cry of rage or excitement, the chief leaped toward me, swinging his torch so close it swept up against my cheek. Now, I made a point, usually, of being nice to the gnomes. But being speared at, darted, sacrificed, and nearly burned was more than I could take. I seized the torch by the burning end, letting the tar and oil drizzle, still flaming, onto my fingers. "That is enough."

I think they expected me to burn.

They expected wrong. See, one of the main problems with being engaged to a half-dragon man was that even the slightest burp or cough could set the bed on fire. Once, Liam had a stomach bug and spent three days in a steel room waiting for the virus to burn itself out.

The gnome chieftain's eyes grew round as the flame guttered out, and he knelt before me. "Forgive us, please. You didn't come for so long we thought you abandoned us."

His round eyes and the droopy hat triggered a memory. "Petri?"

"Chief Petri." He scampered, hopping like a bird, closer and closer, until he stood in front of me. With a deft swipe, he sliced loose the bindings on my body. "Please don't be angry."

"Angry?" I punched at him, narrowly missing his head. "I'm furious. You trapped me in here. You shot me with . . . What exactly are these?" I threw one of them, nearly spearing him to the ground.

Petri looked over the darts, nodding. "Antibiotics, ketamine, and you won't be catching rabies or feline distemper anytime soon. We've missed you so much."

"What happened? The last time I saw you, you were racing monster trucks on the weekend. You were doing so fine." I used Petri's spear to cut loose the last of the vines and rose.

Petri hopped up onto my shoulder, dodging my attempts to grab him in a fist and strangle him until he popped like a tiny sausage in a pointy hat. "Racing got old. Then extreme sports, skydiving without a parachute, and gun-fighting got old. And one day, the shipment of staples didn't arrive on time."

Since Grimm handled all deliveries in Kingdom, I mentally made a note to blame Mikey for everything, which was almost always a good idea. "Staples?"

"So I killed Jakov and took his staples for my own. A few days later"—he swept his spear in a circle—"we found a new way of living. But you didn't come to see us. So we carved a Marissa of our own."

"You could have at least done a good job on the face. Can you get me Fairy Godfather's package? I just want to go home. It's been a bad day." I stumbled through the jungle, ducking vines, back toward the service desk.

"It's a perfect likeness. We made a deal with a demon for a copy of your driver's license. Sent them my mother-in-law and cousin Karl. Stay here, I'll get your package myself." Petri slid down my arm and disappeared into the reeds.

In his absence, a crowd of amazed gnomes gathered around me. Some kneeled, some chanted, but one approached, bowing his head. "Would you be pleased if I cut the heart from an innocent victim and offered it to you?"

I shook my head. "Not really."

His hat sagged; his shoulders slumped. "In that case, never mind." He hurled the oozing leather bag in his hand to the floor, then slouched away, weeping.

After a few moments, a cadre of gnomes returned with a box on their shoulders, following Petri. "Faster! Bring Marissa the package or she will halt the rains for three years." While I didn't exactly know how I'd stop the rain, I had to admire his motivational skills.

Taking the box from their postage-stamp-sized hands, I swung it over my shoulder. "You've done well. I give your chief my favor." Then I knelt beside Petri, whispering, "Which way is out? I have to get back to work."

Petri whistled, a cutting sound that made me wince. White light stabbed my eyes as the jungle lit up, the remains of the post office's ceiling lights giving it the flush of brilliant sun. "This way." Petri pulled at my hand and dashed ahead. "Mind the crocodiles, step over the bear trap." He swept back a blanket of vines, and there, in the earthen bank, I saw the form of a door.

"Bless us with your presence again, soon. Oh, and here." Petri handed me a copy of my driver's license. "Think of Karl every time you use it." Petri pushed the door open, and I stepped out into the crowd, at the emergency exit in the KPS alley. I found a discarded bottle of champagne and rolled it until I got a reflection.

"Grimm?" With my hand on my bracelet, I called.

He snapped into view immediately, his power flooding out through the bracelet once more. "Trouble, my dear?"

"It's the post office. Same as usual. I got the package." I nodded to it, a tight leather bundle bound in black thread. "What's in here?" I knew better than to open Grimm's packages. We had an intern once who opened a package because he got curious about the noises inside of it. Every time I went in that storage room, I spotted another bit of intern stuck to the walls.

Grimm shook his head. "You can open the box when you've returned to the Agency. Not before."

"Never been a big fan of surprises. Just tell me?"

"I've kept the contents safe for four hundred years, stored at the postal service, but the contents are now yours. It is your uniform, you might say. An outfit most appropriate for the handmaiden." With those words, he dashed whatever hope I'd held that what happened earlier was all the result of a bad head injury.

Seven

~

I SAW ARI the moment I opened the Agency door, and gave my best tryout for the Jets, nearly tackling her. I might not have knocked her down, but it would still get me on the team. Alternating between squeezing her until she coughed and wanting to wring her neck, I buried her in a hug. "What were you thinking? You could have been killed." I pushed her back and looked her in the face.

Ari didn't speak. She just looked at me with her witch eyes and trembled. Her voice, when it came, whispered like plastic bags in the autumn wind. "I was supposed to defeat her. I listened to the Fae Mother. She said I would be the last to challenge the Black Queen. She said I could save you."

I wanted to shake Ari until those yellow eyes rolled back in her head. As Grimm pointed out, the Fae speech was almost as bad as Grimm's native tongue. Let ten people listen to the same words, and they'd give you eleven different versions of the same thing.

"Come on. This is no place to talk." I grabbed Ari by the arm, wanting to leave the crowded lobby for a place where every ear wasn't latched on to our conversation. We almost made it, too, before the building's emergency alarm went off, flashing red lights and a fire alarm siren that threatened to split my skull. For the second time in one day, we'd have to evacuate the building. Three more times, and we might match the record.

"Everyone out," said Rosa, pointing to the door.

I left Ari to guard the door while I ushered whining people out into the hall and pointed to the stairs. "Stay away from the elevators." When the last of them left, I pulled the stairwell door closed and sprinted back to the Agency.

Grimm waited in the lobby mirror. "Marissa, there's no reason for the alarms to be going off. No cupcakes, no birthday candles of any sort." The way Grimm's jaw set and his eyebrows furrowed said the Fairy Godfather did not appreciate surprises. "Rosa, bring up the entrance cameras. Something tripped my short-term danger indicators."

Rosa flipped a few switches, and the monitor that usually played Spanish soap operas all day switched to a split screen, showing every entrance to our building along with a Spanish soap opera.

"There." I pointed to the corner. Against the throng of people surging out of the building, four figures threaded their way inward. Their leather cloaks, fur trimmings, and hoods gave away exactly what group had made a fatal decision to attack us. "Huntsmen."

Kingdom's bounty hunters, usually tasked with killing anything that wasn't human and dared attract attention. Their repeating crossbows could pin a man to the concrete or, with a different arrow, punch his heart out through the back of his ribs.

"Picking a fight with Grimm on his turf is suicide." Ari began to crackle as lightning jumped from hand to hand. Anytime Ari was upset or angry, you could power a small city with the sparks she gave off.

A wave of fear washed down my scalp like a blast of cold air. "They're not heading into the Agency proper." Grimm's major mojo stopped at the boundaries. "They're headed into cargo."

"Mikey." We spoke as one. Mikey, grandson of the greatest leader the wolves ever knew, survived a huntsman's attack a few years earlier, and gave the huntsman an overbite that no amount of orthodontics could fix. I thought the other huntsmen had enough sense to let it go. The silver crossbows on their backs said I thought wrong.

"I'm going to go help Michael," said Rosa. "He's such a good boy."

My jaw just about dropped. Rosa grabbed her sawed-off shotgun from behind the desk, loaded a couple of slugs, and limped slowly out the door.

I ran ahead, and Ari trailed me down the stairs, out the side door, and around toward the cargo bay. As I passed the entrance to our underground garage, something came flying out of the darkness, wrapping around my legs. I crashed to the concrete.

"The hunt is over." From the shadows of the garage, a huntsman emerged, older, grayer than the one Mikey tore apart when they last attacked the Agency. Under the enchanted fur armor, he wore a leather vest decorated with animal teeth. In each hand, he twirled silver daggers sporting honed points on the guards.

He strode to the side of the parking garage entrance, staying just inside the shadows. With his attention focused on me, I don't think he ever saw Ari's attack coming.

She hit him with a blast of raw Seal Magic, not even bothering to twist it to an elemental form, throwing him back into the concrete wall. Then she switched her method of attack, drawing Wild Magic from the air around us.

The huntsman rose with a cough, shaking off her spell. The skins huntsmen wore shielded them from minor details like elemental spells or ordinary bullets, so when I pulled out my nine millimeter, he didn't even flinch. I squeezed the trigger, and the bullet ricocheted off of the concrete garage roof above him.

I didn't miss.

The ruined sprinkler over him exploded, gushing water like a fountain. It drenched him, soaking his alligator skin boots so that each step he took, he sloshed. The artificial downpour cascaded down into our garage. A little water wouldn't hurt him any worse than my bullets, something I believe we both knew.

Ari, however, had a creative streak born from her lack of proper training. Huntsmen relied on their enchantments to stop elemental spells.

Those enchantments could stop a blast of pure fire, or a wind colder than the last ice age. They couldn't do a damned thing about the fact that Ari didn't cast a spell at him. She dropped the temperature to fifteen below.

If he'd had an ounce of sense, the huntsman would have held still. Instead, he fought to wrench a foot loose, teetered, and crashed into the ground, where his fur froze him to the wet concrete. He shrieked curses and struggled in vain to free himself while a snowstorm formed inside the parking garage, fueled by Ari's spell.

"Nice touch." I unwound the bolo he'd hit me with and rose, just in time to see Ari cast "Foot-to-Head," a classic spell that worked wonders when one wore steel-toe boots. His furs didn't protect against that either.

Ari hit him with another blast of cold to solidify the ice, then grabbed my hand. "I counted four on the camera. Can I borrow your keys?"

We ran to my car, where I tossed them across to Ari, got in, and then thanked Grimm for making certain I had passenger-side air bags as Ari started the engine and peeled out of the garage, rocketing up the ramp.

Ari, as we may have gone over, was unfortunately a princess. Natural luck, grace and charm that only got better as she aged, and everything from undead sorcerers to Inferno's guardians loved her. The exchange principle, however, meant she gave up something.

Ari *never* drove. It wasn't just the eleven times she failed the driving test. Or the three Agency convertibles she totaled without ever managing to leave the parking lot. Hell, the one time we were in a rowboat, I didn't let her touch the oars because I hadn't forgotten when the captain of the Ellis Island cruise let Ari steer. Hitting an iceberg in the Hudson

River pretty much sealed the deal—the universe didn't want Ari behind the wheel of anything larger than a model car.

The thing was, if you wanted someone run over, Ari was the go-to woman. As we exited, she swung the wheel so hard we fishtailed around the corner, then gained more speed in fifteen yards than I would in two blocks. As we approached the cargo bay at the back of the Agency building, she jumped the curb and aimed at the huntsmen standing at the loading dock.

Anyone else wouldn't have been able to pull it off. Even my mentor, who taught me how to drive badly, couldn't have timed it, but right as Ari reached the bay, the universe reached down to remind her to always take a cab. The passenger-side tires blew out, and we ran over a dolly left carelessly beside a truck.

I wasn't the least bit surprised when our car rolled on its side, passing exactly between two parked delivery trucks, and flattened an extremely surprised huntsman before burying us in a box of champagne glasses destined for Kingdom.

I smashed my way out of the side window, lamenting yet another car relegated to the scrap heap, and whipped my head around as the telltale twang of a repeating crossbow echoed from our cargo bay. Ari lay slumped against the wheel, breathing, but unconscious. It figured, being a princess and all, that the worst she'd get out of this was a headache.

"Grimm, watch out for Ari." He couldn't answer without a reflection, but the pulse of his power through my bracelet meant he heard.

"Move." Rosa's voice startled me so badly I almost shot her. She had her gun leveled at my chest, that same look of lemons dipped in curdled milk, as always, plastered to her face.

I nodded to the door. "You want the left side, I'll take right?"

"No. Stay away." Rosa hobbled on over to the door, peeking inside. She took one half step in, and fired, paused, and fired again, before pivoting out. Then she put the gun up against the wall and pulled the trigger again, blowing a hole straight through the wall.

For the record, enchanted furs are also not terribly helpful against a shotgun slug to the face, which was what one of the huntsmen caught.

The other came rolling through the doorway, and only the slightest glimpse of silver gave me enough warning to throw myself to the floor. A dagger the length of my forearm stuck out of the concrete, and Rosa, she wasn't nearly as fast or lucky.

She'd been pinned to the wall with a spent bolt on the outside of her shoulder. I couldn't tell if it shattered the humerus or not, but based on the lack of gushing blood, it probably missed a major artery. Rosa's shotgun, along with one of her thumbs, lay on the ground in a pool of her blood.

I didn't give the huntsman the chance to finish what he started, squeezing off one shot after another. Problem was, I had the only weapon those bulletproof skins actually worked on. He came for me, pulling fresh knives from the bandoliers about his chest.

And something inside me seemed to scream, a part of me that I didn't know was there. I'd felt something similar before, when my harakathin answered. I waited, hoping that one of them might have survived. Blessing or curse? I didn't care. Either would do.

Come, I willed them. What stepped out of the shadows in answer to my call, I'll never be able to forget. A monster like some sick surgeon had grafted a dozen rotten bodies together, lashing muscle to muscle and bone to bone, without regard for or knowledge of anatomy.

It lurched forward, stumbling and crunching its own bones, gurgling like a fountain of blood ran somewhere deep inside. The eyes on all three of the heads were lit with golden light.

The huntsman took one look at it and decided that between the two of us, it was a lot scarier. He pulled his hood down over his face and began to fling knives, throwing them so hard they exploded out the other side of the creature.

I stood transfixed, trying to find a way to send the thing back to whatever gory realm it called home, but I didn't understand how I'd brought it well enough to punch a return ticket. I glanced back to Rosa, who struggled to pull the bolt from her. As I did, the peephole in the veil drifted into view, and I saw the thing.

A mass of golden light, it shifted, forming a tight series of intricate patterns like Celtic knots. Rosa, too, stood out, her entire body wrapped in a cerulean aura, the same color as the huntsman and Ari. The monster stumbled a few steps closer, and half lunged, half collapsed, tearing at the huntsman with fingers and teeth.

He stopped screaming after what seemed like an eternity.

I can't say the same for me, because as the abomination rose and came toward me bits of fur and a fresh set of arms waved from its torso. Closer and closer it came, and finally I found a way to run, sprinting toward the elevator.

Behind me, it grunted with several sets of lungs, and whistled as it sprinted after me, moving faster on broken limbs than I could run. At the back of the loading bay, I hefted a canister of propane for the cutting torch and threw it back at the thing.

The canister by itself did nothing.

The bullet I followed it up with, on the other hand, did, causing a fireball the size of a pickup truck to explode out. I instinctively ducked. I wasn't faster than a fireball. I barely got my eyes shut before it hit, and if it weren't for my engagement ring, I'd have lost my eyebrows, and possibly my eyes.

The body-blob squealed and whined, crackling in the fire, until at last the spell holding it together dissipated. Ignoring the burns on my face, I limped back to the storeroom. Mikey lay, locked in a death grip with a fifth huntsman, one I'd not seen on the monitor. The two wrestled back and forth, despite the fact that Mikey's entrails decorated the room like confetti streamers.

Furs don't protect against tire-irons-to-kidneys either, which I made sure to repeat until he stopped moving. After I helped drag Mikey's intestines back so he could start healing, I broke the shaft off the bolt pinning Rosa and caught her as she collapsed.

"*Unos Desalmado.*" She repeated it over and over, flinching away from me in fear, unwilling to even meet my eye.

Once, I'd been fooled by Rosa into repeating a lot of very unkind phrases that didn't mean what she said at all. Over the years, my Internet Spanish classes had paid off, and I knew exactly what it was she meant. Soulless Ones.

Eight

~⌒~

AFTER THE AMBULANCE took Rosa away to the hospital, and after I'd woken Ari with a blast from an air compressor, I headed back up to the office, determined to have it out with Grimm. I marched through the Agency door, straight into his office, where he waited in the mirror, hands folded in front of him. Grimm had changed suits to a slightly darker shade of gray silk. His suits often worked like mood rings, but I couldn't tell what this color meant.

I plopped down in the left-hand chair. "When I said look out for Ari, I didn't mean you couldn't help me. Did you see that thing? Do you have any idea what it is?" My rants petered out as he waited, the slightest twitch of his lips telling me how serious the situation was.

"Yes, I knew what it was. The Hebrew name would be *golem*, meaning 'half formed,' though, as you could see, it is indeed formed. Sculpted, one might say, from discarded flesh." Grimm paused, and the door on his office slammed shut, sealing me in.

"Rosa called it one of the 'soulless ones.' That make sense to you?" I kept my gaze fixed on him, watching his every movement.

Grimm looked down, nodding. "Yes. A body without a soul to guide it. A spell bound to human flesh and let free to walk among men. I do not believe it wanted to harm you. They were traditionally used as guardians."

"I wasn't taking any chances. And how, exactly, does a spell control a body? Or a pile of bodies?"

"Your blessings were intelligent, and alive. Imagine the chaos capable if they had flesh to wrap their form in. Spells are alive as well; though, like blessings, they lack free will. They must be given directives, and will follow them blindly." Grimm turned around, staring away from the mirror.

"Why would anyone create something like that?"

I thought he wasn't going to answer. I'd asked him questions before that made him go silent for hours, like "Why did you tip the pizza man fifty thousand dollars?" and "Can you explain why people listen to boy bands?"

I was just about to leave him to his meditation when Grimm spoke. "Because my daughter shares similar interests to my own. She seeks to create spells that will be her servants and fashion bodies for them."

Of the numerous admissions in that statement, I'm not sure what alarmed me most. That the Black Queen was creating more of these things or that Grimm so much as admitted he'd done it before. "That doesn't answer the question. Why?"

"She wants what she cannot have. Servants with both unquestioning, infallible loyalty to her, and with the initiative to guide themselves beyond simple instructions. She will fail, as I did, but not before she unleashes more of her creations on the world." Grimm whispered, so low I barely heard, "She seeks to violate the laws of magic."

The laws of magic. Some of them were pretty easy to understand. "Magic may not magic oppose." So spells aimed at each other usually went wildly wrong, shearing away like magnets of the same pole. "Magic may not to magic give rise." You couldn't create a spell that cast a spell, and so on, and so on. That only left the third law. "Magic may not magic command." Usually this meant you couldn't have one spell fire another, but it had all sorts of side effects. Magic sensors, for instance, couldn't trip on spell creatures because it would be two forces of magic commanding each other.

A knock at the door interrupted what would have been a very awkward conversation. Grimm glanced to the door. It unlocked itself and opened as Grimm intoned, "Come in."

Through the door stepped Mikey, in his wolf form. He had to bend over and turn sideways to fit through the door. "Magrraaahahah." He shook his head, losing a little length on his snout.

"Mariiffaaa, I garfaaahahhahm." Putting his claws beside his head, he began to shrink, and shrivel, the fur on him retracting inward like a backwards time-lapse video. "Marissa, you need to do something about Ari."

"I'll schedule her MRI shortly," said Grimm, his tone saying the matter was settled.

Mikey shook his head. "She won't come out of her office, and she's killing me with her sobbing. Hey, congrats on making handmaiden." Mikey gave me a thumbs-up, an idiotic grin on his face.

After a moment he still hadn't apologized or caught his own mistake. My hands shook and my face turned red. "Do you have any idea what that means?"

"Yup." Mikey nodded. "We wolves worked for the Black Queen last time, before Grimms there had her killed. I hear she was way ahead of the times in workers' benefits."

Grimm's mirror began to glow in a way that said Mikey was about two words from getting hit by lightning or changed into a very hairy, toothy toad. I grabbed Mikey by the hand and ran from Grimm's office, spinning on my heel as he followed, and delivering a kick to his crotch that left Mikey curled in a ball on the floor.

"Don't. Ever. Say. This. Is. Good." With each word, I landed another kick to him, letting my tears loose and daring the nearest temp worker to intervene. I left him in the hall and went to Ari's office. Inside, Ari slumped over, her head down on her desk.

I patted her on the shoulder. "We didn't get to talk."

"I'm sorry. I didn't mean for it to happen. I was supposed

to save you." Sobs punctuated her statements, but her dead eyes couldn't cry.

I sat across from her, taking her hand. "I've been through worse."

She glared at me, sending a chill down my spine. "Don't joke about this. It's not funny."

"I know. But I still tell myself I've been through worse." A wave of self-pity threatened to drown me, so I changed the subject. "Where's Wyatt?"

"He ran home to his mommy." Ari's tone didn't carry the contempt I would have used. "He's asking Ms. Pendlebrook for all the information she has on the Black Queen. And I suspect he's going to take a few princes out for drinks and ply them for information on what happened to the High Queen."

When Wyatt's mother served as High Queen, she had access to secret files from Kingdom's Government. "Wyatt drinks?"

"Milk, juice, and soda water when he has his floss and toothbrush handy. He'll buy other people alcohol, but sparkling apple cider is pretty hard-core for him." Ari shook her head. In two years, I think Wyatt not only hadn't passed second base, he'd run back to home plate a couple of times.

On the other hand, with twice-a-week therapy sessions, he could now sit beside Ari without breaking into sweats, and as long as she didn't look at him, I'd seen him kiss her at least three times. The fact that his earliest memory was of a witch killing his father didn't help their relationship.

Ari looked up at me and seized my hands so tightly it hurt. "I will fix this. I will do whatever it takes to free you."

The bell on Ari's desk rang, and a moment later, Grimm swirled into view. "Marissa, I hate to interrupt, but I've spoken with Liam. I need you to go to his workshop, my dear. He's working on proper armament there."

"You find anything on the souls?"

"Not yet. Keep an eye out on the way to Mr. Stone's and if you run across them, you can do something about it." Grimm disappeared before I could comment on how unlikely I was to meet stolen souls while traveling across town.

Then again, this was the city, and I'd seen just about every-thing else on the subway from time to time.

I didn't really need any encouragement to go see Liam, even though the only place he could afford to buy was on the south end of the city. Two buses, one cab, and zero souls later, I finally reached Liam's workshop.

When we rebuilt it, he insisted on using wood from old houses, scavenging and salvaging for months, but the result was that his studio, the thing he loved before he loved me, was a work of art. Looking like a combination farmhouse, barn, and industrial smelter, its gray wooden walls had never been repainted. They still held stripes of whatever color the original building was.

I hauled the sliding door open, and the blast of classic rock and the heat of the forge washed out over me. I'd visited dwarf forges a few times. Dark places, filled with smoke and piles of broken material. Liam lit his forge with fluorescent light and kept the floors clean.

He leaned over the grinding wheel in the corner, throw-ing sparks against the floor like a shower of fire.

I walked up behind him and ran my hand up his back. Once Liam focused in on a task, the world might burn down around him and he'd never know.

He didn't so much as flinch, or take his eyes off the edge, which he held at an angle, working the blade.

While he ground it, I ran my hands over his muscles, feel-ing the tension and strength that held the metal just right. After what seemed like an eternity, he turned off the grinding wheel and set the blade down. "It's ready. Grimm?"

I wanted a few more moments alone, but Grimm appeared in an antique silver mirror Liam kept on his office door.

"Sir, show me the blade." Grimm's eyes shone with excite-ment.

Liam picked up the sword, a long, thin two-handed weapon. He swung with ease, cutting arcs through the air, spinning and slashing. Two years of theater and performing *Macbeth* could teach a man a lot about how to look pretty with a sword.

"What do you think? Handle was ruined, and there was

no way to save the original edge, but I was able to reuse the metal." He held it out for Grimm's approval.

Grimm shivered and closed his eyes, nodding. "Looks don't matter. It's a message as much as a weapon. My daughter will understand the meaning."

I put one hand on Liam's biceps, turning him toward me. "How about filling me in on the meaning?" Exactly what these two had planned, they hadn't shared. I had ways of making Liam talk.

"Marissa, this blade is ancient," said Grimm. "And it's one the Black Queen has an intimate history with. She will recognize it, and the message I'm sending."

Liam flipped the sword over and handed it to me.

I never did like swords. No matter how I swung, I couldn't manage to get the pattern, the fluid movements that I'd seen him use. "Is this the sword that killed her?"

"Yes, my dear." Grimm crossed his arms, a thin smile on his face. "Created for her death, kept by my own sentimentality, and given new purpose by our master blacksmith. She aims to use you as a shield, but I will find a way to kill her, just as I did before." The way Grimm said that made me shudder, and sent a chill down my spine, even in the forge. Grimm disappeared without so much as a good-bye.

I carefully placed the sword on a rack, afraid I might break it.

"It's stronger than it looks." Liam walked up behind me, brushing past, and took it. Holding it at eye level, he dropped it on the floor, where it clattered against the concrete. "Flexible. Sharp. Able to endure almost anything." He put both hands on my shoulders, and I returned his gaze. "Like you."

I melted into his arms like a pat of butter in a hot skillet. At work, I could be the sharp-tongued, hard-ass lady in charge. Around Liam, I could be someone softer. More innocent in some ways. Much less innocent in others. I wrapped my arms around him and put my head on his shoulder, breathing in the scent of smoke he always carried. "I'm afraid of her."

"She's the Black Queen. You have reason to be. Grimm and I are going over handmaiden lore, all of it. And I'm going into Kingdom to speak with the doorman at the Court of Queens. There's so much of this stuff people don't pay attention to. The details matter." Liam ran his hand down the back of my head, sliding his fingers through my hair.

The doorman kept the history of the court. Enforced the rules of the reigning queen. Bestowed and took away titles. For a jolly little fat man, he wielded a lot of power.

"While you're there, could you ask him to take back the title?" I'd gotten into an argument with a psychotic queen and wound up with a royal title I could neither accept nor get rid of. The doorman insisted it was my due payment, and Grimm still believed he'd find a way to make money or magic off of it.

Liam shook his head, his stubbly chin brushing my forehead. "I was thinking we could go together. In the morning. Let's stay here tonight. Order takeout. Talk." In the back corner, a tiny bedroom and kitchenette were the final remnants of Liam's bachelor life, when he'd lived here, working iron into sculptures.

I'd never cared for it, but now that I didn't know how long we'd have, I didn't care where we stayed, as long as we stayed together. "Yes."

Nine

~∾~

I SLEPT BETTER curled up next to Liam than I dreamed possible, waking when the sun rose high enough to shine through the skylights of his workshop. Liam lay propped up on his elbow, watching me. I rubbed my eyes and shook away the last vestiges of sleep. "Why didn't you wake me?"

Liam leaned over and kissed me on the forehead, his rough stubble scratching against my skin. "Grimm said to let you sleep. Take a day off. I told him about going to talk to the doorman today. You know anything about Ari's 'shortcut'?"

I did. Despite her protests, Ari was, and would remain, a princess for her entire life. I'd kid her about it, but it felt like teasing her for having acne or some other disease she couldn't help. As a princess, the Court of Queens was always open to her. No matter where in Kingdom the door to the court might actually be, Ari's closet would lead straight there. "Yeah. I've got a key to her house. We'll take the fast way."

Liam glanced at his phone and swore under his breath. "Oh, crap. Can we stop by the apartment?"

"Of course." I put one hand on his cheek. "Anything you want."

Liam put his fingers in his mouth and whistled, a sound that would have made a freight train envious. In response, footsteps like a ferret scampered across the roof of his workshop. A moment later, the front door opened.

"Yes, my liege?" Svetlana's lilting voice drifted into the bedroom. "What is your desire?"

The way she said *desire* made me desire to hit her with a cross. Even Grimm had admitted that while Svetlana's kind of vampire wouldn't be harmed by religious symbols, if I sharpened the edges of one and swung it at her, odds were she'd understand. "Was she on the roof all night?"

"I put a packing crate up there and ordered her to stay out of sight." Liam rose and shouted, "Today's your appointment, right, Svetlana?"

Svetlana opened the door to the bedroom without even knocking and walked in.

I glared at her to deliver my "Knock before entering, or better yet, burst into flames and die" look, and my mouth dropped open. I'd been raised not to stare, but some situations simply demanded a stare or two. The leathery-skinned hag in our doorway wore Svetlana's white tennis outfit but, other than that, couldn't possibly have been the same woman. I mean vampire. Her once-golden hair hung in thin white strands, and she had enough liver spots for a pack of leopards.

I glanced to Liam. "Is that—"

"Yes." He didn't look toward me. "I meant to tell you, it's time for Svetlana's antiaging treatment. If she doesn't get it once a year, she'll turn to dust."

"She needs blood." I glanced around, wondering where exactly I'd left my purse. And my gun. If she turned to dust, I'd hire a maid to clean the place and consider it money well spent.

The hag, I mean, Svetlana's lips drew back over withered gums. "Never. I require much more refined treatment. And soon, my liege."

"We're heading right over." Liam rose and shut the door, letting me scramble to get dressed. "I was going to surprise you with a vacation from her. I know how you feel about her."

I slipped on my pants and bra. "I know how everyone else

looks at her." And in the part of my mind that was rational, I knew how Liam never did. The problem was, the part of my mind reacting to her wasn't rational, and didn't care.

We took the bus back to my apartment, and Svetlana got the senior discount on all three legs.

When I unlocked the door, she pushed past me, surprisingly fast for a woman who looked to be in her second century. "I already have the supplies, my liege. And the equipment."

When Svetlana moved in with us, we had a tense first night, with her demanding to lie on the floor beside our bed. I objected to a grown woman, particularly one who never slept, lying awake at night, just watching us. So she grudgingly existed in the front bedroom, where we now headed.

I wouldn't have recognized it as my guest bedroom. Inside, humidifiers saturated the air to the point where a goldfish could have survived, swimming through the air. Lush tropical plants lined the walls. Oranges and pomegranates still on the tree, pineapples in short pots. The carpet had been replaced with grass, pure wheatgrass, but what really got my attention was the bed.

Or the lack thereof.

The bed, left over from the days when Ari lived with me, was gone. In its place lay a crystal coffin. At the top of the coffin stood a machine that resembled a lawn mower combined with a food processor.

Svetlana walked over and handed me a sheet of paper. "Follow the instructions. It is so easy, even you could do it." With that, she began to strip. And if I'd been envious of Svetlana's figure before, the only green-eyed monster in the room was the one getting naked. Let's just say there was no part of her body not heading south for the winter. Liam had never shown any aversion to the female figure, but even he looked away.

Svetlana opened the coffin and worked her way in, creaking and cracking at her joints like an army of senior citizens doing jumping jacks. "Begin."

I read down the list. "Twenty-four pineapples." With Liam's help, I dumped them one at a time into the machine, which started on its own, spewing chunks of crushed pineapple into the coffin. Next came one hundred and thirty pomegranates, thirty-five gallons of yogurt, and most of the wheatgrass. By the time we were done, all the fruit trees lay bare.

Liam left the room and came back with a jar full of Maraschino cherries and a bottle of gin.

"Martinis?" I looked around to see what we could use for garnish.

"Hoping to give her a little color and some personality," said Liam. He dumped the cherries in, followed by the whole bottle. "Last step is to turn on the grow lights." With his foot, Liam nudged a switch. Twenty thousand watts of spotlight lit up the coffin, which was basically a vampire smoothie. I hoped the electric bill was covered by our agreement with the vampires.

I stepped out of the tropical room of horrors. "Give me five minutes."

"Five minutes as in three hundred seconds, or five Marissa minutes?" Liam shut the door behind him. "If it's Marissa minutes, I've got time to watch the first half of the game."

"Five If-You-Know-What's-Good-For-You-You-Keep-Your-Mouth-Shut minutes."

After I'd showered and put on some fresh clothes, we drove over to Ari's house, recognizable as the only house where the lawn clipped itself, the ivy that covered the front never dared cross the windows, and generally speaking, you expected a singing animal to pop up at any moment.

"Man, she's done a number on this." Liam ran his hands along the fence, a fence he helped weld back in place after a few demons nearly tore the house apart. Last time Liam came here, the house was the lair of an undead sorcerer, my lawyer.

I unlocked the front door, almost looking for Ari's pet hellhound, who wasn't going to be showing up, since he was even deader than before. "We have to go up to her room."

Liam followed me up the stairs, where pictures of Wyatt and his family covered the walls. Ari's own family would only find their pictures on walls entitled "America's most bitchy" or "Wanted for extreme betrayal."

Say what you want about Ari, her bedroom was a complete

pigsty. In fact, the three little pigs would have been embarrassed to wallow through that room. I kicked a shipping box of "As Seen on TV" items out of the way, a testament to Ari's favorite hobby: online shopping.

"Somebody likes cheese-o-matics." Liam moved the kitchen appliances over to the side. The stack wobbled and then crashed into a pile of coal-powered fondue sets.

"Somebody had a crush on Billy Mays." I opened Ari's bedroom door, and immediately regretted it. A wave of absolute crap collapsed outward, knocking me over.

"How much would you pay to set this whole place on fire?" Liam tossed a "whirl-a-meal" to the side and helped me to my feet. "Don't answer yet, there's more."

"Very funny. Just push all this onto her bed. We have to be able to close the door for it to work." I began hurling folding boards, collectible china plates, and an entire collection of "Faces of Abraham Lincoln, Volume 3, Second Edition" beer mugs out into the room.

"Where are she and Wyatt going to sleep?" Liam didn't seem terribly worried by the question.

"If he slept here at all, it would be under the smoothie blender that also makes corned beef." Of course he couldn't. Wyatt still had the spell of a witch on him, a lock of his hair given freely by his mother. He couldn't sleep anywhere outside of the wards Grimm built, or the witch could claim him. "I think that's enough." I stepped onto a pile of NASCAR bathrobes, took Liam's hand, and waited as he closed the closet door.

Fumbling in the darkness, I felt for a doorknob at the back of the closet. "Hold on. We aren't going to Narnia."

"Good. You know my rule for talking animals." Liam made the mistake of letting a talking rabbit bond with him the first year we were together. It took half the Agency staff to hunt that thing down and kill it, even with Grimm helping. "If it talks to me, it goes on a plate with biscuits and gravy."

No wonder I loved him.

The door at the back of Ari's closet swung open, and I stepped out into the entrance to the Court of Queens. Never mind that the last time I used it, it opened to an entirely different place.

Behind a velvet rope stood a portly man shaped like a barrel, his arms far too short, matching only his diminutive legs. He held up a monocle to peer at us, and smiled at me, sending a wave of trepidation through me. "Handmaiden. So wonderful to see you return. Have you come to prepare your queen's quarters?"

"Not exactly." Liam pushed me to the side, walking right to the edge of the rope. "We're here to talk to you."

Liam got exactly the look *I* got last time I was here. The same look you give a potato salad that's sat out in the sun for three days, with more black flies than black pepper on it.

"You don't belong here. The handmaiden is not permitted guests, and you are not a queen's guard." The doorman spoke dryly, without threat. As a manifestation of the court itself, he might actually be able to take Liam in a fight. I wasn't eager to find out.

Liam sighed, smoke blowing from him in a thick cloud. The more agitated he became, the more his curse would come out. "I don't want to fight, and I don't want a pedicure. Can we just sit here and talk to you?"

The doorman crossed his arms and tilted his head to the side. "I am an animus of pure magic, born to give refuge to the women of royal families and their select servants. When you leave, this place will no longer exist, until another calls me into being."

"Please," said Liam. "I can't imagine anyone who would know more about the spells that bind a queen and her handmaidens, or the traditions, than you. I'll stay out here while Marissa relaxes."

"I'll what?" Spas remained a location of mystery and terror to me. It wasn't that I didn't get facial masks; it was just that the masks were usually gore from blasting yet another fairytale creature. Long nails, too, might be good for clawing, but I did more climbing than clawing. "I don't—I mean, you wouldn't—"

The doorman cut me off with a glance to Liam. "*If* the hand-maiden were to avail herself of my services, I suppose I'd have no choice but to remain present, and conversation does help pass the eons. If the gentleman would like a seat, I can oblige."

I didn't see him perform magic. I didn't hear a spell, or see the light, but one moment there wasn't a chair behind Liam, and the next moment there was. Not the most comfortable chair ever, but a nice, wooden one that Liam could definitely break over someone's head or set fire to, if need be.

The doorman unhooked his rope and waved to me. "The spa is open, and we're serving chocolate-dipped fruit."

I gave a terrified look to Liam. I'd always been more comfortable in Sergeant's Guns and Ammo than Macy's. "This is so not me."

"Marissa," said Liam. "I've got a ton of questions, so I suggest you *take your time*." He nodded to the doorman, whose dour expression said he didn't appreciate Liam's presence any more than a wad of chewed gum.

The doorman clipped the rope behind me, and, hand on my back, guided me down the hall and around the back of the court, to the spa. I turned to cast one pleading look to Liam. "Mr. Doorman, aren't you going to stay and make sure Liam—"

At the velvet rope, an identical copy of the doorman stood, hands behind his back, nodding to Liam as he spoke. I glanced back to where the doorman stood beside me. He shrugged. "Consider me an excellent multitasker. I'll get to work on your feet immediately." He ushered me to a salon chair, then shook his head, *tsk*ing. "I haven't seen this much dead skin since the last zombie invasion."

AFTER THE PEDICURE, after the thermal spa, after a haircut and facial massage, after more time with a chocolate fountain than should be legal, I finally gathered my clothes. Well, I tried to. When I opened the bag, my normal clothes were gone. The outfit that remained was silk, long sleeved, with onyx buttons, that fit like it had been tailored to me.

I tried them on, admiring myself in the mirror, while the doorman nodded appreciatively. "Do you like them?"

"Love them. *Love* is the word." I wondered why Ari never came here.

The doorman smiled, a wide grin splitting his round, fat face. "I knew you would. They are a gift from your queen."

I bolted for the tunnel leading out of the court, leaving my bag, my purse, everything behind as I raced for the door. I came to the velvet rope and skidded to a stop.

There, Liam lounged in a leather recliner, watching what looked to be next year's Super Bowl on a plasma TV the size of the wall. Beside him, the doorman rested in an identical recliner, sharing a bowl of popcorn as he droned on, talking with his hands as much as his mouth.

The doorman looked up at me and leaped to his feet, brushing popcorn off. "You forgot your purse, handmaiden." He reached down behind his podium and brought it out.

Liam sat up in his chair, set down the frosted mug of beer in his hand, and wiped his face. "You need to hear this, M." He nodded to the doorman.

"Your fiancé asked, quite politely, where the queens are."

You would think that in all that time, it would have occurred to me to wonder why I didn't run into any of them. I'd chalked it up to good luck, but, in retrospect, that'd never been my kind of luck. "And?"

"None dare enter the court. For now, we operate under the standing rules from the old High Queen. The first to enter lays claim to her title."

Ari steadfastly refused to discuss the court every time I brought it up. If getting there first laid claim, I figured we'd have queens camped outside the door like some sort of Black Friday sale. "So why isn't anyone here?"

"The first to lay claim will face the rest as challengers, unless they have already given their allegiance. So, I would expect they are preparing." The doorman turned to look into his empty domain. "Aligning, arranging. The one who gains the support by admission of all the others will be the new High Queen."

A chill sent every hair on my body to full alert, as a possibility occurred to me. I'm certain the look showed through, because Liam gently took my arm, pulling me closer. I took a breath, then spoke. "Was Isolde ever High Queen?"

At her name, the doorman turned back to me, a look of displeasure on his face. "Isolde never cared for my comforts. My rules limited her too much, and she valued her power above all else. When you arrived, wearing her ring, I assumed that you would serve as her representative."

Liam scratched his chin, making a sound like sandpaper as his fingers rubbed the stubble. "What do you mean, limited?"

"I set certain rules. You may not bring outside magic here. She is welcome in my walls, but as a seal bearer and queen only." He nodded, as if repeating a rehearsed speech. "She must check her father's power at the door. Not that she has any need of it. I would wager her the match in magic of any queen, living or dead."

"So all I have to do is get her to come here, and she's cut down to size." My muscles tensed, as that old familiar determination set in.

The doorman shook his head. "She will never enter, nor does she need to. She has you."

Liam spoke before I could. "Tell her about the handmaiden rules."

If Liam had asked the doorman to explain basic addition, the doorman would not have looked more bored. "A queen chooses her handmaiden. A princess's mother chooses the princess's handmaidens." He looked to my hand, where I wore the Black Queen's signet ring. "Normally."

Liam cut in, his patience wearing thinner than the socks I threw out of his drawer when he first moved in. "Ari's mother kicked her out of Kingdom. The High Queen, with the support of all the others, can banish any other queen. Strip her of her rights. Can't change her nature, but we think it would break the handmaiden's bond. Right?" He glanced to the doorman.

"I have never seen it done. The other queens would turn

on her in an instant." The doorman's frown threatened to pull his mouth off.

"But it's possible?" Liam's tone made it clear, as statement more than a question.

"I suppose—" The doorman cocked his head to one side, then his eyes lit up, and he smiled. "Sir, please step aside."

Liam did, and the recliner, TV, everything but the mug of beer disappeared.

"Handmaiden, sir, please show proper respect." The doorman strode down the hall to the double doors we'd entered through. "We welcome our first claimant to the title of High Queen."

Bright light from the double doors made silhouettes of the figures who stood there. The doorman bowed low, but his deep baritone echoed through the hall. "It is recorded. For the title of eight hundred and seventy-fifth High Queen, I accept your claim."

He turned and walked down the hall past us, opening the velvet rope for the three figures. The queen was tall, taller than her handmaidens, taller than me, and she swept down the hallway in an impractically long dress, her handmaidens trailing behind.

Then the swish of fabric stopped, and Liam growled, catching his breath, and his hand tightened over mine like iron.

I looked up, letting the overhead lights confirm the face I'd dreaded seeing, and yet, somehow expected.

The doorman nodded to me. "Your Highness, I present Marissa Locks, Handmaiden to the Black Queen."

She ignored him. Her eyes never left mine, but her mouth pulled back in a tight smile. "Indeed."

The doorman, perhaps sensing my murderous intentions, stepped between us. "Handmaiden, you may bow before Gwendolyn Thromson. For now, High Queen."

Ten

WE WON'T GO into how, exactly, I got myself thrown out of the court. I managed to keep my purse, a bag with my old clothes, and two fistfuls of hair from Ari's sisters, which I yanked out before Liam and the doorman wrestled me away. Ari's stepmother ranked high on the list of people I'd willingly commit violence against.

The fact that she'd tried to kill both me and Ari on occasion might have factored into it. Then again, using her own step-daughters as handmaidens didn't score her any points either.

"You could've handled that better." Liam sat on the curb with me while we waited for a bus to take us out of Kingdom. The doorman had ejected us into an area even I didn't visit very often, and, judging from the diesel bus, one of the lower magic areas.

"I would have, if you'd grabbed the doorman instead of me. I was this close to taking one of her eyes out, and if I'd had my gun, I would have shot her dead." In the silence that passed between us, my own words sounded foreign. I put a hand to my mouth, feeling to see if my lips were the ones moving.

Liam reached over, putting his arm around me. "Easy. Deep breaths."

In the warm sun, I'd begun to shiver. "I don't know where that came from." I pulled at the silver signet ring on my finger for the millionth time, rotating it. Though it turned freely, if I tried to remove it, it clung to me as if glued on.

"I know a bit about things that whisper to you. About impulses, and urges for violence." Liam seldom spoke of the curse, acting as though it were just a cold sore that flared up under stress. His patient, calm attitude had as much to do with keeping it firmly in check as with his genuine good nature.

"I hate her."

"Ari's stepmother, or the Black Queen?"

"Yes." I stood as the bus approached. A hybrid magic-diesel, it pulled to a stop with a puff of rose-scented exhaust. "Tell me you found out what you needed to. I don't do spas. I didn't think I did chocolate fountains, and frankly, I need a workout to sweat all the frilliness off." I had so much to do with my life that didn't involve being pampered, including finding a couple of souls gone AWOL before the Adversary started searching for them on his own.

Liam chuckled as we boarded the bus and sat next to me, taking the aisle seat. That way the freaks that rode public transit would have to sit next to him. "Trust me, that was not a waste of time, but I need to consult with Grimm and Mrs. P. I have some ideas about how to deal with your bond to the Black Queen." Liam drifted off into thought, rubbing his chin for a moment. "Oh, and speaking of Grimm, he called while I was researching. We need to get back to the Agency. Having a sword is one thing. Being able to use it is another, and he's arranged for lessons."

The thought of learning to use a sword seemed crazier than everything else I'd gone through. "I did pretty well in hand to hand. Who's supposed to teach me?"

"I think I'll let Grimm explain that one." Liam leaned over and meshed his fingers with mine.

* * *

BACK AT THE Agency, Ari sat in the kitchen, picking at a salad as much as eating it. When she saw me, she almost ran over, then a look of fear crossed her face, and she dropped her gaze in classic "Ari is guilty" fashion. I knew it by heart because I'd caught her watching the home shopping channel with my credit card several times when we lived together. "M. Are you okay?"

I walked over and slid onto the chair across from her. "I'll be fine. It's not your fault."

"It is. I had Grimm check, and he won't answer my questions about the prophecy. He'd tell me if it were true." Ari put her head down on the desk. "Where's Liam?"

"Helping the cargo guys catch a fire salamander that escaped its crate." Being largely fireproof thanks to my engagement ring, I suppose I should have been helping. The kitchen door swung open, and Mikey dipped his head to lumber through, carrying a pot, ladle, and a few plastic bowls. He grinned at us with teeth that for once weren't pointed.

"Marissa, I want you to try this and be honest. What does it need?" Mikey brought me a bowl of steaming beans and meat.

The scent of basil and rosemary made my mouth water. I chewed for a moment, savoring the texture. "Salt. Definitely needs more salt."

If I'd hit Mikey with a hammer, I couldn't have made him sadder. I know—I'd hit him several times with a hammer and it barely even dampened his mood. "Philistine. Ari, your turn." He handed her a bowl of her own.

Ari scrunched her nose and took a bite. "It tastes gamey. What is this? Deer chili?"

Mikey shuffled his feet, rubbing his thumbs against his fists. "Sure. Deer. You'll eat it if I call it deer, right?"

Ari gagged slightly and spit a bean across the room, then rushed to the sink, where she did her best supermodel impression. "Michael Seth Langhorn, that is *not* funny. I'm already on probation, if I start eating people . . ." She rushed from the room, probably off to gargle some battery acid.

I took another bite.

"So?" Mikey slid backwards across a chair, keeping his eyes on me. "Give me your best guess. What is it?"

I added a bit more salt. "You could at least make it difficult. Basil, rosemary, and thyme with white peppercorns."

"The meat." Mikey's smile revealed razor-sharp canines.

"Honey badger. Next time, give me a challenge." I licked the edges of the spoon, then stopped as the grin spread further and further across his face. "No?"

He shook his head. "I couldn't get honey badger. So I used regular badger and marinated it in honey to compensate. I'll leave a bowl on your desk for Liam." He walked out of the kitchen, taking his chili and smile with him.

I've never found anything that makes a wolf happier (besides eating an unsuspecting stranger) than good food. I polished off my bowl and wiped my face, only to find Grimm watching me from the napkin dispenser.

"Marissa, if you don't mind, I have arranged training. Go to the third floor." Grimm faded out without waiting.

Now, our building, it's had a bad run. Partially it's the neighborhood, and partially it's the economy, but mostly it was from folks who didn't like the Fairy Godfather and decided to do nasty things to us. Just the usual things—trolls knocking holes in the walls, huntsmen attacking, or that time the whole building was covered in bees. One by one, most of the other businesses found good reasons to break their lease, and Grimm always bought them out.

The third floor contained nothing but burned-out office furniture and the remains of a wedding cake shop. What exactly happened we won't go into, but let's say that there were quite a few couples who had cupcakes at their wedding.

When I stepped out of the stairwell, into the remains of the third floor, I wondered how exactly the building hadn't collapsed. Piles of broken drywall, overturned desks, and heaps of filing papers littered the floor. Drips of water from the fire sprinklers left everything mildewed and rotten.

"Grimm?" My voice echoed in the empty space. I approached the remains of a destroyed window office and looked out on the city below. The people there hurried about like ants, wrapped up in lives that never involved evil queens or demon apocalypses. Since I was only three floors up, large ants, like the ones I'd helped exterminate in the sewers last year.

The slightest whisper of air, the thinnest edge of shadow caught my attention. I instinctively ducked, then rolled to my feet and leaped away as a blade passed within a hairsbreadth of my throat.

The figure in front of me wore loose black leggings and a sleeveless top that revealed muscles practically carved of steel. He swung the sword back and sheathed it across his shoulders without even looking. With one hand, he swept back his mask, revealing salt-and-pepper-gray hair, with narrow eyes.

I gave the customary bow. "Shigeru."

He returned it. "I have accepted Fairy Godfather's offer to teach you swordsmanship."

"I don't think you can teach me to be a ninja overnight."

"No." Shigeru picked an iron bar from the rubble behind him and tossed it to me. "We begin with basic strokes. Your lesson is complete when you can hit me."

"Just call me Grasshopper." I caught the bar in the air and swung it like a baseball bat, aiming to end this as fast as it started.

Shigeru fell backwards, twisted, and kicked my legs out from under me. "Don't overextend. Keep your center of balance, even if it costs you force on your blow."

I rose from the floor, spitting out drywall dust. This time, I swung straight down at him.

Shigeru slipped to the side, pulling on my arm so that my own momentum threw me forward. "Force on chopping strokes is down, not forward."

From my vantage point on the mildewed carpet, it was clear this day would be full of bruises and failure.

TECHNICALLY, MY LESSON never ended. That is, I never once got a blow in on the master ninja. I think at the point where I could no longer get up, he took pity on me. What really ticked me off was that he never even needed his own sword. Didn't matter how I swung, stabbed, or chopped; I wound up kissing carpet.

When he finally dismissed me, I was so tired, I rode the elevator up. Ari stood in the hallway, waving good-bye to a couple she'd been counseling, and rushed to put her arm under me.

I winced at a dozen bruises. "Careful. First day of sword lessons didn't go so well."

Ari muttered under her breath, practically pulling me through the lobby and to my office. Then she flicked the mirror like a bell, causing it to ripple. "Grimm, you get in here this instant."

He coalesced in the mirror, causing the waves to stop. "Ah, I see your lesson went as expected. Arianna, calm yourself. Marissa, if you don't mind, I'd like to offer you healing. You have very little time and much to learn."

My mouth turned up in a smile as I remembered the warm, buttery feeling of having all my wounds washed away in a flood of magic. Then my eyes snapped open, remembering the *other* way. "This is going to hurt, isn't it?"

"Pain is how you know you are alive, my dear." He looked almost sympathetic for a moment. Then his power swept out from my bracelet, and the healing started.

If my teeth hadn't been clamped down on my tongue, I'd have painted a soliloquy of swearing capable of boiling coffee at ten paces. Dry ice pressed against my skin wouldn't have hurt worse. As the bruises faded away, the burning deepened until my breath became ragged and my stomach curdled.

Then the pain faded away, and I opened my eyes to give Grimm a weak smile. "No big deal."

Grimm nodded. "I'm proud of you. That was one, let's fix the other sixteen now."

I don't know if it took hours or seconds to heal the rest of my injuries. I can tell you healing the minor fracture in my arm did not feel like cold. No, to replicate that I'd need to stick a red-hot poker into my arm and hold it there.

When Grimm finally pronounced me fixed, sweat covered my body, and I shivered and ached. Ari reached into the shopping bag she carried everywhere, pulled out a washcloth, and dabbed my forehead. "I'm so sorry."

"Me too. This morning was great. Liam and I went into Kingdom and talked to the doorman." I smiled, remembering my pampering session. When I opened my eyes, Ari's gaze left chills. It wasn't the yellowish, dead eyes in her head. The fear on her face, that scared me.

"You went into the Court of Queens when there was no High Queen?" Her voice trembled with fear or anger.

"Yes. The doorman wasn't willing to discuss handmaiden lore with Liam unless he was otherwise occupied. Guess who got to be the distraction?"

Ari kicked my desk, startling me. "Do you have any idea how dangerous that was? The High Queen sets the rules for the court. If you were in a bubble bath when someone laid claim to the court, they could declare the bubble baths be filled with lava."

"Calm down. There wasn't a High Queen, so the doorman said the old rules still held. But there's a claimant now. The first one to lay claim arrived right as Liam and I were leaving." Technically true.

Ari sagged back into my chair. "Grimm, did you know Marissa went into the court this morning?"

Grimm didn't appear for more than a minute, uncomfortable seconds ticking by. "Yes, young lady, I knew. There was no High Queen at the time, and none of the claimants would dare risk my daughter's wrath by assaulting her handmaiden."

The tension drained from Ari's face and shoulders like a wave. "I'm sorry. It's just that I don't want you getting caught up in the battle for High Queen."

I glanced to the mirror, catching Grimm's eye. "You know who arrived as I was leaving, right?"

He nodded. "When you were thrown out by the doorman, I believe you meant."

"Wait—who laid claim?" Ari snapped up like a spring, looking between us.

I bit my tongue, trying to figure out how to say it without upsetting her, and finally concluded nothing short of a lie would help. "Gwendolyn."

Eleven

~⚬~

ARI'S STRING OF curses would have melted the walls. Her auburn hair stood up on end from the sheer amount of electricity coursing over her, and she alternated between shaking the building clean to the foundations and hyperventilating. "I. Will. Not. Let. Her." Ari clenched and unclenched her fists with each word.

I believed there was good in almost everyone, but in the case of Ari's stepmother, the only way I figured that good would ever come out was with the help of an organ-harvesting team. And in Gwendolyn's case, her heart was so black, it would probably be shipped straight to a coal-fired power plant. I tugged the grounding strap at my wrist tight and patted her shoulder. "I know. I hardly think this is a coincidence. Isolde makes her move, the old High Queen dies, and now Gwendolyn has a shot at High Queen. Wasn't that why she teamed up with Fairy Godmother a few years ago?"

If Ari's smile could power the entire Agency building, her anger could electrocute every death row inmate in the country. She set her jaw and narrowed her eyes. "When I see Gwendolyn, I'm going to do more than just pull a few hairs from her head."

"Your sisters are acting as her handmaidens." Ari had already dealt with enough, but I figured better to go ahead and get everything out in the open. "Stephanie and Rachel. You probably don't want to involve them."

At her sisters' names, Ari bit back a sob. "Steph I believe. Rachel would never get mixed up in something like this. What happened to Sirena?"

Ari had so many sisters I'd never bothered learning all the names. Red hair, blue eyes, and bad attitude, that was how I recognized a Thromson. "Feel like a family visit? They need to know what they're getting into. If something happens to Gwendolyn, I'd guess it won't be pretty for them."

Ari shook her head. "None of them called after Gwendolyn banished me. No email. No texts. They've made their choices, and I've made mine."

I wanted to protest, to argue, and tell Ari that family shouldn't be given up so easily, but Grimm didn't give me a chance. "Marissa, we should have you try on your uniform. I had the sword retrieved from Mr. Stone's forge, and time is short."

"But I didn't learn how to use it. All I got were bruises." The only thing I'd learned from my lesson was to keep my mouth shut when I fell, because while mildew might be related to bleu cheese, it wasn't nearly as tasty.

Grimm ignored my comment completely. "I'm certain the essence of your lessons came through. Go to wardrobe. I've ordered your clothing laid out for you, my dear."

When I emerged from our dressing room, I looked like a Navy SEAL crossed with an undertaker. The cloth itself weighed me down, not quite stiff or flexible. The dozens of loops, pockets, and belts left me confused.

I stuck a thumb in one of the loops. "What exactly were all of these for?"

Grimm pointed to different points on my outfit as he spoke. "Poison, daggers, scrying crystals, and the other usual equipment for handmaidens. I had this custom made for an agent.

One day, I'm going to sell the secret of the fiber construction to the military for a pretty penny." Grimm looked over at Liam. "Would you mind stabbing Marissa through the heart?"

Liam scrunched up his face for a moment, like he did when I caught him ignoring me, and he was trying to figure out if I really asked him to crush a testicle. "No."

"Excellent. I need to illustrate to Marissa the protective nature of her uniform. While many in Kingdom may wish to harm her, it will take more than bullets or blades to do so." Grimm tilted his head toward me. "Now stab her, right through the heart."

Liam stood up, shaking his head. "No. I said no. I'm not going to try to stab Marissa through the heart, and for that matter, I'm going with her when she goes to meet the Black Queen. The doorman said they burned Isolde once. I'm betting a dragon can do it again."

I'd never heard Liam's tone set like that, so determined, so almost angry.

"You must not, sir. You have no idea what she might do to you." Grimm folded his arms across his chest, pacing back and forth. "The curse within you leaves you more susceptible to her power. Unless you'd like to willingly serve her."

Liam approached Grimm's mirror, as though the Fairy Godfather could be cowed like a school-yard bully. "The only way I'll be serving her is on a plate, to Mikey and his poker gang."

"Sir, if you wouldn't mind, I'd like to show you something in my office. Marissa, I'll need you as well." Grimm faded out.

I wrapped my arms around Liam's waist, pressing myself to his back.

He spun and picked me up, wrapping his arms around me. "I can't lose you." Only then did I hear the fear he'd masked with anger.

"Grimm will think of something. Come on." After disentangling the three loops that had caught on Liam's belt buckle, we walked to Grimm's office, where he waited in his mirror.

"Thank you for your patience. Mr. Stone, I'd like to educate you on why avoiding exposure to the Black Queen is essential." Grimm looked over to me. "Row twenty-three, column five, Marissa."

A location on the armory wall, the wall that made up the entire east side of Grimm's office, composed entirely of boxes in various sizes. Some contained bullets that could kill anything, some chamomile tea. I counted off the boxes, and slid a shoe-box-sized chest from the wall, carrying it back to Grimm's desk.

"Go ahead, open it." Grimm watched Liam, not me, as I slipped it open.

Inside, like an old friend tied up in the back of a van and left to die, sat a gleaming hunk of steel. I recognized it, and anxiety rippled from my spine down to my fingertips. A silver-plated nine-millimeter pistol Grimm chose for me when I first came to work for him. Nothing like the gunmetal-blue one I carried these days.

That gun had been a friend when I had none, my weapon of choice for nearly seven years, perfectly balanced for me, tuned by a gunsmith to fit my hand exactly.

Liam reached over and picked it up. "I thought this was lost."

So did I. I'd taken it with me through the mirror, when I picked a fight with a fairy and killed her. I'd hoped it was lost, because just seeing it made me ill.

Grimm's gaze dropped to my trembling hands. I'm sure the sweat on my face gave away the feelings I sought to hide. He glanced back to me. "I found it while cleaning up after one of Arianna's training accidents. Marissa, would you mind taking that from Mr. Stone?"

I closed my eyes and reached out, but touching that steel made me almost retch. I clenched it in my fist, willing my fingers closed, and opened my eyes, triumphant.

Grimm spoke past me, to Liam. "I believe the words Fairy Godmother said were 'You don't like that gun.'"

And the truth was, four years later, I still didn't.

"You want to throw it away." Grimm repeated words I'd

never told him. Words I'd never told anyone but gave voice to the ache in my arm. "You need to throw it."

I don't remember my arm moving. Just the crash of metal hitting the armory wall, and then throwing myself at Liam like a frightened child. Four years later, Fairy Godmother's words still held sway over me. "I thought that spell ended when Fairy Godmother died."

Grimm's voice came from behind Liam as he stroked my head. "It wasn't a spell. I told you, a fairy can change your nature. Change your desires, and decisions. Mr. Stone, while my daughter is not a full fairy, I assure you, she would wield a similar power over that curse."

I pushed away from Liam, not liking the implications. "You said that only applied in a fairy's home realm. I went through the mirror to Godmother."

"What I said was the person who returned would be only what she made them. And, my dear, has it not occurred to you yet? Isolde was born on Earth. You are in my daughter's realm."

"And Isolde has Fairy Godmother's power." If I screamed inside, it would have echoed in my hollow mind. The forces aligned against me held every advantage.

"Perhaps. But I doubt she understands it, and given that mastering my own abilities took more than one eternity, I question her skill at using it. The point is that exposing Liam to the Black Queen would be sheer folly." He spoke to me, looked at Liam. "My daughter cannot change people at a whim. She would whisper, each time bending you ever so slightly. When one day you woke up and decided to offer her your allegiance, it wouldn't be a change. Just the acceptance of something natural."

The idea of the Black Queen worming her way down into Liam's brain made me ill and angry at the same time. "I'll go alone." If I'd known what effect those words would have, what would happen, I'd never have spoken. As the words left my mouth, I doubled over as if punched.

I tried to speak, but gasps were the only noise I could make. Liam caught me as I fell, lifting me like a sack of flower, his eyes lit up with hellfire. "What's happening to her?"

"Mr. Stone, I must get her into Kingdom immediately. She's

being summoned. The farther a handmaiden from her queen, the more powerful the summons is. Take her to the portal." Grimm disappeared, leaving Liam to practically sprint through the halls, plowing over Mikey and sending Ari flying back into the kitchen.

The cold stone of Grimm's portal slab touched the back of my neck, and then the world split into rainbows. Like traveling through a kaleidoscope on LSD, the light wrapped around me, and when it folded back like a flower petal, I fell six feet to the ground.

Thank Kingdom a pack of singing rabbits chose that corner to begin an impromptu serenade. Without them to break my fall, I might have crushed my neck instead of theirs. And here, in Kingdom, I could actually stand up. A ravenous hunger filled my gut, but at least I didn't have to imitate a troll's punching bag.

I rose, wiping rabbit fur from my clothes, and caught my breath.

"Head to the fountain, my dear." Grimm took on the same tone he used when coaching me through an ogre's den. I'd learned to pay attention, because my life might depend on it.

The fountain, a giant, round, wishing-well-like contraption, stood before the main palace. A few years earlier, when they built a new castle to consolidate the government, they left the old one and moved the fountain.

I walked to the edge, looking down into dirty water filled with coins, beer can tabs, and broken glass.

"Place your hand on the side of the fountain and walk counterclockwise." Grimm shimmered in the water, watching me.

The rough granite skipped under my hand as I walked, tracing the stone like high-speed braille. All the way around I walked, and as I came back, my heart skipped a beat. The stone beneath my fingers turned cold, ice-cold, and when I glanced into the water, the koi had teeth.

Forcing myself to look up, I saw the castle, as cold and impervious as always, but cast in shadow. Low Kingdom, where evil and darkness held sway.

And I heard her voice.

Clear, distant, like a song and a shriek, calling me. The longer I listened to the sound, the more melodic it became, and the less the crowds of creatures bothered me. A pity I wasn't dressed for normal work. In Low Kingdom, my black business suits made more than style sense. I fit right in with the crowd, wandering through streets packed with goblins, past the shadow of a troll whose bridge collapsed.

I knew where I'd wind up long before my feet led me there.

The old castle.

The original one, built Grimm only knew how many hundreds of years ago. I wandered across the bridge, walking right up to the gate troll.

A hulking, heavy creature, he bent far over to snort at me and show yellow teeth the size of soap bars. Judging from his stench, a bar of soap the size of a minivan couldn't have cleaned him up. "No pass."

I held up my hand, showing the handmaiden's mark.

The troll knelt down, bowing his head, then rose and placed knobby fingers on the doors, hauling them open despite the corrosion.

With the voice of the Black Queen calling me, I found my way through the labyrinthine hallways in record time, emerging at the main banquet hall to find torches lit everywhere.

"I'm here." My voice quavered more than I wanted, my courage quelled by the fact that I'd walked into the den of darkness alone. If Grimm could hear, he didn't speak.

The ranks of dark warriors standing before me didn't turn to look. Instead, they kept their eyes fixed forward. I slid between them, working my way to the front to see. And nearly screamed.

The Black Queen stood at the front, dressed in a black dress like thistledown that shimmered purple in the torchlight. Her face held that unearthly beauty that kept my eyes locked on her; her eyes were covered in enough eye shadow to make up a circus.

Before her knelt a woman, dressed in gray, with a black

sword across her back. Her golden hair cascaded down her back, getting tangled in the woven leather sheath, no doubt.

"Rise, handmaiden," said the Black Queen, and took the woman's hand. The Black Queen looked over to me, a faint smile playing across her lips.

The woman dropped her hand, and a fleck of blood dripped from it where she'd received the handmaiden's mark.

Isolde gestured to me, a smooth swipe of her hand that seemed to both draw attention to me and dismiss me at once. "Kyra, meet Marissa. Marissa is my other handmaiden."

Kyra turned toward me, and this time, to my credit, I held in the shock. "You." Yeah, I should've had something better to say. I just didn't expect to *know* this woman. I spent an entire New Year's Eve chasing her once, after she boosted a pair of magic slippers with a serious security system on them.

She knew me too, her lips pulling back in a grimace. "Me."

I looked over to Isolde, willing myself to not be sucked in by her beauty, forcing myself to focus on her eyes. "What is she doing here? Don't you already have me?"

Isolde swept down the stairs to stand before me, radiating menace and anger. "She came willingly. Prepared. Eager, and asked that she be allowed to serve in return for a favor. How could I refuse her? Why would I refuse her?"

Death told me once that he waited to introduce himself when the Black Queen chose handmaidens. Waited until only one remained. The history books I'd read said Isolde took on dozens of handmaidens during her rise to power. When the time came for her to conquer a new nation, she forced her handmaidens to fight it out among themselves. Only the strongest, the most violent and cruel, would survive to lead her army. She allowed nothing less.

I thought of myself as bitterly honest, not cruel. Strong? That was a matter of more than muscle. Strength could be the courage to face a shaman gone insane from exposure to nature's raw power. Strength could be forcing myself to fulfill my debt to Grimm despite my family abandoning me.

I *was* strong. And ever since I'd agreed to serve Isolde,

a desire for violence crawled into my dreams and thoughts, ready to turn every disagreement into a bloodbath. Maybe Isolde underestimated me.

I looked at Kyra, seeing in her blue eyes acceptance, knowledge, even eagerness. "You know what happens now?" I put one hand to my sword, the other into my jacket, reaching for my gun.

"No." Isolde stepped between us, her words like a glacier, freezing me in place. "I decide when the culling occurs. I set the terms, I choose the conditions. Until I give you leave, you will treat each other with grace and respect." Her gaze locked to Kyra. "Kyra, what would you have of me in return for your service?"

Kyra's mouth opened and shut, and she wouldn't meet the Black Queen's gaze. "May I have time to consider my request? I—I don't wish to waste your power."

Isolde smiled, reminding me more of a shark. Then she turned and ascended back to her throne, a garish black wooden chair that would have hurt to sit in for fifteen minutes, let alone all day. "Of course. Whatever you ask for, I will give you. You have my blessing, and leave to arrange your affairs."

We waited while she left. Then I stood in silence. Behind me, the army of warriors stood like statues, not breathing or moving.

"So what now? You said I had until the new moon." I didn't move toward her, but I refused to look away.

Isolde flicked her hand, and her clothes melted across her, taking on a more formfitting shape, with pant legs. "I never specified which moon. You would think, given your history with contracts, you would understand the concept of fine print. Come, handmaiden." She turned on her heel and walked down a hall, leaving her army. "Do you understand why I chose you?"

"Fear." I glanced her way, biting my lip to keep her beauty from mesmerizing me. "Fear of Grimm. You needed something to use against him, to keep him from repeating the last time he put you in time-out." My words might have been brave. The reality was I nearly fell to my knees under her stare.

She lashed out, striking me across the face so fast her

hand blurred. "I fear no one and nothing. You have no idea why I wanted you. Perhaps you should ask my father."

I spat blood out, barely missing her dress. "I'll do that next time I see him."

I saw her hand move. I just couldn't quite react fast enough to stop her from seizing me by the jaw and twisting my head. She held up her other hand, the nails turned black, pointed. I'd seen them like that once before, when her arm was a tangled knot of bone and root called the Root of Lies. "Are you familiar with how these thorns work, handmaiden?"

I was. They grew toward any lie, tearing it from the heart of the liar. "I know. I'm not afraid, because I tell the truth."

She held up one finger, tracing a path down my chin, between my breasts, where she stopped. My heart raced with adrenaline, waiting for her to finally kill me. And the thorns grew, cutting into my breast, forcing between my ribs, teasing a shriek of pain from my lips.

I fell to one knee, a trickle of blood soaking my bra.

She knelt, taking my hand, pulling me to my feet. "Now you may ask my father anything. The thorns inside will wait."

I shook my hand loose, clutching my chest to stem the bleeding. "I told you, I don't lie."

The look of pleasure on her face would have given the Marquis de Sade chills. "Those thorns won't listen to your lies, handmaiden. They're tuned to his."

Twelve

ISOLDE SMILED WHEN I jerked my hand to my heart. "Ask my father anything. See what answers he gives when he knows the cost." She turned and walked across the hall, then stopped. A frown besmirched her face as her eyes narrowed. "Before we attend to business, show me your sword."

I fumbled at my side, wondering why it always looked so easy to draw a blade in the movies. I drew mine and advanced on her, holding the blade before me like a shield. "Recognize it?"

Only the slightest twitch in her eyes betrayed the emotionless mask of her face as Isolde nodded. "Indeed. Father still hasn't learned to use a scroll, or, what do they call them? Phone? He's still using objects as his messengers and his messages. Two can play that game."

"I've got a message of my own I'd like to deliver." Closer and closer I stalked, still keeping the sword between us.

The thing was, I'd gotten smarter over the years. Most of the time, anyone who let you attack them wasn't really afraid of being attacked. One thing I'd definitely learned from Shigeru was that a calm opponent was the one I should fear most.

So I didn't swing or stab. I just moved to the right position, the sword tip within inches of her.

"Really?" She held out her hand, palm first. "Do you really believe you can kill me?" With a flick of her wrist along the blade, she laid her palm open like a slice of lunch meat.

I dropped the sword, gurgling in shock and pain, as my own hand split open, my blood gushing.

"You are my handmaiden, and I your queen. We share fates." Isolde rubbed her hands together, golden light falling from them into sprinkles of glitter. She held up her palm, showing smooth white flesh, while mine pulsed blood with each heartbeat. "Think before you threaten me."

I clutched my hand, willing the blood to stop, trying to ignore the pain. The white-hot brand of fire in my hand made it hard to think, hard to speak. I didn't see her approach, and couldn't have fought back when she took my hand if I had to. I looked away, afraid, ashamed of my fear.

"This simply won't do." Isolde pulsed with power, like an electric generator, and inside, something like a spotlight switched on, shining with the warmth of a million suns. The stabbing pain in my palm melted away, letting me open my eyes enough to watch the skin smooth together, turning pink, then healthy tan. The spotlight turned on me, healing the thorn wound in my breast, soothing the aches and pains and tension.

Too soon it faded away, leaving me under flickering torchlight, before the Queen of Evil herself. She wore a haughty smirk like the latest fashion. "Does my father not grant you respite from your wounds?"

He did, but not like that. Grimm always said that addiction to magic-based healing was worse than heroin, people cutting and wounding themselves just to experience it over and over. At that moment, I'd have given anything to bask in that feeling for one second longer.

Isolde released my hand and paced past me, picking up the sword I'd dropped. She swung it overhand, smashing it to the ground.

With a spray of sparks, it glanced off the stone and lay humming on the ground. Isolde held out her hand, and the blade leaped to her. This time she swung with both hands, a blow that shaved the edge off the corner of her throne.

Before I could laugh or even smile at her failure, Isolde hurled the sword overhand, flinging it like a dart across the room. It struck a mirror on the wall and sank through the glass, disappearing.

She dusted off her hands and looked to me. "Let Father have his toy back. That sword is inadequate for one of my handmaidens." She held out her hand, and the fingernails from it grew longer, twisting, bending together into a blade laced with hooks and thorns.

With her other hand, she broke the blade off, swinging it toward me. "This is a handmaiden's weapon." In her palm, the blade shriveled away to a rotten husk, leaving only a black bone handle. "Take it from me."

Honestly, I still struggled to push the memory of being healed from my mind. Every inch of me craved that feeling, the warmth which made pain a distant memory. I shook the desire from my head, forcing myself to take a step, commanding my hand to reach out.

I couldn't avoid brushing her palm when I took it from her. I expected her to feel cold to the touch, like metal. Instead, she radiated fire. Rolling the handle into my fist, I clenched it. Thorns burst out from the bud at the end, resuming their wicked shape. The outer edges gleamed with reddish-black poison.

"Come with me, handmaiden." Isolde turned her back to me, seemingly unafraid of the blade I held. Then again, to stab her through the heart would be to kill myself. Without even meaning to, I willed the thorn blade to dust and slid the handle into one of the zillion loops that festooned my uniform.

"Where are we going?"

"To settle old debts." Isolde paced off down the hall, and I followed. I didn't feel her summon a portal. We were walking down a hall, then we weren't. The interior of the castle raced away like shadows fleeing light, leaving us standing in a ghetto of Low Kingdom.

The crowded throngs of monsters, hags, and hangmen reacted rather poorly to their queen's return. Shrieking, screaming, running in blind terror, they trampled one another to get out of her way, leaving the dead and wounded in their wake.

Isolde stalked down the street, thorns growing up from the cracks in the concrete to finish off the wounded, until she finally reached a shop door.

One I recognized.

The Isyle Witch, bound shopkeeper in High Kingdom, oldest and most powerful witch in Low Kingdom. The witch who first saw the handmaiden's mark on me, and longed for the Black Queen's return. I hated her shop, avoided talking to her except on business.

"You aren't truly mine yet." Isolde didn't bother to look at me, peering through the shop windows. "But you will be. When you have nothing left to live for, nothing and no one to love, you'll give yourself to me."

The thought of willingly serving her made me sick. "I've read all about your handmaidens. Murderers. Maniacs."

"Not at first. We start with the simple. The deserving. The guilty." Her smug tone made me worry. She reached out, tearing the hinges off the door without touching it. "Cariah, I have returned. Come out, and answer me."

I'd never heard the Isyle Witch's name. Never even thought of asking it, let alone calling her by it. Her title came from her hometown and, in truth, was the only way I'd ever heard her addressed.

The witch shuffled to the door of her shop, her yellow eyes wide, her toothless maw split in a crazed grin. "At last. I beg your forgiveness, but I am bound to this wretched shop. I cannot leave it." She knelt, splitting the gray rags that draped her.

Isolde shivered, a mask of rage contorting her heavenly beauty. "When my armies were destroyed, where was my High Queen? When the seal bearers attacked, why did my greatest sorceress not defend me? When I lay burning in the infernal flame, you hid in the forest. For that, you deserve death."

The witch's grin turned to fear, her face slack. "Alone, I

could not defeat them. A single witch against the Fairy God-father, I would have died."

"Then or now." Isolde raised one hand; thorns grew from the gutter toward the shop doorway, wreathing it. Then she turned toward me. "Should she live or die? What say you, handmaiden?"

Nothing, if it were up to me. Let the two of them kill each other, far as I was concerned, and leave me out of it.

The witch turned her gaze toward me, her eyes reminding me so much of Ari, scarred by Wild Magic. "Remember? Remember how I have aided you?"

And she had. When Grimm's mirror lay broken in a thou-sand shards, I'd gone to her for fleshing silver to repair it.

The witch pressed herself to the door of the shop, the silver bonds on her wrists glowing white-hot as the wards pinned her in. "I will give you anything you ask for."

She'd given me quite enough already. A love potion that nearly ruined the best relationship in my life. One I'd used to wake Ari from a coma, making certain Wyatt loved her. And at that thought, I knew what I wanted. What I'd accept, in return for her life.

"You have something of Wyatt Pendlebrook's. A lock of his hair. Give it to me." The words felt filthy in my mouth. Black-mail for a life, but after two years, Wyatt and Ari still couldn't spend more than a couple hours together without him retreating to the safety of his warded home.

The witch's gray hair flared up like tentacles. "That child was mine by right, to raise and love."

"Fine. Keep the hair. If you're dead, it won't mean much." I reached for my belt, and the sword, praying she would yield. As my fingers touched the grip, she groaned, a cry of pain and sadness.

"I will give it to you." Broken, defeated, she released her grip on the shop door, sagging downward. She turned and shuffled back into her shop.

Isolde watched me, her lips drawn back with pleasure, her eyes approving. "I knew I chose correctly. Come." She glided into the shop, and I followed, arriving just in time to see the front counter explode into fragments, clearing the way before her. The curtain dividing the front of the shop from the back caught fire, fluttering into ashes.

The back of the shop resembled the warehouse of God. Among rows and rows of wooden shelves, a thousand jars sat. Some glowed; some bubbled; some held things that moved if I let my gaze wander to them. It stretched into the darkness for an eternity.

I ran to keep up with Isolde's effortless glide, and rounded a row of shelves to an alcove. A room, of sorts. Along one side, boxes and a straw mattress formed a bed; along the other, what was either a chamber pot or a fresh fruit arrangement two months past its date.

The witch knelt in the center of the room, her hands outspread, chanting. With each word, the stone beneath her bubbled and rose, like a swamp geyser in granite. At last, a bubble rose and held its shape. She burst it with a knobby finger, revealing a stubby wooden chest.

When she opened the lid, rows of spells lay cradled in sheep's wool, but her gnarled fingers skipped over them, drawing out a rough leather bag. "Take it, handmaiden."

I did, pulling it from her fingers, slipping it into my bra. "I say let her live."

"Your recommendation is noted, handmaiden." Isolde folded her arms. "Now kill her."

"I said to let her live." My tone made it clear that I wouldn't be accepting substitutions.

"And I, as your queen, order you to kill the witch."

If I hadn't spent so much time around Ari, I might have died right there. The witch didn't speak a word, just pulled in raw power from the air. Unlike normal magic casters, witches could draw on the Wild Magic, which permeated everything. Anyone with a healthy sense of self-preservation avoided confronting them. I dove to the left. The air sizzled above me as a jet of flame exploded from her mouth, incinerating the spot where I'd stood.

"Do something!" I looked for Isolde and found her floating, translucent, a few feet away.

She shook her head. "If you are incapable of handling the slightest problem, you are unfit to serve."

A conflict with Kingdom's most powerful witch ranked as "impossible" in my book, not slight. Witches drew on Wild Magic, from the world around them, and the longer they lived, the more powerful they grew. This one had three hundred and seventy years on me.

This time she didn't throw elemental magic at me. The Isyle Witch waved her hands, sending a rolling wave through the stone floor.

I ran.

Oh, trust me, I'd killed things that couldn't die. I'd faced things with more than one face. The issue was, most of the time, running away still ranked top on the list of solutions. Particularly if who you ran from couldn't cross a shop boundary.

I sprinted back through the warehouse as shelves toppled behind me, sending wave after wave of jars crashing to the ground. At the doorway to the front of the shop, I stopped short.

A wall of thorns blocked the exit, grown so solid I couldn't even see through to the front.

"Running away doesn't solve anything." Isolde drifted like a ghost, passing through shelves to float in the doorway.

I disagreed, taking off down the back aisle, narrowly avoiding a blast of pure force that threw everything, including the shelves, straight into the wall. I didn't bother hunkering or hiding; I'd seen Ari look straight through doors and walls, and Ari wasn't twenty-four, let alone four hundred. Behind me, the witch chanted, drawing magic from the air to channel it into a blast of electricity that made the air crackle.

"Come out, girl. I'll make it quick." Her voice echoed through the room. I made it back to the alcove that served as the witch's abode and stopped. Isolde might not have cared one way or the other if I lived, but she had a point. Though the warehouse went on into the darkness, my only hope was to stand and fight.

Where better to arm myself than the storeroom of Kingdom's most powerful witch?

And where would she keep her most powerful weapons, other than in her secret chest?

I flipped open the lid and grinned. Inside lay glistening triangles of crystal. Spells. Not the cheap walnut-shaped spells Grimm gave his agents. These were works of art, built by a master of spell-craft. I took three, stuffing my pockets.

"Hey, Raisin," I yelled out into the darkness, wrapping my fingers around one of the spells.

In the silence, her shuffling footsteps grew louder, until at last she appeared. "I should have killed you when you entered my shop the first time. You are unworthy to be her handmaiden."

If it were up to me, I'd never have entered her shop at all. I held out my hand, pointing my fist at her, and smiled when she squinted, recognizing what I aimed at her. "Any last words?" I didn't wait. The whole point of asking was to get her mind off on some sort of retort. I triggered the spell without giving her a chance to reply.

From my palm a column of smoke burst, uncoiling like a snake toward the witch, smoke hardening to scales, steel gray.

The witch didn't blink. She didn't even raise her hands, but the spell *twisted*, tearing a furrow in the stone floor. "How dare you use my own armory against me?"

"You want to know?" Casting the spent spell to the side, I drew another and triggered it. A luminous fog billowed out, drawing a sharp hiss from the witch.

While her spells weren't labeled, the way she held her arms in a cross before her told me I'd drawn something far more dangerous. Then she raised her hands, and *pushed*. At least, that's the motion she made, and in one sick moment I knew what she meant to do.

A gentle wave of air pushed the cloud, sending it back toward me. I scrambled backwards, running into the wall, as the witch gathered enough magic to create a tornado. I pulled the last spell, setting my mind on the witch, focusing.

I'd never had any ability with magic. I could barely pick a card from a deck.

But something Ari had said over and over came to me. Focus.

I did.

When I detonated the spell, what I willed, what I demanded, was that it destroy the witch, blasting her into a million wrinkly pieces. I remember the light as the spell triggered. I'm guessing the noise was an explosion, judging by how my ears rang.

It threw me like a rag doll, back through a shelf, crushing a dozen jars, leaving me crumpled on the floor.

The witch's laughter filled the room as she completed her spell. Ignoring the luminous cloud, she threw the gale straight at me, shattering, tearing, and destroying everything.

Glass cut my scalp, splinters blew into my face, and yet, I'd survived. In front of me, a narrow sliver of shelf stood, shielding me from the blast, but with one follow-up, the witch would finish the job.

Or maybe not.

Trickling from a bag on the top shelf, a familiar gray powder covered everything still standing. I forced myself to crawl to the shelf, reaching with bloody fingers for the bag. Like a woman in the desert finding an oasis, I dumped it over my head, covering myself.

Bone dust. Made from the bones of some unfortunate victim, murdered, then ground up to a powder. The secret Kingdom's boogeyman used to kill royalty for hundreds of years.

I staggered to my feet, listening to the witch chant behind me.

I didn't care. I'd been a firsthand recipient of the bone-dust treatment, and when she unleashed her spell, it didn't even slow my limp toward her. Too late, she realized her error.

Too late to stop me from sinking my fist deep in her stomach, and following it with a knee to the face, and toe to the ear. Finally, I doused her in the last of the bone dust, sealing her power inside her for longer than I planned to be around.

Lying on the ground, helpless, she seemed older. Frailer.

"Well done, handmaiden." Isolde's voice scared me so badly I bit my lip.

I turned to face her, forcing defiance through the pain, making myself stare her in the eyes. "I'm done here."

"Kill her."

"I won't."

Isolde's eyes flashed the way Grimm's did when I angered him. I'd done it so often Grimm didn't often react to me anymore. Isolde, on the other hand, was a spoiled brat, not used to hearing the word no. "You will. I order it."

"You can do what you want to me. I'm not a killer." I spit out bone dust, nearly managing to hit her in the face.

Her face contorted with rage, scarring the mask of beauty until she looked like a rictus of pain and anger. "Darling." Her voice changed in a way that made me choke more than the dust in the air. "My first command to you is given. Kill the witch." I spent so much time panicking over her voice, I almost didn't notice when I took the first step.

My feet moved of their own accord, and my every effort couldn't stop their movement. I limped to the witch, kicking her with my foot to roll her onto her back. "Stop." I couldn't command. I could barely beg, and my body continued without me.

My hands drew the thorn sword, which blossomed to its purple and black glory like the kudzu vine from hell.

And I slammed the blade into the Isyle Witch's chest.

Over and over.

Only when her body lay a ruined mess did the compulsion leave, my hands dropping the sword. I fell to my knees in a pool of the witch's blood, shaking from pain, fear, and shock.

"First you kill the guilty." Isolde knelt to whisper in my ear. "It is how we begin."

I'm not sure who I spoke to, her or myself. "I don't murder people."

"Who is the liar now? Your hands took her life. Her blood covers you. Handmaiden, would you like me to heal you?" Her voice held no trace of Fairy Godmother now, only her honey-sweet song.

And I did want it. To be free of the stabbing pain that took each breath from me, the burning in my fingertips. I hated her for knowing I wanted it, hated her for offering. "No."

"Another lie. Cariah was wrong. You are most suited to me. Tell my father, when you see him, that this ends when he decides it does." Isolde held out her hand, and in it she held my thorn sword, now just the ebony hilt. She dropped it in front of me.

"That's the message you dragged me through Low Kingdom to deliver? You complain about him not being able to use a scroll." Each word took a separate breath, but I wouldn't let that deter me.

She knelt over, so close I could smell the scent of roses and cinnamon on her. "No, Marissa. That's not my message. You are."

Thirteen

SHE WAS GONE in that instant, reclaimed by a blossom of white light, leaving me to drag myself out of the storeroom. On the way out, I took the rest of the witch's spells, slinging them in a burlap sack. Though each weighed no more than a sparrow, my shoulder screamed if I tried to lift it off the ground.

The thorns which had barricaded me in the storeroom crumbled at my approach, leaving the floor broken and buckled. As I stepped past the tattered curtain dividing the storeroom from the front of the witch's shop, a prince waited. He tapped his fingers impatiently on the countertop. Given the lack of magic shine on him, obviously one of the lesser families, probably just as much of a jerk. He looked at me, covered in bone dust and blood, and raised his lip in a sneer. "Do you have any idea how long I've been waiting?"

And the next thing I knew, I'd drawn my sword. Without the compulsion, it felt like wielding a bowling pin, but the effect was exactly what I'd wanted. Part of me screamed to swing it forward, cutting into his neck. The other part of me quivered in terror, wondering when killing arrogant princes became part of my accepted repertoire. "Leave. Leave now. Pray I don't make house calls."

The prince's eyes widened and he stumbled backwards, tripping over a cage full of Himalayan fruit bats. With a cloud of chiropterans behind him, he fled from the shop, stumbling at the doorway, and leaving a single glass loafer. When the door slammed shut, I limped over and locked it, staring through the glass. Though Isolde had blown out the door to the witch's shop in Low Kingdom, the door existed in two places at once. Since the prince came from High Kingdom, the portion of it from that realm remained locked there, and outside dancing flowers and singing animals waited. At the same time, if I focused on the door frame, the crushed bricks and twisted metal of Low Kingdom flickered at the edge of sight.

I washed bone dust off my face using water from the aquarium in the corner, then found a mirror shard and called for backup. "Grimm." I'd have said more, but even that word hurt.

He flickered into the mirror, then into every single surface in the shop that could hold as much as a sparkle. "Hold on, Marissa. Help is on the way."

IF LIAM HAD waited even a moment, I would have unlocked the door. Instead, he ripped it out of the frame and rushed me. "Are you bleeding?"

His grasp sent shivers of joy and shooting pain through me.

Behind him, Ari came, dressed in navy blue, not bothering to hide her witch eyes from the curious crowds gathering. "Put her down, I need to work."

Liam reluctantly released me, calling to a group of men in blue uniforms who flooded the shop carrying automatic weapons. The head mercenary pulled out a pocket compact, oblivious to the fact that Grimm's face shone everywhere in the shop, and reported in. "Site is secure. We'll hold until the entrances are repaired."

"Grimm's worried about the spells in here getting stolen." Ari ran her fingers back and forth in the air above me, then gritted her teeth. "This won't feel like when Grimm does it, but it should fix your fractures."

Liam let go of me for a moment to look around. "You need me to call an ambulance?"

"No, I'll take care of her." Her fingertips sparked and fizzled, and while her red hair stood out from her head, I didn't feel even an ounce better. Ari shook her head. "She's covered in bone dust. Until we get it off, magic is off the table."

Liam lumbered over to the aquarium and heaved it off the pedestal, dumping the entire thing on me, drenching Ari in the process and sending two frogs down my blouse.

"I was going to ask you to go get the wipes from my car." Ari glared at him with witch eyes, but her anger seemed lost on him. Then she began the magic, pulling power from the air, channeling it through herself and using it to heal me.

First I could breathe. Then I could sit up. Then I could feel my fingertips. I still shook, from shock and fear, and clung to Liam like a frightened child. I pointed to the burlap bag. "That is for you."

Ari took it from the floor and peeked inside, then gasped. "Grimm, are these—"

"Not a word, princess." Grimm risked calling Ari by her title, but the edge in his voice made it clear what I'd dug up worried him. "Marissa, where did you find these?"

"From the witch's private stash. I tried to use a few of them against her."

"Marissa—" Grimm and Ari spoke as one, then stopped. Ari studied one of the spells, turning it over in her hands. "These aren't just spells. They're almost lessons in magic. The way they're put together, the craft—I'd never have *thought* to do something like this."

"Nor would you have the skill," said Grimm.

Ari nodded. "Not yet. But now I know it can be done. Sometimes that's the most important part."

Grimm wiped his forehead. "That is what worries me most, princess. Some forms of knowledge should not be held by humans. At least give me your word you will store them in our vault until you better appreciate what you hold in your hands."

Ari glanced to me. "Are they really that dangerous?"

"Yes, princess," said Grimm, using Ari's title just to keep her attention. "I would buy them from you if I thought you would sell, just to keep you safe."

I didn't care about the money. Magic and I had never gotten along, so I focused on something that did work well with me. Liam. I pushed myself up next to him so the hellfire inside him warmed me, and shut my eyes. When he carried me to the car, I curled up in the backseat, and tried to forget.

BY THE TIME we got to the Agency, I insisted on walking myself, but conceded to using the elevator just this once. The doors opened and we crowded in, pushing a man to the back. It wasn't until after the doors shut that the man spoke. "Marissa, have you found my souls?"

Liam swung around, his skin growing scaly, and fire lighting in his eyes, while Ari's hair crackled and stood on end.

I shoved myself between them, holding out my hands. "Don't." Then I slammed the Stop button, holding the elevator and ignoring the ringing. "I've been somewhat busy, but the other day I crossed the city looking for them. I haven't seen hide nor hair of the Mihails. Are you certain they'd be looking for me?"

Neither my fiancé nor my best friend stood a chance against the Adversary in a throwdown. Even the harbingers of the apocalypse preferred to avoid confronting him, at least according to Death.

"Dead certain. And while I'm touched by the soul you liberated earlier, that wasn't one of the ones I asked you about." Nickolas slicked back his gray hair, making the bald spot on his head look that much larger.

"It wasn't exactly my plan."

He pushed toward me, his breath minty and hot. "I can't give you much longer. Find them, or I'll make you wish you had."

And that was exactly where things went to Inferno in a handbasket. I think that what Nickolas meant to do was pat me on the shoulder. I know both of the people in my corner took that as a threat.

Liam grabbed the Adversary by the throat and threw him back, slamming him into the elevator wall so hard the panel cracked. Ari didn't wait, hitting him with a blizzard-in-a-box that left him encased in solid ice. I hit the elevator button like a monkey on crack, slamming it repeatedly.

The ice began to hiss and crack, an ominous red glow lighting the entire elevator. The elevator jerked to a stop at the next floor. As the door creaked open, I shoved Ari out, dragging Liam behind me. I felt mildly bad for the telephone salesman who got on. As the doors slid shut, a cloud of pure blackness blossomed inside.

"You can't do that." I turned on Liam and Ari, neither of whom had the slightest idea what sort of offense they'd just committed.

Liam shook his head. "The hell I can't. If you think I'm going to stand around when people threaten you, you can think again. If I'd have been there when she tried to take you—" Liam's voice broke. "I won't let her take you."

We climbed the stairs the rest of the way to the Agency. Grimm waited for me in his office.

"The Adversary was in our elevator—" I halted as his power rushed over me, pouring out from my bracelet like a lead blanket.

Then his eyes narrowed, and his mouth opened. "I've arranged an unfortunate elevator accident, and a sacrifice of six hundred goats. Don't say another word, my dear. Not a single word."

Liam and Ari looked to him, fear in open parade on their faces.

Grimm looked away from me, to them. "My daughter has implanted a thorn near her heart. Typically triggered by lies."

I spoke before they could ask. "Not mine, this time. Yours."

He faded out of the mirror, a look of shock and pain on his face. When he returned, he showed no emotion whatsoever. "Of course."

"She had me kill the Isyle Witch." Though I wanted to lie, no lie would change the facts.

Grimm nodded. "The last of her supporters. Her death was ordained the day she deserted my daughter."

Liam knew how I felt about murder. I'd killed people in self-defense, yes, but never when I had a choice. Ever. He took my arm, but I resisted his pull. "Isolde made me kill her."

"Marissa, you need not justify your actions. I understand."

I threw off Liam's hand and pounded the desk. "No, you don't. Isolde called me darling."

Grimm continued his blank look, waiting.

"Fairy Godmother called me darling. Isolde ordered me to kill her, and I couldn't stop myself." The memories welled up like tears of the mind.

Grimm's sigh went on forever. "Sit, my dear. I will finish healing you as gently as I can. And while I have always respected your right to privacy, for your own sake, I must insist on something. It is time you finally told me everything Fairy Godmother said to you."

LIAM DROVE US home that night, after hours and hours of questioning. Every detail. Every secret I'd ever kept about how I nearly died the day I fought with a fairy came out. How I'd tried and failed to kill her with reaper bullets. How I almost managed to kill an immortal being with a blade. And how in the end, only the knowledge that my adoptive mother never loved me let me trick Fairy Godmother into a fatal lie, which let the Root of Lies tear into her.

I'd never told anyone, not even Liam, how close I came to losing myself. Or that I feared the loss of my identity more than death itself.

At home, Liam tucked me into bed after a hot shower. I thought for sure he would slide in beside me, but instead he left the bedroom. I blinked twice, and the clock said nearly two in the morning. Stretching sore muscles, I rose from the bed and looked out into the kitchen. Liam sat out in the recliner, a mirror in his hand, speaking in hushed tones of worry.

I'd never seen him so serious, so I went to the bathroom and opened my medicine cabinet, where Grimm waited for me. I put one hand on his mirror. "Tell Liam whatever he needs can wait. He should come to bed."

Grimm bit his lip for a moment, considering his words. "Mr. Stone and I are discussing your predicament, and the nature of the handmaiden enchantments."

"Since when did my artist boyfriend become a Kingdom-lore geek?"

"Marissa, you underestimate him. His lack of familiarity brings fresh insight, and his knowledge of old Gaelic drinking songs gives him a keen edge in magical research. That said, I forget at times that humans require recharging."

"Good night, Grimm." I flipped the light off. It popped back on.

Grimm still stared at me. "My dear, I will not let you come to further harm if I can control it."

I panicked, thinking of the thorn waiting by my heart. My hand raced to my chest, then my cheeks turned red. Grimm knew I doubted him. This time, when I turned the light off, he left me alone.

WHEN I WOKE the next morning, Liam was gone. The smell of bacon drew me from my bed, though living with Svetlana gave me at least enough smarts to make sure I put on a robe. When I walked out into the kitchen and saw Ari, I could have stepped back in time.

She looked up at me and gave me that gigawatt smile. "Morning, M. Pancakes and bacon, ready."

I took a plate and sat down at the table. "Did you see my man?"

Ari brought her own plate over and joined me. "He and Wyatt went into Kingdom."

At Wyatt's name, I gasped. "My purse. I'm not going to the department of licensing again." I looked everywhere for it. It had my wallet, my gun— "And Wyatt's hair was in my bra."

Ari frowned, raising her eyebrows.

"The lock of hair his mother gave the witch. She asked—" I caught myself, choking. "She asked what I wanted to spare her life. I said the hair." My tears added to the salt content of the bacon. "Then I killed her anyway."

Ari pulled the dish towel off the makeup mirror on my table. "Grimm, Marissa says Wyatt's lock of hair was in the clothing she left at the Agency."

Grimm cocked his head in surprise, and slowly nodded in agreement. "I'll need your boyfriend present to unravel the spell. He and Liam will return around noon, which is when Marissa and Liam will be leaving."

"Leaving?" we asked together.

"Yes. Meet at the Agency. I'll have the armored truck arriving at the same time." Grimm faded out without waiting for further questions.

When he was gone, I turned my attention back to Ari. "So why are you here?"

"I thought maybe you could use some company." Ari blushed, making her hair look even redder. "This is all my fault. I would never have challenged the Black Queen, but I thought I understood the Fae Mother. I was certain she said I would be the one to defeat her. And I wanted you to be able to stop living in fear."

"You challenged her. Maybe just by doing that, you've made sure she'll be defeated. And if we're going over blame, let's start with the fact that you being a witch is my fault." I never said that. Not out loud, though it was true by any and every measure. I'd helped Ari learn magic before she bonded with her Realm Seal, and in doing so, injured her soul in a way that could never be repaired.

Ari closed her eyes. "No. You didn't know what helping me learn magic on my own would do. You didn't tell Queen Mihail to try to kill us, and you would never have let me try to contain a magic apple. I thought I could defeat the Black Queen. I really did."

I took her hand in a grip like a vise, determined that no one, not fairies or evil queens or postmen, were ever going to take away the people I loved.

Fourteen

WYATT AND LIAM were waiting at the Agency, along with Mrs. Pendlebrook. To my annoyance, I still didn't know her first name. When she saw me, she nodded.

I should've said something, but Liam was just past her, and I had priorities. "What's this I hear about us leaving?"

Grimm interrupted, appearing in the lobby mirror. "Please proceed to ritual room number four." His voice had that hollow sound like automatic elevators, history teachers, or other life-less things.

Wyatt took the opportunity to show what two years of fear therapy could do, taking Ari's hand and only shuddering slightly when he looked at her.

In the ritual room, the leather bag with Wyatt's hair lay on a propane barbecue grill, along with a lighter.

Grimm appeared in the mirror at the head of the table. He looked at Wyatt. "Take the draw and light the fire."

Wyatt's quizzical look said he didn't understand the term "draw"—in essence, a physical shell for a magical binding. The hair served as the key element to a binding meant to make Wyatt serve whoever held the spell. Every night at midnight, the binding still activated, but as long as Wyatt spent the night within the wards and celestial crystal, he remained free another day.

With the witch dead, he'd be drawn to whoever possessed the draw, which wasn't going to be me, if I had any say in it. I'd spent six years in service to Grimm, and so understood Wyatt's predicament more than he knew. No, today he'd be free.

Wyatt picked up the bag, and after several failed attempts with the lighter, Liam spat into the grill. His spit erupted into a flame, which blistered the paint. Best I could tell, you could burn the draw with almost anything, but grills met an important requirement for Grimm's spell ingredients—they were cheap.

"Now, the ritual must be completed quickly," said Grimm.

Wyatt reached into the bag and pulled out a hank of waxen blond hair, the same color as the stuff still attached to his head. "What now?"

Grimm closed his eyes, and the air in the room shimmered. "I've broken down the spell's shielding. This won't last long." Which meant that for a brief window, the hair could be destroyed, taking the spell with it and leaving Wyatt a free man. A spindly, pacifistic, free man.

Wyatt tossed the hair into the fire, and the sickening stench of burning hair filled the room. But so did the stench of roses. In the fire, the leather bag pulsed, beating like a heart, faster and faster. My own pulse rose in time, as an unearthly squeal erupted from the bag. The squealing died to a whimper as the leather curled and blackened, then disintegrated.

And I swear, if anything, the magic shine on Wyatt grew stronger. He'd always had a stream of magic boiling off him like glitter almost as strong as Ari. Now I wouldn't want to guess which one of them gave off more raw magic. The man was still beanpole thin, but he looked somehow *more*.

Wyatt fidgeted, his gaze darting around the room, then cleared his throat. "If you don't mind, I'd like to turn off the grill now. The operations guide advises against indoor cooking, and carbon monoxide poisoning can occur within minutes." Wyatt pointed to the handle.

Around the table, four separate sighs of relief came out.

Whatever else he might be, Wyatt was still Wyatt. He turned toward Ari, closed his eyes, and leaned forward, smashing his mouth up against hers. And let me tell you this—from what I saw, Ari could kiss like nobody's business. After what seemed like an eternity, he came up for air. "I did it! I kissed her!" A gleeful grin covered his face. Then slowly the grin faded, and he began to search his pockets.

"Fairy Godfather, have you any mouthwash and soap?" The panic in Wyatt's voice was thick enough to frost a cake. Obsessive-compulsive didn't begin to cover his issues with personal contact.

"There are two bottles under the kitchen cabinet. The green label is drain cleaner. The yellow is mouthwash. I recommend the yellow." Grimm didn't even mock him as Wyatt rushed from the room.

"Young lady, I don't have words to thank you." Mrs. Pendlebrook put her hand on my shoulder, and gave me the first approving smile I'd ever received from her. "I have promised Fairy Godfather any and all assistance I can render. I can never repay my debt to you."

"Do you know what I did to get that spell?" I wasn't in a mood to hide anymore.

"I do. Don't ask me to say I'm sorry the witch is dead, and I won't lie to you. She killed my husband, so you have my thanks, Marissa, and my aid, where I can offer it."

I wanted to say something awful. To say she should have been the one to wield the sword, but before I could speak, Grimm cut me off. "Marissa, you are needed on the seventh floor immediately."

I knew better than to wait. Grimm used *immediately* for "someone left the lights on" and "someone is about to be murdered." I couldn't afford to take chances.

With every ounce of energy I had, I sprinted up the stairs to the seventh floor. Once, there'd been a stock and bond trading firm on that floor. A tragic accident involving an army of wooden puppets and a pyromaniac woodcarver convinced them to move out, and Grimm snapped up the lease. The air still stank of burned wood and bank deals.

I noted the lights left on and headed for the light switches, swearing Grimm could have used a temp worker for this.

Only the slightest whisper of sound gave me a warning, just enough time for a thought. In one heartbeat, the thorn sword hung in my hand. In the next second, it blocked a steel blade just inches from my head. I stepped back, bowing to the figure in black. "Shigeru."

"It is time for your next lesson."

"I don't think I ever got through lesson one." I stepped back as he advanced, trying to keep a concrete pillar or two between us.

Shigeru nodded. "Today I will strike back."

I was completely screwed. I sprinted for the stairwell, and in the time it took me to slide across an abandoned desk, he stood between me and it. And I attacked. Letting the sword guide me as much as I guided it. I held a weapon with centuries of death locked inside, and this time, I wasn't going to be kicked and whipped. Every slice, every chop and stab, I moved faster than thought, letting the blade's own murderous instinct guide me.

And always, he dodged, bending like a tree in a storm, then rolling up to kick my legs out from under me.

A single flash of steel scored my arm. I pressed my hand to it, swearing at the pain. He'd cut me. Not enough to kill. Just enough to hurt. Enough to enrage. Tears coursed through my eyes as I rose, and this time, the cries for blood that echoed in my heart joined those in the blade as I hurled myself forward. This time, I wouldn't be taken by surprise. I let the blade whisper to me, guiding my arms and legs, until its voice became my own. Faster and faster, I swung it, this time backing Shigeru up.

And in one second, he stepped inside a thrust, smashing my wrist with his pommel, then following it up with a cut across my thigh.

"Come." He beckoned. "Strike me once and this is over."

I knelt on the floor, hands on my arm and thigh, alternating between weeping from pain and rage. Every whisper of the sword said this next time would be different. That this time I could take him. But every ounce of my experience said this was a lie no different from any other the Black Queen spoke. I threw the sword down. "No. I won't."

Without a word, Shigeru advanced, swinging his sword from side to side in lazy strokes. And the blood that made my hands sticky said he wouldn't hesitate to use it. This time, though, I waited, watching, until the last moment, when his blade came across, and I could duck under it, scrambling to the side. I had time for one glance upward and a leap to the left, then two steps back to avoid a flurry of blows.

Shigeru switched to stabbing, blows that came straight toward me, and this time, I dodged just enough to let the blade pass. As he swung overhead, his sword sliced open the fire sprinklers and sent a shower of sparks from the light mixed with filthy water.

I did the only thing I could.

I dove headfirst at him, hitting him in the shins, and knocking us both into a heap.

My lungs burned like the air was molten metal, and every ounce of me screamed in pain.

Beside me, Shigeru rose and picked up his sword. I couldn't move another inch. Couldn't stand to save myself. I opened my eyes to face Shigeru.

"We are done." He sheathed his sword and walked over to pull a long muslin cloth off of a mirror. Grimm waited inside the mirror, his arms crossed.

"She has learned today's lesson." Shigeru bowed to Grimm, then turned and left.

"Marissa—"

"I don't understand." I rolled over, letting the fire sprinkler mask the tears on my face. "I don't understand what he's teaching me. If he's teaching at all. I can't keep doing this." My throat couldn't give voice to the pain that soaked every inch of me, making my entire body shake.

I stood up, my teeth chattering. "I can't take any more lessons."

Grimm nodded. "I've arranged a business trip of sorts with Mr. Stone. But you cannot go looking like that."

"No." I wrapped my arms around me. "No more healing. I can't take that either."

In response, the mirror lit up. Golden light poured out, sweeping through the room like a spotlight. Where it touched me, the skin knit together, and bruises faded. But unlike when Isolde healed me, it didn't leave me craving more when the light faded away.

"You've always been capable of that?" I worked the kinks out of my elbow. "And you kept saying you didn't want me addicted."

Grimm nodded. "I have always been capable of local temporal disturbances. I've allowed you to heal at an accelerated rate without the risk of addiction, but the cost can be counted in weeks of your life."

Weeks. Gone in seconds. "How dare you?" I wiped tears from the edges of my eyes. Trying to decide if cursing or screaming better fit the tornado of emotion inside. "What gives you the right?"

Grimm spoke before I could. "Necessity. The auguries are quite clear, Marissa. If you do not learn from Shigeru, you will die in the culling, like so many of my daughter's handmaidens before you." He looked away from me. "I've taken a month. If it means your survival, it is a worthwhile trade. Liam has been waiting patiently downstairs for what must seem like months to him."

I trudged down the stairwell to the front lobby, where Liam waited.

He crossed his arms. "What was the emergency? You've been gone for nearly an hour." He took my hand and pulled me toward the door. "We've got to be going."

Grimm appeared in the front door. "Sir, I've made arrangements with the guards. Take car number three."

I wanted to say I needed to change, but the blood that had covered me had turned to brown crust. Liam probably figured I'd gotten sprayed with chocolate pudding again. So I followed him out, down the stairs to our parking garage. "You want to tell me where we are going?"

"No." Liam opened the car door and slid behind the

wheel. As soon as I was in he pulled out, sparing only a glance at the bags in the backseat.

We rode in silence for nearly thirty minutes. Keeping secrets wasn't Liam's strong point. He'd buy me a present, meaning to surprise me, and blurt it out within minutes of seeing me every time. I put my hand on his arm. "Again, you want to tell me where we are going?"

"Right here." He turned into the private airport, driving right onto the tarmac. A Piper Cub sat on the runway, the pilot waiting, and Liam waved to him.

"We're flying?"

"Yes, and you don't have wings." Liam hefted the duffel bags from the back and walked over to the plane.

Minutes later we were in the air, and I took the opportunity to rest my head against him. I could do anything with his support, even find a way to live with myself after what happened in Kingdom. With his chin on my head and my ear on his chest, I rested until the plane landed.

We touched down in a rainstorm and ran through the deluge to a rental car waiting at the strip. Again, Liam drove. As we passed highways and turned onto streets, my anxiety rose. I knew where we were. "I'm not going in there." We sat outside my mother's house. My house, once.

"You are." Liam pulled over to the curb and turned off the ignition. The pelting rain played like snare drums on the roof. "I did some research. You aren't the first handmaiden who wasn't willing."

He had my full attention now.

Liam slipped one hand over to take mine. "She said the same thing to them. First you kill the guilty. Then you kill the innocent. Last, you kill the ones you love. When you die inside, you'll do whatever she wants." Liam spoke softly, barely audible above the rain. "You've already killed the guilty."

"You really think I'm going to kill someone innocent?" How he could think I'd be willing to do that made me angry, hurt, and afraid, all the things I went to him to get away from.

Liam turned to me and took my hand, though I held myself stiff. "I think she's going to find a way to put you in a situation. I think it will be a lot harder if she doesn't have access to people—"

"What?"

"People you might want to kill. You haven't talked to your mother, ever. Not as long as I've known you. When you talk about her, in your sleep—"

"I talk in my sleep?"

He shook his head. "Who did you imagine Fairy God-mother as before the Root of Lies killed her?"

I let silence be my answer. Not because I was angry with him. Because I was angry with me. How could I not have seen that coming? My mother traded me to Grimm for a wish. It saved my little sister, but cost me six years of my life. "So what do we do?"

"These bags are cash. We go in there and convince them it's in their best interest to move." Liam opened the door before I could protest, slung the duffel bags over his shoulder, and marched up the sidewalk to the house I grew up in.

Liam rang the doorbell before I could get there.

My little sister answered the door. Hope. The reason I'd taken the deal with Grimm in the first place. In my memories, she was still two years old, not nearly twelve. She looked at Liam and shook her head. "Dad, there's a vacuum cleaner sales-man here. We don't want any." Without waiting for an answer, she slammed the door.

Liam grabbed the doorknob and ripped it out of the wood, shattering the door.

I ran to him, grabbing him and pulling him back. "I'll do this. Let me do this. Please. Go wait in the car." I watched him amble up the sidewalk. He'd been trying to help in his own way. I couldn't fault him for that.

"Marissa?" My dad stood in the front doorway, his gaze going from the broken door to me and back again.

"Dad." I waited, and sure enough, Mom came out. Her black hair had sprinkles of gray, and crow's-feet surrounded those blue eyes, the color I always wanted my eyes to be. "Mom."

She didn't speak, which was good, because I had so much to say to her that I didn't want to say.

"I brought you this." I nudged the bags with my foot.

Dad gave me an uneasy glance and looked back to Mom. "A Christmas card would have been okay."

"You know I don't celebrate holidays." I looked at Mom. "Or birthdays. It's cash."

Dad unzipped the bag with care. He probably still remembered the surprise birthday gift he gave me that turned out to have an Egyptian cobra nestled inside. Based on the look on his face, if I'd brought him Mikey's lunch box, he wouldn't have been more shocked. "Why?"

"You need to go. Now preferably, sooner if possible." I tried to keep my voice calm when all the pain of leaving them kept coming up.

"Why would we leave?" Mom let go of the doorpost and slithered out beside Dad. "What did you get yourself into this time?"

"I'll answer your question if you answer mine. Which royal family are you related to?"

The look of disgust on her face made me wonder if it wasn't Queen Mihail's family. I didn't have time for games. "You knew about Fairy Godfather already. You knew about harakathin. You don't have the shine, so you are related to someone who's royalty. Who is it?"

Dad turned on Mom, his eyes narrow, and waited.

"My sister married into the Sixth Royal Family." Mom choked the words out.

"What do you know about the Black Queen?"

She shook her head. "Children's stories. A myth, like Santa Claus."

"Saint Nicolae doesn't come out much, thank Kingdom. Now, you look into my eyes and tell me if you still believe the Black Queen is a myth." I stared at both until they turned away.

Dad shook his head. "Marigold, honey, I can't just leave. What will I tell people?"

I bristled at his pet name for me. I wasn't his little flower, hadn't been for a decade. "Tell them you won the lottery. Tell them your daughter did. Don't tell them anything, just don't be where I can find you. I need you to move somewhere and then not contact me. It should be easy for you." I regretted those last words the moment I spoke them, but hardened my resolve.

"You failed me. You could have said no to Mom. You could have called me, or come see me. But that doesn't matter. Do it for Hope. Take the money and take a vacation. Go to Portland, the Fairy there is really territorial. Go to Moscow. They have great vodka."

Dad picked up one of the duffel bags, stooping under the weight.

Mom waited until he'd dragged one inside with Hope's help to speak. "What do your problems have to do with my family?"

"The Black Queen will be looking for people. People I'm angry with. People who hurt me. People I might not have a problem killing." I let the last bit sink in. "If you ever loved me, take a vacation. If you love Hope, do it for her. You'll be safe in the domain of another fairy. If I were you, I'd head straight to Portland."

Then I left them, praying that the next time I came here, it wouldn't be in the company of evil. We were still in the air when I saw Grimm, reflected from the cockpit window. I nudged Liam awake and opened my compact. "You need something?"

"I need you. I have a feeling I know what my daughter is up to."

Fifteen

~⌒~

WHEN WE MADE it back to the Agency that evening, I wasn't at all surprised to see Ari, Wyatt, and Mrs. Pendlebrook in Grimm's conference room. Grimm waited until we were seated, then cleared his throat to kill the chatter. "Four hundred years ago I had my daughter beheaded by a prince, torn to pieces by the combined might of Kingdom's seal bearers, and burned in the infernal flame while I held back her power."

Grimm paused, looking at me in particular. "While I cannot be certain what else her aims are, I believe she's taking action to prevent that from occurring again. Her first move was against the Court of Kings, where she quelled the commanders of Kingdom's military. Her second move was against the High Queen."

"I'm betting my bitch of a stepmother is her lapdog." The way Ari spat *stepmother* made *bitch* sound like a term of endearment.

"Whether she does so with my daughter's blessing or only as her unwilling pawn, the end is the same. I have no doubt Isolde means to keep the court divided long enough to settle other accounts or unified under her loyal servant."

I counted off on my fingers. "Okay, so the kings are out of play, the queens are busy. What next?"

"She kills any prince foolish enough to be found and destroys Kingdom's army, lest it be mobilized against her." Grimm turned toward Wyatt. "She's already had five princes killed, and no doubt will move against more soon."

"I have no interest in Kingdom politics." Wyatt's voice wavered in fear.

"Given your family's history, she won't care. Prince Edward Pendlebrook is a name that she will never forget or forgive. Your ancestor helped me end my daughter's reign of terror."

Grimm looked to Liam. "I regret to ask you this, Mr. Stone, but it is essential that whoever is killing these princes does not do away with all of them. I once arranged for you to guard a court of vampires. Now I ask you to guard a single prince."

Ari put her hand over Wyatt's. "I can protect him just fine."

"You are needed elsewhere. I need to focus on completing your training. Mr. Stone—"

"Is staying with Marissa." Liam's statement trailed off into a growl.

Grimm shook his head. "Not where I'm asking her to go." He looked over to me. "My daughter cannot kill you without endangering herself. Were she to release you, she would be open to my full wrath. I ask that you return to her and attempt to find out how she is killing princes. Her arrogance may be her downfall."

Liam leaped to his feet, his face red. "Or you could just give her what she wants. Have you thought about that? How about you get off your lazy ass and fix this instead of sending everyone else to do your dirty work?"

Grimm looked down at the table. "I have told you that fairies cannot approach each other. That their powers repel. There is, however, a way. I can change myself so that we attract. In essence, we will be irreversibly drawn together in the equivalent of a magical supernova."

Liam's grip on me tightened further. "Won't that hurt Marissa?"

"No, sir," said Grimm. "As long as the handmaiden's bond is broken, I believe she will survive. When Marissa is free of my daughter, I will end this myself."

We sat in stunned silence, all of us waiting for someone else to speak. I finally found my tongue, hanging out of my mouth. "And you die."

"In a manner of speaking. The resulting entity, given a few billion years, will coalesce into a new fairy. So you see, Mr. Stone, I do intend to do my part."

Liam stayed standing, stayed focused on Grimm. "And how exactly do we get her free? Did any of the ideas I came up with from the doorman work?"

"You might say so," said Grimm. "Your visit did give me the key to a possible solution."

"Me." Ari sat up, her shoulders back, her mouth set in a straight line. "There is no High Queen. So I challenge my mother, and everyone else, to a duel. When I win, I become High Queen and order the doorman to strip Isolde of her title the same way he did Irina Mihail. That breaks the handmaiden's bond."

Mrs. Pendlebrook looked like she'd been slapped. She took off her wire-frame bifocals and studied Ari. "Arianna, while your magic is impressive, I do not believe you are up to the task of taking on every other seal bearer and hired hag in the court."

"I will be. Grimm is going to teach me Battle Magic." The ease with which Ari spoke of magic designed to wound and kill made something inside me quiver with fear, and the darkest part of me tremble with excitement.

Grimm's face clouded over with worry. "For four hundred years I have not taught an apprentice. I can train Arianna in magic no queen of this age has faced." He glanced over to Ari. "But there will be a cost, princess."

"I'll take out a mortgage on the house."

"Young lady, though you bear the scars of Wild Magic, you are not evil. The sort of spells I will teach you are not the tools of defense. They are designed to rend and maim, to kill and make an example of your victims. To use them willingly against another person will stain you in a way I cannot change." Grimm's tone shifted to one I'd never heard, cold and dark, calculating. "Even binding the magic requires sacrifice in a ritual so foul it cannot be spoken of."

Ari closed her eyes and clenched her fists. "I'll do what it takes."

"No." I slammed the binder of menus we used for long nights down on the table, causing Ari to crackle with lightning. "I won't let you do something like that to yourself. Not for me."

"You can't stop me."

"Consider your choice, princess." Grimm's use of Arianna's title always infuriated her. "Once Isolde is dead, the other queens will unite against you at the first opportunity. And if you flee, you will be forever an outcast, reduced to hiding in a hovel lest some prince decide to slay you as a weekend hobby."

Mrs. Pendlebrook raised her hand, looking to each of us to make sure we acknowledged her. "Arianna will always be welcome in my home. If my reasons for taking the throne were so noble, perhaps my Charles would be alive today. Fairy Godfather, can you adapt the wards on my house to protect her?"

My frustration built up like a wave inside me. "You aren't listening. I'm not some damsel in distress, in need of a prince to rescue me. I've been in worse situations before. I'll handle this."

Liam spun on me, his face twisted in anger. "What is *wrong* with you? We are trying to make sure you survive."

I reached out to put my hand on him. "And I am trying to make sure surviving is something I can live with."

Liam kicked his chair back into the wall and stormed out, smoke pouring from his mouth and nose. I sat, unsure why everyone stared at me. Finally Grimm spoke. "Go after him. He's taking the elevator to the roof."

"No rituals." I spoke to Grimm, but locked gazes with Ari until she looked away. Then I ran for the stairs, praying that a decade of cardio could get me to the roof faster than the balky steel death traps building management called elevators.

I hit the roof escape door right as the elevator chimed, and grabbed Liam the moment the doors opened. He was literally steaming as his body temperature rose to the point of transformation. "Stay. Don't go flying off." We'd fought on occasion. It was the only thing that gave his dragon curse enough gumption to actually use the wings.

Liam crossed his arms as he stared. "When you rescued that baby last month, did you blame the mother for setting her down in a patch of flowers full of pixies?"

That wasn't the question I expected of him. "No."

"And the couple who had that talking koi in the pond, did they do something wrong?"

"Don't be ridiculous."

Liam put his hands on either side of my face, callused hands from hours spent in his studio, swinging hammers. "Every day, every week, every month of the year you're out solving someone's problem or saving someone from mistakes. So why can't you accept that we might want to save you?"

I couldn't answer. I didn't have words.

"That *I* might want to save you?" The pain in his voice, the fear, found a partner in my heart.

"I've never been the type to be rescued. I don't know how."

"You could learn."

I blinked away tears. "I can't let Ari do that to herself. You can't let Ari do that to herself. Grimm, I don't know about. This all begins with him, maybe it ends with him, but I won't let Ari harm herself for me."

"I'm not sure she has to." Liam's voice, almost a purr-growl, made me curious who was speaking—Liam, or his curse. "There are other rituals. Other choices, but we'd need time."

"I can buy you that time. Isolde is scary, but nothing I can't deal with."

He wasn't fooled by my false bravado. He'd never been fooled, not from the moment I met him, somehow seeing through it to the me I worked to keep hidden. "I have a few ideas. I just need time."

Pulling my compact from my pocket, I flipped it open. Grimm waited there, without even being called. "So how does this work? She isn't summoning me."

"Go home. Get some sleep, and tomorrow you can report to her after breakfast. A handmaiden may always approach her queen without being summoned, but you need to be at your best to deal with her." Grimm faded away, his command given.

Liam put his arm around my shoulder, and together we found our way home and into bed.

I WOKE WITH a start, unsure what had roused me from my sleep. Beside me, Liam rumbled like a chain saw committing a redwood massacre, wisps of wood smoke tinting his breath as he exhaled. I slipped from the bed. My stomach turned flips and knotted in a feeling almost like the pull when Isolde summoned me before.

I dressed in the dark and, after lacing up my running shoes, slipped out into the three a.m. darkness. The streets are never really empty; the traffic never stops. At night the garbage trucks and delivery vans and construction vehicles come out like vampires and ghosts, afraid of a little sun and a few million people.

I ran without purpose, letting my feet guide me. When they tired, I stepped on board the first bus, losing myself in the swirl of passing lights and gazing out the window, while I worried about how I'd retrieve stolen souls. The Mihails hadn't been pleasant people in life. I doubted the afterlife improved their dispostions.

More than anything, I worried about how I'd survive the Black Queen. Though Grimm often spoke of how I needed to take care of myself, a nervous excitement flowed into me from Isolde's manacle.

This foreign feeling reminded me of the time Grimm found a building maintenance firm that would charge us half what we paid before. Something had the Black Queen so pleased her feelings washed over into me, and I doubted it was that she'd found a good deal on shoes.

So I switched buses and rode to the gates of Kingdom. A bare street corner for anyone not associated with magic. More like an interchange for me. Outside the gates, I held my bracelet tight and looked into a shop window. "Grimm. Something's going on with the Black Queen. I can feel it."

He appeared, a faint reflection of his normal splendor, blotting out the "SALE PRICES" writing in the window. "Has she summoned you again?"

"No. But I feel something. Something exciting, or happy." The possibilities that could excite the Black Queen made my stomach churn.

"You are bonded to her, and it stands to reason that the bond works both ways. Do not show her fear or respect, Marissa. She is due neither, but do not provoke her without reason. I will let you pass the gates unassisted." Grimm held out his arm toward the street corner where the gates split Kingdom from the city.

I ran for them, head-on, straight through them, as a maelstrom of darkness and shadow burst outward, coating the city streets with oil and transforming the streetlamps into torture chambers where unlucky pixies burned, lighting the way into Low Kingdom.

Behind me, the gates stood barred, covered in sharp glass and thorns. I had no intention of leaving that way. My biggest worry were the denizens of Low Kingdom. Early morning was like nine a.m. for the hags and hangmen.

The streets of Low Kingdom stood empty. Only the occasional bat flittered from building to building. No drunken carousing, no screaming in the night as creatures devoured one another.

With each step, my feet crushed broken glass, the loudest noise in the city. The crawling feeling like a roach on the back of my neck said I wasn't alone. I just couldn't see whoever kept me company. So I planned a distraction. After rummaging through a trash mound, I took out a liquor bottle and hurled it far down the street. The darkness swallowed it, but the crash of breaking glass echoed. If whatever kept me company didn't know where I was already, it would head for the noise.

Like the patter of distant rain, footsteps rushed my way. Too late, I spotted the third-story windows, where faces pressed against the windows. Hags watched below with fear in their eyes. Not looking at me, but at the darkness beyond.

I backed up against the nearest building, where fingernails

and molars jutted from the brick, keeping my eyes on the intersection ahead.

The monster that emerged from the darkness galloped on six feet, springing along like a cheetah. Its malformed body consisted of six legs grafted onto a torso. The pale white flesh might once have belonged to a human, but no man had that many pelvises. The shoulders jutted outward, hosting arms laced with thick muscle that ended in hairy hand-feet like a gorilla.

I held very still, hoping it couldn't see me.

It hissed, bare teeth jutting from a jaw without lips, snorting air into a nose without cartilage. The neck, what remained, had fused together, locking the head forward, so it had to twist its entire body to look from side to side.

Then it stopped, staring into the darkness.

If I'd tried to run, I would have died on the spot. Instead, I turned around and climbed, using the brick edges as handholds to pull myself up. At the first story, I grabbed the fire escape, ignoring the mangled bodies that hung from it, and swung myself on.

Below, on the street, the abomination skittered back and forth like a hairy cockroach. Unable to look upward, it couldn't stare at me, but I figured it knew full well where I'd gone. It lunged forward, hands grasping at the brick, gradually turning itself upward, until it fixed me with a dead gaze.

And began to climb.

Not that I waited around. I leaped and pulled down an escape ladder, raced up it, and hauled the ladder up behind me. Below, a clang told me the abomination had reached the fire escape. With three times the climbing equipment, it would beat me to the roof handily. So I stopped.

I waited.

I listened as it clambered over metal railings, grunting and huffing. When it climbed onto the landing beneath me, I was waiting. When it pulled on the ladder, I jumped. Not up. Down, landing with all my force on the edge of the ladder.

The fire escape ladder swung like an axe, crashing into the metal, cutting the fingers off the abomination like a meat cleaver. It screamed a cry that echoed in the city streets, flipping backwards, pulling mangled flesh from the metal floor.

I charged straight at it, knowing this would be my one chance. I'd seen Liam tackle people before, his shoulder lowered, his legs acting like pistons. Liam weighed twice as much as me, but I had adrenaline and surprise on my side. I hit it in the chest, knocking it back to the railing, and pushing it over the edge.

It tried to grab the fire escape as it fell, but its weight tore its last fingers off. It hit shoulder first into the ground, and didn't rise.

After a good twenty minutes on the fire escape to catch my breath, I finally climbed down, and followed the churning in my stomach through the streets of Low Kingdom until I arrived at the castle. From outside, her presence called to me like a beacon.

Going in didn't really seem like a good idea. In fact, the longer I stood outside, the more it seemed like this was a horrible idea, and that if I pinched myself enough, I'd wake up to find the smoke alarm going off, or something normal.

Instead, from the darkness behind me, a thunderstorm of feet echoed. On the moat bridge, I looked back. Abominations lined the street by the thousands, in grotesque shapes and sizes that suggested each came from at least three different people.

Though the streets of Low Kingdom seemed empty, the people weren't gone.

With a chorus of gurgles and strangled hissing, the crowd surged forward, but I didn't look back. I lunged past the sleeping troll, hurtling into a tunnel of darkness.

Sixteen

〰

OUTSIDE, THE TROLL roared, swinging his club so that it thudded against the ground. Maybe he was angry with me. Maybe he was angry at the crowd of abominations setting foot on his bridge. I wasn't going back to ask. Instead, I made my way with ease through the labyrinth of the castle, that alien feeling of joy growing stronger with each step.

When I walked down the wide staircase to the main banquet hall, I should have felt fear. Instead, I could barely keep myself from dancing. Isolde sat at the head of the room on the carved wooden throne. Before her, two women knelt.

One I recognized, and my anger overrode the forced joy. "Gwendolyn Thromson. I thought I might find you here." Ari's stepmother kept showing up wherever disasters went down.

I didn't miss the surprise on Isolde's face as I approached. She didn't know everything.

Isolde beckoned to me. "Handmaiden. Come and bow."

"No." I'd sooner bow to a statue of myself at the post office than the Black Queen. Grimm said not to provoke her, but some things were nonnegotiable.

Isolde put one fingernail to her arm, tapping it against her elbow. "Bow."

"Never."

Her fingernail turned black and lengthened, taking on a purple sheen as it grew into a hooked thorn. She plunged the thorn-nail into her own flesh, and my arm tore open. Now, the number of times I'd been crucified, burned, or nailed with a pneumatic nail gun should have left me whistling, but along with the tearing, a burning like poison coursed down my arm.

I fell over, curling up in a ball, desperately fighting for breath. When the pain subsided, I opened my eyes to see her standing over me. Her own arm had no traces of a wound, and her fingernail no longer resembled an eagle's claw. "That wasn't so hard, was it? Rise, handmaiden, for tonight we celebrate. While I didn't require your presence, I assure you, one more is an easy accommodation."

She put her hands together, forming a triangle, and hummed a tone filled with power. Vines grew from the center of the table, blossoming out into domed silver platters and goblets of wine. "Come."

Gwendolyn rose and took a seat at one side of the rectangular table.

The other woman rose, and I couldn't squelch the gasp that escaped me. Kyra's hair, once blond, hung in a braid that reached to her toes. What really got me wasn't the hair, as much as her face. I'd memorized her features, chasing her from store to store one New Year's Eve. Her face, too, had changed, both familiar and beautiful in a way that left me amazed.

Kyra waltzed over and curtsied. "Greetings, sister. Do you like our queen's gift to me? I am a vision unlike any other." Before I could comment on how long that hair was going to take to wash and brush, she walked to the table and took a seat at the Black Queen's right hand.

I didn't want to sit beside her. I didn't want to sit in the same *castle* as Gwendolyn Thromson. Isolde turned toward me, her brown eyes lit with a sparkle that said she enjoyed the flavor of my discomfort more than any wine. "Since you invited yourself, don't be difficult."

Far as I could tell, difficult was the only thing I knew how to be. Liam always said that what I lacked in height I made up for in pure stubbornness. I reminded myself of why I was there, and took a seat.

Isolde held out her hands, gesturing to our plates. "I've taken the liberty of conjuring you a meal to remind you of your loyalty. Eat, and remember: There is always more I can take from you."

I took the silver dome off my plate and my stomach convulsed. Before me sat a heap of spaghetti in a worn yellow bowl. The silverware had spots that were either unwashed food or soap scum, and the drink, a bottle of cheap beer.

Liam's favorite meal, from his favorite restaurant.

Across the table, Kyra's look of horror told me I wasn't the only one surprised. On her plate sat an array of chicken nuggets, fish sticks, and carrots. The sippy cup on her platter held what looked to be apple juice.

Gwendolyn's place setting was empty, without as much as a glass.

"Eat." The Black Queen sliced her own food, a steak drowned in butter and garlic.

Leaving the silverware on the table, I picked up a handful of spaghetti and slurped it into my mouth. Slimy and cold, it might have just been served from the bowl at Froni's.

"How do you know what the meal should be?" Kyra chewed a chicken nugget, the edge in her voice unmistakable as she stared at Isolde.

"I don't. I simply told the platters to remind you of what you stand to lose if you fail to serve me." Isolde continued with her steak, as if we discussed the weather. "Continue to eliminate princes, and I'll have no reason to question your loyalty."

"As you command, my queen." I'd seen that look on Kyra's face. Worn it myself on more than one occasion. The sort of determination that says "I will do what I have to, and pity the people who stand in my way."

I glanced over to Gwendolyn, who sat with her hands folded before her on the table, and spoke to keep myself from spitting. "You're on one hell of a diet." I strangled the urge to shove my fork into her eye.

"Jealous? I have nothing to lose, but if I waver, I get nothing." Contempt dripped from Gwendolyn's lips like spittle from a rabid dog. "I cannot be threatened. Only rewarded. How is that insolent stepdaughter of mine doing? The one who challenged our queen?"

"She's fine. Training harder. Getting stronger."

Gwendolyn nodded. "When the matter of High Queen is settled, the first edict I will give is to have all witches put to death. We'll see how strong she is then."

Without a pause I flipped my fork over and drove it through the flesh between her thumb and forefinger, nailing her hand to the table. Wyatt once told me that applying pressure there would help with headaches. There was probably a fine line between "helping" and "causing," a line I burst across without ever looking back.

Gwendolyn screamed, but the rage that filled me, the desire to tear her heart out and feed it to the dogs in Low Kingdom, made it the sweetest of music. I delivered a right hook across her cheek, then rose and seized my chair, swinging it like a baseball bat. As I did, the air around me boiled in a feeling that told me a spell had activated nearby.

The chair exploded against a body like a brick wall. My eyes followed the wall of flesh and muscle upward. Another abomination, this one humanoid, loomed above me. Far too large for a normal man, it looked like someone had fashioned it from an ogre, then wrapped the body in human skin. On top of shoulders as wide as a table hung a mockery of a human skull, twisted. Then it spoke. "Marissa."

I struggled to keep the spaghetti I'd swallowed down, because I knew the voice, a monster of a person whose outside now nearly matched the hideous person inside. "Prince Mihail."

He shook the head, causing pink slobber to swing from the jaw. "Not anymore. You poisoned me."

Technically, I'd like to point out the apple poisoned him. I threw it, but not at him. Convenient that he forgot that tiny detail. "You tried to kill Ari and me. You had it coming." I couldn't hide the shaking in my hands or the fear that crawled up from the depths of Inferno to make its home in my spine. "I have it on good authority you pulled a prison break."

Monster Mihail leaned over, bending for what seemed like an eternity to bring his face to my level. "When I have a proper new body, we'll talk again. When I've killed everything and everyone near you, we'll talk." With a hand the size of my head, he tore the fork from the table and lumbered to stand behind Gwendolyn.

Obviously Gwendolyn hadn't lived through enough pain, because a simple stab through the fleshy part of her hand left her shaking. She spat on the table. "My guardian will tear your arms off if you lay a hand on me again."

"The souls," I whispered, more to myself. And the rest of the situation clicked into place for me. I turned back toward Kyra. "Where is Irina Mihail? Step-bitch here got the prince. I'm guessing you have the Queen of Crazy as your pet."

"She's been looking forward to meeting you again." Kyra narrowed her eyes at me, then closed them, concentrating.

This time around I recognized the spell activating. Most spells came with aural or visual hallucinations. This one smelled like burned fish, which I usually associated with some form of summoning. When a hulk the size of Prince Mihail's modern monster lumbered from the shadows behind Kyra, I wasn't at all surprised. I stepped up onto the table so that I could at least look her in the eye.

Irina Mihail's fresh body had the same basic semblance as the one that her son wore, with the addition of gargantuan breasts that resembled bowling balls in leather sacks and served absolutely no purpose. The hatred in her eyes burned like a coal fire, and her lips cracked as she drew them back to smile, revealing rows of pointed teeth.

I wasn't impressed by the twelve-foot-tall psycho ex-queen. I'd sent her to hell once, beating a demon at his own game, and I could do it again. "I figured you'd be hanging out with step-bitch, not following a low-class thief."

Irina-monster worked at it, mouthing the words over and over again, but when she spoke, the clear Russian accent sounded like she'd never died and gone to hell. "I chose this.

Remember, when the culling comes, I will be there to defend her, and to end your miserable life. Wrath, Marissa. I have it stored up for you."

Kyra whistled, calling her pet back. "I have work to do. Tonight we will finish the fourth and fifth houses." She looked back to me. "What about you? Did you receive a guardian?"

Guardian. I finally made the connection to the creature from the Agency. I didn't exactly want to bring up that I might have destroyed my guardian on account of not knowing it was mine. Also on account of not keeping monstrosities as pets, unless you counted the cat I once owned.

"Marissa declined my generous gift." Isolde spoke, her voice commanding I turn and look back to her. "So I have selected a different one for her. Something she needs more. Go, my servants. Make ready my way."

At last, I knew where the missing souls were. And I knew why they hadn't come looking for me like the Adversary expected. Now the question was whether or not the news would appease him long enough for me to figure out a way to kill them.

Kyra rose with a bow and stalked off down the tunnel, her nightmare guardian following. I can't say where Gwendolyn went, because I couldn't take my eyes off the Black Queen.

When their footsteps faded to silence, she released me. "A man's meal. You fear the loss of your boyfriend most."

"Ari loves that place." As I spoke, the thorn near my heart shifted, and my blood ran cold. But this lie was my own, not Grimm's.

"A good lie, but a lie nonetheless. Remember, I am the Root of Lies, you cannot fool me. You love a man, though I cannot divine even his name. Does my father interfere?"

"I hope so."

"Did you like my guardians? I've been practicing here on the denizens of this miserable plane. My father can form bodies so wonderful they look natural. My efforts are but a shadow of his. That's all I ask of him. A body, a perfect one, made as only he can." The pain and eagerness in Isolde's voice gave her away.

"He won't ever do that. Grimm says your mother has to move on."

A blast of elemental magic tore the carpet from under me, sending me rolling across the floor.

Isolde's voice came out a shriek. "Sticking Mother in purgatory for my sins was not letting her move on. When I master the secrets of flesh, I will make her new bodies forever. She will never grow sick, never die, and never leave me." Her hair stood out from her head the way Ari's did when Ari cast spells.

"You shouldn't have stolen souls from the vault. The Adversary knows what you did. He'll—"

"Do nothing," said Isolde, "beyond order some servant to retrieve them. Did he threaten to take out his anger on innocents? I cannot be threatened so. And I care nothing for the queen and her son, but their hatred for you was too delicious to resist. Now, let us arrange for your gift."

"I don't want anything from you."

"No, but you do want something." Her words hit me harder than any fist. When she spoke, Fairy Godmother's voice echoed, the same words she'd said to me when I first met her. "You are unpresentable, unfit to be my proxy." For a moment, I thought she meant to remove the queen's ring I wore. A ring only she could remove.

She paced toward me, and I couldn't help shrinking back. "Where is the brave Marissa I heard so much about?" She cast her hand at me, throwing a wave of glitter at me, and I flinched.

Nothing. Nothing happened at all. Well, not quite nothing. My clothing transformed into an old-style ball gown. Taking a single step required more effort than walking a marathon. The dress featured enough fabric below my waist to act as an emergency flotation device. I looked up to see Isolde walking away, returning to her throne. When she'd taken her seat, she folded her hands before her. "Go home, handmaiden. Return to this man of yours, and find out if he truly loves you."

* * *

I MADE IT out of Low Kingdom and back to my apartment in record time, terrified that she had cast some spell on Liam, or kidnapped him. When I threw the apartment door open, he jumped from his recliner, spilling beer all over the carpet.

Relief swept through me. "Thank Kingdom you're here."

Liam looked at me sideways and took a step away. "Who are you, and what are you doing in my apartment?"

Seventeen

I DIDN'T SPEAK. Couldn't speak. Liam continued to move until the bar no longer stood between us. "Where is Marissa? Are you the other handmaiden?" His voice deepened, the curse speaking through him. "I'll *cull* you now if you are."

"It's me." My own voice sounded foreign. More musical, less whiny. "Marissa."

Liam shook his head. "Sure, and I'm the King of Jersey. If you've harmed her, I won't leave enough of you to feed a cat. If you know where she is, now would be a good time to say so. While you still have a tongue." He picked up a meat tenderizer off the counter and advanced on me.

I held up my hand, to show him the handmaiden's mark, and his engagement ring. My skin, smooth and tan like it had never been, bore no scares. My fingers were bare. "Grimm!" I shrieked. "I need you."

He burst into the living room mirror, a look of horror on his face. Then he looked to Liam. "Stop, Mr. Stone."

Liam wavered, his gaze flipping between Grimm and me.

Grimm shook his head. "You don't want to harm your fiancée."

"That isn't Marissa." His gaze roved over my body again, fixating on my face. "Is it?"

I went to the mirror, and Grimm faded out, letting me see. The person who looked back at me had brown hair, true, and brown eyes. Her hair hung past her shoulders, silky, with gentle waves in it; her complexion looked like the one I'd always wished I had; her eyes normal sized instead of part bat. The person who stared back was me as I'd always dreamed I might look. "What happened?"

I touched a hand to my face, making sure my cheekbones really did angle out like that.

Grimm reappeared, alternating between rage and frustration. "It is a lie. My daughter's talent at work, lies so real you can scarce tell them from the truth. Lies that become real, if embraced. Mr. Stone, take Marissa's hand. I will do what I can to unravel the web and prove who she is. If Arianna were available, she too could confirm Marissa's identity. Her spirit sight would not be fooled by such trivial changes."

I watched Liam approach from the mirror, the look of confusion on his face as he reached for my shoulder. "I'm ready."

Grimm's power surged out like a river, swirling around me, buffeting me like a hurricane. The woman in the mirror flickered. Vibrated. Split, like double vision, until both of me looked back. My face, as I always knew it, and the one she'd given me.

Liam spun us around and wrapped me in his arms, nearly crushing me. "I couldn't tell."

I looked over his shoulder at Grimm. "You said you would protect me from her changes."

Grimm shook his head. "I *am* protecting you. Your personality is mostly intact, with a minor influx of bloodlust. Such illusions, however, *you* must reject to prevent them from becoming real."

The problem was, it didn't feel like a lie. Different? Sure. But maybe good. "I found the missing souls." I waited, but Grimm seemed neither surprised nor impressed. "And Kyra. She's killing the princes." After I recounted my experiences in the old castle, Grimm remained silent, lost in thought.

My thoughts, on the other hand, fell to the man right in front of me, and the way he looked at me, almost frightened, or excited. Liam let me go, just a little, and put one hand beside my face; with the other he traced my nose and lips, his eyes wide with wonder or fear.

I batted my eyes at him. "Am I beautiful?"

"Always. Still." Liam closed his eyes and leaned in to kiss me, and it hit me that he didn't have to lean so far. I was at least three inches taller. His lips brushed mine, and I drank in the heat that radiated from him, kissing him back the way I always did. "It's you. It's really you."

I peeked open my eyes to see Grimm gone from the mirror. On any other night, we'd have Svetlana sitting on the couch, watching us with Olympic-class boredom. With her still locked in her fruit smoothie spa treatment, we could relax.

I pulled Liam toward the bedroom, eager to hold him in my arms. With both hands, I shoved him backwards into the room, showering his face with kisses, but found my mouth didn't fit—to kiss his ears and jaw, I had to bend my head until my neck hurt, and his attempts to kiss me back had him licking my nose or my chin, until I bit his lip ever so gently.

His hands roved over me, exploring curves I'd always wanted but never had. The frustration mounted, as I attempted to take off my shirt, only to find it stitched to the skirt Isolde transformed my clothes into. I tossed Liam's T-shirt onto the fan, and fought with the laced front of what might have been an attractive top three hundred years earlier.

The tension in Liam's body grew like a spring as we fought with the clothes, until I shoved him onto the bed. "Give me a moment." I dashed out into the kitchen to the silverware drawer.

After a few moments, Liam joined me, stripped to the waist, and used a steak knife to saw the lacing on my top apart.

And walking hurt. Every step, as my breasts bounced, pulling the skin on my shoulders tight. We sat on the bed, and I bit my tongue as his sandpaper-like hands traced my nipples, which never seemed to react like that before. Where before, the trace of his thumbs around my nipple sent electric chills from my chin to my pelvis, now his fingers reminded me of dragsters with snow tires making laps. I finally understood the term *aching nipples* from those vampire romance novels Ari loved, and the term would never conjure the same image for me. I slid Liam's hands to my hips and pulled his jeans down, as he thrust his tongue into my nose for at least the tenth time.

As his hands traced my hips, they rose. A murmur escaped my lips, and a clink sounded from my crotch.

Yeah, that definitely put the lovemaking on hold. I reached over and switched on the lamp, wriggling out of the skirt bottom. The panties, definitely fur on the inside, had woven chain mail, with a tight metal cord at the top sealing them on.

"Oh, come on." Now it was my turn to be frustrated, as I fought to slide the formfitting steel panties past my hips.

Liam stood up, a frustrated snort escaping him, and marched out in his underwear. A few minutes later, he returned with pair of bolt cutters. "I got them from the building superintendent. Suck in your stomach."

He slid the bolt cutter in at my navel, making me tremble for all the wrong reasons, and flexed his gleaming muscles. When he pulled back the bolt cutters, a gasp of relief wracked me. I yanked the chastity panties off, yelping as the frayed wire scratched me.

Finally, I could take Liam to me, his powerful body gliding over me, just as he always did, ramming my thighs. The noise I made wasn't a moan of pleasure, I'll tell you that for sure, but by now I'd become so frantic I didn't care. Liam smoked, his sweat boiling from his body, and only the asbestos weave in my sheets kept the bed from catching fire as I forced myself on him.

Twenty minutes later we lay in a puddle of sweat and fire, nursing bruises and scratches.

"That was—" I searched for words.

"Painful. I think I bent something."

I had bruises of my own and no sympathy. "Well, if you'd stop imitating a jackhammer you'd feel different." Faint bloodstains marked the edge of the asbestos sheets. "Are you bleeding?"

"Your nails are like daggers. You know you don't have to carve me like a goose."

I sat up, frowning. "Well, I'd like to remind you that big breasts are still attached breasts, despite your attempts to pull them off."

"I was trying to arouse you. And what's with the noises? It's like being in bed with a pack of Chihuahuas." Liam sat up in bed, putting his arm around me.

"Says the man who oinks at the end. I thought you were part dragon, not one of the three little pigs." The moment I said it, I regretted it. Truth was, I'd seen less fumbling at a Jets game sponsored by Astroglide. Sex was something learned, that grew. This was more awkward than the time Grandma got up on the Thanksgiving table and did a striptease, begging us for tips.

"I'm going to take the bolt cutters back." Liam steamed as he put on a bathrobe and stomped out. I searched without success for a bra that would fit my new body, stretching my sports bra until I looked like a sausage about to burst.

When Liam came back, I was waiting in the living room. "I'm sorry."

He wouldn't look at me. I put one hand on his chest, careful not to scratch him. "We'll get better."

"I loved you the way you were." Liam looked up at me, biting his lip.

"And now?"

"I still love you. I may not be able to wear briefs for a couple days, but I still love you." He followed me back to bed, where I spent the night discovering I couldn't roll onto my stomach anymore. So I spooned him, feeling the pulse of his heart.

Eighteen

THE NEXT MORNING I went shopping before going to work.
Forget underwire—I went with under-girder, and found a set of
black blouses that didn't strain to restrain me. I made it into the
Agency, rode up to the front door, and walked into a mutiny.

In the lobby, on crutches, stood Rosa, surrounded by our
cargo workers and most of the Agency temp staff. Grimm
stood in the lobby mirror, his hands folded behind his back,
a look of concern knitting his brows together.

Rosa looked at me, and her eyes widened. "Out." Rosa
swore at me in Spanish, her face turning red along with the
normal brown. "Get her out."

"Do we have a problem?" I took a few steps toward Rosa,
suddenly appreciating how the sway of my hips kept eyes focused on me.

Rosa couldn't hide the fear on her face. The tremble in
her hands or the way she glanced to Grimm as if he'd help
her. "I won't work with her anymore."

Grimm spoke quickly in fluent Spanish, his Rs rolling
like the purr of a cat.

I'd taken Spanish lessons for the last four years for a reason.

I kept my gaze on Rosa. "Of course I'm not dangerous. You trust the Fairy Godfather's judgment, right?" The thought of finally slapping her rude face made me smile. The thought of what my nails might do made my smile a grin.

The look of fear on Rosa's face spread, like a contagion, through our staff, faster than the flu. Rosa always treated me like rotten fish, but the others—I signed their payroll checks on time and we got along. The staff door opened, and Mikey emerged from the back, standing a head taller than everyone else.

He walked around the crew, sniffing the air. "I knew I smelled fear. That or too much cardamom in my stew. What's everyone afraid of? Marissa's fine by me." He leaned down and sniffed me. "You smell different. You get a haircut?"

Before I could berate him for not noticing that my hair was the *least* of my changes, someone else spoke. "Working with a handmaiden of the Black Queen is suicide. I'm off the job while she's on." Big Bill, our head hostage negotiator. And a chorus of other echoes as the people I'd taken care of turned on me like a pack of wolves. I could deal with wolves, with only a flame-thrower and a clip of silver bullets. The clamor rose until Grimm reached forward, clawing his nails along the mirror.

The shriek that came out made me wince and grind my teeth, and I took it better than most of them. "That is enough." Grimm crossed his arms before him, his eyes flashing with rage. I waited for him to start transforming dockworkers into frogs. And waited. He glanced to me and nodded. "Marissa, would you mind going to Arianna's house and checking on her?"

"Yes. I'd mind a lot." I put my hands on my hips. "Rosa, I'm sick of your attitude. I'm sick of you treating me like elf-droppings, and I'm sick of you threatening me. Get the hell out of my Agency. You're fired."

"It's not yours." Rosa limped toward me, raising a crutch like a club.

"Really? Did I ever sign it back to Grimm?" I looked over to Grimm, catching the surprise that washed over him. Rosa, on the other hand, should've known better. She helped me sign the ownership papers while Grimm was unavailable. "Get out."

"I'm not afraid of you." Rosa wasn't a very good liar. She looked through the crowd, then whistled.

The crowd of dockworkers slowly parted, not the flee-in-fear reaction of people who've found something deadly in their midst. The what-in-Inferno-did-you-roll-in response to something that smelled like a demon in a Dumpster.

Two people in filthy bathrobes walked forward. "We're here to, ummm, curse you if you don't leave voluntarily."

"I remember you." What I remembered was that their magical prowess left everything to be desired. "Those are Agency robes you stole, aren't they?"

"Would everyone please stop?" Grimm's mirror surged with light, flashing the room white.

I opened my mouth to tell him to go visit the Adversary, but the ringing in my ears grew louder. He'd killed all sound.

"Rosa, there is a call waiting on line two I want you to take. Enchanters, if you leave the building immediately, I won't transform your underwear into poison oak. Michael, I want express shipments out within the hour. Everyone else, return to your stations or clear out your desks."

The crowd began to shuffle out the doors, while Rosa dragged her fat, wounded ass back to her corner counter.

"Marissa, I understand your sentiment, but now, more than ever, it is vital that the Agency continues to operate. I'm offering you personal leave until I've dealt with my daughter. When she is gone, you may make any changes you desire." He looked to Rosa as he spoke.

I stormed toward the Agency door, so angry I couldn't have spoken even if Grimm had let me.

On the ground floor, as I dashed out of the building front door, I ran into Liam and Ari, who kept Wyatt huddled between them. Liam had gashes on the side of his head and blood running down the front of his shirt. He caught me by the wrist, and without thinking, I tripped him, sending him face-first into the pavement. Only after he crashed to the ground did my actions register. "Oh no." I held my hand over my mouth.

The result of a moment of rage, a flash of frustration, and a decade of training. Liam pushed up off the floor, blood welling from his mouth. He didn't say a word. The silence hurt worse than any words.

Ari stepped between us. "Wyatt, go with Liam, give him your handkerchief for his nose." Ari shoved her boyfriend away and took me by the arm, staring at me with witch eyes. "Grimm told me you had a spell cast on you. He didn't say it was this. This is awful."

She looked back to Liam and Wyatt. "Keep out of trouble. I think I can help."

"I want to go to work." I tried to shake Ari's hand off and she crackled with static electricity as though shocking me had become a viable option.

Ari shook her head. "Not like this. This lie wrapped around you, it's getting comfortable. Settling in. Grimm may be the Fairy Godfather, but this is mostly Seal Magic." She ran her eyes over me again and clucked her tongue. "This is how you wanted yourself to look?"

"No." I swallowed, remembering how I felt when I first saw myself in the mirror. "Maybe."

Ari didn't answer. She just put one hand on my shoulder and pushed me out the front door. We walked for blocks in silence, the dense crowds having enough sense to get out of my way. "I didn't ask her for this."

"Please, Marissa. I'll bet you didn't need to ask. Don't you always say you are happy with who you are?" Ari and I reached the waterfront and began the trudge toward the gates.

When we arrived, Ari grabbed her bracelet, the only thing keeping her mother's banishment at bay, and took my hand. She surged forward, dragging me into High Kingdom.

This time, instead of a parade, people drifted away from me. Talking beasts fell mute as I passed. After we'd walked several blocks, I had a feeling I knew where we were headed. "Tell me we're going to a doctor."

"Not exactly." Ari crossed the street, cutting off a Kingdom policeman on horseback without so much as an "excuse me." The Isyle Witch's shop lay a few doors down. The occasional passerby reached out to run fingers along the red brick replacing the ruined doorway.

Standing in front of the shop, Ari stopped and looked both directions. Like anyone could tell if someone was watching in the middle of the crowd. The rush of magic into her left frost on the concrete.

I wanted to take Ari's hand, but past experience said interrupting her while casting a spell was a great recipe for getting knocked on my back.

I didn't even notice when the spell started.

Ari always favored lightning bolts, fire, and frost. This magic reached out, gently, subtly. The crowds passing by shied away, completely oblivious, even though they pushed and shoved like a kindergarten class chasing a gerbil made of sugar.

"Hold on." Ari seized my arm, then yanked me forward, straight into the brick wall.

My head jerked back, like I'd slammed into the actual wall, and the world spun. Ari kept on pulling, nearly wrenching my shoulder off, and I slipped through the wall. All in all, the experience was no different from all the other times I'd been buried in wet concrete.

We emerged in darkness, to the sound of scampering paws and slithering scales. I meant to reach for my gun. Instead I picked up the thorn sword, awkward as always.

"Be," Ari whispered, and a burst of light lit up the room, causing a dozen nightmares to retreat to their cages. "I told Grimm this wasn't closed down right. All of you, back in your cells." Ari went around the room, latching cages, closing doors, until she looked around and nodded, as if to herself. "Let's see what I can do."

"You've been here?"

"It's where Grimm took me to train yesterday." Ari sat the witch's cauldron upright and shuffled through the ingredients on the back shelf, seeming to toss them at random over her shoulder. "We'll start with the balance statement from my credit card bill. Nothing says the truth like facing the music. And this, this is skin from a supermodel the morning after a shoot. Pure truth."

Ari turned and pointed under the counter. "Hand me that bag." After I did, she opened it and took out a plastic stick.

"Positive pregnancy test. No way to lie your way out of that one. This won't be easy."

"Is anything ever?"

Ari spun, her hair wheeling out from her head like red spokes. "Listen to me. Grimm told you the lie would become true if you didn't reject it."

"Yes." I remember him saying that. I also remember being so eager to try out the new me I didn't care.

Ari left the cauldron and walked over, appraising me like a chunk of ham. "Did you?"

"Did I what?"

"Reject it."

And the feeling inside me, the sick sadness, said everything. Because part of me liked the way I looked. It hurt like hell, and I felt like an alien in someone else's skin, but at least part of me liked the skin. "I don't know if I want to."

"Liam doesn't care what you look like." Ari kicked over a cage, sending leathery bats squealing, and sat on the cage side.

"I do." I spent the first six years working for Grimm alongside a woman so beautiful she stopped hearts or tore them out, often literally. I spent six years knowing I was *never* the most beautiful woman in the room.

Ari turned and hit the cauldron with a blast of ice three times the thickness of anything I'd ever seen her produce, then followed it up with pure hellfire, leaving the cauldron boiling. Waving her hand, she stirred the brew until it steamed. "That should do it. You know there's no magic in the ingredients, right? They just help me fold and sculpt the spells."

She rose and walked back over to the cauldron, and beckoned. "Come on, M."

I went, begrudging every step.

"Here." Ari stood across the cauldron from me. With a wave of her hand the water became still. Ari's reflection showed her dimpled chin, her red hair in ringlets.

And me. Not just one of me; three of me. The me inside, the plain girl who never turned heads, she stood in the middle. On one side, the handmaiden me, lovely and elegant, stacked like a pile of pancakes, with lovely eyes and hair like brown honey. The third me made me ill, a gross exaggeration of both of the others. The third me had filthy brown hair, squinty eyes, bulbous breasts, and teeth like crooked tombstones.

Ari pointed to the third. "That is the lie she wrapped you in." She took a silver ladle from beside the cauldron and dipped it into the real reflection. The liquid came out amber, scented like honey, smoke, and cupcakes. "Drink this and reject it."

I closed my eyes, my hands clenching the sides of the cauldron, and opened my mouth. Like a sick child being force-fed castor oil, I waited till the ladle brushed my lips.

The lie smelled like happiness, but tasted like the bitter bile of failure and held the cloying stench of death. I forced my eyes open and clasped the ladle, gulping the vile brew out until it was gone.

In the cauldron, regular me and beautiful me were gone. Only the lie looked back at me, blinking when I did not, grinning a toothy grin.

"I reject you." I spat the words out, letting tears join them as I refused the Black Queen's offer. The lie screamed, clawing at the surface of the water. I jerked away. Could it break the surface?

"Hurry," Ari hissed. "I can't hold it long. Choose the truth, or live someone else's lie the rest of your life."

I put my hands on the cauldron and leaned over, staring back at it. "I reject you. You are not me, or any part of me." In my mind, I forced memories of my true face. My true eyes and ears and lips.

As each took form, the lie shrieked again like I'd stabbed it with a fondue fork. It thrashed, making the surface of the cauldron bubble and boil, but the longer I held to the truth, the weaker it became. I shut my eyes as the false image of me began to bleed into the cauldron, staining Ari's brew a foul crimson.

"That's it." Ari put a hand on me, and I opened my eyes. The cauldron showed a ragged, bloody lump of flesh, like a placenta, writhing at the bottom. Then I caught a glimpse of myself, the outline.

I hadn't changed back.

Nineteen

I GRABBED ARI by the wrist, trembling. "Why didn't it work?" With each second, I became more frantic. Now I couldn't remember why I thought changing how I looked could ever have been a good thing.

"I said it was mostly Seal Magic. A tiny part of it is Fairy Magic. *That*, you have to give back to the caster." Ari selected a steel flask from the wall, and ladled a measure of the brew into it. "This will prevent her putting another lie in place."

Ari drew a copper cover over the cauldron. "I'm going to like it here. Grimm says even if the other queens turn on me after Isolde is gone, I can live out my life here safely. Kingdom always has need of a witch."

The thought of Ari trapped behind the glass, sleeping on the straw mattress in the middle of a warehouse, made my stomach turn, and gave my determination an edge like diamond. "No rituals. No killing spells. Not for me. I might look like some killer handmaiden, but I know what I am, thanks to you." I put one hand on her. "I know who you are too. The Ari I know doesn't even think about killing with magic."

Ari turned away. "I will fix this. I will strip the Black Queen's title and her right to handmaidens. I'm almost ready."

Grimm had spent years training Ari with only mild success. Now Ari wanted me to believe she'd acquired skill equal to Kingdom's most powerful seal bearers in a matter of days. "You never even passed your driver's test."

"I didn't want that the way I want this. I'm going to get you out of here. We're going to go find Liam so you can apologize. Have to remove the wards for a moment." Ari held out her hand, pointing with three fingers at the shop front. A pile of bricks caved in, letting sunlight filter in from High Kingdom.

The doorway flickered.

One moment, it showed High Kingdom, passing crowds in fancy dresses. The next, it showed Low Kingdom, with chain gangs dragging the streets while jeering taskmasters swung whips.

"That's freaky." I couldn't take my eyes off the jagged opening. The glass doors of the witch's shop must have served to stabilize it, so that one could leave the appropriate way, but without them, what was left looked like an unguided portal.

Then Low Kingdom snapped into place, and held.

"Get down, someone's approaching." Ari threw her hair forward, covering her face, and I huddled down behind the counter.

"We're not open." Ari's voice came from the front of the shop.

A woman answered, her voice muffled. "Please, I've been searching all day. I need something." Her voice came clearer as she moved closer, sending shivers through me.

Kyra. Her boots clopped against the stone floor inches away. "I have to find some unicorn essence."

I nearly choked. "Essence" was a marketing term made up to make the substance palpable to people who'd never seen a real unicorn. Once you saw one, with the gangrenous sores covering it, and smelled the stench of decay, the fact that it had a horn didn't do much for the memory.

The dry scratch of a quill on parchment came from just above me, then Kyra spoke. "And these, if you have them."

"I said we're closed." The crystal aquarium on the counter reflected a flash of white as Ari froze over the exit with solid ice. "But I guess one customer won't hurt." Ari's voice pricked with worry and, to my chagrin, concern. "What exactly are you trying to assemble?"

The soft pad of Ari's running shoes came closer to the counter, and she leaned over, studying the list. "I won't make you a possession spell."

"That's not what this is. You get the ingredients, I'll work the spell myself."

"Sure you will. Sweetheart, I'd have trouble with this one. Unicorn goo, the heart of a gnome, ogre marrow, and frail heart. Is it to counter some sort of disease? This won't cure it—the binding agents aren't right." Ari stepped around behind the counter, giving me a glance that told me to shut up and hold still.

"There's no cure. I need something to help control it." Her next words came out a whisper. "Please, it's for my son."

That helped me with the whole "shut up" thing. I couldn't have spoken if I had to. Kyra had a son, a young one, judging from the meal she'd enjoyed, chicken nuggets and apple juice.

"You should go to your queen for spells. Most of them tend to be territorial." Ari kept her voice clear, though her hands on the countertop trembled.

For a moment, silence held sway in the shop. "I don't want her involved. I'll pay double your rate." The desperation in Kyra's voice worried me. I'd seen what desperate people could bring themselves to do.

I shook my head, looking up at Ari, trying to catch her eye. With one foot, I stretched out to tap her leg.

Ari ignored me. "You have to do something for me if you want my help."

"Name your price."

Ari turned without answering, and walked into the back room.

Though I hid beneath the wooden countertop, a voice inside me whispered that Kyra could see me. Not because I could see her in a reflection, but because she stood so close I could hear each breath, tense, like a tiger preparing to spring.

I could stab her. From what I'd seen of the thorn blade, it would cut through the counter like butter, straight into Kyra's chest. She'd never know what hit her. Without even meaning to, my fingers curled around the handle of that infernal blade.

I don't mean I pulled it out of my purse, or out of my pocket. I thought about using the blade, and I had it. That's all it took to summon it to me. And the longer Ari kept me waiting, the greater my desire to use it grew. Assuming the blade would honor my wishes.

That tiny voice inside me told me over and over that all I'd have to do is jerk it in her direction. The blade would do the rest. The image of her collapsing in a pool of red brought a smile to my lips, and shot a bolt of fear straight through me.

I threw the handle away, realizing too late what I'd done.

It hit a glass vase on the floor near the entrance to the storage warehouse, ringing it like a bell.

Kyra caught her breath, and the shop went silent.

With my knees drawn against me, I pressed myself up against the counter. Only then did it occur to me that Kyra, too, kept a blade of thorns. She would use it, if our positions were reversed. In my head, I rehearsed the motions I would take. Swing myself up, using the counter, roll across the counter and into her.

From there it would be clutch fighting, clawing, biting.

I could win.

But if she managed to speak, to call, to summon the Black Queen, Ari would die in a heartbeat. No story I could conjure would fool the woman known as the Root of Lies.

So Kyra wouldn't get the chance to speak.

I braced myself, crouched instead of cowered.

"All right." Ari swept out of the back room, her arms full of vials. She paused, sensing the tension in the room, then stepped to the worktable. "This isn't exactly what you ordered, but I'm guessing we're up against some form of autoimmune disease. So we're going to use regular marrow, and add a touch of wort instead."

I forced the air out of my lungs to keep from yelping.

The whole time Ari worked, she chattered like a rabid

monkey. A rabid monkey tasked with cleaning the cauldron, refilling it, and adding a list of ingredients that made processed cheese look pure.

Kyra answered in one-word grunts, as she paced back and forth, her boots scuffing the floor.

After Ari cast the spell, after she'd poured it into a golden flask and dipped the top in wax to seal it, she held it in one hand, away from the counter. "I give you this, on one condition."

"I said name it."

"Leave the Black Queen's service. I can put you in touch with someone who can help." Ari held the potion closer, her fist wrapped around it.

"I can't." The anger in Kyra's voice could have painted the entire shop red. "I am bound to her, body and soul. Her word is my command, her will, my life."

Ari couldn't hide her shock, staring at Kyra. "Why?"

"I thought she could help. I pledged myself to her, meaning to ask for a cure, but now I don't want her anywhere near my son." A golden cloud of glitter dusted the counter as something thumped on it. "Take your payment, witch, and give me my potion." Now iron resolve braced her words. I'd used that tone myself more times than I could count.

"You could break free—"

"I don't want to." A fist slammed into the counter, and Ari dropped the potion. It rolled to my feet, clinking in the dust. "I want my potion. I want to leave, and I want it now, before I kill you."

I gripped the counter and prepared to leap upward. One chance. It wasn't like Kyra didn't have it coming. At that moment, it hit me. I was planning a murder of my own. On my own. With fists clenched, I closed my eyes. I wouldn't move unless she did.

Ari reached out her hand, drawing the potion through the air to her. She set it on the countertop and stepped back. "Take it. Get out of my shop." Ari raised a hand, and the smell of burned dust filled the air as she melted the ice blocking the doorway.

Kyra's footsteps clopped away, leaving me a complete

wreck. I'd have liked to sit beneath the counter and catch my breath, but Ari grabbed my hand the moment Kyra was gone and pulled me up. "We're going back to the Agency."

"You shouldn't have helped her. Every minute she spent looking for that potion was one more minute she wasn't doing something for the Black Queen."

Ari turned back to me. "She doesn't have a fairy keeping the Black Queen out of her mind. You've seen what the Black Queen can do to your body. Imagine what it's like to have your mind change."

"You don't know what I'm feeling, except angry and violent." I thought of my old gun, in a box in Grimm's office, and shuddered. "When did you put the shine on your spells? You could have been Miss Magic two years ago."

"Four years ago, yesterday." Ari turned toward me, and pulled her hair back. Ari's once-perfect complexion held lines I hadn't seen before, and she wiped her eyes.

"You've only worked for Grimm four years."

"No. I spent four years practicing with him, yesterday. Time isn't the same in his realm. Judging from the number of birthday cakes he brought me between tests, I'm guessing I'm twenty-six."

Four years of Ari's life passed in one day of mine. I couldn't cope with the thought of that, couldn't bring myself to acknowledge it. Four years of constant training. And four years without friends, or the human dishrag she called a boyfriend. "Does Mrs. Pendlebrook know Wyatt's dating an older woman?"

Ari rolled her yellow eyes—I could tell because the crimson blood vessels that contrasted with the yellow moved when she did. "I missed him more than I could say. Wyatt has to help me get ready to bind the spells." She pulled me by the hand, leading me to the shop door. As she approached, it locked onto High Kingdom.

A creature straight out of my nightmares lumbered past, pausing to look at the broken brickway before continuing on.

"That's one of Isolde's creations." I swore, reaching for my gun.

"In High Kingdom." Ari held out her arm and a broom

whipped to her hand, a gnarled handle with twigs bound to it. "Why aren't the police taking care of it?" She lifted a mirror from the side.

We called together. "Grimm."

The mirror went blank, then his face faded in, and his eyes popped open. After all these years, I recognized the signs of Grimm busy foretelling the future. "Ladies, High Kingdom is not safe."

I checked my gun and nodded. "Police?"

"Overwhelmed. I am currently counseling the army to act, but without the kings to command them, they have only agreed to mobilize and gather." Grimm shook his head, disappointed. "By the time they respond it will be too late for far too many innocent victims."

Just past the three laws of magic lay another rule of the universe: Never underestimate the ineffectiveness of a bureaucracy.

Ari and I exchanged a glance that said everything, and she nodded. Together, we stepped past the pile of bricks, which zipped themselves up behind us with only a glance from Ari. The screams from every direction, the roaring of abominations, alarms, and sirens blasted us.

We'd stepped out of the shop and into a war.

"Where to first?" I looked to Ari, since she now packed more heat in her fingertips than all of my ammo put together.

"I think—" Ari stopped as a delivery truck went sailing through the intersection. Behind it, a couple cowered on a building stoop as one of those abominations lumbered nearer.

I didn't think, just squeezed off a couple shots, nailing it in the shoulder. I'd seen mosquitoes with more effect than my bullets, but it did do the one thing I wanted.

The abomination turned to look at me, opening jaws that held other jaws, baring each row of teeth at me as it gurgled.

And then it charged for me.

Twenty

MY CUNNING PLAN began and ended at "get the monster's attention." The next plan I formed on the spur of the moment. It involved running, more running, and maybe some hiding, if I survived that long. I dashed down the street and hid behind a singing flower cart for just a moment, which was all the time it took for the abomination to kick the cart clean through the building window behind me. The cart sang "So Long, Farewell" right up until it smashed to pieces with a falsetto shriek.

If you need a partner, you'll never regret bringing a witch to the party. I was used to feeling Ari breathing in magic and throwing it out as fire, ice, or lightning. I expected her to use the broom in the normal manner, flying by the monster to keep it busy.

Instead, she held the broom like a guitar. With a strum of the broom twigs, it threw a ball of green light at the monster. A distraction, I thought, until the orb blew a chunk the size of a guinea pig out of the monster's chest. The abomination obviously came from the same line of design as the body Prince Mihail was sporting, looking like the entire offensive line of a football team mashed together.

Ari strummed a few more times, knocking the abomination on its deformed rear end. With a few more bolts, it shuddered to the ground and didn't rise.

I gave the pointy end of Ari's broom a fresh dose of respect. "I thought witches rode those."

Ari tossed me the broom. Instead of some magnificent weapon, I held a bundle of dry wood and twigs. "I tried exactly once while Grimm was training me. You want that between your thighs? I'd rather use it to focus."

I handed the stick of doom back to Ari and glanced around, finding a parked car to call Grimm from. "Grimm, how many of these things are there?"

Grimm appeared in the side-view mirror, then jumped to an unbroken widow display. "Six more, but they are scattered several blocks apart, wandering aimlessly."

A few blocks down the street, I spotted the beginning of a plan. An armored truck nestled against the curb, with the engine still running. "Come on." We sprinted to the truck.

The last time I had to hijack an armored car, the guards weren't kind enough to leave it running. This time around, I hopped into the driver's seat, snapped my seat belt, and rolled away from the curb the moment Ari leaped in.

With Grimm in the rearview mirror calling directions like the world's most magical GPS, I used the sidewalk to bypass clogged streets. As I approached the first abomination, I wondered which was tougher, the monsters or the machine. For the record, eight tons of Detroit steel will beat down a monster any day. We plowed over the first abomination without losing speed. The second one almost got a chance to run before I crushed its skull with my patented "parallel park of death." As we rounded the corner on another, Ari rolled down the window and leaned out, her broom resting on her shoulder.

If she ever went out for the majors, they'd need to invent a new kind of ball, one that wouldn't get blasted to smithereens by a wooden broom. Like a country girl on a mailbox rampage, Ari swung her broom right at a creature's head and, as far as I was concerned, scored a grand slam of gore.

The rain of flesh left its head stuck on my windshield in a hail of wet flesh.

"Where are the other two?" I looked to the mirror for directions, while Grimm closed his eyes in concentration.

"Two blocks west. Arianna, please avoid friendly fire."

Though abandoned cars filled the streets, I managed to avoid taking the subway in an armored car, instead crushing parking meters, which yelped like dogs as I ran them over.

One block over, the traffic jam stood so thick only a monster truck could get through, and I didn't have time to call the post office, so we left our ride and ran on foot.

The sound of crushing metal and breaking glass led me to the corner, where an abomination of flesh, a nightmare wolf, and the man of my dreams fought.

The abomination, like the rest of the Black Queen's work, barely resembled a fourteen-foot human. Its rib cage lay bare, with jagged, thorny spikes jutting from every angle.

The nightmare, an eight-foot-tall, four-foot-wide wolf, I recognized as Mikey.

Liam had let the curse take over entirely, becoming a dragon the length of a station wagon, with reddish-green scales and a mouth that could have swallowed a shopping cart.

The abomination's hands ended in clusters of bone spikes, like a medieval morning star attached to each wrist. It swung them overhand, missing Mikey by a paw's width and crushing the hood of a sports car.

Mikey looked over at us and howled. I hoped it was a welcome howl, rather than a "Hey, fresh food" howl.

Liam's head snapped our direction, and he hissed in a way that either meant "What are you doing here?" or "Don't you owe me an apology?"

Both of which were excellent questions.

Lining up her broom like a sniper rifle, Ari strummed off a few rounds of explosive light, which tore the flesh from the abomination's shoulder. To my horror, the flesh grew back like pink tongues of muscle, then the bones lengthened, forming armor over the wound.

The abomination spun in a circle, bashing Mikey across the

street and through a door. His return blow hit Liam's dragon head with a thunk that made me pray his brain was only the size of a peanut, shielded by half a ton of meat and bone.

The monster came for Ari. The other abominations had wandered, destroying, smashing as they saw fit. This one recognized a threat when it saw one. It leaped onto the roofs of cars, leaving an entire row of cabs looking about like normal as it sprinted toward us.

I moved to the side as I fired, hoping to give it an iron overdose with each bullet. Bullets in the ribs barely bothered it; bullets in the knees, however, got its attention. It swerved, coming after me.

I would have run.

I didn't get the chance.

As I turned, my foot slipped on an expanding floor of ice that burst like a white oil slick from Ari's finger tips. The wave of ice solidified under the abomination right as it brought its foot down, sending it face-first to the ground just like me.

The sheer mass and momentum kept it moving, sliding like a bone bulldozer straight into me, plowing me along in front of it.

Ari didn't watch. She didn't look; she kept her eyes closed, her hands moving before her like magic was cloth she could braid. And maybe it was, as a wall of light snapped outward like a barrier. I slid through it without a scratch. The abomination plowed into it like Ari's wall was made of stone.

Then those damned laws of physics cut in.

I think, if Ari had time, she could have created a soft wall. A spring-loaded one, something to absorb the force and redirect it. Instead, all of the momentum went straight into the wall, then hit Ari. She flew like a rag doll.

The glass storefront behind us had been destroyed already, and Ari sailed through the air, crashing into a rack of glittering ball gowns. Her wall of light disappeared along with her consciousness, leaving me two feet from the monster.

It raised a head, and I put a bullet into each eye. The eyes grew back, tiny sparks of fire lighting the darkness of its pupils. And the bone armor enchantment took over. Thick bone grew downward from the eye socket, sealing over the eyes, leaving them blind.

The abomination swung its hands up to its eyes, shattering chunks of bone away long enough for it to see me, and it rose to one knee, reaching for me.

"Stop!" I screamed at it, my voice echoing in the empty street.

It did.

"Stand." I gave the order, and it rose, heaving blasts of breath from diseased lungs. The stench of its morning breath reeked like a thousand buffet dinners gone bad.

I looked at the cursed mark on my hand. What had the history books said? The handmaidens commanded the Black Queen's armies. The handmaidens ruled over all of her creatures. "Do not move."

From the street corner, Liam stumbled in my direction. The loss of consciousness had caused him to revert to his normal form. Naked, but normal. I held my arm out in front of me, as if the mark could shield me from the abomination.

Mikey growled like he'd gotten a dozen years' rabies shots, and came hurtling toward us, leaping onto the abomination's back, tearing into its flesh. The abomination convulsed but continued to obey my command. After a few moments of tearing flesh from it only to have the flesh regrow, Mikey dropped to the ground on all fours, then changed, becoming more wolf man than wolf.

"Little help?" He looked to Liam, who nodded.

With claws like meat cleavers, Mikey tore the abomination's ribs back. In the cavity, a heart like an elephant's palpated, humming with saffron energy. That was how we'd killed the others—when I ran them over, it crushed their hearts.

Liam reached in and tore the heart loose, then vomited on it, fire that seared and blackened the flesh until it finally stopped moving.

I threw myself at him, wrapping my hands around his chest. "I'm sorry. Ari's helping me get rid of the lie— Ari!" I let go of Liam and ran for the storefront.

Inside, Ari lay nestled in a pile of fashionable clothing.

When I shook her, she opened her eyes. I'd seen this look before. Spell exhaustion, caused when Ari pushed herself too far, too fast. Liam stepped through the glass, letting scales cover his feet to keep them from being sliced up.

"Here." I took a lace gown from the pile and threw it to him. "I'm so sorry about what happened."

"We'll talk later." Liam tied the dress around his waist and gathered up Ari like a bag of tenpenny nails and walked out, with me following.

Mikey flexed his muscles, tearing a Kingdom mailbox from the concrete and tossing it over his shoulder.

"What are you doing with that? The gnomes will be furious." I shook my head, glad it wasn't me this time.

Mikey gave the box a shake, and a muffled shout rose from inside. "Wyatt was with us when those things attacked. I used to do this to nerds all the time."

I tried not to laugh, and failed. "Grimm? You can come out now."

He appeared in half a dozen taxi mirrors, a look of satisfaction on his face. "Well done. Now, if you—" He stopped, looking around. "Marissa, where is the sixth creature?"

I looked around, frantic, and listened. The streets still stood silent. I can't tell you why I looked behind me. Call it instinct, maybe training, or would it be so awful to say that for once the universe let me have a little luck? I turned to the west just in time to see a taxicab come sailing straight toward me.

Twenty-One

I RAN TOWARD the flying cab, not away, knowing that Wyatt-in-a-box and my triathalon-training best friend would be so much meat for the abomination. Liam might be able to do something, or might not, since he usually needed a nap between transformations. And of course, holding still would have left me in the path of an unexpectedly airborne cab.

As I rolled to my feet, thankful I wouldn't have to tip the cabby for a ride I didn't want to take, I saw a familiar form. "Prince Mihail." The cab exploded behind me in a crush of glass and metal.

He'd gotten an armor upgrade, obviously, looking like a knight in bleached bone as much as a swamp monster. "Marissa." My own name sounded foul on his lips, as if their speaking dirtied me.

"I command you to stand still." I raised the handmaiden's mark to him.

He shook his head. "I don't work for you. I only take orders from the real handmaiden. Much as I'd like to kill you now, I have something more important to do. I have to deliver the news."

"You do that. Tell Isolde we killed her army. Tell her we'll kill the rest. If I can do this with an armored truck and a witch, imagine what black-ops spell casters with tanks are going to do." I continued toward him, hoping that Liam wouldn't leave Ari unprotected to come to my aid.

"You think this is her army? The death of a few experiments? That's not news that matters. I have to tell our queen, I found the one she's looking for." Monster Mihail turned and plowed through a brick wall, disappearing through the building. The explosion one street over as he came out rattled my teeth, but I kept my focus where it belonged. On my friends. On my fiancé. "Grimm, where are the police? I need an ambulance. And a can opener."

"Law enforcement are hiding, as well they should be. I'll notify the district chiefs to sound the all clear." Grimm's failure to note the fact that his agents were neither military nor deputized worked out in Kingdom's favor more often than not. We weren't concerned with or beholden to most laws.

"Do we have casualties?" I looked up and down the line of wrecked cars. In High Kingdom, the folks there carried a sort of luck that often left them safe in the face of disaster.

"Yes. Leave them to the first responders. Take Arianna and Wyatt to his mother's home, not the Agency. The morale situation there is best dealt with by me alone." Grimm disappeared before I could weigh in on the subject, despite the fact that I had opinions like anchors to share.

Mikey borrowed a cab, and with Ari in the back and Wyatt in the trunk, we clunked our way back to his mother's house. Every single bump we hit, that boy managed to complain about, though with the trunk and the mailbox, he didn't complain loudly.

MRS. PENDLEBROOK WAS waiting for us in her yard, a parasol shading her from the sun. She opened the gate so that Mikey could carry in Ari, and watched without emotion while Liam pulled the mailbox from the trunk.

I caught her eye and crossed my arms. "What are you

doing here? You're supposed to be under the Fairy God-father's protection."

Mrs. Pendlebrook looked down for a moment and shook her head. "I appreciate his hospitality, but I would rather live out my life here in my home. This house has become a part of who I am. I'd rather die here than live anywhere else." She turned sharply away, cutting off the discussion.

Liam gave her his usual goofy grin, which evaporated under her gaze like spit on a cast-iron griddle. "You have a hacksaw in the toolshed, Mrs. P.?" The fact that he was still wearing a dress didn't faze him.

"Don't be ridiculous. Downstairs, in the basement, you'll find a plasma cutter and a set of diamond drills. Be careful not to get the hem caught, young man." With that, she spun and marched inside, probably off to make tea and crumpets. I'd never eaten a crumpet, but if anyone would have them, it would be Mr. Pendlebrook.

Liam brought a toolbox out of the basement and worked to cut Wyatt out of the mailbox while I swung on the porch swing, thinking about Prince Mihail's words. "The one" could be Mikey. As a wolf, he'd always been clear that his first loyalty was to the pack, and his second loyalty was to his stomach.

Or Ari. I wouldn't put it past Isolde to hold a grudge. In fact, I expected her to have spare arms just for grudges.

Worst of all, he might have meant Liam. Strictly speaking, not Liam, but the curse he carried. The only reason the Black Queen would seek out Liam on his own would be to have wrought iron bent into a nameplate for her castle door, or maybe a few steel roses.

She had to be after the curse.

Prince Mihail meant to gain its power once. I wouldn't take bets on which he hated me for more: poisoning his body with a magic apple or giving away his chance at true power.

After far too many yelps and complaints from Wyatt, Liam finally cut the post office box open and helped Wyatt out. Wyatt would need to gain a hundred pounds to have a leg up on a string bean, but what he did have going for him was Prince Magic strong enough to give Ari a run for her money.

"I'm going to apply bruise cream. Afternoon, Marissa." Wyatt nodded to me as he disappeared into his mother's house.

Liam followed Wyatt up the steps, but detoured to sit beside me. He knew I loved the porch swing, because it reminded me of our second date, when he showed off some of his iron work, and I admired some of his iron muscles.

He patted the iron chains. "I could make you a swing like this."

"Yeah, we could take out the kitchenette, eat in the swing at breakfast. You think the super would mind?" I laid my head up against him, not wanting to talk curses or queens.

Liam wrapped his rough hands around mine. His fingers, thick with calluses, made mine feel like twigs. "He didn't complain when we had asbestos tile installed in the bedroom. He'll keep his mouth shut unless I saw off a support beam. Which I won't."

"Marissa, Mr. Stone, would you mind joining me for a moment?" Grimm watched me from the crystal windowpanes. If I didn't know better, I'd say he regretted interrupting. Not that the Fairy Godfather ever admitted to regretting anything.

Inside, Grimm waited in a full-length dressing mirror that looked like it came from Victorian England, by way of the local thrift store. "I finally understand my daughter's goals."

Liam stiffened, his muscles rippling like iron. "And?"

"The Court of Kings is quelled, and what few princes remain are under my protection at the Agency. I believe she means for Gwendolyn to rule the Court of Queens. That leaves only Kingdom's army. She will not suffer them to interfere."

I looked over at Liam, unsure what this could possibly have to do with him. "Your point?"

"Those creatures were a test, a trial run. Without leadership, without purpose. Her next move will be with reason. She will destroy Kingdom's military in two days, when the full moon makes a portal easier."

Liam nodded. "So you are calling out the army."

"No." Grimm shook his head. "They will not answer to me. Without the Court of Kings, the military is paralyzed. By the time they act, it will be too late. The horde of abominations she means to unleash will kill everything in their path."

Ari came from the kitchen, a teacup in her hand, a white bandage wrapped around her head. "We didn't fare well against them one at a time. What makes you think we'll do any better against a horde?"

Grimm paused, his eyes closed, his hands clenched. "Arianna, I will give you weapons I forged for my own daughter, but never allowed her to touch. They will amplify your powers." He looked to Liam. "Master Stone, do you recall the potion I gave you to guard the vampires?"

Liam nodded. "All dragon, all the time."

"Not just dragon." Grimm vanished, and a creature appeared in the mirror. A creature the size of a city bus, that looked like the great-granddaddy of dragons. "You've always been trapped in an intermediate state. This will allow you to take the true form."

I put one hand on Ari and one on Liam. "And I can command her creations. Make them easy to kill."

All three of them spoke at once. "No."

Grimm shot a warning glare to Ari and Liam, then looked back to me. "When you invoke the handmaiden's authority, you accept the Black Queen. Her hold on you becomes stronger. I have shielded your mind from her invasion, but if you choose to give her entry, I cannot prevent it."

Liam turned toward me. "We'll take out Isolde's garbage and give Kingdom time to organize."

"Grimm, what's left of Prince Mihail was there. He said he'd found the one the Black Queen was looking for. Was that Mikey or Liam?"

Grimm's eyes looked to my chest, no doubt thinking, as I was, of the thorns waiting at my heart. "Neither. She seeks the power of the curse. The man it is attached to matters nothing to her." He looked back to Liam. "Now, sir, do you understand why I cannot allow you to confront her?"

Liam nodded, a nearly imperceptible shudder working through him. "Did you think about my theory?"

If I had ears like Mikey's, mine would have perked up at that comment. Liam tended toward the "Smash first and ask questions later" line of thinking. His theories usually formed around "What was that guy thinking?" while watching football.

Grimm nodded. "It seems logical, near obvious. And indeed, it fits with what Marissa described."

I scratched my head while I tried to figure out what I'd missed. "Described what? You two been smoking something?"

Liam leaned over to whisper. "Do you trust me?"

"Of course." The fact that he had to ask offended me more than the question.

"Then let him do this." Liam stepped away and gave Grimm a thumbs-up.

Grimm's eyes narrowed, and his power streamed out from my bracelet, rushing over me. "I'd like you to try to resist me."

My body went cold, and I took a step toward Liam. That is, my feet moved, dragging me along with them. My muscles listened to some other master, and all my effort, all my force couldn't make them stop, not even for a moment. "I can't."

"You must." Grimm redoubled his efforts, and against my will, I ran, a prisoner in my own flesh, drawing back my fist.

I swung in a haymaker, a punch that would have knocked a few teeth out of Liam's mouth. He caught my hand, right as Grimm released me.

My knees buckled, and I sagged, letting Liam catch me. He held me up against him as I shook, fear and anger mingling in confusion.

"Well done," said Grimm. "I had to command every movement, every step. You claimed you could not stop me, but in truth, it took the might of my will to force you." A single tear of glitter ran down Grimm's cheek. "I'm sorry, but I believe Mr. Stone is correct."

I pushed away from Liam, looking to Ari, and noted she looked as lost as I felt. "About what?"

"You agreed to serve Fairy Godmother. It is not only a handmaiden's bond by which Isolde commands you, but the power of a fairy's contract. By consuming Fairy Godmother's power, my daughter has assumed her debts, and in this case, her agreements." Grimm nodded to Liam. "You were correct, sir."

Liam sat on the coffee table, making it groan. "And the other part?"

"I cannot say." Grimm looked back to me. "But it makes sense as well. Marissa, when you first met Fairy Godmother at the funeral ball, what did she offer you?"

That was years ago. A different me, a different time, when I'd gone with Ari to her father's funeral. Like all other celebrations I attended, it ended in disaster. "Work. Just like everyone else." I wiped tears from my eyes, remembering how she made me feel. Insignificant. Wrong.

Grimm nodded. "And she set the terms."

In my mind, I heard her voice, like my grandmother and a grade school teacher rolled together. "I don't keep people. Three tasks, and you'd be done." And when I faced her, through the mirror, in the realm where Ari practiced magic, her words came back to me. I was hers. I agreed to it. "So Isolde can make me do anything."

"Only two more things. She may only command you by the power of a fairy twice more. I will not allow her to force you into a deal again. My power will prevent that." Grimm's image flashed around the room, as he looked at the windows, making sure we weren't being spied on. "And so I ask you to return to her."

"What?" Liam grabbed me, as though I'd be sucked through a portal right then and there.

Ari shook her head. "You're spending too much time in a mercury mirror. It's poisoned you."

"Hear me out." Grimm returned to the mirror. "Marissa is bound to Isolde both by Fairy Godmother's power, and as a handmaiden. Either one alone, I can deal with. Arianna can take the position of High Queen and strip my daughter of her title. I can join myself to Fairy Godmother and destroy us both."

"But not both at once." Liam's voice sank, despair flooding into it. "If you kill Fairy Godmother while she's still bound . . ."

Grimm bowed his head. "Her survival is not guaranteed

in either case, but I believe that once her agreement is completed, Marissa will suffer only the handmaiden's bond. Isolde's death may destroy her mind."

"Not going to happen." Ari spoke in a voice like steel. "It's time you taught me those spells."

"I'm not letting Marissa go." Liam wrapped his other arm around me. The sweat steamed off of him.

"Use your head for a moment." Grimm's tone sounded like an angry judge. "My daughter will not kill Marissa, not while she needs her as a shield. Every moment Marissa is with her is one more moment for a slip of her tongue. 'I command you to get me that glass.' 'I order you to kneel.' Let her waste her power over Marissa."

"Let's go." Ari walked toward the mirror, ready to step through it.

And the mirror shattered as a hammer flew into it, throwing Grimm's image into a hundred pieces. "That is enough foolishness." Mrs. Pendlebrook strode across the room, grabbing Ari by the arm. "You have no concept of what you are undertaking."

"Spells. Black Magic. Power." Ari spoke through gritted teeth, unbowed.

Mrs. Pendlebrook put her hands on Ari's cheeks, looking straight into Ari's witch eyes without fear. "Forget the magic. The court. High Queen is not a position one walks away from. I escaped, with the help of the Fairy Godfather, but I was neither a seal bearer nor a witch."

"And yet here you are." Ari took Mrs. Pendlebrook's hands from her face. "I caused this. I don't want the position, or the power. I just want Marissa set free. Gwendolyn will never allow that."

"No," said Mrs. Pendlebrook, "but do you truly understand what it means to immerse yourself in that world? Your family will become targets. Your friends, collateral for blackmail. Your strongest supporters will fear you and dispose of you at the earliest opportunity."

Ari turned away. "I don't care what happens to me."

"I care." Wyatt beat me to the words by a millisecond,

and for once, he spoke without quavering. "I care what happens to you more than you could possibly imagine."

Mrs. Pendlebrook grabbed Ari's hands, forcing Ari to face her. "Think of those who would go on without you. Or are you still believing that your mother died of natural causes?"

I'd seen Ari take a punch easier than those words. Wyatt's mom could take down a heavyweight with that tone. Ari jerked away, shaking her head. "No."

"Yes, young lady. Not the first time, nor the last, that a disease-causing potion will be used to remove a rival. That is the Court of Queens."

"Who?" Ari snapped her head up and hissed the word.

"Given your mother's conflicts," said Mrs. Pendlebrook, "I'd put money on Tegra Ambuwe."

Queen of the Seventh Royal Family. Mother to a girl I'd seen in Ari's photo albums. Murderer.

Mrs. Pendlebrook rose to drive home her point. "Arianna, this is the nature of the court. Did you not guess why your mother delayed training you in magic? She wanted to shield you from those who would see you as an ally to be obtained or an obstacle to be destroyed. I know right before she fell ill, Tegra approached her, asking for her loyalty—and yours."

Wyatt and I moved at the same time, from opposite sides, both trying to comfort Ari. Her hands shot out at us, bursting with yellow light that threw me back into the couch and froze Wyatt in place. She opened those witch eyes, looking at me, and for the first time in nearly two years, fear tap-danced down my spine when she gazed on me.

"Grimm, did my mother die of natural illness?" Ari looked at the mirror over the mantel.

If seeing Ari with two of us in a spell-lock surprised Grimm, he hid it well. "I don't know, Arianna. Allow me time to look back. I warn you, though, I specialize in the future. Past divination is not my normal proclivity."

After a moment, he nodded. "I cannot divine the exact nature, but her disease was at least assisted, if not implanted. What are your plans, princess?"

"Arianna, revenge is not in your soul." Wyatt stepped

forward, fighting the spell. I know she let him. The girl could pin a truck in place if she desired, but he took one step after another, until at last, he reached out to brush her cheek.

The spell pinning us evaporated, and she folded into his arms, wracked with sobs. If witches could cry, she would have worn tear trails on her cheeks.

I tried to slip out without them noticing. Easier on Liam if he didn't realize I was going. Easier on me. Almost made it to the car. The door groaned open behind me, and feet whispered across the marble porch. "M. I'm sorry. Come back."

I wanted to be angry with her. Using magic against me, that hurt. Letting Wyatt be the one who comforted her, that hurt more. We weren't sisters in the normal sense, but I thought we were as close as two people could be. Wyatt wouldn't even look her in the eyes.

She jumped down the stairs and ran to me. "I'll go with you to the fountain."

"No. Stay here. Stay safe. Just make me a promise, okay? Don't ask Grimm to bring her back. He'll say no." If I could have taken Ari's pain, I would. Pain and scars, however, were the two things everyone carried themselves.

"M, this all started because one woman couldn't let go. I'm so angry, I want to turn someone into a frog, but I can't change what was. You keep telling me to be what I am. I don't have to be what my mother was." She looked back to the house, and then to me.

I gave Ari a hug and headed into Kingdom. At the gates of Kingdom, I stopped and took Ari's potion from my bag. It tasted like cheap scotch and vomit, the flavors blended surprisingly well, but the buzz in my system said I wouldn't be catching any more lies from Isolde.

I stepped through the gates, ready for the horrors of Low Kingdom. Instead, the streets burst into gold. Gold drenched in blood. Fires raged, filling the sky with oily smoke.

Kingdom burned.

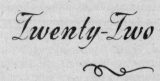

Twenty-Two

I SET OFF at a sprint, running up the streets toward the fountain. It originally sat in front of the old castle. When they built a new home for Kingdom's government, they moved the fountain brick by brick.

On the way there, I ran past destroyed buses and through showers, where beheaded fire hydrants shot water into the air like geysers. When I finally rounded the corner two blocks from the fountain, I stopped short.

The new palace lay in ruins, a smoking crater. I picked my way through the broken glass and debris in a haze. I caught glimpses of faces in the windows high above, but when I looked, the skittish onlookers drew their curtains. With one hand, I ran my fingers over the stone of the fountain, unwilling to look away from the destroyed palace.

As I completed my circle, Low Kingdom flashed into existence.

And burned as well. Vast mounts of rubble lay where buildings once stood.

"Grimm." I found a shard of glass and turned it to catch the light from burning rubble. "What happened?"

Grimm appeared in the glass and surveyed the carnage as I turned it from side to side. "She means to destroy both High Kingdom and Low Kingdom. Their fates are meshed together, so what happens in one affects the other. Those buildings must be rebuilt, or their counterparts will collapse as well."

Both layers of Kingdom overlapped the city, where millions of regular people lived regular lives. And that gave rise to a far worse thought. Every bit of real estate existed in three planes at once, which was the only reason I'd ever come up with for the astronomical rent. "If a building collapses in both High Kingdom and Low Kingdom, what happens to the real one?"

Grimm shook his head. "Your question tells me you already suspect the answer."

"Why is she doing this?"

"Marissa, I swore an oath to my wife the last time I let her die: I would never resurrect her again. And I keep my promises. The heart of my daughter was never known to me, but I believe she thinks if she can just push me far enough, I will change my mind."

I'd only known Grimm for a decade or so, but that was more than long enough to know his tone. He wouldn't give Rouge Faron a new body, ever, no matter the cost.

I sprinted all the way to the old palace, the only place someone as traditional as Isolde would consider home. The gate troll lay dead; his corpse wedged the castle doors open. I clambered over and slid down his shoulder blade into the darkness.

Inside the palace, the air hung still and damp. The torches guttered few and far between as I made my way to the center hall. There, Kyra stood, her head bowed, with the monster that was once Prince Mihail looming over her.

Blood dripped from Kyra's face, a gash that ran down her forehead and across her cheek.

Isolde stood on the throne steps before her. "Once more I will ask. Why do you have the stench of foreign magic on you? You reek of most curious spell-work."

Then her gaze flicked to me, and her eyes narrowed. She stared, her gaze boring into me, as her face contorted with rage. "What have you done, handmaiden? Where is the gift I graced you with?"

I looked down for a moment at the figure she'd granted me. The complexion, the voice. A face that could turn heads and the curves to fill out the clothes I could never wear.

A lie, all of it, no different from the one Ari helped me kill.

"I don't want it. I refuse your gift. I return it." As I said the words, my stomach wrenched and the world warped. My clothes sagged on me; my pants almost fell to the ground.

Isolde passed Kyra without a glance, stalking toward me. If eyes were coals, hers would have caught fire and burned me to ashes. I returned her gaze, refusing to cower in the doorway. I expected a spell, but got a fist, followed by a foot to the rib cage.

"That lie was practically your twin, handmaiden. Fairies cannot work Seal Magic, so do not claim he was behind this. Who helped you break my enchantment?"

I pushed up onto my elbows, spitting out blood. "I did it. Been studying sorcery in my spare time."

"You cannot command magic."

"I've been practicing." I rose to one knee. "You should see me pull a rabbit out of my hat."

Isolde kicked my side, knocking me to the ground again. "This time, I will wrap the lie around you so tightly you will embrace it or die." She snapped her fingers at me, showering me in glitter.

And again.

A strangled cry of rage escaped her throat as she willed me to change.

"Magic may not magic oppose." I recited the first law of magic, which Grimm drilled into me over and over. With Ari's potion on board, Isolde's creation couldn't take hold. "The truth is bitter, but I'll take it any day."

"Give me one reason I shouldn't snuff you out like a spell gone wrong." Isolde's voice shook with anger.

The floor shook as Monster Mihail lumbered over. "She knows the dragon man. I saw him with her, years ago. And today." He leaned down and grabbed me by the ankle, hanging me upside down. "I could shake the answer out of her."

Isolde stood, her hands behind her back. "Tell me where I may find him."

"Make me." I set my jaw, ready to bite my tongue off before I would speak Liam's name.

Isolde opened her mouth and then stopped, covering it with her palm. "You . . . desire my command. What trickery is this? What has my father told you that brings this madness?"

"He's told me all about you. A frightened little girl, crying for her mother." I saw the backhand coming this time, just enough time to brace myself.

"You know nothing about me. Nor does he, and I will prove this to you. Answer me one question, and I will grant you anything except your freedom." Isolde stepped forward, so close her breath chilled my forehead. "What was the lie by which I knew my power? Which was the first one I ever told?"

I knew better than to guess. If you only had one bullet, you made certain it was a solid shot. I kept my mouth shut, reminding myself: Grimm valued knowledge over anything, even magic.

After a moment, Isolde stalked away. As she did, she spoke again. "And I give you another choice. You know the keeper of the curse. Bring him to me, and I swear on my power I will let you go."

I'd sooner see myself dead. "Never. I'd rather die."

"Kyra." Isolde beckoned to her. "Your dalliance is forgiven. Tomorrow I will grant you command of my army, to do my bidding. I lift my restrictions on the culling. If you see Marissa again, and she does not have the dragon with her, you may kill her."

Kyra knelt and bowed her head. "Yes, my queen. And if she does bring him?"

"Then no force on earth can save you from the wrath of that curse. And if I control it, no army on earth will stand against me. If my father will not do as I ask, I will burn his precious Kingdom to the ground and reign over the ruins. Sleep well, my handmaiden." With those words, Isolde faded away, leaving only a fading trace of her lovely form.

Prince Mihail raised me up by the leg, shaking me. "Mother will be disappointed if she doesn't get to kill you."

Disappointing Irina Mihail ranked high on my list of goals. When he dropped me, I rolled, letting the impact sweep through me, and as fast as I could, I limped away. I'd almost made it to the tunnel when Kyra called after me.

"Don't come back."

I fled into the darkness and destruction.

BY THE TIME I made it back to my apartment, Liam was home, waiting for me. I rushed to him, looking him over. "The Black Queen is looking for you."

"I know."

"She let me go. Wants me to bring you back to her."

Liam put one hand on my chin and gazed into my eyes. "She offered you your freedom in return for me, because she wants the curse, right?"

"How—how did you know?"

Liam leaned over and kissed me on the forehead. "I've been reading the history of her previous reign, and she's not very original. I'm glad you are back. The real you. The beautiful you."

I wanted to take him in my arms and hold him, and forget about what I'd seen, but the images of burning buildings and rubble flashed behind my closed eyelids. "Grimm, she's proclaimed Kyra the handmaiden and is bringing an army for her to command. She says she's going to wipe Kingdom clean."

Grimm snapped into the living room mirror above the fireplace. "I see. And her commands for you?" The anticipation made Grimm's voice tremble.

"Nothing. She *knew* I wanted her to. Tell Ari her potion saved me from another lie."

"I will do so. There is only one place where the form of summons she needs could work. She must bring forth her army on the Plain of Agony, at the far western edge of Middle Kingdom. From there, they will tear through the populated portions of Middle Kingdom and invade High Kingdom."

"Wait." The feeling in my gut told me I'd missed something important. Some key element that Grimm, in his usual manner, would simply leave unexplained. While I didn't doubt his theory, his explanation didn't make sense. "Isolde's about as evil as a woman can get. How could she or any of her servants pass into High Kingdom? You can enter Middle Kingdom from either High or Low, but won't the spell keep you locked to whichever one you came from?"

"Indeed, it would," said Grimm. "But my daughter knows the secrets I used to split Kingdom apart. She knows the back ways and hidden paths that bridge the two. For all I know, she may be planning to have her handmaiden unravel the pillars holding them separate and merge both planes of Kingdom together."

Liam tensed, and his teeth ground, his skin steaming slightly. "Won't that hurt the people in both parts?"

"You might say so," said Grimm. "The carnage of colliding realities would be magnificent, and Isolde's armies would slay all who survived. But at the boundary between layers, we will be waiting."

I pushed back from Liam and turned to look at Grimm in the living room mirror. "I'll be waiting."

"No!" Liam and Grimm spoke at once, then stopped and looked at each other. After a pause, Grimm tipped his head to Liam.

He wrapped his arm around me. "M, you'll be the target of this handmaiden's fury if you are there. I can handle a hundred of those abominations bent on just destroying things. If they were all after you, I wouldn't be able to concentrate on killing them." He leaned his head over and whispered. "Please. Let us handle it."

"You'll call out the army, right? A line of tanks like the Thanksgiving Day Parade? A battalion of ogres?"

Grimm shook his head. "My daughter has already moved against them. Everyone higher than a captain is *quelled*, but even Isolde had the good sense to leave the ogre handlers alone."

The ogres of Kingdom, with six arms and barbed tails, bonded with their handlers from the moment the ogres chipped out of their tombs. Once, and only once, I'd seen the aftermath when an ogre's handler died and the ogre survived. Only ten tons of wet concrete and a veteran captain willing to make a final sacrifice let us put a stop to the trail of bodies.

I opened my mouth to name this as the suicide it was, when the air in the apartment crackled, like lightning struck the building. Wood snapped and crashed in the kitchenette, and I went sailing through the air, tossed onto the couch by Liam.

He leaped over the bar, scales studding his skin, and his fingernails stretched into long black claws. I'd seen him get lizardish more times than I could count, but this time, the sight made me thrill in a way that frightened me.

Snarling, Liam slammed into something in the kitchen . . . and stopped. His breathing calmed, slowed. "A fridge. Someone dropped a fridge in our apartment."

And a sick feeling in the pit of my stomach told me I *knew* that fridge. I stalked over and threw open the door. Inside, a wheel of cheddar sat on a glass platter. A note taped to it said "Stay away from the Agency." Our staff had signed it all over with notes of encouragement and explanations about how they'd see me dead if I showed my face again.

I snatched the note, counting names. "Those bastards. How did they—"

"Enchanters." Grimm cut me off, his eyes flashing with rage. "I have a personnel problem to deal with. I believed we settled the matter earlier, but I believed wrong."

Liam looked inside and shuddered. "I'm not touching that thing."

"A wise decision. I'll arrange for movers to return the extra appliance next week. In the meantime, if you two could excuse me, I'm going to arrange a mandatory after-hours morale event for my employees." Something about Grimm's tone told me it wouldn't be bowling or golf.

With Grimm gone, the apartment fell silent, until the ice maker in the Agency fridge turned over, dropping ice cubes with a crash.

"Easy, now." Liam spoke over my shoulder, now, once again, so much taller than me.

"Nothing is easy."

He wrapped his hands around my waist. "Loving you is easy."

MY NIGHTMARE BEGAN like they always did: I woke up. At least, I became aware. I think I was awake already, leaning over Liam as he snored in bed. My hands traced his chest, following the curves of his muscles down his abdomen and back to his heart.

The heat of his skin made the asbestos-weave sheets Grimm got me glow white-hot. My hand stopped above his heart, feeling it beat beneath my fingertips.

I opened my mouth to whisper "I love you," and what came out sounded like I swallowed a garbage disposal.

And Liam answered, mumbling in his sleep, in that same language.

I fought the nightmare, my own limbs sluggish. I could jerk my hands, but not control them, flinch, but not look away. Again, I spoke words, guttural, inhuman, and again he answered, this time, clearly.

I focused on the tips of my fingers, and the nails turned black, growing outward. They twisted, curled, until my index finger ended in a thorn the length of a steak knife. And my shaking hands turned back to him, sliding along his skin, the razor edge so sharp he would never know what cut him.

And right then, I stopped believing it was a dream.

While my hand worked its own magic, carving in red, my brain screamed in terror, because the cuts weren't some lazy torture attempt. They formed an engraving, the basis for a binding.

With a flick, I cut the last crossbar into the sigil and watched as blood seeped to the edges. Spell power gathered around me, and I fought to close my eyes, winding up squinting. Unlike Grimm's control of me, this I could almost overcome.

Inch by inch I warred with my own flesh, pulling my hand back from Liam. With the last of my will I forced my fingers to brush the golden bracelet on my wrist. The word that came from my mouth sounded like "gruaaahham," but the *intent* was what mattered. I meant to call Grimm.

A beam of white light blasted from my bathroom, bounced off of the makeup mirror on my desk, and hit me in the chest, throwing me back onto the headboard.

My ears rang with the Black Queen's laughter as her presence receded.

Liam sat up, throwing off a tangle of covers and shielding his eyes from the spotlight. Blood ran in trails down his skin from the cuts on his chest. "What in Inferno is going on here?"

"Mr. Stone, remain calm." Grimm's voice came from everywhere.

I remained unable to move, barely able to breathe, until at last the wave of light snapped off, letting me sink to the bed. My fingers crackled when I moved my right hand, thorns crumbling like broken leaves. "She tried—" My voice caught in my throat. "Was that a command?"

Grimm appeared in the makeup mirror, his gaze locked on Liam. "No. You wear her signet ring. The phrase used in the Court of Queens is 'present by proxy.' I suspect she was present."

Liam looked down at his chest, just noticing the blood. "She was going to kill me."

"No. She was going to bind you to her will." Grimm spoke in the tone of gravediggers and undertakers. "It is time for the contingency plans we discussed."

Liam shook his head. "No. I didn't agree to that."

"We are past the point of agreement, Mr. Stone. My daughter did not seek your agreement. I ask for your cooperation. It is no longer safe for you to be in Marissa's presence."

"What?" I tried to think of something better to say, but that one word was pushing it for the moment.

Grimm closed his eyes and looked down. "Isolde had no reason or desire to watch or act through you, until she saw you as access to Liam's curse. Now there is no way she will stop. Her army of abominations is a second choice at best. She would rather she commanded a dragon."

"Take it off. Please." I pulled at the signet ring for the

millionth time. Like always, it remained both loose on my
hand and impossible to remove.

"My dear, I would, were it in my power. Mr. Stone, I can
keep my daughter's attention away only as long as I am present
here. By the time you reach the curb, I'll have a cab waiting
to take you somewhere safe."

Liam shook his head, but I knew that shake. I'd seen it when
we fought and I won, when we argued and I won, when we
discussed, and I won. He'd go. Instead, he turned to me, coming
so close I could smell the woodsmoke on him. "Tomorrow. Ari
will challenge the Court of Queens tomorrow. Just this once,
I want you to do something for me."

I blinked away tears. "Anything."

"Stay here. Stay away. For once, let me rescue you." He
didn't wait for me to answer, slinging a T-shirt over his shoulder,
and stepping into a pair of pajamas. "I'll come for you the second Ari takes over."

Moments later, the front door opened and closed, and he
was gone.

"I need your help, Fairy Godfather." I sat up on my bed,
my hand to my bracelet, ignoring the swirl and pop that told
me he'd appeared in the mirror.

"I'm sorry, Marissa."

"You should be. Why don't you just give her what she
wants? What is one life, if it saves millions more?" Tears
came to me, and I didn't try to hold them back.

"Out of love for my wife, I will not break my oath." Grimm
put his hand to his forehead. "This world is not meant to be a
long-term destination for humans. Think of it as a bus stop with
an eighty-four-year layover. Humans are born, they grow and
learn, and they move on."

"Does it even matter to you that people live or die? Isolde
asked me something. She asked me what her first lie was.
The lie by which she knew she had power. She's promised
to give me anything but my freedom in return."

"If you believe I do not care who lives or dies, then my
daughter has already managed to convince you of one lie."
Grimm crossed his arms. "But I don't know the answer to her

question. I don't know what my daughter's first lie was." He looked up at me, and shook his head.

I threw a pillow at the mirror. "The Fairy Godfather does *not* admit to not knowing. He says, 'I can find out.' You want to tell me you could figure out 'Rumpelstilskin' as a name, but not your daughter's first lie?"

"Yes, that's precisely what I mean to tell you. And truth be told, Marissa, I couldn't figure out that odious little goblin's name either."

"I've read the file. She came to you and asked for his name."

"And I attempted to determine it. I was able to rule out so many options. Mary, Thomas, Jason." Grimm ticked off names on his fingers to himself. "So many names I could be certain were *not* the answer."

"So you sent her in there blind? Random names from a hat?"

"Yes. No." Grimm conjured an image of the girl, her golden hair and tan complexion giving her a beauty marred by the fear in her eyes. "I gave her a list, narrowed down the choices for her, and told her to listen. Sometimes, all we can do is make an educated guess and hope for the best."

"You're not helping."

Grimm's exasperation boiled over, making his image tremble. "I'm doing what I can, my dear. Listen to my daughter. The human heart yearns to speak truth, and her actions might tell you as surely as her words."

"Do you ever do any magic? You know, for a Fairy Godfather, you seem allergic to actually working a spell or two."

"I am doing something right now. Something I'm about to devote all my attention to. Arianna and Liam are now the focus of Isolde's attention. Liam because of the curse; Arianna, because my daughter has deduced her involvement in killing the lie."

I thought I couldn't feel any worse. I thought wrong, so wrong. "You have to keep both of them safe."

"I will do what I can. But it will take all of my attention. I appreciate the situation, your solitude, and desire to have someone to speak to. I will not be responding to summons of any sort until this is resolved. The auguries say that if you remain in the apartment, no harm will come to you."

"And if I leave?"

Grimm flickered for a moment, and returned, his face gray and sweaty. "I am a fairy. I may ask questions and receive answers, yes or no. I know only that if you stray, you will command a massacre. You will commit a murder."

Twenty-Three

~~~

I CAN'T SAY Grimm's predictions that leaving my apartment would make me a murderer did much for my peace of mind. "You didn't ask if I stay or not?"

Grimm shook his head. "I don't believe in asking questions that can only lead to frustration. Stay calm. Be patient, and I assure you, deliverance is close at hand." With that, he faded out of the mirror, leaving only an afterimage.

I crawled back into an empty bed, heaped covers over me, and tried to sleep.

TWELVE YEARS OF routine woke me before the alarm could, then refused to let me go back to sleep. Gray dawn light barely lit the brick wall outside my window. I couldn't help worrying. The list of questions I worried about ran longer than Ari's credit card bill. When would Isolde hand over control to Kyra? How would Ari and Liam handle a hundred of Isolde's abominations when one nearly killed Ari last time?

I rolled out of bed, went out to eat breakfast . . . and froze. On the kitchen table sat an empty bowl, a spoon, and a box of cereal. Running all the way back to the bed for the gun under my pillow would leave my back exposed, so I took one careful step after another backwards to the bed, felt around until I came up with my gun, then worked my way back to the kitchen. No one in the living room, so I padded over to the guest bedroom, where Svetlana slept in her coffinatorium. The crystal coffin still showed what was either a rotten corpse or a six-foot-long, 135-pound tuna fish sub sandwich.

"Marissa, breakfast is the most important meal of the day," said an old man's voice, from my kitchenette.

I spun, ready to fire.

The harbinger Death, manifesting as a Chinese senior citizen, sat in one of the two remaining chairs, waiting at my table.

I set my gun down on the counter, safety on. "You here to take me?"

"I wish." Death rose, took a carton of milk from the fridge, and poured it into my bowl. "I heard the Black Queen has agreed to cull her handmaidens, and War wants to have a word with you."

The harbinger War once tried to turn me into a killing machine. At least, that's how I interpreted his gift, which I put on layaway. "I'm not interested."

"He's giving pointers to the other handmaiden. You'd be foolish to refuse him."

I took a seat and poured my cereal. "Kyra might be interested in killing everyone. I'm not. And we have a plan to kill her army."

"Marissa, in that history of the Black Queen you read so much, it never says anything about the armies." Death turned to look at my bookcase, where one of the few surviving copies of a book on Isolde's reign rested. Written by the mad historian Ian Brachus. Rumors of how it was printed in blood or bound with human skin surrounded the book, but from what I could tell, this was simply clever marketing. The faded black ink didn't match any of Ari's grimoires, most of which were printed in blood, and thanks to the first car I owned, I knew exactly what tanned human hide looked like. But I thought I owned the only copy remaining.

"You've read Brachus's account of her reign?"

"No." Death blushed slightly, turning his pale yellow skin a slightly darker shade. "But I witnessed many of the events firsthand. Those I missed, I caught up on by reading over your shoulder many nights. After learning what happened last time, I figured you'd put a blade through the other handmaidens at the first opportunity."

I stowed away the urge to ask why Death had spied on me, in favor of a more urgent question. "Why would I do that?"

"The culling is meant to make sure only the most terrible of her servants is rewarded. After each culling, the surviving handmaidens received abilities far beyond mortal power. And this time, the Black Queen has the power of a fairy with which to bestow gifts. Forget her abominations. It's Kyra herself you should be afraid of." Death stared at me. "Your cereal is getting soggy, Marissa."

"Does Grimm know?"

"Of course the elder fairy does, but I suspect, like everything else to do with his daughter, he underestimates. Don't make his mistakes. Don't underestimate Isolde or her servants."

"I've faced Kyra before. I can handle her. Hell, Ari could handle her without using spells."

Death shook his head. "Not once Kyra claims her title as the only handmaiden. If you run away, she wins by default. You can't let that happen if you want your friends to survive, and I can only think of one way to prevent it."

"I can't fight her. I can barely use my sword. And she'll have control of an army. And all those powers." My frustration mounted, fueled by my inability to find a way to fix this.

"She doesn't get the title or the powers until after the culling, if you challenge her. Talk to the harbinger War. Accept his gift. People are going to die anyway, Marissa. I suspect you'll be a kinder, gentler overlord than she will."

Death disappeared with a pop, leaving me alone with a bowl of mush. As I slurped my way through a breakfast I wasn't really interested in, I couldn't help wondering if at any moment Isolde might be peeking through my eyes.

If so, I hoped she liked looking at the dregs of milk and sugar.

The signet ring formed a link, allowing me to act as a proxy for her. The gold bracer on my wrist, no doubt, would let me call to her. Why on earth I'd want her here wasn't a question I had a good answer to, since even Grimm wouldn't take time off to answer me.

That's when it hit me. Carefully putting my hand on the bracer, I thought of her and her perfect face, ageless beauty. "Isolde." After a moment, I spoke again. "Isolde, are you there?"

Her presence crept into the mirror, draining down it like oily sludge, then she faded into view, wavering like an old television. "By what right do you disturb me?" The anger in her voice confirmed my theory. Like Grimm, she wasn't omnipresent. To deal with me, she had to focus her attention my way.

And that kept her from wherever else and whatever else she might want to pay attention to.

"What is your command, my queen?" The disrespect in my voice left no room for misinterpretation.

"I have no command for you at this moment, only suggestions. You could relax, enjoy yourself. Or perhaps you'd like to visit the Court of Queens in my stead?"

My hopes sank, knowing I couldn't trick her into a half-hearted command. But I still had one chance to make a difference. I could keep her distracted. "Grimm told me what your first lie was."

"You cannot know . . ." Her eyes widened. Her power reached out, streaming up my arm like a swarm of ants, and she nodded. "You *do* lie. When the matter between my father and I is settled, I will deal with you. Until then, take care of yourself, handmaiden. I do have a suggestion, but of course, the choice is yours. I suggest you stay far away from Kyra. Her eagerness to obey is commendable. Her desire to kill you is all-consuming."

With that, she slipped out of the mirror, not a controlled disappearance, but almost like falling out.

"Isolde." I continued to summon her, pushing for her attention.

What hit me next was a flash of vision. A burst of consciousness. I'd reached her, through the handmaiden's bond or my deal with Fairy Godmother, I couldn't say which. Isolde could ignore me, but she couldn't shut me out.

She moved through a forest, dark oak trees like giants shrouded in fog. And everywhere, abominations loomed. These made the ones we faced in Kingdom look like puppies and kittens. From the bone armor covering them, to ropes of muscle bulging from their backs, these things were built to annihilate.

Isolde—we—moved out of the forest, and behind her, the abominations came, shaking the ground as they lumbered forward after their creator and owner. She glanced back, then turned. As far as the eye could see, abominations lumbered among the trees. Not a dozen of them. Hundreds.

I shuddered, and Isolde shivered too. Her hands reached up, touching her cheeks, and a bolt of lancing pain ejected me from the vision. I don't know if I fell or was thrown off the chair, landing in a pile in the kitchen.

She knew I'd been watching. What I'd seen.

"Grimm!" I screamed, holding on to the bracelet, begging him to answer. Again and again, until my voice became hoarse and the neighbors pounded on the walls. If someone ever killed me, so long as he did it quietly, they wouldn't intervene. Heck, given the number of problems I'd had with the neighbors, they might take up a collection and send my killer a gift basket.

I LEFT THE apartment without looking back. Thoughts of Grimm's warnings didn't so much as slow me down. Not because I'd forgotten. I couldn't forget. Because I'd rather risk my own death than that of the people who mattered to me.

They had to know what was coming.

I drove to Liam's workshop first. His bachelor's bedroom there had hosted many a warm night where we lay in bed, drinking wine and talking. My key still worked, but inside the hearth was cold as ice, the forge unfired for days. Liam's bed, as well, stood neatly made, with no sign of him.

A dresser drawer stood slightly open, and a glint of gold

inside caught my eye. I'd always lived by the rule that I couldn't, wouldn't pry too deeply in Liam's pre-me days. I expected to find a copy of "Busty Babes from 'Bama." Instead, I drew out a single gold coin, thick as my hand, as big around as a dinner plate. Hieroglyphic-like characters ringed the edges. Vampirese characters.

I'd seen the coin once, right after Svetlana moved in. Liam did some contract work guarding vampires, and as a reward, gained that coin.

The coin that represented their debt to him, a debt that by all rights should have included everything they owned. The vampires objected to this, and so for now, Grimm continued negotiating on Liam's behalf.

I'd made him hide it after watching Svetlana drool at it more times than I could count. The thing was, while Svetlana might be undergoing reconstructive surgery, she had ways of finding Liam that bordered on supernatural. I knew, because I'd made a few efforts to lose her over the years.

From Liam's collection of tool bags, I stole a heavy leather bag and slipped the coin into it, locked up the shop, and headed to most likely hideout number two, Ari's apartment. Now that it was no longer haunted by an undead sorcerer, the basement made a nice guest room.

My key let me in, and I smiled when I heard the clink of dishes in the kitchen. I ran through the living room, around the corner, and nearly plowed over a short, balding man with salt-and-pepper hair.

"You?" I stared at him. "What are you doing in Ari's kitchen?"

The Adversary looked back at me. "An act of pure evil. I've moved every item in her kitchen to a different place and switched all the drawers."

"And?" I crossed my arms and tapped my foot.

He turned away from me. "I put three socks without matches in her laundry basket. I stole them from a woman in Illinois. It's going to drive her crazy."

"How in Inferno did you get in here?" He shouldn't have been able to cross the threshold. Demons and most other celestial entities couldn't enter someone's home without an invitation. What mattered wasn't the words, but the intent to allow them in.

"That sweet little princess invited me in. Tried her charms." He looked around, to see if anyone was watching. "They don't work on me, but she doesn't know that."

"If you harm her, I'll find a way to kill you too. People said fairies couldn't die until I killed one. I wouldn't bet against me." I leaned over him, using my inch of height to try to intimidate the Lord of Destruction. I had a history of picking fights with entities I couldn't possibly hope to win, but when my family and friends were threatened, reason went out the window.

"Oh, please. Your righteous fury is very touching, but you needn't worry. It's so much more entertaining to torment Ari with everyday evils." Nickolas Scratch rolled his eyes. "Also, I brought her a pet."

Ari's last dog, a hellhound named Yeller, had been kicked out of Inferno for being a runt and not devouring souls fast enough. "She doesn't want a puppy."

Nick turned and walked to Ari's staircase, where a produce box sat. "How will she feel about three of them?" He opened the box, and three puppy heads with glowing red eyes poked out.

"She'll kill you. I wouldn't bet against her either."

Nick reached in and lifted out a single body attached to all three heads. "These guys were getting picked on for not devouring the damned fast enough. I couldn't help thinking of her. The other day she told me how much she missed Yeller, or as we called him, Hellhound 122387548."

Even standing in the presence of the master of Inferno, my blood turned to ice. "When did you see her?"

"She invited me over to talk about Black Magic. Wanted my blessing for some rituals that I haven't seen for a while."

"Please tell me you didn't say yes."

Nick shook his head. "That's not up to me. Or you. The princess will make her own decisions."

"Do you know where she is?"

Nick unplugged Ari's television and bent the prong so it wouldn't fit tightly. "No idea, but if you catch up with her, tell her to be careful. I wouldn't wish those spells on anyone, but I won't stop humans from performing them if it's their choice."

I left the devil in my best friend's living room, feeding pairs of her designer shoes to a single puppy, and drove to Wyatt's house. Technically, his mother's house.

She met me at the door, her face lined with worried wrinkles. "Young woman, you are too late. They left to prepare for the ritual a hour ago."

"Where? When?"

"I believe they intend to dispatch a few wandering monsters, then . . . perform a secret ritual." She sat down on her porch swing, looking lost.

"Where is Wyatt?"

"With Arianna. You know, he truly loves her." A tear glistened at the edge of her eye.

"I know."

"Then go home, and wait, just as I will. My son will not come home after this. I know it." She hung her head.

I ran for the car, decided that come hell or high water, I wouldn't be the reason my friends died. I could try to meet Liam and Ari at the bridge, but that would only help if I had a column of tanks to back them up. Thing was, I knew someone who might be able to pull it off. I just needed to make Grimm pay attention to me, and the Agency, that was his baby. Odds were, he'd be paying at least partial attention to what happened there. As fast as the traffic allowed, I raced there. When I pulled into the parking garage, I ran past the cargo workers and straight into the stairwell. From there, I made it up to our floor in record time.

I stood in the stairwell, planning my next move. Service entrance, secret entrance, or front lobby—no matter which way, I was likely to encounter hostile employees. One employee, in particular, was hostile before, during, and after I worked with her.

I reached for the stairwell door and it blew open, hitting me in the face.

"Hands up." Rosa's voice boomed in the stairwell.

I opened my eyes to find a shotgun pointed squarely at my head.

Twenty-Four

"ON YOUR KNEES, hands in the air." Rosa spoke without waiting for me, taking a step into the stairwell with me. The better to blow a hole straight through me.

"I need to speak to Fairy Godfather." I forced my eyes to stay open, still seeing pixies from where my head had an unexpected meeting with the door.

She shook her head. "He isn't answering us anymore."

Those words hit me harder than any shotgun blast, ever. Not their content. Their length. Rosa avoided speaking in complete sentences where I was involved. Grunts and baleful stares were as much her native tongue as Spanish.

"He's helping Arianna and Liam with a ritual. I need to find them. Please."

Rosa hefted the shotgun, holding it with her off hand, since there was no way her wounds had healed. "This is all your fault. I told him, make the *girl* be a shopkeeper. Make the girl be some princess's handmaiden. But does he listen to me? No. He says, 'Rosa, be nice to the new girl. She'll be my new agent.' You never fooled me." Rosa slipped the safety off, peering down the barrel at me.

I struggled to keep from lunging at her, held in place only by the knowledge that even in her stitched-up state, she could pull the trigger faster than I could grab her. "I'm sick of you blaming me for everything. I never did anything to you."

"You brought another fairy down on us, and a crazy queen, and hordes of demons. The wheel of cheese had your name on it. You cause nothing but trouble."

Now, the demons, I was guilty as charged. Tricked, but guilty. The crazy queen, sort of, but then again, the queen's son had planned to toss Ari out a window after marrying her. The fairy was going to cause trouble to begin with, but the cheese, that was not my fault.

I gathered myself for a lunge, and nearly shrieked when the stairwell door pushed open.

Mikey poked his head in through the door, standing so tall he grazed the exit sign. "Everything okay in here?"

"This doesn't concern you, Michael. Go back to cargo." Rosa swung the shotgun around in his direction. "Go on."

"Marissa, last time I checked, humans are lousy at regeneration." Mikey looked over to me.

Rosa bumped him in the chest with the barrel. "Get out, Michael. This doesn't concern you."

The darkest part of me leaped to the fore, screaming to do what it did best. Watching her turn her beef with me on other people made me so angry the world went white. My upraised hands turned to fists, and my right hand closed around a familiar weight. The thorn sword handle, called by my anger.

"Rosa, I said you were fired." I waited, and as she swung back to me, I summoned the blade, driving it through the middle of her shotgun like it was licorice.

Her gun roared and exploded in her hands, the shells disintegrating. I lunged to my feet, slamming her back into the wall, and bore down on the shoulder with stitches.

Rosa shrieked in pain and collapsed in front of me. She didn't get up.

The sword in my hand called to me, for blood and vengeance. Revenge for every time she'd treated me like trash or ignored me. She'd given me more curses than an army of sailor witches, and more evil eyes than a convention of auditors with glasses.

The shadow me wanted to kill her. It was right, it whispered. She deserved it.

With that thought, the Black Queen's words came back to me. How it would be easier and easier to kill. With a gasp, I threw the sword down the stairs, where it clattered against the metal.

Mikey sat down on the stairs, motioning for me to join him. "She really doesn't like you."

"I know, and as much as I want to repay her for treating me like crap, I don't have time. I have to find Liam and Ari."

"They left thirty minutes ago through the portal. They even brought that string bean of a boyfriend with them." Mikey reached over and checked Rosa's for a pulse. "Good news is, she's too mean to die. Bad news is, she'll still be as mean when she wakes up."

"What were they going to do with Wyatt?"

"Heck if I know. Magic is a bunch of gibberish, but I'm guessing from the way he looked, he's the sacrifice in the ritual to give her power." Mikey caught the look of fear and shock on my face and shrugged. "Hey, it's the best he could do. You know, he mentioned wanting to do his part, and the blood of a prince ought to do the trick. You know, Black Magic ain't free."

I stood, and stumbled down a couple of stairs. "Then I'm too late. Kyra is taking over an army of those abominations. Death told me I had to stop her, but I don't have an army. I don't even have an agency."

Mikey nodded. "Isn't everyone trying to rescue you? I mean, that's the point of all this, right?"

"I've never really been the type to get rescued." I let gravity lead me down the stairs. When I last looked back, Mikey was still sitting on the stairwell next to Rosa, lost in thought.

DESPITE GRIMM'S PREDICTIONS, I made it back to my place without being mangled by anything or anyone. I'd formulated a new plan along the way. One that involved my taking a suitcase full of cash and purchasing shoulder-mounted rocket launchers, then surprising Ari and Liam. Nothing says I love you like rocket-propelled weapons.

In the empty apartment, I wallowed in tears and cereal while I made a few cell phone calls to my black-market arms suppliers. While I waited for back-alley deals to come together, I poured a bowl of cereal and drowned my loneliness with milk, sugar, and processed grain.

The knock at my door I dismissed as an errant Jehovah's Witness, a Girl Scout selling cookies, or the fire department, here to tell me that once more, my building was on fire. I didn't care. The problem was, whoever it was kept knocking.

And knocking.

"Go away." I didn't get up.

"Marissa, it's me." Mikey's voice caught me off guard. The wolf had never come to my house. Not ever. The fact that I still shot him on occasion probably factored into it a little.

"Go away, Mikey."

"I'll let you shoot me. Open the door so I can come in and talk to you. I figure you shouldn't be alone." He resumed pounding, so hard it made the door flex with each blow.

"Not by the hair on my chinny chin chin." I could make a pig of myself in private. I reached over to pour some more milk, aiming for that perfect cereal sugar sludge, when the door exploded.

I leaped to my feet, frantically searching for my gun. As the drywall dust settled, a hulking form, eight feet tall, black fur with a gray stripe down his back, emerged, tossing the doorknob to the side. "I'll huff, Marissa, and puff, and kick the door in." He spoke in his true voice, the guttural growl of a wolf.

"Go away," I said. "You don't want to be here. Probably not good for you."

He changed, melting slowly back into Intern Mikey instead of Monster Nightmare Mikey. "Marissa, come on. I'm a wolf. You're the pet of the most evil queen ever. We can totally hang out. Matter of fact, if that bitch shows her head, I'm likely—"

"Don't." The fear came for real, a sharp tingling cold that radiated from my spine. "Don't say a thing. Today, Kyra will claim her army, receive who only knows what kind of powers, and kill most of Kingdom. I can't stop her, but I'm getting ready to make a stand of my own. I'd rather you didn't get killed."

He grinned, his teeth still sharp. "I knew you cared about me. Sure, you've emptied more rounds into me than a target dummy, but you always keep your rifling nice and clean, and you use high-quality ammo. I'm hungry."

Feed a wolf. Always feed a hungry wolf, to keep them from feeding themselves. "Cereal? I have—"

The look on his face said cereal wasn't what he had in mind. He loped into the kitchen and threw open my fridge. "Sweet Kingdom, Marissa. You need to hit the grocery store. And the butcher." He turned around and grabbed the other fridge door.

"Don't mess with that." I threw a spoon at him. "That's from the Agency. Sent here as a warning."

"You got free food? Sweet. You know, Fairy Godfather made me keep my lunches in my private fridge. I wasn't allowed to go near this one."

Most wolves considered hunks of rotten meat good dining material. Grimm's arrangement for a private fridge for Mikey probably saved us a number of conflicts, and I'd personally ordered all the interns to stay away from the main one after altercations with the cheese claimed too many lives.

Mikey wrenched the door clean off. Now Grimm would make me pay for a new fridge. "Marissa." The growl in his voice shook, as if he fought an internal battle.

"Don't touch it. It might be the only thing worse than the Black Queen."

Mikey reached inside and slid the wheel of cheese out, gingerly carrying it over to the table. "Where did you get this?" His fingers ended in long claws, and with each breath, ripples of fur grew out from his skin, then retracted in.

While he fixed his gaze on the cheese, I slid the chair back, forming a plan. Straight to the kitchen, out the window, jump. Three stories down to the Dumpster—I might survive. I glanced up at him one more time and found red eyes fixed on me.

"Don't move, Marissa." He reached out with one monstrous claw and put it on my shoulder. "Don't run. Answer the question."

I did my best to ignore the threat of disembowelment and poured a mountain of cereal into my bowl. "My first birthday after I came to work for Grimm, he threw a party. Only one he ever threw that didn't end in a disaster. Next morning, we found it in the office fridge, with my name on the box. You don't want to pick a fight with the cheese, Mikey. I've lost count of the number of people who died trying to remove it, or sample it."

Mikey laughed, a guttural growl and howl combination. "Lupa's Tears were not meant for humans." He held up a claw and ran it along the top of the wheel, cutting into the rind. In response, a gash like an axe wound opened up across his head, gushing blood. Mikey licked the tip of his claw and shivered as the wounds closed. "It's time I had a slice."

Mikey rose and walked into the kitchen, going through my drawers. "Go on, ask."

"No, thank you." Ignorance really is bliss.

"Don't want to know what you had in your fridge? Lupa's Tears, Marissa. The holy grail for wolves. Made from the breast milk of Lupa herself, when she suckled the first wolves." He drew out a serrated knife and walked over, twirling it.

"Why is it called her tears?"

"We wolves are born with full sets of teeth. If you had to breast-feed six of them, you'd cry too." He slid out the chair, becoming more and more wolf with each moment. Then with a single, swift movement, he stabbed the cheese.

His eyeballs exploded, ruining my cereal.

Mikey waited until they took shape again, and cut. As the knife slid, bones crushed in his chest, and for a moment he turned blue, gasping for air. With a fork, he teased out a wedge onto the plate. "Care for a bite?"

I shook my head, as he spit out a tooth onto the plate.

"Your loss." With that, he cut into the wedge, spraying blood out his back, and put the bite into his throat. The sounds, the carnage, the spray of flesh, all meant one thing. There was no way in hell I'd get my deposit back.

*   *   *

I CAN'T SAY how long I hid under the table, while Mikey turned my apartment into a disgusting painting made from his own gore. While it might have been only minutes, I would have sworn it took hours. My cell phone rang exactly once, and Mikey threw it straight through the window. When his chair squealed, scraping back across the floor, I nearly screamed too.

Mikey threw the table off of me and roared, shaking the walls, and probably convincing the neighbors that Liam and I were fighting. I looked up and marveled. His fur, tinged with green, rippled with muscles. Mikey always had the bodybuilder figure, but that cheese gave him power like I'd never seen.

"Come." He grabbed me by the shoulder, slicing through my blouse. "Forget whatever you had planned. It's time to make things right, and get you an army of your own."

Twenty-Five

GOING ANYWHERE WITH a wolf is usually a bad idea. Going anywhere with a wolf who can't control his own changing, even worse. To top things off, as we raced down the highway at more than a hundred miles per hour, I held a wheel of the most evil cheese on earth in my lap. From what I could tell, the cheese was one of the "Do unto others" variety, so I held it with utmost care.

We made exactly one stop, at a costume store, where Mikey fit right in, wearing what the owner said was the gnarliest wolfman costume in history. And he was so right. Mikey repaid his compliment by actually paying for a costume instead of stealing it and daring the owner to shoot him.

While I belted myself in, Mikey tore open his bag. He slipped something out, a grin on his face so wide I could see every tooth in his mouth. Throwing open the driver's-side door, he slid in and tossed the costume into my lap.

"Hell no. Inferno no. No. I'm not wearing it." A "Little Red Riding Hood" costume sat in my lap, with crushed velvet hood and gold belt. "I made that mistake once."

It took Grimm a few dozen pigs and several months to gloss

over the fact that I paraded into a wolf town dressed as the queen of the wolf genocide. The real "Red" Riding Hood's hood was white as snow, when she started her crusade. Every time she killed a wolf, she drenched her cloak in its blood.

Mikey didn't take his eyes off the road. "Red took Lupa's Tears from us. Stole the source of our power and reduced us to pathetic animals."

"Alternate plan," I said. "You want to be their leader, you take it back." Mikey originally came to the Agency to kill me and bring back my heart. I hoped the wolves' most beloved cultural treasure would do the trick as well.

He shook his head. "No. You're a villain among my pack for daring dress like her on a negotiation run. Bring this back, and you'll become something else. A legend."

I EXPECTED THE guards waiting off the interstate. They let us drive through a cattle gate once Mikey flashed his canines. I got no attention, since I guess we were "Wolf and guest." Or snack. What I didn't expect was row after row of RVs, vans, and the occasional tour bus. The fields surrounding the wolf village had become one vast parking lot, like Wolf-stock. Dark clouds hung overhead, spraying the occasional band of wind-whipped rain.

"Where did everyone come from? Are they all—"

"Wolves? Yeah. The family's been gathering ever since the Black Queen came back. We bring in six tractor trailers full of pigs every day just to keep everyone fed." Mikey waved to a scraggly wolf with patches of mange. "I went to high school with him. And that one over there, she was my first . . . friend."

"You're gathering. To fight her?"

Mikey pulled his lips back into a wide grin. "Come on, Marissa. How long have we known each other? Wolves aren't exactly hero material." He clicked a button, and the doors locked. "You'll want to stay in the car until it's time." Hail plinked off the windshield as Mikey pulled to a stop.

The wolf village lay in a wide bowl of fields, a combination of old Amish and trailer park, wooden cabins and cinder-block barns. At least, it did the last time I was there. Now bonfires crackled around the edges, with furry figures gathered under pop-up awnings.

Mikey rolled down the window and stuck his head out, letting out a howl that would have made every vampire in Transylvania shiver. Wolves took up the cry, baying across the fields, howling until the noise split my ears. When the last plaintive cry died out, growling replaced it.

Mikey rolled up the window and looked over at me. "Get dressed. Whatever you do, don't get out of the car until I give the signal." He reached into the backseat and pulled out a wooden box. One he'd filched from my office. "Keep this handy."

I opened it, taking out a silver dagger. The blade twisted from the hilt to the tip like a corkscrew. One of Evangeline's knives, enchanted to stop wolves from regenerating. When I first joined the Agency, Evangeline showed me the ropes. She'd died fighting with the old Fenris, hell-bent on revenge. I kept her knives to remind me that retreat was always an option. Asking for help was always an option.

The silver blade in my hand reminded me of Evangeline. Foreign, frightening, and yet comforting. I nodded to Mikey, and he rolled the vehicle through the crowd, down toward the bonfire at the center. When we stopped, Mikey got out, changing as he did. From the tips of his toes to the alert ears on top of his head, he looked more like his grandfather than I could stomach.

Just looking at him, I couldn't stop the memories of Evangeline fighting with Fenris. Her gift, her skill, made her move faster than any human had right to, and it hadn't been enough. How could I hope to do any better?

A passel of wolves gathered around Mikey, though the tallest still stood a foot smaller than him. Their wagging tails and yipping barks made it clear they followed, and obeyed, his every word. When the same mangy wolf man Mikey waved to earlier pushed his way through, he brought a microphone.

Mikey tapped it, and the speakers amplified it like thunder. He growled, and the gathering fell silent, except for the patter of rain and distant thunder. "My family, I have returned. The Black Queen has come, calling us together."

A chorus of howls answered, yipping that echoed across the hillside.

"But," said Mikey, "we will not answer her call." The yipping and howling died out, replaced with the odd growl.

"Last time, we wolves answered her call. We acted as her army. And when the blood was spilled, who died? Wolves. When she was gone, who was left to be hunted like stray cats? The wolves. This time, we will remember what she did." Mikey's fur stood up, spiky from the rain, and water dripped from his tail.

Through the crowds, another wolf came. He didn't push so much as the wolves stampeded to get out of his way. Flashes of white fur among the bonfires were all I saw, until the crowd parted. He walked on four feet toward Mikey, then changed, shifting into a wolf man almost as large and wide. "I say we go to her now and take our rightful place."

Mikey shook his head, flinging water everywhere. "She already has an army, one she created. One of abominations, spells stitched into bodies. She has no need of wolves. And wolves have no need of her."

The white wolf drew himself up to full height, looking more like a polar bear than a wolf. "My great-great-great-grandfather was her commander in chief."

"And following him led us to where we are today, Snowball. We're weak. Mangy. Reduced to eating the young and helpless. Our greatest treasures were stolen while we warred on her behalf." Mikey flexed one claw, showing off the green tint at the ends, an infectious disease that only the most powerful wolves carried. "But they are lost no longer."

He flexed one tinged claw at me, and I scrambled to put on my hood. Part of me wanted to start the ignition and drive away, running over as many wolves as I could in the process. Mikey could easily be setting me up to die for the crimes of a woman long dead.

But I ran my fingers on the hilt of Evangeline's knife. Would she still be alive, if she'd let me help, trusted me? I tied the hood beneath my chin, wrapped the cloak over Lupa's Tears, and stepped out into the rainstorm.

Little Red Riding Hood, for the record, was an awful bitch, even by my standards. Killing people, sometimes that was necessary. I'd signed on Grimm's behalf for government assassination contracts, and killed Rip Van Winkle myself. Those were cases where murderers made a mockery of the law and left a pile of bodies in their wake. I agonized over every one, even if it wasn't my hand on the trigger. Red, on the other hand, took joy in the process. For her it went far beyond protection, beyond retribution, clear into genocide.

All eyes remained on me as I walked through the crowd. Whispers turned to growls, but the red hood all by itself repelled the wolves. And enraged them. The wind whipped my cape and drove rain into my eyes, leaving me almost blind as I struggled toward Mikey. The angry growls rose louder than the wind.

When I reached Mikey, he put one claw on my shoulder. "Four hundred years ago, Little Red Riding Hood stole our power and scattered our people. Four years ago, Marissa Locks killed my grandfather, the Fenris."

My blood ran cold as the falling rain as I waited for his next sentence.

"My orders were to bring back her heart. And so I have." He drew back my hood, revealing my face. "But I decide who I kill. I give the orders. I am the Fenris."

Snowball raised a claw toward me, but Mikey stepped between us.

"Why would anyone follow you?" The white wolf's ears flattened back on his head, and he bared his teeth. "You've grown softer than a vegetarian sausage."

Mikey looked over his shoulder at me. It was time. I pulled back my cape, revealing the cheese. Though I'd watched Mikey slice a wedge from it earlier, the cheese had regenerated, becoming whole.

"You'll follow me because I've made a deal with Red Riding Hood herself. The return of Lupa's Tears, in return for our help." Mikey took the platter from my hand, and held it high so that everyone could see. "I've already tasted of it. Follow me, and you can too."

A mountain of white fur leaped upon him.

The cheese went flying back, striking me in the chest. I caught it at the last moment, cradling it from the ground. Before me, Mikey and Snowball rolled, savaging each other, tearing flesh and bone, spraying blood.

And by all bets, Mikey was losing. Though his wounds healed within moments, Snowball tore new ones, blind to his own injuries. It wasn't that Mikey didn't tear into him. It was just that he seemed about as well matched as me versus Shigeru in a sword fight.

With a heave of his feet, Mikey threw Snowball back and leaped to his feet, then pounced.

Snowball sidestepped his pounce and kicked Mikey right into the bonfire. Mikey's fur caught fire and his skin crackled, but as he tried to leave, Snowball blocked him, knocking him back into the embers. Silver, like Evangeline's daggers, was a great way to kill wolves. Fire was a close second.

Each time, Mikey took longer to rise, and less force to drive back. The stench of burning wolf meat filled the air. He looked through the fire to me, his eyes pleading for help against a monster I didn't stand a chance against.

One last time, Mikey rose and crawled, unable to stand, trying to leave the flames. And Snowball waited, his lips bared. As Mikey reached the edge of the fire, Snowball drew back his foot, to kick him in the head.

Snowball never saw me coming. Never saw the silver dagger I drove through his spine and held there, one arm locked under his chin, the other gripping the dagger handle as I used my weight to work it back and forth.

Snowball spun, and stumbled back and forth, swiping at his own head with claws that could carve me like ham. Then one claw caught my fluttering cape, and he pulled on it, yanking me forward.

With my legs wrapped around him, I held on. Even as I choked and the world turned gray at the edges, I twisted the blade, driving it forward.

When he fell backwards, I didn't have time, or the presence of mind, to let go. Beneath four hundred pounds of animal I lay pinned, until at last darkness took the pain from my lungs.

Twenty-Six

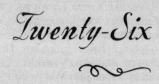

I WOKE TO rain on my face, puddling in my eyes. A monster huddled over me. *My* monster. I opened bloody lips, and croaked when I spoke. "Mikey?"

Patches of charred flesh covered him, mixed with new fur. He shifted enough to speak, his voice coming out a half growl. "You have no idea how much this hurts."

"Thought you liked barbecue."

"Eating it. Not being it." He wiped at his chin, brushing away streaks of blood.

Snowball's corpse lay a few feet away, his chest torn open. I didn't want or need confirmation on what had happened while I took a lack-of-oxygen nap. A few yards farther away, wolves lined up to take wafer-thin slices of Lupa's Tears, howling and gurgling as the cheese struck back at them.

I sat up and untied the hood that nearly got me killed, rubbing the tender patch under my neck where Snowball almost pulled my head off. "Any more challengers?"

"Nah." Mikey grinned, and while his mouth was open, a fresh tooth burst from the gums. "I gave my best friend a slice of the cheese and no one else wants to risk the both of us. They'll follow me anywhere now, which means they'll follow you anywhere. We're your army now and forever."

"No." Now it was time to reveal the other part of my plan. "Killing Kyra's army won't be enough. I can't leave the Black Queen with anything. You follow me until her army is dead. The moment it's over, I want your word you won't accept an order from me. Just disappear."

Mikey looked up to an old wolf, one whose fur had turned silver, where it hadn't fallen out. The elder wolf barked, short and choppy, and Mikey nodded. "You have yourself a deal."

"Get everyone into Middle Kingdom. Meet me at the west edge of the Plain of Agony." I stood up, brushing mud from my rear.

"Where are you going?"

I walked over to Snowball's corpse and wrestled out Evangeline's dagger. "I once watched a friend of mine die because she wouldn't ask for help. I'm not making that mistake. I'll call in every favor I can get my hands on."

Mikey whistled, and in response, a black wolf the size of a moving van lumbered over. "Kent, you're looking better after the cheese." The pattern of his fur reminded me of the mangy wolf from earlier. "Round up the packs. We're taking a road trip into Middle Kingdom, to the Plain of Agony. We'll meet you there."

We left the Pack of Packs behind, heading back into the city.

From the wolf village, we drove straight to my apartment, where my neighbors went out of their way to avoid eye contact with Mikey, even in his human form. My apartment door lay on its side, where I left it, and in the meantime my neighbors had helped themselves to my TV.

In fact, Grimm's spellbooks were the only things they hadn't touched. I kicked open the door to the guest room, where Svetlana basked under grow lights; her skin held a light green hue under the shell of her coffinatorium.

From my purse, I took out the debt coin, and tapped on the crystal.

Her eyes flew open, locking on the coin, then her gaze darted to me. "Go away. I am not yet ready."

I flipped the clasps on the coffinatorium, opening it to let the steamy atmosphere out. She didn't bother trying to cover her once again perky breasts, even under Mikey's hungry gaze.

"I'm here to make you an offer. You owe Liam everything, but you help me out, and you are free and clear. I hold the debt now." I clenched the coin in both hands, knowing this wasn't exactly true.

"Pomegranates. I crave pomegranates." She shimmied from her coffin and opened a crate of fruit. "What is it you want?"

"I need fighters. Warriors. Ugly sons of bitches to help me kill something that's already dead twice over. Abominations made of magic and flesh." I handed her the coin, more than a little creeped out at how her nipples grew hard as she gazed at it.

"You have them. I will bring ten of our finest warriors."

"Plain of Agony, west side. Don't kill the wolves. And what happens to your liege?" She'd always called Liam that.

"He is nothing to me now. We will be ready." She walked off to get dressed, her every step turning Mikey into a puddle of goo as disgusting as the ooze draining from the coffinatorium.

"Let's go." I grabbed him by the shoulder and dragged him out behind me.

In the hallway, he stopped, and honestly, I figured he was going to head back for another peek. Then he shook his head. "I was thinking—"

"Really? Tell me, what color are her eyes?"

Mikey blushed. "I mean, before we got here, I was thinking. We could use all the help we can get, right?"

He'd certainly been paying attention before our encounter with Svetlana. "Go on."

"I think we should make another stop." Mikey waved to me, and I followed him.

WHEN HE PULLED into the storm drain entrance, I started to wonder if Mikey hadn't had quite enough time to recover from his charcoal makeover. Mikey trekked to the trunk and came back with a pair of muck boots, which he handed to me.

"You don't need a pair?" I slipped mine on and stepped out into six inches of sewage.

"I'm good." He trotted off barefoot into the sewers, and I did my best to keep up.

After several turns and twists, Mikey stopped and sniffed the air at each corner, then headed onward at a trot. If you've ever imagined sewers as wide-open spaces, with room to stand and nice wide sidewalks, you would be unpleasantly surprised by parts of the normal sewer system. Unlike Kingdom, where you could drive a boat through the tunnels, at each turn, the ceiling dipped lower. If Mikey couldn't have walked on four legs, his head would have bent backwards. We reached one junction, where feeder pipes dripped slime, and Mikey stopped. He stood, changing back, and whistled. The tunnels echoed the whistle, farther and farther away in the darkness.

"We don't need an alligator. Unless you have an army of them." Come to think of it, we hadn't had giant alligator problems for at least a couple of years. I stepped up to give Mikey a pat on the back, and froze. From one pipe, a pair of glowing red eyes stared back at me. And another pair, and another. I held still, very still, as all around me, glowing eyes gleamed back at me.

"All the alligators got eaten a few years back." A low hum shook the surface of the sewage stream. Mikey looked down at me and nodded. "She's here."

Splashing footsteps echoed from the tunnel ahead, and the humming became louder. Recognizable. The words of "Mary Had a Little Lamb" erupted from my lips, as from the sewer ahead, a woman emerged.

Six feet tall, white complexion, and more hooks on her body piercings than a tacklebox, she wore her black hair in a bouffant cut. Around her feet a flock of deadly poodles danced, yipping and licking her feet. Their razor-sharp teeth gleamed in the light of Mikey's flashlight.

He ignored the poodles and picked up Beth, giving her a hug that seemed more than a little personal. "Hey, sweet thing."

"Down, boy." Beth hummed on her kazoo, and he almost dropped her. "Marissa."

"Beth." Last time I'd seen her, she was supposed to run a few thousand poodles off into the bay. Instead, she disappeared, taking all the poodles with her. I never doubted she'd show up again, but I didn't exactly expect these circumstances.

"We were wondering if you might be interested in helping us out." Mikey knelt and tickled a poodle under the chin, ignoring the chunks of flesh it tore from him.

Beth bent over, petting her darlings, before she turned back to us. "And why would I do that? What could you possibly offer me?"

Air freshener, for certain. A supply of antibiotics, real silver jewelry instead of that cheap crap she favored. I could offer her a lot. But there was one thing, in particular, I knew she'd want. "First pick. Every year, first choice of the poodles. For as long as I work at the Agency."

For the last couple of years, we'd had trouble disposing of even small groups of poodles. Sometimes things went according to plan, with only a few casualties before we could destroy them. Other times, our mercenaries would arrive to find only the remnants of her rampage.

"First call. They all belong to me." Beth stepped up to Mikey and hummed.

"Plain of Agony in Middle Kingdom." He kissed her, then rubbed his muzzle on her head. "I'll bring the big dogs. You bring the small ones."

"One condition." I interrupted their cuddle time, earning growls from the entire room. "When the battle is over, you bug out. Don't stick around."

Beth shrugged. "It takes me hours to groom them for bed anyway."

I couldn't wait to get out of there. When we slogged our way back to the car, I figured it was time to reveal the last recruitment drive. "Next up, let's hit Kingdom. We've got exactly one stop left, and then it's time to rally the troops."

On the way there, I tried repeatedly to contact Grimm, but I didn't even get so much as a glimmer. By the time we pulled past the gates into High Kingdom, I halfway expected the raging fires and mass chaos in the streets.

Singing flower vendors fought with animal-companion shopkeepers, and ladies in ball dresses sported black eyes and bruises as they fought to the death over breakfast.

Mikey drove on the sidewalks as necessary, employing an "if they didn't want to get run over, they would have moved" philosophy. He watched a mob chase a gingerbread man down the street and whistled. "The Agency hasn't been able to move any groceries in for the last week. Even worse, no champagne for two and a half days."

"Take me to the post office. And stay clear when we get there."

Mikey whined. "I'm an eight-foot-tall nightmare wolf. You think you can do better than that?"

I laughed and stepped out of the car. "You aren't bad for a wolf, but I've got you beat. In there, I'm a goddess."

I threw open both doors to the Kingdom Post Office, and bellowed at the top of my lungs, "Gnomes, I command you to come forth. I am Marissa, Bringer of Death, and I demand your obedience."

Drums burst into a beat, rumbling so loudly they shook me, echoing down the streets of Kingdom, until at last the rumble cut off, and a single purple gnome stepped out. He turned and knelt, showing my signature on his rear end. "What would you have of us?"

"I'm going to hunt giants. Monsters twenty times the size of a single gnome. Abominations made of flesh and magic, too foul for most spell casters to create. I ask for your aid." I bowed to him, and Petri's eyes grew wide. "In return, I will make sure that the office supplies are forever refilled. Each warrior will receive his own stapler and his body weight in staples. Two reams of paper to the gnome who fells one of these monsters, and a box of paper clips for every eye."

A waterfall of tiny shouts accompanied the mass of gnomes who burst forth, waving letter openers and wearing baby-wipe loincloths.

Petri pounded his letter opener on the ground until the group fell silent. "It is our honor to serve."

"Thank you. I have one more request. When the battle is done, you will disappear into the shadows and await the delivery of your spoils."

"It will be our greatest priority to stamp out these monsters. To the mail trucks!" Petri shouted, and they rushed off. I dashed off the address, Plain of Agony, Middle Kingdom, and stuck it to the back of Petri along with a page of stamps. Behind me, Mikey stood, a look of absolute shock on his face.

I patted him on the arm as I got in the car. "Told you I was a goddess."

Twenty-Seven

❧

THE MOMENT WE turned off the road in Middle Kingdom, we arrived at the Plain of Agony. Lush green grass spread as far as the eye could see, split only by a sparkling stream where trout leaped.

Here and there, glowing groves of trees bore fruit day or night. Only a few pesky rabbits hopped to and fro, frolicking in the grass while they waited for a wyvern to devour them.

Oh, sure, at one point the Plain of Agony was a vast wasteland of mud. Back then, lost spirits roamed the cursed ground, tormented for eternity, while a river of boiling mud killed every living thing for miles.

If you give the lost souls a book of sudoku puzzles and get the battery manufacturing plant upstream to stop dumping raw acid into the water, you'll be surprised how nice a place could turn in a few years. Of course, all the maps had "plain of agony," and the locals all gave directions like "If you reach the plain of agony, you've gone too far."

So the name stuck. A row of RVs stood along the edge of the plain. Around them, wolves stretched and scratched while they waited. Others chased rabbits who were definitely not equipped for what big teeth they had. A dozen yards away, a group of vampires munched on fresh apples of the non-exploding, put-you-into-a-coma type. Most fearsome, however, were the mass of white poodles, all laying like tiny sphinxes before their mistress.

I called the leaders together for a huddle and laid down my plan. "Kyra will have her army by now, but they have to march from the edge of the plain to here, then up to the castle, and out into High Kingdom. Our job is to make sure they don't make it there."

Svetlana spit out a peach pit and wiped the glistening juice from her lips. "And what will we be killing?"

"Abominations. Dead flesh reanimated and lashed together into something sort of like a giant. Driven by spells." When I added the last part, she recoiled.

"Disgusting. We will tear them to pieces."

I nodded. "Gnomes and poodles are good for removing flesh, which you'll have to do. Take out the heart or off the head, either will kill these things. Hey, where are my gnomes?"

Beth jerked her thumb over her shoulder toward a pop-up tent, where a phalanx of gnomes mounted up on poodles. "Twice the tiny terror."

I meant to point out that my plan involved the gnomes using mail trucks, but before I could speak, Svetlana held up her hand. She peered out across the plain, into the horizon. "They come."

And they did.

A cloud of dust rose on the horizon, and it looked like a tidal wave of misshapen flesh, thundering along, straight toward us. The abominations sprinted like Olympic runners, each step covering twenty feet.

"Ready!" I summoned my thorn sword, wishing my gun packed larger bullets, and braced myself for the onslaught.

Closer and closer the wave came, their eyes bulging from their heads, running so wild they crashed into one another, only to rise and take off again. Twenty paces out the wolves ran to meet them. My wolves leaped onto the leaders, tore their stomachs open, and left them thrashing on the ground. My gnomish army swarmed out behind the wolves, covering the downed creatures.

I swung the blade up and leaped forward as the first one came at me—

And bounded clean over me. One by one, they thundered over us like a herd of gazelle, sprinting past us and plowing into buildings in Middle Kingdom. A few dozen thrashed on the ground before us, as wolves tore their hearts out and tossed them to waiting poodles.

"Do we chase?" Mikey roared, his hands covered in blood.

Like that was going to work. They moved so fast a chase was useless. "We'll never catch them. I didn't expect them to run away from us."

Svetlana shook her head. "Not us. They run as prey run, driven by fear."

"Fear of what?" I spun from Middle Kingdom to look out across the plain, and I knew what would drive an abomination to terror.

Shapes the size of true giants lumbered across the plain. Each more than a hundred feet tall, each laced with bone and thorns. A body that size couldn't have a single heart. It would have dozens, each of which had to be torn out to kill it.

Isolde had taken her lesser abominations and stitched them together into these, a nightmare's nightmare. Where the flock before had run wild, these marched in rank, keeping time.

"We can't fight them here—three steps and they'd pass into the populated parts of Middle Kingdom," I shouted, hoping the others could hear me.

Mikey nodded, and the wolves took up a howling, followed by the poodles and the unearthly shriek of a thousand angry gnomes. He ran to me, hefted me onto his back like a backpack, and crouched.

Kingdom help me, I gave the order. "Charge!"

We fanned out across the plain, rushing forward so my hair flew out behind me. Mikey shifted, his feet gathering in leaps and bounds as he tore ahead, then he spun and rolled me into the grass as he leaped for the first one.

With hands the size of a pickup truck, it tried to grab him. Each finger was made of a body molded together, sewn into a misshapen digit. The problem with grabbing him was that Mikey moved way too fast. By the time its fists reached where Mikey had been, he was already climbing its rib cage like a ladder and burrowing into its chest.

The abomination stumbled and fell, raking fingers at its own chest, and that gave me the key. "Take out the feet. Drop them and then kill!" With that, I ran forward, slicing the big toe off of the one Mikey attacked, then following it up with a cut to the Achilles tendon.

Like a gore worm, Mikey erupted from its back, sliding down the spine. "There's too many hearts. I can't kill them all at once."

I whistled, and waved for a pack of poodle riders. "Gnaw through to the hearts. Get a vampire to listen and tell you where they are."

Around me giants fell, crippled, and yet the waves of monsters went on, farther than I could see. I grabbed Mikey by the fur and nearly lost my bowels for it as he spun, a look of feral rage on his face.

I shouted to be heard. "This isn't going to work. We have to cut off the head."

Mikey's gaze locked on the head of the abomination, and he growled like a bulldozer.

"Not like that." I pointed farther out to where two smaller abominations marched, and the diminutive human between them. "That's Kyra. Get me to her. If I am in charge, I can command those monsters to hold still while we kill them."

Mikey changed into a full wolf, and I slipped onto his back, clutching fur as he leaped onto a still-moving body. Three bounds later, he stopped a few yards from Beth. She focused on humming "The Battle Hymn of the Republic" on a bullhorn.

I shouted over her hum. "We're going after Kyra."

Svetlana stopped tearing flesh from an abomination to join us and nodded. "Bring the small ones, and let us make it so."

With a pack of gnome cavalry, a handful of wolves, and a blond vampire, we set out to put an end to the assault. Moving among the creatures proved easier than I feared. While these were more intelligent, their ponderous size meant we'd passed under they before they could even begin to reach us.

And that was the key. These weren't warriors. They were destruction machinery, built to tear down every building in High Kingdom and Low Kingdom. Grimm said the city was self-reinforcing, but that meant the destruction of a building in the city wouldn't crush the corresponding one in the other layer of the city. The destruction of two of the three would resonate.

The Black Queen truly meant to wipe Kingdom clean, and most of the city as well.

I leaned forward to explain to Mikey right as a blast of orange spell power hit us. Mikey blew to the side like a puff of cotton. I flew headfirst for the ground, managing to hit shoulder first and roll like a rag doll. I struggled to my feet, and at last found Kyra.

She'd grown even more beautiful than before, her blond hair turning crystalline silver, her chin coming to a graceful point. And she fired spells from her hands like bullets. One caught a gnome and exploded him into a mist of blood and office supplies.

Then she turned her gaze to me. "Do you like my army? And my powers?" She raised her hands at me, and I tensed, knowing I couldn't possibly dodge.

A burst of purple light blinded me for a moment . . . and that was all.

I opened my eyes to find my fingers still attached and my brain mostly functional. She unleashed her spells on me again and again, which made for a pretty light show, but a lousy weapon. I held up my wrist, showing the handmaiden's mark. "Your powers don't work on me. And I have an army of my own."

Behind Kyra, a smaller abomination lumbered. One I recognized, somewhat. The fleshling Irina Mihail inhabited. She'd upgraded, sporting a set of teeth that no longer fit in the mouth, and a bone bra to hold the hideous flesh bags on her chest. "It is finally time for my wrath, Marissa." Her teeth made the words nearly impossible to understand.

"No. The unworthy handmaiden is mine. Kill everyone with her." Kyra spoke with authority, and Monster Irina turned away, heading for the grass where Mikey lay. Poodles covered him, their ears flattened back, their eyes wide, and a few yards away, Beth turned her megaphone on Irina.

"Down." She hummed into the microphone, and only experience kept my knees from bending. Half a dozen poodles collapsed at her command, then leaped back up.

The Monster Irina, on the other hand, shook her head from side to side, like she'd had a short nap, and continued on.

And that was the point at which Kyra came for me. With a cry of rage, she charged, her thorn sword in hand. I already had mine, shaking it back and forth in an attempt to trigger the blade. No matter how I squeezed it, the thorns wouldn't respond.

"Mikey!" I threw the handle toward him, and he caught it offhand. In his grip, the blade erupted, locking together into an ebony sword.

He glanced down at it and shook his head. "Ummm, thanks, but I'm fine." Mikey lobbed it like a javelin toward me, coming distressingly close to my feet.

I seized the sword and turned to face Kyra, but as I raised it, the pain of Shigeru's blows hit my shoulder. At least the memory of them did. Instead of swinging my blade up to meet her blow, I waited and sidestepped, letting her momentum carry her past.

She lunged back, slinging the blade in an arc, and this time, I ducked and moved behind her, my blade at the ready.

Like a river in motion, Kyra danced a ballet of blades, where each lunge flowed into the next and every swing set her up to strike again.

I couldn't hope to match her skill, but the longer she attacked, the more natural my responses became. Step and turn, duck and push her away.

This was what Shigeru meant to teach me. Not how to strike a death blow. How to avoid one. How to bide my time, as the battle, if you could call it that, roved from side to side.

Because Kyra tired.

The thorn blade might have been magic, but that didn't mean it weighed nothing. With every blow, she took longer to recover her balance. Each time, I stepped farther away, and she lost more momentum. One wild overhead swing sent her blade flying, and she scrambled after it, sure I was at her back.

I wasn't. My momentary distraction turned into a full-blown horror, because when I looked up, Monster Irina held Beth by the neck in one fist, and Mikey by the head in the other. Poodles hung like chains from Irina's flesh, gnawing without result on her armor-like skin.

She shook them. Whipping them back and forth like rag dolls. Beth's arms jerked once, then went limp.

Mikey's ears flattened back, and the whining howl of grief that rose from his chest pierced the battle din. Foam dripped from his lips as he whipped his hind legs up, raking her tendons with his hind claws until she dropped him. Poodles ringed Irina, gnawing on the bone armor that covered her, but it was the eight-foot-tall Dire Wolf who spelled death.

If Kyra had managed to keep her mouth shut, I would have died right there.

Instead, her cry of rage gave me the one moment I needed to see the blade coming and spin to the side. And while I didn't stab her, I did bring my own blade around, sliding it across her exposed calf muscles while she strained to stop her own momentum.

Kyra collapsed forward, her legs useless.

Mikey's roar pulled my gaze to him. Locked in a death embrace with Irina, she squeezed his ribs between her hands, attempting to crush him. When she opened her mouth, he shoved his claw down her throat.

She bit the arm off cleanly.

Blood showered everything, spurting from Mikey's shoulder, while she continued to crush him. And her face froze. Her eyes bulged, and her mouth fell open. The skin on her chest rippled and moved until a claw burst through it, the remains of her heart still dripping from it.

Mikey limped over and drew out his arm, pressing it together at the joint.

Kyra, on the other hand, made no effort to move. Not even when I rolled her over, her sword in my left hand, my own in her right. She looked up at me, blood spattering that crystalline hair, and wept. "Please. Don't go after my son—"

"I won't." How could she think that? But putting myself in her position, if she had won, she wouldn't stop with my death. "Yield."

She nodded, and a flush of power swept over me, then drained as quickly as it came. My hands didn't glow purple. My eyes didn't see through lead. I held up my hand and commanded, "Lie down. Do not move."

I hadn't realized how far from the battlefront we'd become. While I waged my own private battle, the war machines had continued their march. At the far edge of the plain, their hazy forms kneeled, waiting for death.

"End this quickly. Please." Kyra's plea turned me back toward her.

"No." I looked around, wondering where Mikey went. The pile of gore that once housed Irina Mihail still oozed onto the grass, but the wolf and his piper were gone.

"You promised."

I threw her sword away, and mine after it. "I'm not a killer."

"My queen will save me." The crazed smile on her face couldn't come close to knowing the truth. Too late I realized what she meant to do, grabbing the golden bracer on her arm. "Come to me."

In that instant, Isolde was there, a vision in black, her face so majestic it made me want to kneel, her eyes so deep they contained the secrets of the universe. She looked at me, and at Kyra.

I waited for the rage.

Instead she smiled. "So the culling happened after all. An army for an army. A handmaiden for a handmaiden. It makes no difference to me." Then she looked over to me. "Finish it."

Kyra's mouth fell open in shock, gasping, as the certainty of her doom took hold. "My queen."

"The next words shall be your last." Isolde looked down on her like a dying dog. "Kill her, Marissa."

"Do it yourself. I may be your handmaiden, but I'm not your assassin." I turned to leave, and the compulsion seized me.

"My second command to you is given, darling. Finish the culling with her death."

My hands and feet moved without my prompt. I stumbled to where I'd thrown the sword and seized it. I fought the compulsion, making the tip waver, but my gaze darted to the Black Queen, and the shock, surprise on her face. Grimm was right. She'd meant to order me to kill, but calling me darling, even Isolde knew that wasn't right. She mouthed the words to herself over and over, her gaze distant.

Seized by the compulsion, I stepped forward and drove the sword through Kyra's heart.

Her body arched up as much as the blade would let it, pain driving her eyes wide open. Then she slumped against the ground. Her eyes gazed upward, vacant, her limbs limp.

"Now you may take your army and finish what she could not." Isolde spoke behind me, and I spun, my blade ready to claim her life, and my own if need be.

The Plain of Agony contained only monster corpses, a few dead wolves, and an overturned mail truck. "I have no army. And neither do you." I'd demanded my army desert me for exactly this moment, and this reason.

Now anger twisted her face as she understood the depths of my deception. "You planned this."

"I did."

"You've accomplished nothing. I will still rule Kingdom, and see it burn. Tonight my pawn settles the matter, and I will take her oath of fealty." Her face said one thing; the tone in her voice, the quaver, betrayed the lie.

Gwendolyn. And with her name came another. Ari. I couldn't let the Black Queen attack her again. "No."

Isolde's eyes lit up. "Fear. I feel it in your words. What is it you fear? My triumph? No. Trust me, girl. I will find what you fear, and use it to mold you into my tool, my weapon."

"I'm not afraid of you." And in that moment, it was the

truth. "You promised me anything I wanted, for a simple answer."

As she looked at me again I almost fell into those eyes, that face that seemed unearthly.

"Of course, handmaiden. At your leisure, you may guess."

I gathered my courage. "I know what the first lie you told was."

"Really? Are you sure? Tell me, handmaiden? What were the words with which I knew my power?"

I looked at her. An educated guess, Grimm had said. But I thought about what she'd done to Kyra. About what she'd done to me. Now I *knew*. "Your first lie was to yourself. You said, 'I am beautiful.'"

Twenty-Eight

~~~

ISOLDE TURNED HER back to me, hiding the shock I'd already seen. "What is your wish, handmaiden?"

"I have your signet ring. Let me be your proxy to the court and receive the oath from Gwendolyn."

"You desire the court. And here I thought the lust for power had no hold on you." She paused, and the manacle on my arm hummed. "No, you think you can challenge my plans by doing so. You are mistaken, so I honor your request, and you will visit in my stead. The final challenge begins in less than two hours. Do not be late, my murderer."

My blood boiled at the word, though the stains on my sword condemned me. I gritted my teeth, hissing at her. "I'm not a killer."

When she turned back toward me, the serene smile on her face made me want to tear it off her face. "It seems I'm not the only one lying to myself. You've killed for me twice. I can't compel anyone to do *anything*. I can give you reasons, but I can't take away choices."

Before I could answer, before I could act, she summoned a portal around herself, and faded into nothing. Could it be that she truly had no idea of Fairy Godmother's power? If so, it might be the key to her undoing.

The Plain of Agony became the Plain of Despair as I forced my sore muscles to stand, and limped back toward Middle Kingdom. It wasn't until I crossed the stream dividing it that I became aware I wasn't alone.

At the corner of my eye, something moved to and fro, never quite in focus. I closed one eye and looked through the veil. A surge of blinding light hit me, causing me to flinch.

"I didn't expect you to look for me that way, Marissa," said the harbinger Death.

I walked on, limping. "Leave me alone."

Death stepped into being alongside me, and slipped his arm around my shoulder. Though he appeared as an eighty-year-old Chinese man, he supported me like I was made of rice paper. "I'm finishing up. Collecting souls. Listening."

"Listening to what?"

"Stories. Sometimes when people die, all they really want is to know someone will remember their life. So I listen while they tell me. Some have only a few words. Some talk for what you would call years. Then they go with me." Death opened his right hand, where an orb of light like a firefly rested. "I collected Irina Mihail for you."

"Then drag her straight to Inferno."

Death stopped, forcing me to as well. "I can't. If I take her back that way, people will know she was missing. I'm going to give her to you. You can give her back to the Adversary next time you see him." Death pressed his palm to mine, and the globe of light stuck to it.

Despite my best attempts, I couldn't shake it off. It was just like the time I had a live lobster glued to my palm, only more disgusting.

"Marissa," said Death, "do the same thing to her son, and you'll have the Adversary off your back."

I pushed Death away, throwing his arm off me. "Gnomes died. Wolves died. Beth is missing."

"Ah, the piper. She took a stroll with me a few minutes ago."

I'd held out against all hope that maybe she'd only been

injured. That Mikey had rescued her. As the thought of yet another death sank in, my anger rose. "Don't talk about this like it's some simple errand."

"Marissa, for me, this is. You should know, the piper liked you a lot. Couldn't stop talking about how you helped her."

"I have to help Mikey arrange a funeral service." A tear rolled down my cheek, followed by another, and a river.

Death reached into his pocket and pulled out a handkerchief. "I wouldn't worry about that. The wolf did what she wanted and fed the piper's bones to her dogs. Honestly, I don't think she would have gone with me otherwise. She really loved them."

I looked around, and found myself at the edge of the plain just outside of Middle Kingdom. "How did we—"

"Don't ask." Death pressed a business card into my palm, an address in Middle Kingdom. "A princess choked to death on a cherry stone a few hours ago. Her closet door is still connected to the court."

"I'm not going to the court. Ari and Liam should be somewhere here." I tried summoning Grimm again and again, to no effect.

Death put his hand on my wrist. "I cleaned up after their mess earlier. You know those two think they saved the city? It's all a matter of perspective, I suppose. Anyway, your princess friend is preparing for her return to the Court of Queens. If you don't hurry, you might miss it."

I almost said thanks. But I hesitated one moment, and Death was gone.

The corpses of building smashers lay scattered throughout Middle Kingdom, along with purple stains where the occasional gnome met their crushing end. People peeked out of windows at me from time to time, but most of them had the good sense to hide.

Though I called to Grimm over and over, he still wouldn't answer. I imagined him guiding Ari through a ceremony meant to give her the power to tear apart her challengers, and found the strength to run through the streets.

When I finally found the address, thank Kingdom, Isolde's

creations hadn't reduced the entire building to rubble, or finding a fourth-floor closet would have been difficult.

I knocked twice on the apartment door, then kicked it open. Inside, the stench of sour milk combined with death, a smell I followed to the bedroom. There, carton upon carton of vanilla ice cream, and a mound of banana peels remained as evidence.

She'd eaten herself to death on sundaes and shakes rather than answer the summons to court. I picked up the silver scroll and read her name. "Jardain, Princess of Cream." All the whipped cream in the world hadn't protected her when it was time to choose a new High Queen.

Ari warned me throughout the years that I'd never seen the court at its worst, and I'd never understood why she feared it. The only thing Ari feared more than the Court of Queens was her credit card bill. So, sword in hand, I stepped to Jardain's closet. A mountain of empty ice-cream containers cascaded out when I opened the door.

With a kick and a shove, I cleared the doorway and smashed the door shut.

For one moment, I stood alone with the hum of flies in the darkness and the smell of ice cream gone bad. Then the door in front of me swung open, and the doorman of the court stood, waiting.

"Handmaiden, will your queen participate?"

"It's just me." I stumbled, stepping out of the closet, but the doorman caught me.

He nodded over his shoulder. "The arbiter's booth is open, though none remain neutral. I'll just tidy this up." He produced a trash bag and began to gather cups and spoons from the floor, but stopped to grab my hand as I stepped away. "You may observe, but not interfere. This is no longer a place of peace."

I emerged from the tunnel to the main amphitheater in the court, where princesses and queens engaged in a combination catfight and debate. Gwendolyn's faithful used magic, muscle, and a fair bit of hair pulling to make the last few resisters submit. The entire ceiling had transformed into a thundercloud, which threw flashes of lightning to illuminate the war below.

Taking the stairs to the arbiter's booth, I caught Gwendolyn's eye. She couldn't intimidate me. I held up my fist. "Gwendolyn, I was sent to receive the oath of the High Queen. Not a pretender."

Gwendolyn looked over at me and pulled back her hood. Her face drooped like she'd had a bag of strokes for breakfast, her wrinkles had wrinkles, but her eyes still shone with magic. "The last of the court will kneel in moments. Bear witness to my ascension, and carry my oath of loyalty to our queen."

The gallery filled with raucous laughter where the witches watched, but they had no say in the matter. Gwendolyn's followers dragged a young girl to the center of the court. She couldn't have been more than twenty, but Gwendolyn's faithful beat her until she collapsed.

"Do you acknowledge me as High Queen?" asked Gwendolyn.

Blood dripped from the girl's mouth as she nodded. "I do. Just stop."

"Are there any other challengers?" asked Gwendolyn. She looked to the Witches Gallery and to the broken and beaten who lay on the floor of the court.

The door of the Court of Queens blasted open, sending the doorman flying. Liam, in dragon form, threw the guards into the wall so hard their bones snapped like breaking branches. Beside him came Wyatt, carrying a rapier that glowed with purple light.

I glanced to the doorman, waiting for him to eject Wyatt and Liam, but a glint of silver on Liam's claw caught my eye. And Wyatt, too, wore a band of white gold. I supposed there wasn't technically a law against having male handmaidens.

Behind them, a figure wrapped in white came through the door. She threw back the veil on her head, letting red hair spill out, and stepped to the front. Directly into the storm, Ari walked, without fear. "I challenge you for High Queen, Mother."

"Ari," said Gwendolyn, "I am surprised to see you here.

You have no standing to challenge me. You have been cast out of my family. Indeed, it is curious that you can enter Kingdom at all. If Fairy Godfather were not interceding on your behalf, we wouldn't be having this conversation."

Ari walked toward her stepmother. "I've lived my life afraid of what I was. Afraid of what you might make me, or what I might become, Mother. No longer. I'm ready to be what I am." Ari drew back a sleeve to show her golden Agency bracelet. "Grimm, I quit." She threw it on the floor and it disappeared in a flash of glitter.

I waited for her to fade from view, since her stepmother's banishment stripped her of her right to enter Kingdom without Grimm's assistance.

She didn't. "I am not a frightened girl anymore, Mother. You will call me Arianna. You will kneel before me."

Gwendolyn gestured, and the storm struck with a thousand bolts that poured down on Ari like rain. "You are worthless. So suffer like the rest."

I was blinded for just a moment by the lightning. Then as my eyes cleared I saw her, standing at the center of the court. The lightning had burned her train away, but it hadn't touched her. "Really, Mother? I was Princess of Clouds before you disowned me, but no longer." She held up a hand, where a golden band shone. "Wyatt and I got married a few minutes ago."

Gasps rang out across the court, and even the Witches Gallery fell silent.

"My name is Arianna Pendlebrook, Queen of the First Royal Family." She looked to the doorman.

He bowed. "Your Highness, I will record it. Arianna, Queen of Clouds."

Ari laughed, that same laugh she'd always had, but it came from deep down inside. "No. My stepmother was right about one thing. Let it be recorded, doorman. I am the Witch Queen."

The court gasped. My chest ached from how long I'd been holding my breath. Above us, the Witches Gallery moved in unison. They kneeled, and then rose with a raucous cheer.

If I'd been Gwendolyn, I'd have figured out how to kneel. Or how to run. Anything but stick around and fight it out with a woman who had just won the loyalty of every witch in Kingdom with a single sentence.

Instead Gwendolyn invoked a subtle spell that made me shiver. Shadows blossomed beside her, and then she looked up to the hulking mass of flesh now standing at her side. Prince Mihail, whose abomination body sprouted thorns like a cactus. Gwendolyn croaked out her command. "She is unworthy to die by my hand. Slave, kill my daughter."

He lumbered forward, his jaw hanging to one side in a disgusting grin. "I've been waiting to do this for a long time."

Ari stumbled backwards, then ran, hiding behind the hulking dragon who happened to be my fiancé.

"What's the matter, Ari?" Gwendolyn's taunting voice echoed. "Did you not bring a decent monster of your own? Dragons are so four years ago."

Liam roared in answer, and slithered forward. Over the years, practice had given him fine control of his lizard body. Each step coiled and uncoiled his body, allowing him to lunge forward and slide out of the way without pause.

Prince Mihail, at last the monster on the outside he'd always been deep down, ran for Liam. Unlike the building crushers, Mihail could leap and turn with deadly precision.

Liam dodged one blow, then snapped back, his teeth gleaming white.

And whipped his head away, hissing in pain. Blood bubbled from the edges of his jaws where the thorns covering Mihail had slashed through Liam's scales.

I'd seen steel blades break on Liam's scales.

Seizing the opportunity, Mihail swung with both arms, flailing like a pinwheel, trying to dice the man I loved more than anything into hunks of meat. I lunged forward to jump over the railing, and hit a barrier like invisible concrete. Cold as ice, hard as stone, it sealed me into the booth.

I could only watch as Liam slithered back and forth, whipping his body in circles to avoid blows that barely missed. Mihail charged, swinging his fist overhead, and Liam surged forward, taking the blow full.

I cried as the thorns cut into him, knowing what it meant

to be torn by them. And he belched fire, a gush of living flame, straight into Mihail's face, engulfing his eyes.

Prince Mihail staggered backwards. The thorns on his palms tore flesh from his skull as he clutched his head. The problem with being a living cactus was that taking out a contact had to be near impossible. Liam limped away, each step leaving bloody claw prints, and sagged to the ground.

I pounded on the barrier, screaming, and hurled myself against it over and over. Though it bruised my fists, I might as well have struck it with a plastic fork.

Then Mihail rose and, with a rip, tore the skin from his own head. His skull stared back with inhuman eyes as he rose, ready to reengage. With two lumbering strides he closed the distance between them, ready to tear Liam apart.

Mihail drew back one foot to kick Liam.

And fell over, clutching his knee. Beside him, Wyatt stood, his rapier bloody. "Violence is rarely an acceptable method for resolving conflict." He walked along Mihail's thrashing body, stabbing carefully at elbow, shoulder, and knees. "However, I must concede that this is an exception."

Mihail rolled onto his stomach and swiped at Wyatt. "I've got a thousand of those pig stickers, weakling."

"Really?" Wyatt leaped in, stabbing twice at Mihail's shoulder, then turned and sprinted toward Liam, who struggled to get to all four feet.

And Mihail rose, the flesh on his head turning purple as it solidified. "Now you both die." He raised a fist, to show off.

And stopped.

The thorns covering him had retracted, leaving only smooth, dead flesh.

"What spell is this?" Mihail turned to Gwendolyn, looking for aid she would never offer.

Wyatt sheathed his rapier. "Acupuncture. You'll find your qi is blocked at several key points. You may find it difficult to concentrate, summon spikes, or perform sexually."

And before Mihail could respond, Liam was on him, claws and teeth tearing, ripping, shredding. I'd seen Liam as a dragon before, but never like this. Never as the primal force of destruction. Mihail thrashed and screamed, but without his thorns, the monster prince was no match for the oldest curse in Kingdom.

When all the flesh was torn from Mihail's arms, Liam pinned him down with both claws, and rumbled like a volcano. The river of flame that gushed out onto Mihail's head continued until the stone beneath them glowed white-hot, and Mihail's skin caught fire.

When Liam stumbled away, the remaining mass of flesh didn't move. Lurching from side to side, Liam made his way back to Ari, coiling about her the way he once protected me.

Ari stepped away from him, one hand on Liam's nose, and raised her other hand, beckoning to Gwendolyn. "I'll take an old-fashioned dragon any day, Mother. Submit now, and I will forgive you. You are no match for me."

Magic surged in on Gwendolyn, distorting the air around her. With a shriek, she channeled the power out. Waves of fire and ice burst from her palm.

Instead of blocking them, Ari pressed her palms together and held still as a blast of steam left her face damp.

Gwendolyn threw a bolt of lightning that practically greeted Ari like a dog meeting his master. Each spell took longer to build, and each seemed easier for Ari to block. I waited for Ari to actually do something on her own.

And waited.

Raising her hands, Gwendolyn surged with power, and when she opened her mouth, smoke billowed out. The cloud swirled out, separating into columns, which then solidified into snakes the thickness of fire hydrants. Her spell serpents lashed toward Ari, hissing.

From behind Ari a crevice opened, spilling red light and sulfur. A stream, a torrent of hellhounds burst from the ground, each dragging a serpent down to Inferno.

Gwendolyn leaned on her staff, her breath ragged, her eyes an ominous shade of yellow. "So you have learned it is not raw power which matters, and yet I can't help but notice you take no action. Are you afraid of harming your dear sisters, my handmaidens?"

Of course. If Ari turned her spells on her stepmother, her sisters would suffer through the handmaiden's bond the same way I did whenever Isolde was wounded.

"Let them go, Mother." Ari spoke in a tone of quiet command.

"On one condition," said Gwendolyn. "You agree to match spells with me."

"No!" I shouted from the arbiter's booth, drawing the ire of both. Ari obviously had more power than Gwendolyn. She probably had better spells too, so agreeing to a duel like this made no sense. Each of them would pick one spell, and only one, then pit them against each other.

"No handmaidens," said Ari. "No interference. Just you and me?"

"One spell for each of us," said Gwendolyn.

I had no doubt what spell Ari would be forced to use.

"I agree, Mother. Choose your spell. My decision is already made." Ari bowed her head, concentrating, rippling with power.

The floor of the court beneath them erupted into crystalline walls, isolating them from the rest of the court. No force in heaven or hell could breach the barrier. Perhaps I could trap Isolde inside—or myself. If the handmaiden's bond could not pass the wall, I might have a way to break free.

"Good." Gwendolyn spoke in another voice. A dark voice, like a well of evil in a human skin. "I, too, have had a teacher." The syllables that burst from her throat next could not have been spoken by human lips. They stained the air, as if sound became visible, a black mist that enveloped Gwendolyn. When it lifted, she could barely stand, her back hunched and twisted. Trails of blood dripped from her eyes.

Yellow eyes. Witch's eyes.

"Mother, you've taken evil into your heart for nothing more than power." A note of pity hung in Ari's words. "Submit now, and I will let you go."

Gwendolyn cackled, a noise like a dying rooster. "I have learned the spell of oblivion, as have you. We die together."

"The only ritual I chose to perform was my marriage vows. And you can only learn my spell by traveling through the mirror, Mother, but I didn't learn this from the Fairy Godfather." Ari risked a glance to me. "You might say I learned it from Marissa."

I stood, shocked into silence, trying to understand her meaning. Magic and I never got along. I once failed to pick a card, any card. I had scars from my attempt to use bottled spells. I was so worried about what Ari meant, I almost missed the shift, as Gwendolyn befouled reality with her magic.

The spell swept out from her, a tide of death, a wave of bones and beetles, the smell of the grave and the sound of closing caskets. Like a landslide of darkness, it rushed toward Ari, cracking the stone floor below, sloshing off the crystal walls.

The wave arced up, rising to near the ceiling of the court, and then hurled down at her.

Ari unleashed the spell she'd been casting, not out at Gwendolyn. Back onto herself. Light like a thousand flash photographs blinded everyone in the court, leaving me seeing only spots. Through the veil, though, I saw what she did.

As the well of death swallowed her, Ari became, for one shining moment, *possibility*. Like every choice, and every chance that could ever happen, all at once. She multiplied outward, becoming herself a thousand times over, from a thousand different choices. An Ari who never learned magic, an Ari who learned Seal Magic from her mother. An Ari wrapped in darkness from Wild Magic, and one dead, murdered by Prince Mihail on their wedding night.

Together, that universe of Ariannas combined their magic, snuffing out the darkness and death like a candle flame. When the darkness ebbed, only one Ari remained, the Ari I knew.

Gwendolyn fell, her dark ambitions destroyed.

The crystal barriers retracted, and the doorman approached Ari, then kneeled. "My queen, shall I have the evil one executed? Her use of Black Magic forswears my protection and violates Kingdom law."

Ari looked at her stepmother, broken and twisted, and turned her back. "It is her choice. If she chooses death, I will not stop her. If she wishes to live, let her be bound to a shop for the rest of her life. My Kingdom has need of a witch."

The doorman seized Gwendolyn by the wisps of white hair that remained on her head, dragging her down the hall toward an exit. When he'd left, the other queens approached, kneeling before Ari, one at a time.

"What is this?" asked the Black Queen, coalescing beside me in the arbiter's booth. "A new challenger? Or an old one, grown wiser?"

"You said I could receive the oath—"

She chuckled. "I lied, Marissa. It's what I do. Tell me what spectacle this is?"

"A new High Queen," said Ari. "Though it appears there is a question as to your loyalty, Princess Isolde. Shall we settle it?" Ari walked toward the arbiter's booth, her previously destroyed dress spreading behind her as wisps of magic coursed along it.

The court rose from their knees and fell behind Ari, some literally hiding in her shadow, some standing in solidarity, others out of fear of being left alone.

Ari's confidence, her skills, her sheer presence told me what the outcome of this would be. "You'll never beat her."

"Silence," screamed the Black Queen, and my tongue stuck to the roof of my mouth. She turned back to Ari. "Kneel before me in your mother's stead, and I will give you her power and more. Resist me and I will finish what I started the first time. My handmaiden cannot save you again."

Ari looked at her with a look of pure disdain. "I have matched Gwendolyn's power, I bear that of a seal, every seal bearer, and witch in Kingdom. We shall finish our duel of magic, Isolde. I challenge you. I want a rematch."

Rage boiled on the Black Queen's face, a scowl that looked like she would tear Ari's throat out with her teeth, but I saw the fear that it concealed. The Black Queen, scourge of five hundred years, was *afraid*. She knew I saw it, her slit-like eyes darting to me, loathing me. "You are unworthy of the honor. Handmaiden, kill her."

"I won't do it," I said. "I won't kill anyone else for you."

She hit me with the back of her hand, and I let her, let it split my lip and bruise my cheek. "You *will*." Then her eyes flicked back and forth between Ari and Liam. "The queen or the dragon? Who shall I have you kill first?"

"Neither," I said, and drove the dagger in my fist toward my chest. My body locked cold, frozen in place by her power.

The Black Queen began to giggle. "I *told* you I'd find what you feared most. I understand now, Marissa. Your boyfriend, your best friend. Who dies first?" She shrugged. "Leave the queen for later. My third command to you is given, darling. Slay the dragon."

"No!" I cried, but the compulsion came upon me. I fought it with every fiber of my being. Every inch of my muscle and ounce of will I had. My feet moved at her command, dragging me forward out of the arbiter's booth.

"Stop," I said, begging the Black Queen for a mercy she did not have.

She ignored me, a look of shock and surprise on her face, one hand covering her mouth. She'd heard Fairy Godmother's term for me. She *knew*.

My hands took the thorn sword from my side. The most I could do was make them tremble as I marched toward Liam. Then he began to change.

"No, don't do that," I screamed through clenched teeth, but he did. Scales melted into skin, his face grew shorter, and paler, until at last it was only Liam, and still I advanced.

"Run," I said. "I can't stop her."

He looked at me with those brown eyes and smiled. "I know, M. It's going to be okay. That's her third command."

I thought for a moment he had some spell. Some binding or trick, or *weapon*, and then I realized what he meant to do, and I screamed.

"It's going to be all right," he said. "I love you."

Then I stabbed him. Right through the chest, with a strength beyond any I had ever known. I drove the thorns right up through him so they stuck out the other side, and then I tore it out, covered in his blood. Liam fell at my feet. Dead, by my hand, and the compulsion finally released me. I collapsed over him, finally free to cry the river of pain that came from my soul.

"Now kill the High Queen," said the Black Queen. But the manacle on my wrist broke open and dropped to the ground.

I looked up at her, my pain mixed with rage, preparing to lunge at her.

Ari spoke in the silence. "As High Queen I order you stripped of your title, and the privileges that go with it. Does my court concur?" As she spoke the foundations of the castle shook and a hurricane blew through the room.

The doorman snapped into existence with a thunderclap, radiating menace.

Isolde's eyes widened, a look of panic on her face. "Nocte." With one word, she froze the court.

I no longer cared if I lived or died, so long as I took Isolde with me. With my hand on my bracelet I called him. "Grimm. *Kill her.*"

Plaster fell from the ceiling as the ground trembled.

Isolde whirled, looking everywhere. "Yes, Father. Come and insult me from your mirror, if you can even manage that. Taunt me and order your puppets about from the safety of the glass."

The walls flexed inward, and every bit of glass in the palace exploded into a powdered mist. Grimm's voice thundered in answer from the stone itself. "I come."

A ray of blinding light leaped from Ari to the Black Queen, wrapping around her. In flashes through my left eye I saw her in her thorn tree form, struggling against Ari's binding. In the center of the room a ball of light like a miniature sun began to grow. I had seen it before, when Grimm came to me, in Fairy Godmother's realm. Grimm wouldn't be coming through mirrors, or watching from a distance.

With a cry the Black Queen forced herself to stand. Then she held up her hands and began to chant, each word growing louder, each syllable gathering power. The sun in the room was so bright my eyes hurt with them closed. Then the Black Queen screamed: *"Nocte!"*

A wall of darkness swept out from her, engulfing me.

I opened my eyes to nothing.

Twenty-Nine

NOT COMPLETE NOTHING. As the moments passed, my eyes adjusted. The room was not black, but the color of the world at twilight when the sun has just set. No sign of Isolde or the miniature sun that would have become Grimm. I knelt on the ground and tried to cradle Liam's body, but I couldn't move him. The same dark gray that wrapped everything else covered him as well. Finally I lay down on the concrete, stretched out beside the only man who had ever truly loved me, and I wept.

Time didn't have meaning in that in-between place. I can't tell you how long I lay waiting and wishing. At times I nearly slept, and at other times the tidal wave of grief receded far enough for me to almost be aware of where I was. It was one of those moments when I realized Grimm was standing behind me, watching, and waiting.

He looked like when I'd seen him in Fairy Godmother's realm. A proper English butler, dressed in a perfect silk suit, with thick black glasses and silver hair. I looked up at him, gazing into those eyes, which sometimes seemed to be the color of rain, and sometimes that of grass in the field. I looked up and attacked. I leaped upon him, smashing, kicking, and screaming, but the skill that came with the compulsion was gone. I was only me.

He waited, not raising a hand to my blows, until exhaustion set in.

When I could no longer throw punches, I switched to flinging words. "This is *your* fault. If you had been here to begin with, Ari never would have been attacked. Liam wouldn't have died. I wouldn't have murdered him."

Grimm didn't answer until the sobs wracking me stopped. Finally he spoke. "That's not all. Go ahead. Say it."

"She's your daughter. This is all your fault."

"I know that, Marissa. There are not words to express my sorrow, or my guilt. I could not come until Liam was dead and you were free of Fairy Godmother's compulsion."

"You *knew* he was going to die?" My eyes blurred again and I clenched my teeth until they ground.

"Come with me, my dear," said Grimm. He put his hand on my shoulder and I slapped him.

"I'm not leaving him. Go to hell, Grimm." I tried in vain to move even Liam's little finger, but the shadows wrapped around him held him like ice.

"This world is frozen. Paused, one might say. You cannot change it nor affect him in any way. Nor any of the others, for that matter."

Others. I glanced around through tear-blurred eyes. Everyone still stood in the Court of Queens. Wyatt still cowered behind a podium. Ari's hands were still in the air, her face focused as she wrangled magic. I reached out to touch her hand. I'd stolen marble statues less cold. "Are they dead?"

"No, my dear. They are *quelled*. To quell an entire realm has surely consumed all of the fairy power my daughter stole from Fairy Godmother. Even I never cast it on more than a town or forest at once, and that was only for a few hundred years so that the crop blight might pass."

He put his hand on my shoulder again, and this time I didn't fight it off. When he wrapped his arms around me I found, to my surprise, that there was still grief to be had. I can't say how long it went on.

It might have been a hundred years later, or maybe a few seconds, when he finally let me go. "Will you come with me? Please?"

I did. I kept my eyes open as the world slanted inward like a box folding, and then outward again. We stood in the front office of the Agency, and the quell did not hold sway. The lights hummed and flickered like always; the doors opened and closed just fine.

Rosa, however, was missing. Grimm had always had a shelter agreement with her that against all disasters, she and her family would be safe. In her place sat the harbinger Death, filing papers and looking over applications. He rose and nodded to Grimm. Then he looked at me. "Is this is the point where you get angry at me, or attack me, or throw things at me? I didn't kill your boyfriend."

His words cut me like the thorn sword, as if I could ever forget that *I* had.

"This way, my dear," said Grimm. "An audience awaits you."

I followed him back to the main conference room. Inside sat a group of beings I had hoped never to see again. On one side of the table sat Eli, head angel in charge of the city. Across from him, Nickolas Scratch, leader of Inferno himself. On the other side sat Death. I hadn't seen him come down the hall, but Death had a nasty habit of showing up. To his side sat the Fae Mother. I didn't really understand what she was doing here. The others, well, they sort of fit in with the rest of my life.

Grimm walked to the head of the table. I took the seat at the end.

"So tell me, Marissa," said Nickolas Scratch. "What exactly are you going to do to fix this?"

Eli leaned over to pat my hand. "Ignore my associate there. The Authority wanted me to tell you how sorry she is for this situation, and to relay her condolences. She says when your boy finally gets there, you can consider him spoken for."

I glared at Death. "What do you *mean*, *when* he gets there?"

Eli held out his palms. "Seems like he missed his bus or something. Not to worry. Everyone gets there eventually." He looked out the window, at the quell. "Now that, there, that's nasty. No defense against it. Cuts straight to the soul, wraps it up."

I can't tell you what the Adversary's answer was. My mind locked onto Eli's words, going through them over and over, until my tongue finally birthed the question. "Grimm, why didn't the quell affect me?"

In the city that never sleeps, you could have heard a pin drop. Or an asteroid drop, for that matter.

"I'm stepping out for some fresh air." Eli backed out the door. "Nick, you want to come with me?"

Nickolas nodded and walked out as well, followed by the Fae Mother and the spirit of darkness who had once been my lawyer.

I kept my gaze locked on Grimm. "Why didn't the quell affect me?"

Grimm kept his hands behind his back, as he looked out the window. "Do you know the meaning of your name?"

"Of the Sea. Answer the question." I stood, pushing away my chair.

If he knew I approached, he didn't react. "In Latin, yes. In Hebrew, *Mara*, meaning 'bitter.'"

"Answer the question."

Grimm turned, finally, and took his glasses off. "It has another meaning, as well. It means 'wish child.'"

I knew I'd been adopted. Always figured I was yet another drug addict's baby, given to my parents in return for who knows how much cash.

"The quell affects the soul, my dear. And while I can do wondrous things, I cannot make a soul."

I held up my hands, looking at them, I can't say why. "I don't understand." Grimm ran a series of orphanages just because "a baby" was a common wish. "I know about the orphanages. I signed the inspection reports when you were gone."

Grimm sat down in the chair I'd just vacated, and rubbed his glasses on his sleeve. "I established my first orphanage twenty-seven years ago, Marissa. I don't raise the dead. I don't end the world, and until the night your parents came to me, I didn't offer children. Ever."

He gestured to the chair across from me. "Your father and his wife found their way through my wards the old-fashioned way—pure desperation. They showed up at fifteen minutes to six and, the moment I saw them, began begging for a child. In this day and age, we would say Clarisse had no viable eggs. All she knew was that she couldn't have children. I turned them down, like everyone who wished for a child."

"Yet here I am." I didn't sit.

"It was your father's last words that struck home. He said, 'You don't know what it's like. To want a child, to love.' After he lost a fistfight with one of my agents, your parents left the office, and I remained. That night, once my employees left, I retreated to my demesne, and began to wonder. You might say I committed the worst mistake a fairy can."

"Fathering an evil queen who kills anyone and everyone?"

He ignored my jab. "I let my mind wander. I asked myself, 'What if?' What if I hadn't given my first daughter power? What if she'd been a normal girl, with no affinity for magic? What might have been?"

I shook my head. "There is no way on earth I'm your daughter." The thought of it made me angry. No, anger paled beside this fury. I preferred being the child of a heroin addict than something like the Black Queen.

"Your genetic material is a combination of the blood your father left in the lobby and that of one of my most trusted agents. You are not my child, Marissa, much as I might wish it. You are my creation. Building a body, forming flesh, that is the easy part, like assembling a bookcase." He saw the look on my face.

If my life had been any different the previous weeks, or if it had been one whit different from the moment I turned eighteen, I think I wouldn't have believed. The thing was, part of me echoed with betrayal, and burned with the lies that made up my life. The other part nodded inside, like something I'd always known had been confirmed.

The how, the why of my body, those didn't concern me. I'd settled those questions back when I thought I came from an orphanage. I spent six years asking myself who I was. It felt like longer, until I worked up the courage to ask. "What am I?"

"A woman." Grimm didn't meet my eyes.

It couldn't be a lie, or I'd be lying dead from the thorn near my heart. But it wasn't the truth either. "You can't make a soul. Death told me that several times, and I think I understand why now." As a matter of fact, so many things made sense now. Why the Adversary had turned down my attempt to bargain my soul for the end of the apocalypse. Why magic never obeyed my will. Why even the doorman at the Court of Queens couldn't give me Mihail's kingdom.

Why I couldn't have children.

"Tell me. No more half answers. What am I?" I slipped into the chair, taking both of his hands, and waited until he finally looked at me.

"Isolde grew within her mother, nine long months, and in the normal manner, she took a tiny shard of her mother's soul, and grew it into her own. You were formed complete. Alive, breathing, but without spirit to drive the body. You are a wish. Created by me, bound to flesh, and given to your father to raise."

"You made a wish, just to put it into a body?"

"No." He looked down at the table. "Long ago, a man came to me for a wish. Bitter at his ex-wife, he wished that she would never again be able to celebrate, as partying was her favorite vice. He died before he could collect and use his wish, but I kept it. Waiting."

I bit my tongue. "And?"

"For guidance, I bound the wish to itself. It's a subtle trick, one I suspect is quite similar to how the Authority created the first human souls. I swaddled it in the waiting flesh, and when the Agency opened the next day, I dispatched an agent to deliver you."

"So that's what Clara had against me."

"Clara?" Grimm chuckled. "I didn't take on Clara for another four years. Rosa carried you to your parents."

Bile rose up in my mouth at Rosa's name. "She knew what you did?"

"Rosa possesses a unique talent. She knows the true nature of everyone she sees, but I forbid that she tell you."

Now I understood why Rosa never liked me. Why she treated me like furniture. Worse than furniture. The taste of bile in my mouth became stronger. No wonder she detested me. "You let Ari be attacked?" A second later, its companion followed. "Liam *died*." I threw off his hands, pulling mine back. "You could have stopped this, and Ari wouldn't be quelled. Liam would still be alive."

"Not without harming you." A tear formed in Grimm's eye and rolled down his cheek, sparkling gold.

"And that matters? I'm not a person. I'm a *thing*. Another of your experiments. You let people die to keep me safe, Grimm. Beth died. I *killed* Liam, and he chose to let me. You think he would have made the same decision if he knew?" My shouts echoed in the hallways.

Grimm looked up at me, any sign of contrition gone. In fact, his rigid shoulders spoke of rage. "This is *exactly* why I did not tell you. And both of the people closest to you knew exactly who and what you were, Marissa."

When I spoke, my voice came out like a whisper. "How?"

"Arianna's spirit sight can see through your very flesh. She's known since you two traveled to the focus point. Liam came to me two years ago, looking to make a deal of his own. I make you able to have children, he would serve me. He threatened to find another fairy if I refused. If you think it mattered to them one bit, you didn't know either one. As I told them both, I feared that knowledge of your exact nature would make you value your life less. You would make dangerous choices, needless sacrifices."

"Get out." My gun couldn't harm him, but I swore I'd beat him with my fists until he shut up.

"My leaving won't bring Liam back. Now you understand why I no longer grant wishes. I've seen what they can become, and couldn't bring myself to create them, just to die for someone's whim."

Somewhere, a part of me recognized that Grimm spoke the truth. At the same time, I couldn't accept it. Couldn't hear any more. I rushed for the door, leaving everything behind, dashing through an empty lobby and down the stairs.

I ran every morning, six miles, and the ritual had hardened my body to my will. And what I willed it more than anything was to take me away. I don't know how many blocks I covered before I stopped, but it wasn't because my side ached or my lungs burned like fire. I ran through a city of dark gray ghosts, in a world of absolute stillness.

No matter how far I ran, I couldn't get away from the thing I most needed to escape. Me.

I stopped because no matter how far I ran, no matter how fast I went, I was no farther away than before. That, and the sound of moving metal caught my attention. A low, grating, creaking sound, among a world of gray.

I wanted to find a place to curl up and sleep. To forget about everything that had happened. Everything that I'd learned. Problem was, I wanted to find out what was making that noise. So I wiped my eyes, caught my breath, and walked out into the frozen city, listening.

For a couple of minutes, I thought maybe I'd missed whatever it was. Then the sound of breaking glass caught my attention. Like a cat after a laser pointer, I darted through the crowds toward the sound. Only when I reached a street corner and heard yet another window break did I think to be more cautious.

Creeping now, walking softly through the quelled crowd, I saw movement ahead.

A woman.

An older woman. Quite a bit older. In fact, more than anything, she reminded me of Clara, Grimm's oldest agent. Note I didn't say oldest living agent, because, like most of Grimm's employees, Clara died on the job. Whoever this was, for once, I was facing somebody my size, my build. I could only hope that if I lived to be as old as she appeared, my hair would turn that beautiful silver.

She walked through the center of the street, looking at

the crowd, studying the frozen traffic. Then she walked over to a cab and put her hands on it. With a sound like pudding sucked through a straw, the quell retracted, leaving the cab the same dirty yellow as normal.

My jaw dropped.

Walking to the front of the cab, she began to push against it, rocking it back and forth. Then she stopped, turned around, and looked right at me. "Give me a hand with this."

I admit to thinking about running. It's the most sensible thing to do in so many situations. Might be dangerous? Run. Is dangerous? Run. Boring? Run. I wasn't sure what this old woman was, but she canceled the quell with her bare hands. Running should have been my primary objective.

Except that I wasn't concerned about much of anything anymore, least of all threats to my safety.

I slipped through the gaps in the crowd, and approached. The woman had hazel eyes and lips that looked like she wore only gloss. Her simple button-up shirt would have fit a grandmother or a businesswoman.

"Push at the front. We only need to move it a few centimeters." She walked over and set her back against it.

I pulled from the other side, and slowly the cab tires slid a tiny distance.

"That's enough." She stood up, walked to the front of the cab, and looked down the road, to where an unfortunate jaywalker was about to receive a door prize, if the quell ever let up. "He'll still get hit. Can't fix that, since it was his decision to step out, but at least he doesn't die now." With a brush of her hand, the quell returned, wrapping over the cab, returning it to normal.

"I heard breaking glass." It wasn't much of a question. I couldn't think of all the questions I really wanted to ask.

She pointed a few stories up. "I broke that window over there. See that crane? The cable's rusted. I want people looking up, moving that direction for a better look, and out of harm's way." She pointed overhead, to a construction crane. Then she looked back at me. For a brief moment, the fear that kept me alive for years returned. A drive to run, to sprint back to the Agency, back to the lights and the harbingers and the fairy who'd lied to me all these years came back stronger.

"Stick around, Marissa. You have questions." She pointed across the street to a bistro. "I have answers, and perhaps a few questions of my own."

The fact that she knew my name didn't faze me. The sheer number of things that greeted me by name without introduction had ceased to amaze me several years earlier. I might as well have had "Hello, my name is Marissa" monogrammed on every single outfit I own.

I followed her across the street. At her touch, the quell retracted, letting me move people from the chairs enough to sit down.

She walked through a half-open door, and a few minutes later, came back with coffee cups, steaming hot. "Sugar and cream, just like always."

I wasn't clear on whether I should say thank you or be creeped out. We sat in a pregnant silence that could have given birth to quintuplet conversations, without words. Then she put her cup down. "So, would you like me to tell you what you are?"

I thought of all the names that came to mind. "An aberration. A violation of natural law. One of Grimm's freakish experiments."

"I was going to suggest a beautiful woman."

"I'm not." Either of them.

She spit to the side and shook her head. "You sure look like it. Whatever you might have been, you've lived nearly thirty years in *this* world. In *that* body. By *their* rules. The process has changed you. And that is interesting, because it means that you might be able to do something about this mess."

"Who are you?" I finally worked up the courage to ask the question. Most of the things interested in killing me never sat down to coffee first, but there had been a couple of exceptions.

"The final answer on everything. The reason why most things are."

The Authority. The one the angels said I'd be better off not meeting. I tried to think back. What was proper etiquette for meeting someone like that? Bowing? Groveling? Sacrificing an accountant? I slammed the coffee cup down so hard it shattered. "This is your fault. You let this happen."

"Not the tone I expected." She reached over and collected the shards of my cup. "But yes, I let things happen. Of all the things I'm proudest of, it's their free will. It's precious. If they decide to do wonderful things with it, I accept that." She began to fit the pieces back together, looking at the edges. "If they do horrible things, I have to accept that too. I can't go changing people's decisions, Marissa. Ever."

"I'm not a person. You could have saved Liam." Speaking his name brought tears to my eyes, made my throat close up.

"You are, in so many ways, just like every other person. You've lived in that body, as one of them, thought like one of them. Fought like one of them, and the process has changed you. What your Fairy Godfather did was dangerously close to infringing on my secrets. So I consider changing your choices much like changing theirs." She handed me back the coffee cup, every crack perfectly repaired. "I sent Liam your way, you know."

I turned it over in my hands, running my fingers along the smooth surface. "I don't understand."

"On the pier, five years ago." She poured another cup of coffee from the pitcher.

"Why? Why would you do that to him?"

"*For*, not *to*. Oh, if you could have seen your Fairy Godfather's face when he found out. You had your little game of hearts planned. Set the princess up with a prince. Make a little more Glitter. And then the wrong man just stumbles into your trap. I considered it a work of art." She held up a sugar packet and cream cup.

"If I had never met him, he'd be alive." The tears ran like streams now, but my anger fixed where it belonged. On myself.

"You don't know that. You and your friend the queen stopped a war that would have killed thousands. How do you know Liam wouldn't have died there? Together, you ended yet another apocalypse and taught that demon brat Malodin a lesson that is quite literally etched into his hide."

I shook my head. "Liam would be alive."

"You two loved each other. I knew what you were when I sent him your way. And yet I still sent him." Her tone shifted, became cold and serious. "You are *of* this world, Marissa. So I believe that you can fix this situation. You still have the ability to make choices."

Of course something like this was coming. No one acted friendly to me unless they wanted something. "What do you want?"

"I want you to restore their choices. I can't change what Isolde has done because, like you, she is too much a part of this world. But you can. I want you to go to her demesne and end the quell. I want you to kill the Black Queen."

The sheer ease with which she'd manipulated me made me sick. My anger. My tears. All of them setting me up to do something I wanted to do anyway. "I'm not a killer."

"Until an hour ago, you didn't know what you were. Still, there's something in it for you." She looked at me over the edge of her coffee cup.

"Bring him back." My heart leaped, and my will clenched around me like ice.

"No. I set rules for the way things must be. The dead stay dead, Marissa. But if you do this, I'll give you the one thing your Fairy Godfather never could. A soul." She set down the cup and waited, watching me.

"Bring him back. I'll kill her a dozen times if you bring him back. Grimm says souls are limited, but you bring him back, and you can keep it." I tried to force confidence into my voice.

"I can't break my own laws. And souls are precious, that's true, but I created the first ones. That said, I keep a few. There are crimes for which you can lose your soul, Marissa. Crimes for which I would take it."

My skin crawled at her words. "I don't want anything but him. I don't want some serial killer's soul. I just want Liam back."

"You say that like I'd give you the soul as is. A couple of times through the wash, and it would be perfectly new. If I told you the things that have happened between hotel sheets you've slept on, you'd be ill. You could have children—"

I stood up, cutting her off. "No deal. You bring him back, I'll do it. Let me know if you change your mind."

She nodded and rose as well, extending a hand I didn't take. "My offer stands as well. I want you to think beyond yourself, of the people trapped here. Your pain and sorrow will have an end, but several billion lives can neither end nor continue."

I left her there, carefully adjusting chairs.

THERE ARE NO words to describe the alleys of sorrow or darkness I wandered. Lost in a maze of gray, without a way forward or backward, I walked beyond knowledge, finding tears at some turns, and anger at others.

The repetitive rhythm of footfalls gave me an outlet, allowed me to sail through grief, until I finally reached a decision. One that hurt to think of, felt like a new betrayal. And with a clarity of purpose, my feet led me back to the Agency, back up the stairs.

Death saw me come through the doors first, and nodded.

I strode down the hallway to Grimm's office, nearly hitting the Fae Mother with the door when I barged in. Behind me, the soft patter of feet heralded Death joining us.

Grimm had the good sense to keep his mouth shut, until I'd taken a seat. Then I leaned forward, put my hands on his desk, and looked him in the eyes. "How can I kill the Black Queen?"

Thirty

❦

GRIMM CLEARED HIS throat. I looked over my shoulder to see Eli and Nickolas had joined us. "My daughter has expended all of a fairy's power quelling the world. She is weak. But as a half fairy, she has retreated to her demesne."

Now I understood. Though Fairy Godmother's power was gone, Isolde had her own demesne. Nothing could reach her there. Not another fairy, for sure, and probably nothing else.

"Marissa, with the permission of the other fairies, I have collected every bit of magic in existence. You will take it with you into her demesne. And there, you will wish her dead." Grimm's voice echoed in the silence.

"You can't set magic against magic." This sounded like a terrible idea.

Grimm shook his head. "Not true. With the amount of magic I will give you, you could wish me dead. You must enter her demesne, and there, wish. I will do the rest."

"I can't control magic."

"No, but you can ask, and I can act in response. Consider this a more direct form of wish making." Grimm put his hands behind his back. "This is *your* world, Marissa. I can act only in response to your decisions."

"I'm not doing this because of you." I watched Grimm until he acknowledged me with a nod, then I turned to Eli. "Or for your boss. I'm doing this because I want to. All of you, out."

When they left, I closed the door.

Grimm waited with his eyes downcast. "Marissa—"

"Don't. I'm nobody's puppet. I'm not some perfect slave to do your bidding. I don't know what I am." I kept my back to him, leaning my head up against the door. "I decide what I do. I decide what I wish for."

He walked around the desk, soft sounds of feet on carpet, then rested his hand on my shoulder. "Of course, my dear. Though I have told the others that you will wish the Black Queen dead, whatever your wish, I give you my word I will honor it."

I looked over my shoulder at him. "Anything?"

"Of course. Once you are in her demesne, the magic will belong to you. Your wish will be my command." He knew what I was thinking. And accepted it. "Anything. Now, I have a plan to get you to her. It requires a ritual—"

"No." I closed my eyes. "I know you are there. Probably watching with a smug smile. I need help." When I opened my eyes, the Authority sat at Grimm's desk. The look of shock on his face brought the first smile to my face, and a tinge of guilt for it.

"Death told me he has ways of reaching all humans. Is Isolde human or not?"

The Authority nodded. Someone rapped at the door twice, and I opened it, knowing who would be on the other side.

Death slipped past me and bowed his head. "Yes, ma'am?"

She pointed to me. "Death, you will take Marissa—"

The grin on his face reminded me of a small child at Christmas. He turned toward me, a look of glee on his face.

"—to Isolde's demesne," the Authority said, a disapproving frown on her face. "Grimm, have a seat. It's time you and I discussed the laws of magic and your attempts to circumvent them. Marissa, shut the door on your way out. This isn't a conversation you would survive."

I glanced to Grimm, and he nodded toward the door. I couldn't help being worried for him. I walked out of the office, closing the door behind me, and Death followed me to the kitchen. He reached out and patted my hand. "There. That's the soul of that miserable prince. You know, I didn't think I'd ever get a chance to show you life beyond the veil." Death opened the fridge and took out someone's lunch.

"Lunch? Is it poisonous or something?" I recoiled, not wanting to touch the bag.

The look of exasperation on his face made me laugh. "I thought you might be hungry. I'm not allowed to take anyone but humans. So I didn't think you and I would ever get to do this."

A new thought grabbed me, one drenched with fear and driven by morbid curiosity. "What happens to me when I die?"

"I have no idea, but I promise I'll stick around to find out. Could be that you float free, like a spirit. Or maybe you get absorbed back into Fairy Godfather. Can't really say, never seen this before." Death took a bag of chips out and tossed them to me.

"Where is Liam?" I spoke each word slowly, clearly.

"His body's still nailed to the floor in the Court of Queens. His spirit is waiting to see what happens." Death looked around, as if trying to spot something. "Love pins people here all the time. He just needs to see what happens to you, then he'll move on. Though if I could get him to let go of that curse, he'd feel a lot better."

Grimm told me curses dissolved when people died, unless you had the misfortune of getting ground up in a soul sieve. "It was supposed to die with him."

Death began to gesture, almost talking with his hands. "Nah. Body's wrapped around both of them, both of them leave the body. Normally, the curse would just dissipate. Instead, he's holding on to that son of a bitch like it's a life preserver. Really, it dies when he lets go."

"Can I talk to Liam?" I couldn't bring myself to look at him while I asked.

"No. I'm sorry, Marissa. I'd make an exception if I could, but it's not up to me. Are you really going to wish the Black Queen dead?"

Something in his tone made me worried. "That's the plan."

"How well did killing her work last time? Look, it's not my decision, but that woman's got enough hate to last a thousand years or more. Seems like a shame for you go to all this trouble and fail." Death stopped, and right when I thought he'd continue, someone knocked on the doorway.

Grimm stood there, his face pale and haggard, the edges of his suit frayed. "My dear, are you ready?"

I rose, and walked toward him. I couldn't stop myself from giving him a hug. "So how do I carry all the magic in the world? You give me the world's largest vial?"

Grimm shook his head. "I wouldn't want it to be something that you could drop. Close your eyes."

I did, feeling that gut-wrenching sensation that always came when he transported me. When I opened my eyes, I stood on the roof of our building. For the first time since the quell, wind stirred.

"Look." He pointed into the distance, where something moved. A cloud, like a golden thunderstorm, boiled on the horizon. Then another, and another. In every direction, the sky went from gray to golden, and the wind whipped faster, harder.

Fear gripped me almost as strongly as his hands on my wrist, anchoring me against the hurricane as the sky turned bright golden, and waves of glitter washed down like a tornado, swirling around me, almost blowing me off the roof.

I closed my eyes and put my hands over my ears until the gale passed.

The sky once again hung suspended, gray, and motionless. The rooftop looked like the freak storm had never happened. Then I glanced down.

Golden cloth covered every inch of me, like a magnificent wedding dress of gold, including a train that would make walking near impossible. I twirled in it, watching the magnificent cloth shimmer and ripple.

"Does it come in black?" At my words, the color rippled

and became black like an oil slick, rainbows reflecting out as I breathed. Then I grinned and formed a new thought, and it responded. The ridiculous train shriveled up and the dress pressed in, divided, leaving me in a button-down business suit.

"It comes in every form and possibility in the universe. It is pure possibility, absolute power." Grimm adjusted my collar, then brushed my shoulders. "All the magic on earth looks good on you, Marissa. Have you given thought to what you will do with it?"

I knew.

"I'm going to wish her dead." To say the words made me sick and thrilled at the same time.

"Is that truly your desire? I know what it is your heart cries for." Grimm hung his head.

But what I wanted wouldn't help Ari, Wyatt, not even Mikey. "I know."

The roof-access door opened, and Death stepped out. "Marissa, are you ready?"

"I think so."

"Then come back downstairs. I took a look around, and there's a problem." Death let the door shut, and I sighed. Why couldn't anything be easy?

We met in our conference room, the oddest collection of people I'd had the opportunity to meet with there, and that was saying a bit. Death motioned for me to take a seat.

"She has guards. Lots of guards, at the edges of her demesne. I can get you to the entrance, but once you reach it, you are going to be in severe trouble. These things aren't alive, so I can't take them. They're like her abominations, only worse. I think you'd call them lychron?"

At his words, Grimm winced, Eli cursed under his breath, and even the Adversary crossed his arms and spat, burning a hole in the carpet.

I had no idea what they were, having never made it past volume C of the Beast Lexicon, but anything that disturbed angels, fae, and the devil himself couldn't be fun.

"Take a corpse. Give it life. Allow it to hunger for things so unnatural that even demons dislike them, and you have a lychron, Marissa." Grimm put his hand on my shoulder, failing completely to comfort me.

I glanced over to Eli. "I know you only help people who help themselves, but I'm trying. How about some backup?"

Eli nodded, and sat back in his chair, thinking. From time to time, he'd whisper with Nick. Finally, he sat up. "You got it. I'll send a guardian with you. Michelle?" He looked up, as a form of wondrous beauty appeared. Brilliant black hair, olive complexion, and a gigawatt smile.

"Meet the archangel, Michelle." Eli nodded toward her.

"I thought Michael—"

"Really? Are they still misspelling my name?" Her voice sounded like crystal ringing. "Do they get anything right?"

Nick leaned forward. "There's one minor problem. See, I wouldn't be comfortable with one of them going along with you in this kind of situation. Too much opportunity to do something that would unbalance the game we play. So, if you want to take one of them, you need to take one of my boys."

He waved his hand, and a gout of flame exploded from the floor beside him. Nick kneeled down and put his head into it, yelling. "Anyone want to go with Marissa to kill a bunch of lychron?" When he leaned back, hellfire ran down his neck, and tiny wisps of smoke came from his ears.

From the fountain, a shape emerged. Long, spidery limbs that ended in claws, a hunched body with a head that swiveled like a wasp. Malodin. Prince of Inferno, son of Satan himself, and the demon who almost managed to bring about the end of the world. I'd caught him on a technicality twice, and probably wouldn't ever be so lucky again.

"Marissa." He spoke my name like fingernails down a chalkboard. "Still trying to sell a soul you don't have? And Michelle. Miss me already?"

"That will do, boy." Nick snapped his fingers, and the flames evaporated. "You want to take her, you need to take him. Fair is fair."

The looks of rage between the guardian and the demon scorched the air between them. "You have got to be kidding me. Those two are going to kill each other, and quite possibly me too."

"Possible." Eli raised his palms.

"Let me help you out." Nickolas Scratch reached into a pocket and pulled out a jar of orange light. "This here is a part of the infernal flame. I know you've played with hellfire, girl, but this ain't that. This here is what I use to *make* hellfire. Comes right out of my backside every day like Old Faithful. You could torch everything between here and her demesne with that." He handed me the bottle of liquid fire.

As my hand brushed his, the glowing spot that had been two souls jumped to his. Nick held on to one of the orbs and squeezed. And I swear it screamed, a voice of pure pain that echoed in my brain. "A trade," said Nick. "Fair and square."

"Now, Marissa," said Eli, "I would think more than once before you take that. You shake hands with the devil and you *will* get burned." He leaned across the table and held out his hand. "You want me to dispose of that?"

I looked him in the eye. "What are you offering me?"

Eli fidgeted and popped his knuckles. "Well, I don't exactly have anything to offer you, except that warning."

"Thanks, you two." I closed my hand around the bottle and slipped it into my jacket pocket.

"Your funeral," said Eli, but he smiled at me.

"No. I've decided not to take angels or demons with me, but I need to talk with Death, alone." I waited as one by one they filed out, and then looked Death in the eye. "Tell War I decided to accept his gift."

"He always knew you would, once you finally figured out who you were." Death gave me a grin I wanted to smack off his face.

"I'm not a killer."

"You are planning to fight your way into the Black Queen's demesne, then wish her dead. Marissa, denial does not go well with black." Death adjusted his shirt buttons, obviously ashamed by my fine attire.

If my plan worked, I'd be gone before the others came back. "So how does this work?"

"Just like for real. You choose to come with me." Death rose and walked to the conference room door.

I followed him, then froze as he swung the door open, and absolute black stared back at me. Not darkness as in a cave. Nor the empty vacuum of space, which is still somewhere. Nothingness so dark it made my outfit look white. To say I froze would be an understatement.

Death took my hand and pulled gently. "The first step is always the hardest."

Liam. Maybe he was out there, somewhere, waiting for me. I walked into oblivion without fear.

Thirty-One

～⌒～

OBLIVION FELT LIKE walking through a rainstorm. That constant buffeting, the feeling of cold that chilled me through. The only constant was Death's grip on me. The burning cold force clenching my arm normally would have been terrifying. In this nothingness, however, I clung to him, taking comfort in his grip as we rode through waves of absolute nothing.

The storm calmed, and from a distance, if distance still existed, a mountain of light shone, brighter than the sun, even from a world away. It drew me, like a moth to a porch light, then the grip on my arm yanked me away, back into the darkness, the storm.

I struggled against him, fighting to go back, but he steered me onward like a parent dragging his child, until the darkness around me faded from oblivion to mere pitch black. I caught my breath, once again aware I *was* breathing.

"We are here," Death whispered, softly. "We stand at the edge of her demesne."

"What was that?" Even now, the memory of that light faded, and I struggled to cling to it.

"You tell anyone I showed you, I'll say you lied. When he's ready, I'll make sure Liam gets there. All the way there."

The tears that returned mixed with the thought of Liam getting to see that place, and the absolute realization that I would never join him. And that thought was what I needed most for what I did next.

I closed my eyes, looking for that swirly light, like a sunspot, that always waited when darkness came. The gift of War, my reward for serving as apocalypse bringer. He'd said it would keep me from losing so many fights. Before, I'd worried about what it would make me. Now I worried about what I already was. "I accept your gift, War." I said the words, thought them. And the wisp of light dissolved, flooding me.

I opened my eyes to the same darkness. Felt of my fingers. No razor-sharp nails. In fact, this was one of the lamest gifts I'd ever received. "That's it?"

"Marissa, do you remember *my* gift to you?" Death's voice had that tone again, urgent.

I did. Knowledge, he said. Of how love could pin a spirit on earth until the loved one passed. Of how hate could keep one here forever. "I remember."

"Good. You need it as much, if not more. Go do something that makes a difference." Death gave me a push, and I stumbled forward, standing at the edge of a shoreline. As my eyes adjusted, I recognized the patterns of tree trunks and branches before me.

Behind me, nothingness. Not even Death's wizened figure. Before me, a distant outline that looked all too familiar. I set out through the night forest, determined to make an end of this.

"Marissa, thank goodness." Grimm's voice came from nowhere.

I looked around, trying to find a mirror. "Ummm . . . where are you?"

"Your bracelet. I embedded mirror dust into it. While I cannot see, it will allow us to converse. Remember. Get to her, wish her dead."

The sound of feet dragging over wood and stone told me I wasn't alone. Reaching into my pocket, I pulled out the thorn sword.

When I saw what made the noise, I forgot to breathe. Which was just as well, because otherwise I would have screamed. Grimm said you started with a corpse, the active term being "started." Judging from what I saw, you then stripped away anything that wasn't muscle. Then you grafted on more muscle, and teeth like sharks, and claws like eagles.

"What is that? Another spell abomination like myself?"

Grimm's voice tingled in my ear as he spoke. "No. My daughter had made bodies for creatures from a lost realm. These are spirits who hunger only for destruction and death."

The lychron saw me and hissed, shaking itself so that its bones rattled like a diamondback.

"I'm not afraid of you." I hefted the thorn sword. It failed to extend, and I shook it, smashing it against my leg until at last it grew, becoming a black blade.

From the forest around me, answering rattles came, echoing, with the thud of running feet. The first lychron leaped at me, mouth open wide to take a bite of my skull, and before I could swing the sword, before I could move a muscle, the world changed.

War's gift acted like my own private quell. The lychron hung suspended in air, and my hands, they *knew* how to wield the sword. War had given me a sliver of his skill. The knowledge of a thousand years of battle, of a million fights won and lost, coursed through me.

I sank the thorn sword through it, then took its head off, willing it to speed up so that I could see it collapse that much faster. It fell to the ground, a twisted heap of flesh, and pleasure wracked me harder than any drug. Each kill filled me with power, life, and strength, but in the blur of battle I couldn't take time to ponder it. I welcomed the next set of eyes, and the next, and the next, until I stood in a circle, and everywhere I looked, glowing eyes gleamed back at me.

I didn't wait.

I attacked before they could.

Dodging claws, avoiding slices, rolling under spiked tails, crushing bones. With every kill, I grew stronger. Faster. Less human.

The lychron ran, but I ran faster. Through the forest, I hunted them, using the gift of War to slaughter the abominations. That's what I was. One abomination, killing others. With every blow, I left behind the woman I'd always been.

I didn't matter, I told myself.

This was what I really was.

I found the last in a den, a makeshift hole created by its thrashing, and laughed like a banshee, as I recognized the creature inside. Unlike the others, her limbs had no scars, her joints seemed almost natural. Though one leg was longer than the other, and the fingers looked more like a child's than a lady's, I had no doubts about who this was.

She rose, trembles of agony shaking her, but made no movement toward me.

"Rouge Faron." Isolde's mother. Grimm's wife. "That's you, right?"

She nodded, but did not speak.

"Why are you out here? Did Isolde kick you out?" My hands shook as I said the words. Here was the soul that started this all. The woman for whom countless thousands died, hiding in a hovel, in the dark.

"No." She answered in French. Her lilting voice reminded me of a songbird, so at odds with her deformed body.

"You left on your own?"

She knelt down, pressing her knees to the cold soil. "I begged my daughter to cease her madness. To release all those people from her spell. I told her if she would not, then she was no longer the daughter I raised and loved. I tried, but I am so very tired."

Death stood beside her in that instant. Not as the hideous reaper, but as an elderly Chinese man, and took her hand. "Rouge, I'm so sorry this happened to you. I give you my word it won't happen again. It's time for you to rest."

She looked up at him, tears of gratitude streaming down her face from eyes that didn't quite match.

And waited.

Death glanced over at me. "Marissa. I am Death, not destruction. Release her soul from this body."

I shook my head, tears of my own coming now. "I'm not—" The words wouldn't come. In the carnage, and the darkness, I'd killed every abomination, torn them to shreds, cut them to pieces, and in doing so, murdered what little remained of myself. Isolde's creations weren't so different from me, after all.

I hadn't been a killer.

Now I was.

The blade chose that moment to obey my command, slicing through Rouge's chest, destroying her heart. Death shone like a searchlight for a millisecond, then he held in his hand a shrinking globe of light. "This one isn't yours to deliver. I won't let her be returned to purgatory. Not this time." Then he was gone, taking her soul with him. Something I'd never had, and always wanted, without knowing the words to describe it.

Numb with pain and sadness, I dismissed the blade and walked out of her den. One more murder, one more death remained. I should have known what I'd find on the other side of the forest. The Black Queen's demesne was an exact copy of Kingdom's old castle, once the seat of its government. I went there so long ago to stop an insane fairy from causing a war between the realms.

The wooden doors hung open, and inside, torches lit the walls instead of fluorescent lighting. This was the castle, as it had been when Isolde lived there, for sure. Once, I'd been lost in its halls, but now I knew where I was headed. I made my way through to the center of the castle. To the vast feast room.

The lush carpet padded my footfalls, but I slipped out of my shoes and ran on bare feet, watching for her at each turn.

Grimm kept his silence, knowing that his words might betray my presence. Not that I intended to hide.

When I made that final turn and descended to the Grand Hall, I froze. From inside, a soft humming came, like a small child singing to herself. I peeked through the door, to where she sat with her back to me, making herself up in a mirror I swear looked just like the one I saw in the Court of Queens.

"You are here." She didn't turn around to see me. "Come out, Marissa."

I thought of Grimm's words. To wish her dead on sight, but my hands still dripped with lychron blood, and the joy of slaughter still made my heart beat fast. Worse yet, as I looked at her, the tear in the veil aligned before me, and I truly saw her.

Her true form looked like a wooden puppet, carved from the black wood of the thorn tree. Under that soft flesh lay the tree monster I'd watched attack Ari. More frightening, though, was the pillar of black clouds that jetted downward as if erupting from the ceiling.

Hate. Pure hate, with side founts of rage. I'd known a litch, and it looked like a tiny garden hose of hate. This looked like a geyser, drenching her constantly in blackness. No wonder Death couldn't claim her.

The plan was to wish her dead. I made a plan of my own and walked into the throne room.

Isolde rose and turned toward me, giving me another shock. Her unearthly beauty left behind, she looked back at me with eyes I recognized, a face familiar and strange at once. I knew now where Grimm got the other half of my DNA. From his own wife.

"You are wounded?" Isolde looked me over, making me shiver.

Though I dripped gore, none of it was my own. I gave her no answer.

"He has sent you to kill me."

"No." I finally found my tongue. "I came of my own free will. End the quell, and I will let you go."

She glanced at me dismissively. "It seems I was wrong about you. And you reek of magic, more magic than any human could survive. He sent you to wish me dead."

"Yes." It shouldn't have mattered. I'd killed lychron in the forest without a thought, but this was wrong. Different.

And she didn't react like I expected. Not afraid. How could she face death, knowing what would happen?

"Well, then. Get to wishing. It won't be the first time I've died. Nor the last." Setting her hands on her hips, she waited, defiant.

And I couldn't speak. Because what I wanted to wish for wasn't death at all. It was life. One life in particular.

And she knew it. I saw it in her eyes. "Go ahead. If you spare me, I give you my word I will never harm him. Live out your lives here, together. On my power, I swear no harm will come to you or him." The smug tone in her voice, the way she spoke with absolute confidence, cut to my core.

"Handmaiden," said Isolde, "remember: You will experience what you wish for me." She held up her hand, wiggling her ring finger.

I looked down at the ring locked on my finger. I didn't plan on leaving here. When I took Death's hand, I'd accepted there would be no return journey. And with acceptance, I found my voice. "I wish . . ." At the words, the power around me surged. Grimm's promise echoed in my mind. That he would honor any wish I made. Anything.

At that moment, I thought of Ari. Of her frozen in the quell, neither able to go on, nor back. What had she said? That all of this came because one woman couldn't let go. Because of grief. Pain begets pain. I could never grant myself the only wish I truly wanted, without becoming the person I despised.

I knew now how Isolde had built up a fountain of pain and hatred powerful enough to defy death. I could do it myself, by nursing this, and holding on to it, like the seed of anger that would last beyond the bounds of life. And I knew what to wish for.

"I wish you love, for all the hate in your heart. I wish you joy, for all the sorrow. I wish you happiness, for all the grief." At the words, my heart leaped. A wall of memories, a tidal wave of happiness swept across me, across us both.

I felt myself in my father's arms, safe in a thunderstorm, and heard the shout of joy as I scored a goal in high school. The sound of Liam's voice, calling my name, the smell of his hair. Ari's laughter. The pride of returning a kidnapped child to his parents.

How long it went on, I cannot say, but when the wave receded, the brokenness inside me no longer burned. I missed Liam, and always would. But I wasn't that person, and couldn't return to that time.

Across the room, Isolde rose. Her makeup streaked with tears, her hand to her mouth to cover a faint smile that drained to a look of horror. "What have you done?"

From the edges of the room, wry laughter filled the room. Death, laughing. I twisted my head until I caught a glimpse through the veil. The fountain of darkness on Isolde was gone.

"Go ahead. Hate me for it." I advanced on her as she realized what I had done. My clothes no longer rippled with magic. I'd returned to my own clothes, having used all the power on earth to obliterate her grip on it.

"Marissa, what did you do?" Grimm's voice shocked us both.

"Father!" Isolde screamed, looking around. "You cannot come here."

"No, but I can. And this time, when you die, you won't have anything to hold you here. No well of hate. Not stolen power. This time, you will *stay* dead." I took another step toward her, and she cringed.

Isolde balled her fists and stood up, gathering magic. "I am the daughter of a fairy and a seal bearer. You come at me with a stick." The magic rippled across her skin as she gathered power, building a ball of lightning twice the size of anything I'd ever seen Ari throw.

I didn't have time to dodge. The lightning leaped out at me, arcing across me, down my body, and into the ground. Again. And again.

She switched to fire, which dripped off me, the way I'd seen Liam shed it so many times, then ice, which swept over me like a brush of cold air. With a gasp, she stepped backwards, a look of fear on her face like when Ari challenged her.

"Daughter of the fairy. Creation of one. We're cut off from the realm seals here, and without Fairy Godmother's magic, everything you've got comes from Grimm. Grimm's magic doesn't work on himself." I took out the thorn sword, triggering it, only to find it a lifeless stub.

"Nor can you wield my tools against me." Isolde sneered at me, her eyes locked on mine.

She ran at me, and I willed the gift of War to take hold. To grant me inhuman reflexes and the knowledge of a million battles won and lost. The world quickened around me—but Isolde didn't slow.

She moved as fast as I did. Her fist slammed into my chest, knocking me to the ground, cracking my sternum. "You aren't the only one who's ever brought about an apocalypse."

This time I rose more carefully, circling her. The knowledge of how to fight, that all still remained, but I wouldn't be dancing around her while she moved in quarter time.

Isolde came for me, and I ran, backwards, toward the feast table with its heaps of meat.

"What's the matter? You aren't afraid, are you, handmaiden?"

"I hate that term." I hated a lot of things, but not enough to keep me around once I died.

Isolde walked back and forth, keeping me trapped between the table and the wall. "You would prefer 'sister'?"

I never got a chance to answer. Instead she ran at me, only this time, I didn't stand around waiting for something that would never happen. I let her run, let her strike, and stepped just to the side, shoving her on so that she crashed into the table. She recoiled in fear, like a trapped animal.

From side to side she stepped, looking at the table, cringing as she glanced to it. I considered that she might be allergic to venison, or grapes. Or fire. She didn't fear the food. The flames on the candle, that terrified her. I reached into my pocket, pulling out the jar of infernal flame.

If I thought she was afraid before, the terror painted across her face magnified a thousandfold. "You don't dare."

I opened the top. "I do."

"We are linked, handmaiden. If I burn, you burn." The fear in her eyes said she knew I spoke the truth.

"Take the ring off, then." I held up the hand, offering it. A mistake.

In the moment where I couldn't see her, pain blossomed from my knee, and I fell backwards. A steak knife stuck out from my knee, buried two inches deep. Isolde hefted another, and threw it at me, driving it through my shoulder into the floor.

"When I ran errands for Father, I always preferred knives. Let me fetch a crossbow, and I will pin you to the wall for the rest of eternity. But first . . ." She strode over and seized the infernal flame from me. "Your hatred for me is delicious, Marissa."

Isolde nudged the thorn sword hilt toward me. "Oh, how you desire to harm me—with a hand cannon?" Her musical laugh filled the air. "You are a pawn, a tool used by those with power. Here." She placed one hand on the sword, and it shrank, changing, dripping, and running. Changing into a gun.

Not just any gun. A pistol. My original nine-millimeter pistol, which I'd taken with me to Fairy Godmother's realm. Fairy Godmother's words came back to me. "You don't like that gun. You need to throw it." Just looking at it made me shake and want to vomit. Grimm had warned me, it wasn't a spell Fairy Godmother put on me. She'd changed me from inside.

I struggled to pick it up, but my hands shook, and all I could do was push it farther away.

"You see?" Isolde rose and turned. "You are a tool to be commanded, a shadow of a human. Only what your masters make you."

In that moment, I couldn't have told you it was a lie. But I needed it to be a lie. What had Grimm told me? That I never obeyed him. The Authority had said as much. I closed my eyes and felt for the gun with my good arm, wrapping my fingers about it.

The first shot I fired shattered a crystal wineglass on the wrong side of the room.

Isolde stopped and turned back to me, one hand on her hip, the other cradling the cask of infernal flame. "What folly is this? Dare you try to shoot me?"

I squeezed the trigger again, but looking at the steel blue

of my nine millimeter made my hands ache. I fired again, a bullet that glanced off the arched ceiling.

"Oh, what fun we shall have," said Isolde as she crossed the room to take a crossbow down. "I will heal you of your wounds each day, and every day find new ways to bless you with pain. You will be my eternal amusement." She paused, putting one hand on her hip, and held the other to her chin. "But I suppose if you turn that gun on yourself, I might grant you the mercy of death. You've wasted two bullets already. The third shall be your last."

I closed my eyes, taking myself back to the moment at age sixteen I'd agreed to work for Grimm, and asked myself the questions I feared most: Who made me me? Who chose for me? Who decided? And the answer of my life came back in memories. Of every time I'd ignored the easy way, laughed at the right way, and done things my way.

Who decided who I was?

I did.

My gun barked, and the vial of infernal flame exploded in Isolde's hand. It leaped onto her like a thing alive. Pain? No. Pain is a feeling. What coursed through me was an essence. An explosion. A reality. And as Nick had warned me, the infernal flame was alive. It didn't burn one spot. It streaked around, leaving a trail of scorched flesh, and laughing in a voice made of a fire's crackle.

My screams joined Isolde's. The fire on my hand, on my arm, dancing along my elbow, burned her even faster. Her true nature, the thorn tree, had dried in the months since she left Fairy Godmother's realm. Where the infernal flame left streaks on me, it scorched gashes of ash from her, racing up and down her faster than it could consume me. Liam's ring, his gift to me, blunted the heat, shielded me, but she had no such protection. Isolde collapsed to the floor, her eyes locked on me between shrieks. "You can't have my face." She lifted her burning hand to her face, wiping it along her cheek, covering her eye.

My world exploded.

The left side of me saw only white; the right side jerked as the devil flame picked a spot here and there to sear the flesh. Isolde's screams became shrieks, and the pain rebounding on me through our link reached a crescendo, a feedback whine that overwhelmed me.

There was one more thing I had to do.

The quell would break with Isolde's death. Ari and Wyatt would be released. But Liam would still be dead. I needed one more wish to undo the last of the harm my life had caused. "I wish Liam were alive." I gasped the words, flailing against the flames.

"I'm sorry, Marissa. There is no more magic." Grimm's voice came to me across a distance.

But he was wrong. "Whatever I wish for. You swore you'd do whatever I asked." Because despite Grimm's protests, there was one more wish, one who had walked with Death into Isolde's realm willingly.

I wished on *me*.

Beyond worlds, I felt more than heard Grimm speak. A sea of voices all belonging to him, speaking my desire into existence. Now I watched my body from a distance, writhing in pain that no longer reached me. Across the hall, Death kneeled over Isolde, scooping the soul from her body. And standing beside Death, I glimpsed a form I recognized. Liam!

He wore the same red-and-black flannel I bought him for Christmas. I struggled to understand the words he spoke. Hold on? There was nothing left for me to hold on to, but fragments of my being would power the spell that gave him life.

That thought gave me peace to embrace my unraveling. Filaments of white lashed out from me toward him, tracing Liam's outline. Too late, I saw the thing behind him. The dragon curse he'd carried since the day I sent it after him by accident.

I'd always pictured it as a dragon from the history books. Maybe a T.rex with a few more quills and frills. But eons trapped in bodies with humans had changed it. Twisted it so that it resembled a hulking lizard man with oversized canines and a tongue that hung to its waist. It cowered behind Liam, who gripped its claw with one hand. The living filaments from me became a cloud of gossamer strands that exploded outward, wrapping Liam, blanketing him—and the curse. It melted downward into him, wrapping around his soul, embedding itself in the flesh that formed around his soul.

He lived.

As the last dregs of my being drained away, and the world faded, Liam rushed toward my body, changing into a dragon twice the size of what he'd been before, with pearlescent red scales and sweeping wings that folded behind his body. The dragon's tongue lashed out at the fire burning me. And then there was nothing.

Thirty-Two

I OPENED MY eyes to white everywhere, brilliant white, like I had finally made it to the mountain of light Death showed me. No pain. In fact, a chilling numbness covered my body. I tried to sit up, and the bed beneath me crinkled.

"M?" The voice sounded distant. Off-kilter. Blinking, my eyes grew clear, and I saw a face I recognized. Brilliant red hair, yellow eyes. Ari looked down at me and shrieked with delight. "She's awake."

"Dead." I spoke the word carefully.

"No. It's going to be all right." Ari raced out of the room, which, now that I could focus, looked a lot like a hospital room. She returned a few minutes later, towing a doctor.

A doctor I recognized as Pestilence, the fourth harbinger of the apocalypse.

"What are you doing here?" I squinted at him.

"I was making sure you didn't contract any infections from the surgeries. You're welcome." Pestilence looked into my right eye with a penlight and nodded. "Your reactions look good."

I tried to sit up, and flailed.

"Marissa!" Grimm's voice came from everywhere.

I looked around, found a single him I could focus on. "Grimm."

Grimm had returned to the mirror at some point, but he peered out at me, a wide grin on his face. "We only have a moment. I must wake Liam, or he will never forgive me. He hasn't left your bedside for a month." Grimm looked at me, staring again.

"A whole month?" It felt like minutes, though it explained certain aches.

"Surgery takes time."

Grimm's words sank in, and I raised my hand. Starting at my palm, a smooth white streak of flesh traced around to the back of my hand, where it tracked up my wrist, obliterating the handmaiden's mark. When I flexed my hand, only the thumb and first two fingers moved.

"You'll need physical therapy, but there's no reason you shouldn't recover a full range of motion," said Grimm.

That's when I realized I was looking at things sideways. I reached up with my right hand, feeling my face.

Ari grabbed my hands. "Gentle."

My fingertips brushed over a scar that ran from the corner of my left eye back toward my ear. "I want a mirror." I ran my hand over my ear, confirming that most of it was gone. That explained why everything sounded distant.

Grimm spoke slowly. "Let's take things one step at a time. Let me explain—"

"I want a mirror. Get out."

He faded away. I leaned forward to get a better look in the empty mirror. My right eye remained the same milk chocolate brown it'd always been. My left eye, on the other hand, was a shade of pearlescent blue that would look more at home in an oyster, and the hair where I'd been burned grew in almost white.

"What—what did you *do*?" I glanced to Ari, and when I looked back, Grimm had taken up residence in the mirror again.

"Marissa, your wounds were not simple burns," said Grimm. "Magic may not—"

"Magic oppose." I knew the laws. My mentor, Evangeline, had died with wounds that couldn't be healed. She'd always said I'd have scars of my own one day. "How?"

"It was my idea," said Ari. "Just because you can't heal a damaged eye doesn't mean you can't replace it with a healthy one. And the hair you can dye. But the scars . . ." She glanced back to Grimm.

"I can live with." I reached out to take her hand. "I can live with them." Which brought me dangerously close to the question I couldn't ask yet, because I didn't want to know. Not yet. How was I alive?

"My dear, I have a solution for your hearing, though like the eye, it may take time to get used to." Grimm waited for me to look to him to continue. "I assure you, any visual artifacts will become completely normal as soon as the transplanted eye gives up on returning—"

The room door exploded open and Liam burst in. He hurled himself at me, wrapping his arms around me despite my attempts to push him off.

"I thought I lost you forever," he finally managed to say.

And before him, a wave of fear struck me. Of self-consciousness that barely covered "Don't look yet. I—"

He whispered in my ear, "I was here when they did the grafts, M. I don't care what color your eyes are, or your hair. I don't care about any of that. You are beautiful."

"Don't say that." I knew what the mirror had shown me. The infernal flame's damage left me looking as much like a freak on the outside as I now knew myself to be on the inside. "I'll never be beautiful."

He held on and buried his head in my shoulder, whispering, "To me you'll always be."

I SPENT THE next six months in rehab, physical therapy, and getting my body back into some form of motion. With the help of a therapist who was a combination of genius and sadist, I regained use of my fingers one painful inch at a time. My hearing both improved and took a turn for the worse when Grimm supplied me with an earring he claimed came from Selkie craftsmen. I could hear, all right. Sometimes too well.

Eventually I found the courage to believe Liam loved me, and from that, I found the courage to talk to Grimm. One morning, while Liam worked in the forge, I summoned Grimm, forcing myself to look in the mirror.

"My dear, how may I help you?" Grimm gave me a grandfatherly smile. He never talked about business, always insisting that I get better first.

"How am I alive?" The question I'd lay awake at night asking myself over and over.

"Mr. Stone had grown to regard that curse like a friend. His spirit kept it anchored on earth, and when you wished him a new body, he used his reptilian side to put out the flames where your clothing caught fire."

I shook my head. "That's not what I meant. I'm a wish, and wishing should have destroyed me."

"Marissa, I can only theorize, but I've spent many hours contemplating this myself, and I have a plausible theory. I believe that the Authority kept a promise to you. She offered you a soul, for the end of the quell. The death of the Black Queen."

"I turned that deal down."

Grimm nodded toward me. "And then you did what she asked anyway. It is a theory. Arianna says your spirit appears different. Like a master craftsman blended the portions that make you *you* into a soul. So, you remain unique. Speaking of Arianna, will you be meeting her for dinner?"

"Yep. Tonight's poker night for Liam. I hear he's actually playing poker." It killed me to let him go the first time, but I couldn't spend the rest of our time together controlling him.

"Excellent. You two will meet at the Agency. I've made reservations and have a limo ready to drive you to dinner." Grimm disappeared without waiting for me to answer.

When I finally got to the Agency, it felt like coming home. Mikey, directing the cargo trucks in our bay. Rosa, fixing me with evil looks the moment I entered the door.

The two new girls, sitting in Grimm's office, listening to a lecture.

Okay, that part was just a little weird.

"Marissa, meet my newest agents. This is Lisa, and this is Amanda." Grimm pointed to the two, who both reminded me of Gangster Bitch Barbie. "Marissa is my partner and most trusted agent."

I shook hands with the two, watching their eyes lock on my different eye. Grimm hadn't been kidding when he claimed there might be visual artifacts. Sometimes, I saw things that weren't there—at least, not yet. Other times, things that were, but shouldn't be visible. I can't say it made sleeping easier.

"Arianna is in her office, clearing out her desk." Grimm's words caught me by surprise. I'd heard Ari quit, but thought it was like Ari quitting chocolate, or Ari quitting soap operas, or Ari quitting Internet shopping. In other words, a fifteen-minute retirement.

I walked down the hall to Ari's office, where she dumped another drawer out of her desk into a box. And her desk looked surprisingly like my desk. "So, how are you and Wyatt doing?"

She blushed, though that was *not* what I asked. "We're doing fine."

"You managed to get over his fear of 'contact'?"

She turned an even deeper shade of red. "We're working on it. We spend a lot of time together in the Court of Queens."

I snorted. "You mean you've taken Wyatt to the court again?"

Ari looked back at me with innocent yellow eyes. "Wyatt says the Court of Kings has an excellent balance without his interference, and it will take a combined effort to keep the queens in line. He goes there every day, performing binding arbitration of disputes."

"You lend him a shotgun?" Rosa herself couldn't handle the Court of Queens.

"Grimm offered to arm him."

At his name, Grimm flashed into Ari's mirror. "Anything he asked for."

I ran down a list of weapons in my head. "Cat-of-nine-tails? Cat-of-one-tails?"

"A copy of *Robert's Rules of Order, Revised*, and a never-ending tin of butterscotch cookies. A wise man indeed." Grimm nodded, satisfied. "Ladies, your limousine awaits."

I enjoyed the ride. It felt wonderful to be treated as a high-class citizen. Wonderful to be alive. When the driver opened the door and I stepped out, the look of wonder fell right off my face, into the open Dumpster. "Here?"

"Liam recommended it." Ari took my hand, and we walked down the stairs to Froni's.

Once she managed to gag down a warm beer, Ari finally found the courage to talk. "I need your help."

Grimm watched us from the empty napkin canister.

"You need someone beat up? Or shot? I've never been a bruiser, and I'll need to spend a few weeks practicing to get my aim back." In fact, most of the reasons I'd been an agent didn't work.

Ari took a bite of noodle from the plastic forks I kept in my purse. "The Court of Queens is more than I can handle. More than Wyatt and I can handle."

I shook my head. "I'm retiring." I glanced over at Grimm. "Consider this two weeks' notice."

"I wouldn't be much of a Fairy Godfather if I didn't see this coming. I haven't been able to gut a rabbit for two weeks without the entrails spelling out 'Marissa quits.'" Grimm shook his head, exasperated.

"Help me," said Ari. "I'm High Queen, but a queen can't directly . . . influence another queen. Particularly not me." Ari took my hands and looked me in the eye.

"You want someone who they'll be terrified of on sight? There's not one of them that will ever forget me standing with the Black Queen." Then again, Ari's yellow witch eyes didn't exactly inspire thoughts of cuddly puppies. "Don't you already have their loyalty?"

"I did. Right up until I told half the witches I wouldn't let them kill half the queens. And I lost most of the queens when I wouldn't let them bring charges against the witches. You're right on one account. *I* will never control them." She slid her hand over to mine. "*We* will. You and me. The Witch Queen, and her handmaiden, who slew the Black Queen." Ari set her face in that look. The one that said she'd already decided.

"Will you just accept and be done with it?" Grimm's tone sounded peeved.

I wiped the table with an antibacterial wipe, killing off entire civilizations of bacteria and probably committing genocide. Then I wiped down the napkin holder where Grimm watched us. "Who left soap scum on your mirror?"

Ari blew a hair out of her face. "Ignore him. He's been upset with me for weeks."

"What did she ever do to you?" I glared at him.

"It's not what you've done, it's what you are going to do, Arianna. It's near impossible to schedule appointments for our clients with you as is." Grimm put his hand on his forehead.

"We quit," Ari and I said together.

"Yes, yes. I'll see you in two weeks, three days, Marissa. Arianna, welcome back next month, in case I forget to mention it. You two would plan better if you learned to read the future." Grimm's tone grew more agitated with each word. "That's hardly the worst of it. Arianna, must you take maternity leave so soon after your honeymoon? Could you not have staggered this out a bit?"

I stared at Ari. "When are you due?"

She shook her head. "I'm not—"

"Five months, three weeks, one day and twenty hours from now." Grimm glared at Ari as well.

"You said you and Wyatt didn't . . ." I kept my eyes on her as she blushed.

Ari's face remained white as a sheet, and her mouth flopped open and shut. "There was this one time, in the hotel."

Grimm choked. "She told me the same thing. Arianna, are any of these locations jogging a memory? The book closet at *my* Agency? Mrs. Pendlebrook's couch? And why don't you tell Marissa how it was that her desk came to be in your office? Marissa, trust me, you don't want that desk back."

The desk didn't bother me. I could always buy a new one,

assuming Grimm was right about me coming back to work for him. And if he was wrong, it wouldn't matter. But what sent a pang of jealousy through me was the thought of Ari as a mother. Being Aunt Marissa would never be the same as loving a child of my own.

"Marissa," said Grimm. "You have a soul now. I would appreciate it if you take appropriate precautions, so I don't have both of my senior agents out on maternity leave. Now, if you don't mind, I have a double wedding ceremony to plan." Grimm started to fade out, then snapped back in. "Mrs. Pendlebrook demands an appropriate occasion for her son, and, Marissa, try to act surprised. Your fiancé is a loving man, but he should not be allowed to pick out dresses, menus, or, probably, his own clothing."

I sat in stunned silence, drinking what remained of Ari's beer, since she would be on a water-only diet for a while. Ari switched sides of the table to slump beside me. "What do you think? You and me? The Witch Queen and her handmaiden?"

I considered all the possibilities. I'd dreamed of "happily ever after" all my life, but not how I would reach it, or who I'd be when I got there. I had a man I loved, and who loved me back. A best friend who was more like a sister, and one day, the possibility of a family all my own. Maybe happily ever after wasn't a destination or a situation. Maybe it was a decision, made every day. So I made one. "I prefer the term *agent*."

TURN THE PAGE FOR A SNEAK PEEK OF A BRAND-NEW
URBAN FANTASY NOVEL FROM J. C. NELSON

The Reburialists

COMING FEBRUARY 2016 FROM ACE BOOKS!

Brynner

PUTTING THE DEAD in their graves was easy; keeping them there gave me a full-time job. A job that came with hazard pay, full medical coverage, and a life insurance policy that covered every form of death from being buried in a lost tomb to stung to death by scorpions. It didn't cover getting stabbed on a fire escape by a jealous woman. So I climbed the fire escape of a hotel in Greece like the building was on fire (it wasn't) and like my life depended on making it to the top (it probably did).

Beneath me, my date from last night's champagne ball cursed in Greek. The only part I understood for certain was my name, Brynner, and that her name was most definitely *not* Athena. Athena would be her sister, my date from the night before.

I patted the knives sheathed on my hips and checked my messenger bag. Wallet? Check. Passport? Good. Cell phone? Thank god. Fresh pine branch, sharpened to a point? All the essentials. Not that any of those would help me against an angry woman or her sister.

On the rooftop, I crouched behind two air conditioners. They rattled and labored against the summer night.

"Brynner?" She insisted on mispronouncing my name. Briner is what you soak a ham in before you cook it. Brynner, like the grin I'd turned on her the night before, was mine. She looked over the edge of the far side. All I had to do was wait for her to climb down, and I could make a dash for the roof access door.

My cell phone rang from inside my bag, like the worst-timed game of Marco Polo ever.

She spun, zeroing in on the noise. "Brynner." She circled the air conditioner to where I crouched, my shirt unbuttoned, the white bandages across my chest barely concealing fresh stitches.

"Hi . . . Elena."

She pointed the knife at me, trembling with rage. We'd enjoyed a wonderful room-service breakfast until she answered the hotel door and had an awkward conversation with her sister. "What is my name?"

My cell rang again, the emergency tone. I flipped it out with one hand, and kept my eyes on Dimitra. Dina? Now that I thought about it, it wasn't clear which of the two lovely embassy representatives had chased me out the window. "Give me a moment." I held the phone to my shoulder and backed away. Jealous women and angry badgers deserved their space. "Brynner Carson speaking."

A computerized voice on the other end barked out, "We have a situation, asshole. Get a move on to the shipping district. Car's out front." That would be Dale Hogman, field team commander of the Bureau of Special Investigations.

"Call someone else. We just had a situation, and I'm in a bit of a situation myself right now."

Elinda? Athena? She yelled at me in Greek, something about a goat and my mother.

"Is that the native you had draped over you last night? Saw her on the telecast." Dale didn't bother hiding his amusement. Or his familiarity with the scenario.

"Could be her twin from the night before." I'd consumed more than my share of wine even before moving to the more private celebration.

"Love her and leave her. We've got a moldy-oldy on its feet. Trust me, no one else is going to be able to handle this one." Dale cut the call off, right as Etria came for me.

She swung the knife at me in a high overhand arc, not bad for killing a mummy, but not the best way to carve out a man's heart.

I stepped to the side and caught her wrist, spinning her around.

A younger me would have leaned in to kiss her before dashing away. A younger me once got kicked in the family jewels for doing exactly that, so I let her land rump first and ran for the stairwell. Two nights earlier I was a celebrated hero. Last night I was an honored guest, and by tomorrow morning I wouldn't be able to smile at a waitress in the city without getting spit on.

Women talk.

And that was exactly why I preferred my day job, my night job, my going-to-get-me-killed job. I sprinted down the stairs, met the driver at the front door of the hotel, and picked up my bag of equipment from the passenger seat while calling back in to headquarters on my phone. "Brynner Carson. Give me the details."

"Now you're in a rush? Sure you don't want some more time to work things out?" The strangled gasp from the other end sounded like a man's throat being crushed, but I knew better. I'd seen Dale in person enough times to know he was just taking a cigar puff through his tracheal tube.

"I don't think couples counseling will help. I'm five minutes away." I strapped on my Kevlar and titanium body armor while the driver careened down cobblestone streets. "Situation report?"

"Like I said: Corpse woke up a few hours ago. Took apart three guards and half a cargo crew."

We continued downhill into the port, veering past cranes and loading trucks. "Near the water?"

"Better. On a *boat*."

"Bullshit." Even on my first day working for the Bureau of Special Investigations, even on my first assignment, I knew better than that.

Dale waited so long I thought he might've dropped the call. "No. And that ain't the freakiest part. It knows you."

My hands froze, leaving one boot untied. Freakiest part in this particular conversation was a series of contests. Freaky that a three-week-old corpse had reanimated and gone on a rampage? A little. Well, not really. More like an everyday job for the BSI.

Freaky that one had done so on a *boat*? Completely. Contact with living water could drive the Re-Animus straight out of the shell. That scored an eight on the scale of bat-shit crazies, where one would be the homeless guy at the grocery store and five would be us hitting dead things. "How can you be sure?"

"This one's talking."

I yanked my boots tight and snapped my fingers. "Bullshit."

"And writing hieroglyphics in blood."

"Bullshittier."

Dale laughed, a rumbling cough that sounded like he'd need to tweeze a piece of his lung out of his breathing tube. "And if you believe the cargo guys who got away, this one's asking for you by name."

That killed the friendly banter deader than the corpse had been a few hours earlier. Because meat-skins, or the Re-Animus running them, *never* spoke. Though I wanted to sleep in the sun for a month, I couldn't let this one get away.

"Happy hunting. Don't get dead." Dale clicked out.

I rode the rest of the way in silence, wondering where my life went wrong. Probably around eighteen, when I walked into a BSI field office, signed my name, and asked where the nearest dead thing was.

The car pulled to a stop and I got out, a walking armory of wood and religious symbols from damn near every religion on earth, including a few that sane folks didn't practice anymore.

The police stepped out of my way. Sure, the cops might handle normal criminals, but they left the dead to us. Donuts didn't have a habit of ripping your insides out and playing with them. As I passed, they made the sign of the cross, which was fantastic, assuming the meat-skin I was up against had been Christian. Not a bad guess, for Greece.

I tore the cordon out of my way and walked up the cargo ramp alone.

Why it had to be a cargo ship, I can't say. It wasn't just the warren of steel boxes and narrow pathways, perfect for a meat-skin to hide in. It was that I'd always gotten seasick just *standing* on a boat. Hell, I puked in a canoe at summer camp.

So my roiling stomach wasn't due to nerves as much as waves, the rocking sensation at my core wasn't that I was hunting something that killed six men less than an hour earlier. At least, that's what I told myself.

Closing my eyes for one moment, I listened, threading my way through a forest of sound to find the one that didn't fit. Dale hadn't lied. Beneath the undercurrent of traffic and the gentle slosh of waves, a voice like gravel and coffins echoed in the hull of the ship.

Which meant I wasn't dealing with your garden-variety walking corpse. Dale had been right to call me. It was a Re-Animus. An unholy spirit known for animating the dead and tearing apart the living. Again.

It whispered into the shadows, mumbling at times and moaning at others.

Dad always said Re-Animus never spoke, for fear of what might slip out. That the act of stealing a body was so heinous that their very souls cried out to be imprisoned the way they imprisoned others. Controlled the way the Re-Animus did the dead.

Someone never mentioned that to this one.

Stake in hand, I jogged along the deck till I came to a cavernous hole leading to the cargo bay. Imagine a football field inside a boat. Now turn off the stadium lights and turn loose one recently live corpse run by something so foul we had to invent a word for it.

That, right there, is why I looked forward to vacation.

I hopped down stacks of cargo containers, well aware each hop sent a booming echo through the hold. The meat-skin might be dead. The Re-Animus in the driver's seat would have had to be to miss me coming.

And things grew weirder still.

In the distance, at the far end of the hold, a torch flickered. Not a flashlight. The Re-Animus had lit an honest-to-god torch, like a tiki torch. It illuminated a dim circle on the vast hull of the ship, and in the flickering light, the meat-skin shambled back and forth.

Dale called it a moldy-oldy. Meaning someone dead a few weeks. Plenty strong but not exactly a threat, so long as people did the sane thing and *ran*. Away, not toward it like I did. Fresh corpses could be downright deadly.

The ones everyone feared, the mummies, could barely move, let alone threaten someone. The worst they might do is get dust all over you when they disintegrated. This body had all the signs of a grave robbery gone wrong. The grave cuffs still hung from one wrist.

It turned toward my light, one eye sagging and the other wild. And began to laugh. "Carson. Finally." So the Re-Animus was still on board. Fully present. Fully capable. That familiar voice had wailed as I drove it out of a body not three days earlier.

"That is one ugly ride you picked. It's an island. Couldn't you find a tan corpse?" I stayed just beyond the torchlight, hopefully farther than it could leap.

It took a step forward, staggering to the left. "I had a great body. I had a whole collection, if you hadn't destroyed them. We'll settle that some other time. I've come to speak with you, Carson."

"I'm not really in a mood to talk, but I could arrange for a therapist to call you if you want."

The corpse turned away, slouching back toward the hull, where it resumed painting by gnawing a finger and dabbling the blood that oozed out.

Score: Dale, 3. The thing wasn't writing. It was drawing. Technically, it was writing as well, since the pictures were hieroglyphics.

While it had its back turned, I crept up on it as stealthily as I could, my stake drawn. Green pine could suck the power right out of the meat-skin, killing a chunk of the Re-Animus. The key? Getting in the first blow. I leaped forward, driving the stake down in an arc meant to strike just above the shoulder and continue down into the rib cage.

The Re-Animus caught my hand without looking. "Carson, you killed one of my favorite bodies that way not three days ago."

I was in trouble.

The last body was fresh. The last body was fast. The Re-Animus must have spent the last three days pouring itself into this body, building it up for pure strength. Under the force of its grasp, the armor on my wrist crackled and shifted.

It swung another hand around, gnarled fingers grasping at my throat. I didn't wear a titanium neck brace for style, but neither could I keep my feet on the floor as it lifted me higher, then twisted my head so I couldn't look away.

"I came to deliver a message." Its foul breath washed over me, the stench of rotten fish and clogged toilets. "The old man's body molders, and now she stirs. Give back the heart, Carson. Carson's blood took it, she says. Carson's blood will pay if it isn't returned."

He liked to talk, so while I could still breathe, I wanted to set a trap. "Who do I send it to?"

"The darkness follower. The edge walker. The eater who lives in sin and walks in the shadow of the new temple. You cannot trick me into revealing anything, lesser Carson."

And that right there, that pissed me off. With my free hand, I drove a stubby silver blade into the arm holding me, and when my feet hit the floor, I hurled myself at the meat-skin. Four years of high school football taught me how to lead with my shoulder, drive with my feet.

Using momentum to drive a stake through an animated corpse when we hit the hull wasn't covered in physical education, though. Thank god my dad had homeschooled me in corpse killing.

The stake sizzled and popped as it drove the Re-Animus out. Black clouds of smoke billowed into the night. To me, dying Re-Animus always smelled like burning hair. Three breaths later, I stood alone. Me, a once-again dead body, and the lap of the waves.

I snapped a picture of its finger painting with my cell phone and called Dale. "I put our walker back to bed. You've got to see what it was drawing. I'm sending a picture now."

After a moment Dale swore. He'd tweaked the inflections on his voice module to get the curses just right. "You didn't repeat any of that out loud, did you?"

"According to you, I can barely read the instructions on a condom wrapper. Pretty safe bet I didn't read the glyphs. That what I think it is?"

When Dale spoke, his voice trembled, as much as it could, being mostly mechanical. "Wipe it off the walls, get the hell out of Dodge. I'm booking you a flight back to the U. S. of A. We need to talk to the director."

I rolled the corpse over, making sure it was dead for good. "The Re-Animus threatened me. It might just be some sort of curse."

I waited for what seemed like an eternity until Dale answered.

"No. I've seen that pattern before. I think it's a spell."

J. C. Nelson is a software developer and ex-beekeeper residing in the Pacific Northwest with family and a few chickens. Visit the author online at authorjcnelson.com.

Want to connect with fellow science fiction and fantasy fans?

For news on all your favorite Ace and Roc authors, sneak peeks into the newest releases, book giveaways, and much more—

"Like" Ace and Roc Books on Facebook!

facebook.com/AceRocBooks